Raves for *Private Arrangements*

"*Ravishingly sinful and addictive. An an...*"

—Eloisa James,
New York Times bestselling author

❧

"*A love story of remarkable depth...
Entrancing from start to finish.*"

—Mary Balogh,
New York Times bestselling author

❧

"*Enchanting... An extraordinary,
unputdownable love story.*"

—Jane Feather,
New York Times bestselling author

❧

An irresistible new voice in historical romance, Sherry Thomas has
already drawn the praise of these
bestselling romance favorites for her
debut novel, *Private Arrangements*.
Now Sherry returns with another
must-read treat that is truly…

Delicious

"Let me see your face."

"No," she said.

A look of bittersweet longing came over him. He quickly looked away, but the damage—to her—was done.

She'd come to realize that the man in her heart had become less Stuart Somerset than an ideal man she'd invented and re-invented over the years. The real Stuart Somerset was a mystery to her and, more than once, a disappointment: he was nothing of the fearless lover she remembered, but a man very much ruled by—and in thrall to—the conventions of Society.

Sometimes she wondered whether she still gravitated toward him simply because she could not face the fact that her faithful love might have been a mistake—a beautiful mistake, but a mistake enormous and pervasive all the same.

But now, as she gazed upon him, her heart did something strange, a twist, a clench, a fracture—she didn't know what precisely, but yes, the damage was done. She was falling in love with *this* man, this man who wouldn't touch her, kiss her, or marry her.

Delicious

SHERRY THOMAS

BANTAM BOOKS

DELICIOUS
A Bantam Book / August 2008

Published by Bantam Dell
A Division of Random House, Inc.
New York, New York

This is a work of fiction. Names, characters, places, and incidents
either are the product of the author's imagination or are used
fictitiously. Any resemblance to actual persons, living or dead,
events, or locales is entirely coincidental.

Bantam Books and the rooster colophon are registered trademarks
of Random House, Inc.

ISBN 978-0-440-24432-5

Printed in the United States of America
Published simultaneously in Canada

www.bantamdell.com

OPM   10 9 8 7 6 5 4 3 2 1

To my husband. Each day with you
is a perfect beginning to the rest of my life.

Acknowledgments

To the extent that this book is any good, most of the credit goes to my editor, Caitlin Alexander, for refusing to accept anything less than my best work. It is not every editor who can send a sixteen-page, single-spaced revision letter without making the writer quit. And when she tells me to take my head out of my rear end, I laugh and actually listen.

Kristin Nelson and Sara Megibow, for the best spa day ever. And that's on top of the best professional support in the business.

Heidi, for bailing me out in my most desperate hour. Janine, for going over the manuscript with a fine-tooth comb and spotting problems that I'd missed. And Sybil, for doing an emergency read for me when Janine was out of the country.

My wonderful family, for rallying to my aid during the year I was both in school and writing *Delicious*. It melted my heart every time my husband answered to calls of "Mom!" with "I'm Mom." Household chaos was kept down to a minimum thanks to my mother, who came every day to fight a valiant battle against entropy. And how fortunate to have a mom-in-law so lovely that kids always want to visit her for weeks on end!

My sisters at Austin RWA. A better group of friends I've never met.

All the bloggers, reviewers, authors, booksellers, and readers who got the buzz going on *Private Arrangements,* and the talented team at Bantam who launched the book so beautifully. I can never thank you enough.

And as always, if you are reading this now, thank you. Thank you for everything.

"When I write about hunger, I am really writing about love and the hunger for it, and warmth, and the love of it . . . and then the warmth and richness and fine reality of hunger satisfied."

—M.F.K. Fisher

Chapter One

In retrospect people said it was a Cinderella story. Notably missing was the personage of the Fairy Godmother. But other than that, the narrative seemed to contain all the elements of the fairy tale.

There was something of a modern prince. He had no royal blood, but he was a powerful man—London's foremost barrister, Mr. Gladstone's right hand—a man who would very likely one day occupy 10 Downing Street.

There was a woman who spent much of her life in the kitchen. In the eyes of many, she was a nobody. To others, she was one of the greatest cooks of her generation, her food said to be so divine that old men dined with the gusto of adolescent boys, and so seductive that lovers forsook each other as long as a single crumb remained on the table.

There was a ball; not the usual sort of ball that made it into fairy tales or even ordinary tales, but a ball nevertheless. There was the requisite Evilish Female

Relative. And mostly importantly for connoisseurs of fairy tales, there was footgear left behind in a hurry—nothing so frivolous or fancy as glass slippers, yet carefully kept and cherished, with a flickering flame of hope, for years upon years.

A Cinderella story indeed.

Or was it?

It all began—or resumed, depending on how one looked at it—the day Bertie Somerset died.

Yorkshire
November 1892

The kitchen at Fairleigh Park was palatial in dimension, as grand as anything to be found at Chatsworth or Blenheim, and certainly several times larger than what one would expect for a manor the size of Fairleigh Park.

Bertie Somerset had the entire kitchen complex renovated in 1877—shortly after he inherited, two years before Verity Durant came to work for him. After the improvements, the complex boasted a dairy, a scullery, and a pantry, each the size of a small cottage; separate larders for meat, game, and fish; two smokehouses; and a mushroom house where a heap of composted manure provided edible mushrooms year-round.

The main kitchen, floored in cool rectangles of gray flagstone, with oak duckboards where the kitchen staff most often stood, had an old-fashioned open hearth and two modern, closed ranges. The ceiling rose twenty feet above the floor. Windows were set high and faced only north and east, so that not a single beam of sunlight would ever stray inside. But still it was sweaty work in winter; in summer the temperatures rose hot enough to immolate.

Three maids toiled in the adjacent scullery, washing up all the plates, cups, and flatware from the servants' afternoon tea. One of Verity's apprentices stuffed tiny eggplants at the central work table, the other three stood at their respective stations about the room, attending to the rigors of dinner for the staff as well as for the master of the house.

The soup course had just been carried out, trailing behind it a murmur of the sweetness of caramelized onion. From the stove billowed the steam of a white wine broth, in the last stages of reduction before being made into a sauce for a filet of brill that had been earlier poached in it. Over the great hearth a quartet of teals roasted on a spit turned by a kitchen maid. She also looked after the civet of hare slowly stewing in the coals, which emitted a powerful, gamy smell every time it was stirred.

The odors of her kitchen were as beautiful to Verity as the sounds of an orchestra. This kitchen was her fiefdom, her sanctuary. She cooked with an absolute, almost nerveless concentration, her awareness extending to the subtlest stimulation of the senses and the least movement on the part of her underlings.

The sound of her favorite apprentice *not* stirring the hazelnut butter made her turn her head slightly.

"Mademoiselle Porter, the butter," she said, her voice stern. Her voice was always stern in the kitchen.

"Yes, Madame. Sorry, Madame," said Becky Porter. The girl would be purple with embarrassment now—she knew very well that it took only a few seconds of inattention before hazelnut butter became black butter.

Verity gave Tim Cartwright, the apprentice standing before the white wine reduction, a hard stare. The young man blanched. He cooked like a dream, his sauces as velvety and breathtaking as a starry night, his soufflés taller than chefs' toques. But Verity would not hesitate to let him go without a letter of character if he made an improper advance toward Becky—Becky who'd been with Verity since joining her staff as a thirteen-year-old child.

Most of the hazelnut butter would be consumed at dinner. But a portion of it was to be saved for the midnight repast her employer had requested: one steak au poivre, a dozen oysters in sauce Mornay, potato croquettes à la Dauphine, a small lemon tart, still warm, and half a dozen dessert crepes spread with, *mais bien sur,* hazelnut butter.

Crepes with hazelnut butter—Mrs. Danner tonight. Three days ago it had been Mrs. Childs. Bertie was becoming promiscuous in his middle age. Verity removed the cassoulet from the oven and grinned a little to herself, imagining the scenes that would ensue should Mrs. Danner and Mrs. Childs find out that they shared Bertie's less-than-undying devotion.

The service hatch burst open. The door slammed

into a dresser, rattling the rows of copper lids hanging on pin rails, startling one of them off its anchor. The lid hit the floor hard, bounced and wobbled, its metallic bangs and scrapes echoing in the steam and smolder of the kitchen. Verity looked up sharply. The footmen in this house knew better than to throw open doors like that.

"Madame!" Dickie, the first footman, gasped from the doorway, sweat dampening his hair despite the November chill. "Mr. Somerset—Mr. Somerset, he be not right!"

Something about Dickie's wild expression suggested that Bertie was far worse than "not right." Verity motioned Letty Briggs, her lead apprentice, to take over her spot before the stove. She wiped her hands on a clean towel and went to the door.

"Carry on," she instructed her crew before closing the door behind Dickie and herself. Dickie was already scrambling in the direction of the house.

"What's the matter?" she said, lengthening her strides to keep up with the footman.

"He be out cold, Madame."

"Has someone sent for Dr. Sergeant?"

"Mick from the stables just rode out."

She'd forgotten her shawl. The air in the unheated passage between kitchen and manor chilled the sheen of perspiration on her face and neck. Dickie pushed open doors: doors to the warming kitchen, doors to another passage, doors to the butler's pantry. Her heart thumped as they entered the dining room. But it was empty, save for an ominously overturned chair.

On the floor by the chair were a puddle of water and, a little away, a miraculously unbroken crystal goblet, glinting in the light of the candelabra. A forlorn, half-finished bowl of onion soup still sat at the head of the table, waiting for dinner to resume.

Dickie led her to a drawing room deeper inside the house. A gaggle of housemaids stood by the door, clutching one another's sleeves and peering in cautiously. They fell back at Verity's approach and bobbed unnecessary curtsies.

Her erstwhile lover reclined, supine, on a settee of dark blue. He wore a disconcertingly peaceful expression. Someone had loosened his necktie and opened his shirt at the collar. This state of undress contrasted sharply against his stiff positioning: his hands folded together above his breastbone like those of an effigy atop a stone sarcophagus.

Mr. Prior, the butler, stood guard over Bertie's inert body. At her entrance, he hurried to her side and whispered, "He's not breathing."

Her own breath quite left her at that. "Since when?"

"Since before Dickie went to the kitchen, Madame," said the butler. His hands trembled very slightly.

Was that five minutes? Seven? Verity stood immobile a long moment, unable to think. It didn't make any sense. Bertie was a healthy man who experienced few physical maladies.

She crossed the room and dipped to one knee before the settee. "Bertie," she called softly, addressing him more intimately than she had at any point in the past decade. "Can you hear me, Bertie?"

He did not respond. No dramatic fluttering of the eyelids. No looking at her as if he were Snow White freshly awakened from a poisoned sleep and she the prince who brought him back to life.

She touched him, something else she hadn't done in ten years. His palm was wet, as was his starched cuff. He was still warm, but her finger pressed over his wrist could detect no pulse, only an obstinate stillness.

She dug the pad of her thumb into his veins. Could he possibly be dead? He was only thirty-eight years old. He hadn't even been ill. And he had an assignation with Mrs. Danner tonight. The oysters for his post-coital fortification were resting on a bed of ice in the cold larder and the hazelnut butter was ready for the dessert crepes beloved by Mrs. Danner.

His pulse refused to beat.

She released his hand and rose, her mind numb. The kitchen crew had stayed put at her command. But the rest of the indoor staff had assembled in the drawing room, the men behind Mr. Prior, the women behind Mrs. Boyce, the housekeeper . . . everyone pressed close to the walls, a sea of black uniforms with foam caps of white collars and aprons.

In response to Mrs. Boyce's inquiring gaze, Verity shook her head. The man who was once to be her prince was dead. He had taken her up to his castle, but had not kept her there. In the end she had returned to the kitchen, dumped the shards of her delusion in the rubbish bin, and carried on as if she'd never believed that she stood to become the mistress of this esteemed house.

"We'd better cable his solicitors, then," said Mrs. Boyce. "They'll need to inform his brother that Fairleigh Park is now his."

His *brother*. In all the drama of Bertie's abrupt passing, Verity had not even thought of the succession of Fairleigh Park. Now she shook somewhere deep inside, like a dish of aspic set down too hard.

She nodded vaguely. "I'll be in the kitchen should you need me."

In her copy of Taillevent's *Le Viandier*, where the book opened to a recipe for gilded chicken with quenelles, Verity kept a brown envelope marked *List of Cheese Merchants in the 16th Arondissement.*

The envelope contained, among other things, a news clipping from the county fish wrapper, about the Liberals' recent victory in the general election after six years in opposition. Verity had written the date in a corner: 16.08.1892. In the middle of the article, a grainy photograph of Stuart Somerset gazed back at her.

She never touched his image, for fear that her strokes would blur it. Sometimes she looked at it very closely, the clipping almost at her nose. Sometimes she put it as far as her lap, but never farther, never beyond reach.

The man in the photograph was dramatically handsome—the face of a Shakespearean actor in his prime, all sharp peaks and deep angles. From afar she'd watched his meteoric rise—one of London's most sought-after barristers, and now, with the Liberals back in power, Mr. Gladstone's Chief Whip in the House of Commons—quite something for a man who'd spent his first nine years in a Manchester slum.

He'd accomplished it all on his own merits, of course, but she'd played her small part. She'd walked away from him, from hopes and dreams enough to spawn a generation of poets, so that he could be the man he was meant to be, the man whose face on her clipping she dared not touch.

Chapter Two

W e've known each other a long time, Miss Bessler," said Stuart Somerset.

At the Besslers' Hanover Square house, the drawing room had once been a rather ghastly green. But Miss Bessler, taking the reins of the household after her mother's passing, had papered the walls in a shade of carmine that was almost sensual, yet still solemn enough for the home of a former Chancellor of the Exchequer.

Miss Bessler raised a severe eyebrow at Stuart. She looked very fine tonight: Her eyes were bright, her cheeks held a tinge of becoming blush, her Prussian blue gown was pure drama against the crimson chaise longue on which they sat nearly knee to knee.

"We've been *friends* a long time, Mr. Somerset," she corrected him.

They'd met years before she'd made her official debut, when both Stuart and the Besslers had been guests at a weeklong house party at Lyndhurst Hall.

He'd been alone in the garden, smoking a cigarette, thinking of someone else. And she'd escaped from the nursery to watch the dancing in the ballroom, indignant that a mature, clever girl such as herself wasn't allowed to join the fun.

"Yes, we have indeed been friends a long time," he said.

And it had been with pride and affection that he'd watched the lovely child—though she'd always insisted that at only a few weeks short of fifteen, she'd been no child—grow into an even lovelier young woman.

"That's much better," said Miss Bessler. "Now, won't you please hurry and ask the question so I may tell you how delighted and honored I will be to be your wife?"

Stuart chuckled. It was as he'd thought. Mr. Bessler hadn't been able to keep the news to himself. He took her hands in his. "In that case, would you make me very happy by consenting to become my wife?"

"Yes, I would," she said firmly. She looked happy—and relieved, as if she hadn't quite believed until this moment that he really would offer for her. Her hands squeezed his. "Thank you. We both know that I'm not getting any younger."

He still thought her a young woman, because of the twelve-year difference in their ages. But there was some unfortunate truth to her words. At twenty-five, with eight seasons under her belt, she was far older than the usual adolescents on display in London's ballrooms and drawing rooms.

"Not that it would change my answer, because I'm

too practical and selfish to give you up," she said, "but I do hope you haven't proposed entirely out of pity, my dear Stuart—may I at last call you Stuart?"

"Pity is the last of my motives, Lizzy," he said. "There is no one else in all of Society with whom I'd rather spend my life."

He'd delayed looking for a wife until he was old enough to have sired the current crop of debutantes. He didn't want a seventeen-year-old, either on his arm or in his bed. He needed a more seasoned spouse who would not be flustered by the demands of an MP's household. Lizzy was a descendant of an old and highly regarded family, a statesman's daughter, and a gracious and competent hostess. And she was beautiful. She was everything Stuart could sensibly hope for in a wife at this stage in his life.

There were, of course, his more insensible hopes—but he'd had to accept that some dreams were stillborn and some memories mirages.

"I don't understand why you haven't been whisked off to the altar years ago," he continued. "And part of me still feels that I'm asking you to settle for an old man of somewhat dubious ancestry—"

"No. I only wish that it hadn't taken you so long," she said. One of her hands tightened over his, and she looked down for a second. "I only wish we'd been married years already."

Her sentiment surprised him. True enough that there had been a time, near the beginning of their acquaintance, when she'd been a little infatuated with him. But by her first Season, when she'd become the belle of the ball, her sights had been set firmly and ambitiously above a mere lawyer and MP.

"In that case, you'll forgive me for asking that the wedding take place before the opening of Parliament?"

The opening of Parliament was at the end of January. She regarded him again with mock severity. "I don't know if I'll forgive you entirely for handing a wedding of such magnitude to me with only two months to prepare—and for robbing me of a proper wedding trip."

"I apologize in advance for the rush. When Parliament closes, we'll go anywhere you wish. And as to the preparations, I'll put Marsden at your disposal."

She frowned. "Must we involve your secretary in this matter?"

"Only so that you may have time to sleep and dine and bathe once in a while."

"But Mr. Marsden grates on my nerves."

Women usually adored Marsden. Stuart lifted one of her hands and lightly kissed the back of it. "Let him help. I do not wish you to run yourself to the ground."

She grimaced, then sighed. "All right, I will tolerate Mr. Marsden, but only to save you the worrying."

He rose. "Shall we find your father and inform him that he will soon have me for a son-in-law?"

She tilted her head and batted her eyelashes. "Aren't you forgetting something, sir?"

She expected him to kiss her. He sat down on the chaise longue again and pulled her toward him. She lifted her chin and obligingly closed her eyes.

He placed his hands on either side of her face. Her

cheeks were as smooth as the finest powder. And when he leaned in closer, he smelled the fragrance of lily of the valley, the same perfume she'd worn ever since she turned sixteen.

His lips almost touched hers. He held still for a moment, then kissed her on the forehead instead. Strange that they should end up engaged, a middle-aged man too late to the Marriage Mart and a young woman who should have been out of it long ago.

"We are to be married now," she chided him. "You must stop being so brotherly."

Brotherly. Avuncular was more like it.

A knock sounded at the door. They glanced at each other. Stuart rose, expecting that it was Mr. Bessler, impatient for the good news. But it was the butler.

"There is someone waiting to see you, sir. A Mr. Marvin, from Locke, Marvin, and Sons. He says it's urgent. I have him in the morning room."

Stuart forwned. Locke, Marvin, & Sons were Bertie's solicitors. What could Bertie possibly want of him?

"If you'll excuse me," he said to his new fiancée.

Stuart's first reaction upon seeing Mr. Marvin was that the years had not been kind: The solicitor had deteriorated from the rather eminent-looking individual Stuart remembered to this nondescript little old man. Then he realized, no, he'd never met Mr. Marvin. He was thinking of Mr. Locke, with whom he'd conferred twice early in '82, to see if they could come to some sort of mutually acceptable agreement that would allow Stuart, bankrupt from Bertie's five years of relentless legal maneuvers, to bring an end to the nightmare and still hold on to a fig leaf of dignity.

"Mr. Marvin, an unexpected pleasure," he said, offering his hand.

"My apologies, Mr. Somerset, for disturbing you in your hour of leisure," answered Mr. Marvin.

"I assume it's a matter of some importance that brought you here today," Stuart said.

"It is, sir," said Mr. Marvin. "My condolences. Your brother passed away earlier this evening."

"I beg your pardon?"

"Mr. Bertram Somerset passed away earlier this evening. I called on you as soon as I received the news myself. Your man was kind enough to give me directions to Mr. Bessler's house."

Whether Bertie lived or died made little difference to Stuart, except—

"You mean to tell me I'm his heir?"

"Indeed, sir," affirmed the lawyer. "As he never married and sired no children, all his worldly possessions have devolved to you: Fairleigh Park, land in Manchester, Leeds, and Liverpool, a house in Torquay—"

"Excuse me," said Stuart. He didn't need an enumeration of Bertie's properties. They'd fought over every last rock and brick that hadn't been part of Fairleigh Park. "How did he die?"

"The doctor believes it to have been a catastrophic failure of the heart."

"A catastrophic failure of the heart," echoed Stuart.

Frankly he was surprised. He thought Bertie's heart had withered long ago.

He asked the questions expected of him—Would there be an inquest? Who was responsible for funeral arrangements? Did the staff at Fairleigh Park require immediate directions from him?—and thanked the solicitor for his trouble.

Mr. Marvin showed himself out. Stuart returned to the drawing room. Mr. Bessler had joined his daughter. They must have guessed—both waited solemnly for him to speak.

"My brother is no longer with us," said Stuart. "He passed away several hours ago."

"My condolences," said Mr. Bessler.

"I'm sorry," said Lizzy.

"We will have to delay the engagement announcement until after his funeral," Stuart said.

"Of course," said both the Besslers.

"And you'll have your hands full after we are married, Lizzy, for I have inherited Fairleigh Park."

"That is not a problem," she answered. "You know I like to lord over houses, the bigger the better."

He smiled briefly. "Shall we toast our engagement, then? I'm afraid I must leave soon, much sooner than I'd like."

He had a case that would come up before the Master of Rolls in a fortnight. And the necessity of attending Bertie's funeral and seeing to the estate in the meanwhile meant he must start final preparations for the case right away.

Champagne was brought out and consumed.

Stuart took his leave, but Lizzy followed him to the vestibule.

"Are you quite all right?" she asked. "About your brother, that is."

"I couldn't be more all right if I tried," he said in all honesty. "He and I haven't spoken in twenty years."

"It's just that, when I first met you, there were times when you seemed disconsolate. I'd always wondered if it was because of your brother."

He shook his head. "I wasn't disconsolate." Then, more truthfully, "And it wasn't because of my brother."

❧

Stuart lived not in his constituency of South Hackney, but in the elegant enclaves of Belgravia. From the Bessler house, he returned directly home and worked 'til quarter past two, when he judged he'd done enough for the night.

He poured himself some whiskey and took an intemperate swallow. The news of Bertie's death affected him more now than it had earlier—there was a numbness in his head that had nothing to do with fatigue.

It was the shock of it, he supposed. He hadn't expected Mortality, ever present though it was, to strike Bertie, of all people.

Two shelves up from the whiskey decanter was a framed photograph of Bertie and himself, taken when Bertie had been eighteen and he seventeen, shortly after he'd been legitimized by both an Act of Parliament and the marriage of his parents

What had Bertie said to him that day?

You may be legitimized, but you will never be one of us. You don't know how Father panicked when it looked as if your mother might live. Your people are laborers and drunks and petty criminals. Don't flatter yourself otherwise.

For years afterward, whenever he'd remembered Bertie, it was Bertie as he had been at that precise moment in time, impeccably turned out, a cold smile on his face, satisfied to have at last ruined something wonderful for his bastard-born brother.

But the slim youth in the picture, his fine summer coat faded to rust, resembled no one's idea of a nemesis. His fair hair, ruthlessly parted and slicked back, would have looked gauche in more fashionable circles. The square placement of his feet and the hand thrust nonchalantly into the coat pocket meant to indicate great assurance. As it was, he looked like any other eighteen-year-old, trying to radiate a manly confidence he didn't possess.

Stuart frowned. How long had it been since he'd last *looked* at the photograph?

The answer came far more easily than he'd expected. Not since that night. He'd last looked at it with *her,* who'd studied the image with a disturbing concentration.

Do you still hate him? she'd asked, giving the photograph back to him.

Sometimes, he'd answered absently, distracted by the nearness of her blush-pink lips. She'd been all eyes and lips, eyes the color of a tropical ocean, lips as full and soft as feather pillows.

Then I don't like him either, she'd said, smiling oddly.

Do you know him? he'd asked—suddenly, and for absolutely no reason.

No. She'd shaken her head with a grave finality, her beautiful eyes once again sad. *I don't know him at all.*

Chapter Three

June 1882

She didn't know him at all, Verity thought, a ringing dizziness in her head. She didn't know him at all.

"You lied to me," Bertie repeated his accusation, his words as heavy and hard as manacles.

"I did not," she said, trying to keep her voice down to a reasonable volume. "Why would I lie about something like that?"

"Should I even dignify that with an answer?" Bertie was too well-bred to sneer, but the contempt in his voice made her turn her face, as if bracing for a slap.

"I was not trying to trap you into marriage," she said through clenched teeth.

She wanted to marry him, of course. She loved him. And marrying him would rectify all the missteps of her youth and restore her to Society. But her pride was as great as his, and if he thought any less of her—

"'I know something that would make you hold your head up high again,'" he mimicked her. "'You can marry the daughter of a duke.'"

The battle for his inheritance had gone all the way up to the Court of Appeals. And their decision had devastated Bertie. He had not believed that he, the rightful heir, would be evicted from his own town house. Yet he had been, by a horde of constables, and allowed to remove only his clothes.

He could never show his face in London again.

She had been despondent for him, had railed against his brother and the bewigged, berobed old men who wouldn't know a proper application of Common Law if it robbed them in broad daylight. And then an idea had come to her, a wonderful idea that would solve all their problems and salve both their battered dignities at once.

"I told you—"

"They showed me the Lady Vera Drake's photographs, and she was not you. They showed me her tombstone. They even offered to summon the physician who attended her on her deathbed."

"Did you tell them you wanted to marry me?" It would have made all the difference, particularly to the duchess.

He glared at her. "Have you completely lost your mind? It was embarrassing enough for me to go before Their Graces and inquire if this servant of mine could be their late beloved niece. My God, if word ever got around to my brother—"

He took a deep breath. "No, I don't wish to marry my cook, thank you very much, if that's all you are."

For a moment she couldn't speak. Of course she knew that he wouldn't marry someone who was only his cook—though there had been gentlemen who'd married their servants, or even stage actresses, and lived and prospered—still, it tore her to hear him say it aloud. *If that's all you are.*

When she found her voice again, the words that emerged were hesitant and beseeching. "The duke and the duchess are not the only ones who know me. We can find my old governess. Or Monsieur David. They won't lie about me to save their own standing."

"No, Verity." It was Bertie who spoke through clenched teeth now. "I have met and broken bread with Their Graces; more God-fearing, upright, and gracious people I've never come across. What they have shown me is proof enough. I refuse to go along any further with this circus, subjecting them or myself to duplicitous nobodies who would say anything for a guinea."

So he did think her a liar, a duplicitous nobody who would say anything to land herself a prize husband. She wanted to lash out at him. Were she still the Lady Vera Drake he would be quite beneath her. He wasn't even titled. And the manor at Fairleigh Park was a thatched-roof cottage compared to the splendor that was Lyndhurst Hall.

She said nothing. She should have kept her mouth shut all along. She should have known.

Bertie sighed. He moved away from the window, where he'd been stiffly standing, to the embroidered stool next to the bed. "Let this be the end of it," he said wearily, pulling off his shoes and socks. "Now come to bed."

"I'm sorry?" Had he lost *his* mind?

"I said, come to bed," he repeated impatiently.

"I don't think so."

He didn't even look at her. "Don't be childish."

"I don't think it's childish to not want to sleep with a man who believes me an unscrupulous adventuress."

He pulled off his cuff links. "If that's what you are, why should you be offended?"

Until this moment she'd believed that he loved her too. The black sensation in her—was it how a snowman felt on the first day of spring, that the world was ending, that she herself would dissipate into nothingness?

"That is not what I am, therefore I am deeply offended." Her voice rose, as brittle and bitter as burnt caramel. "And I fail to understand why *you* would still want anything to do with me, as apparently I'm such repellent dross!"

At last their eyes met, but the only emotion she discerned in his was a profound irritation. "Fine. Enjoy your umbrage. But refrain from impugning my character. It was never the beauty of your soul that interested me and you know it."

Sometimes, when I savor your dinners, it's more than food. I luxuriate in the beauty of your soul, the sweet mystery and refulgence of it, like an antechamber of Heaven.

Lies. All lies. And she'd believed them.

She forced her tears to remain where they were, welled in her eyes, and bobbed a curtsy—after their first night together, he'd told her she need not curtsy to him anymore. "Good night, Mr. Somerset."

She would never call him Bertie again as long as he lived.

Chapter Four

The day was fading. The carriage, chiming softly, pulled into view. Bumbry, the coachman, had spent the past three days polishing tack, button, and handle. In the wash of lamplight and candlelight through windows freshly scrubbed with ammonia and spirit of wine, the brougham shone as if it were made of jet and onyx.

Verity watched from the solarium. Her father had had a carriage like that, a gorgeous brute the size of an omnibus. By the time she arrived at Fairleigh Park, she'd had quite enough of poverty and backbreaking work. She'd wanted to ride in a fancy carriage again, wear beautiful clothes, and sleep on a stack of feather mattresses higher than she was tall.

At times she wondered how much she'd loved Bertie for himself, and how much because he represented everything she'd lost. But it was not a question that troubled her exceedingly. Would the story of Elizabeth Bennet be half so triumphant and beloved had Mr. Darcy been a mere yeoman farmer? She thought not.

Bertie, like Mr. Darcy, had had ten thousand pounds a year. The Somersets had been a distinguished family since the Hundred Years War—the estate had been granted to an ancestor by royal decree in 1398 for valor in battle. Since then, though no Somerset descendant had as of yet been raised to the peerage, numerous sons had been knighted for service to the crown in war and in peace, the latest being Sir Francis, Bertie's father.

The manor at Fairleigh Park, rebuilt early in the previous century, was one of the finest Robert Adam houses in the land. The gardens, nestled in a crook of the river Ure and nurtured by generations of horticulture enthusiasts, were forty acres of color and idyll, beautiful in every season.

Bumbry reined the team of four to a full stop. Geoffrey and Dickie leapt off their perches at the back of the carriage. Her hand tightened on the curtain that concealed her.

Except for Mrs. Boyce and Mr. Prior, who awaited the new master outside, on the lowest of the wide steps leading up to the front door, most of the other servants had assembled in the entrance hall, under the high blue-and-white ceiling that had always reminded her of exquisite jasperware.

Verity would not join them.

It was not a decision she'd made lightly. She'd thought of little else for days. What did it mean that their lives should intersect again, so long removed from the one night that had set her sky aflame like a rare comet? That he should arrive here one day—the lord of the manor, the prince of the castle—was Fate trying to tell her something? That perhaps it wasn't yet too late, that it was still possible for their broken fairy tale to be made whole?

But fairy tales concerned only virtuous, blameless girls, girls as pure in body and soul as they were beautiful. There were no fairy tales for willful women of impaired judgment who'd brought about their own disgrace and heartache.

The footman pulled down the steps and opened the carriage door. Her heart seized. He'd had eyes dark as the hours before dawn, beautiful cheekbones, and a surprisingly, almost shockingly intimate smile. And he'd wanted her with the force of cyclones and maelstroms—God, how he'd destroyed her resistance.

He alit from the carriage now, all hat and dark, flying cape. She held her breath. He lifted his gaze to encompass the manor that was now his.

She stumbled back from the window, leaned against the nearest wall, and pressed a hand over her chest. Something was wrong. She was supposed to look upon him with no more than a bittersweet wistfulness. Not this shortness of breath or this frantic rush of blood in her ears, like a swollen spring river that had finally broken through the winter ice.

Not when she'd already made up her mind to leave, very soon, perhaps as soon as Bertie's funeral.

She only wanted time enough to give him a gift, a gift that had been in the making—she realized just now—since the hour she first left him, her battered valise in hand, a piece of the cake he'd brought her in her pocket.

❧

Stuart had made only one request to the staff, that they leave Bertie's apartment and belongings undisturbed. For all his otherwise indifference, he found himself somewhat curious for a glimpse into Bertie's final days.

The master's bedchamber, like most of the rest of the house, reflected the vibrancy and sensuality of a different era. The walls were a mellow gold, the ceiling an aged champagne on which had been painted a mural of bucolic charm reminiscent of Watteau's *fêtes galantes*.

Stuart opened a wardrobe. Bertie's clothes. Dozens of shirts, waistcoats and under-waistcoats, drawers full of neck clothes and handkerchiefs—everything in its place.

He pulled out a day coat. It was not for a heavyset man: Bertie had not thickened excessively despite his love of good food.

Mrs. Boyce hovered in the doorway to the bedchamber. Stuart realized the housekeeper was waiting to be addressed. "Yes, Mrs. Boyce?"

"Should we make room in the wardrobe for your clothes, sir?"

"No need." He would stay only three days on this

trip and had brought very few things. "You may see to it before my next visit."

"And that would be, sir . . ."

"In January," said Stuart. He would have planned for a house party had he known he'd have Fairleigh Park before Christmas. But as such, he'd already accepted a yuletide invitation to Lyndhurst Hall.

And his life and his career were in London. After the wedding he'd let Lizzy manage Fairleigh Park and make use of it as she saw fit: She was good at such things. "You may return to your duties, Mrs. Boyce. I'm quite settled."

"Thank you, sir," said Mrs. Boyce, a largish woman with the features of a farmer's wife but the pale, unlined skin of someone who'd spent her entire life indoors. "Dinner is at half past seven, sir. We keep country hours here."

"Half past seven?" Before they'd come up to Bertie's apartment, Mrs. Boyce had offered Stuart tea, and he, thirsty and somewhat hungry, had accepted. There'd been scones and biscuits from the housekeeper's still room and he'd eaten his fill. "No. Have it served at nine."

Mrs. Boyce blinked. "But, sir, if you started only at nine, you would be at the table 'til eleven."

"No, I assure you I'll have finished in half an hour, if not less."

Mrs. Boyce blinked again. "You'll finish twelve courses in half an hour, sir?"

Twelve courses? What in the world? "Did my brother have twelve-course dinners every day?"

"No, only eight, sir. But we thought, since this is your first dinner at Fairleigh Park—"

"Three courses will quite suffice." Bertie might have been mad for his dinners, but Stuart paid little mind to food, if at all.

"But the menu is already set, sir," said Mrs. Boyce, with an air of desperation. "Perhaps you would like to see it?"

"No, I will not need to see it. Inform the cook: no more than three courses."

For a moment, Mrs. Boyce looked as if he'd condemned her to wrestle crocodiles on the banks of the Nile. Then she acquiesced. "Very good, sir."

After Mrs. Boyce left, Stuart closed the wardrobe door and went to the bed. On which side had Bertie slept? He tried the night table to the left of the bedstead. It held two books of philosophy—both by Epicurus, of course—and a few drams of laudanum.

Bertie had never kept a diary, as far as Stuart knew. So the books and the laudanum would be as intimate a look at Bertie's private life as Stuart was allowed. But all the same, he circumnavigated the bed and pulled open the drawers of the other night table.

Those drawers yielded only a folded handkerchief identical to the score of others in the wardrobe. Not exactly a revealing personal item. Stuart shook the handkerchief open.

It wasn't clean, nor was it soiled, but there were irregular translucent spots where the fabric had absorbed some sort of grease. Butter, by the faint smell of it. Stuart lifted the handkerchief to his nose.

Butter and a trace of the pungency of lemon, mellowed by the sweetness of sugar. He examined the handkerchief again. Good, white linen, Bertie's initials in one corner. Bertie had used it to wrap around a piece of cake or pastry. Afterward, he'd folded the handkerchief into a precise square and placed it in the farthest corner of the nightstand, its edges exactly flush with those of the drawer.

Had Bertie kept it for the smell? Stuart sniffed the handkerchief again. An ordinary enough smell. What had it been? A slice of lemon pound cake? He could think of nothing interesting, memorable, or important about the smell of lemon pound cake.

He inhaled deeply, trying to extract some hidden essence from the smell. It remained faint. Yet with every breath he took, the scent grew subtler and lovelier. And suddenly it was the sparkling odor of warm southern climes where lemon trees flourished under cobalt skies.

Stuart lowered the handkerchief, amazed almost as much by the intricacy of the scent as by his imaginative reaction. It was only pound cake, and he didn't even care for pound cake. Yet as he put the fabric to his nose again and closed his eyes, he could very well believe himself in the gardens of a Mediterranean villa, surrounded by potted lemon trees laden with fruit the color of sunshine.

Had Bertie been still alive, he'd be able to tell Stuart why he'd kept the handkerchief, and what it had been that had left behind the alluring, evocative odor.

But Bertie was dead.

Stuart dropped the handkerchief back and closed the drawer.

❧

The dining room at Fairleigh Park was cavernous and drafty. Stuart informed Prior that he'd have his meal in the bright, creamy library instead.

Prior's reaction was a dismay nearly identical to that of Mrs. Boyce's. For a second Stuart thought the butler would clutch his chest and fall over. But the head manservant's training held. "Yes, sir," he answered. "We will have a place set here for you."

Prior and his minions arranged the place setting on the mahogany desk as Stuart annotated a stack of bills on a reading table. He'd already reviewed proposed legislations concerning fertilizers, barbed wires, and conveyance of mails when a footman marched past with a soup tureen.

"Dinner is served, sir," said Prior.

Stuart settled himself at the desk and opened an ironed copy of the *Times* to an investigation of the recent anarchist bomb attack in Paris. Vaguely he was aware that Prior and the two footmen looked askance at one another, as if he were reading not the country's newspaper of record, but a copy of *Fanny Hill*. Then Prior cleared his throat, and lifted the lid of the tureen.

Suddenly the library, which had smelled mainly of old books and old cigar smoke, was redolent of summer, of crisp cucumbers ripening overnight on the vine. Stuart lowered his paper a moment to see what had produced such a potently pleasant odor. Prior laid a bowl of pale, thick potage in front of him.

Stuart took a sip. The sip turned into an explosion of flavors on his tongue, rich, deep, pure, like eating the sunshine and verdure of a fine June afternoon. Startled, he did something he almost never did—putting down his newspaper when he dined alone—and stared into the soup.

Slowly, he lifted another spoonful to his mouth. No, the first sip had not been a deviation. The soup was indeed that good. He tried to taste each individual ingredient: cucumbers, onion, a hint of garlic, butter, broth, and cream. Nothing unusual, fancy, or particularly noble. Yet it was . . . it was sublime.

He cared nothing for food. Hadn't in ages and ages. Food was sustenance, something to keep him alive and healthy, nothing more. A dinner at the Tour d'Argent was no different from a dinner at the lowliest fish-and-chip shop: just dinner.

This was not just dinner. This was as dangerous and unpredictable as the presence of a scantily clad woman in the cell of a monk who'd taken a vow of chastity.

He set down his spoon. Thirty years ago he'd have begged for one more sip. Twenty years ago he'd have been thrilled to discover that his sense of taste hadn't permanently atrophied. Ten years ago he might have taken this sudden reawakening of his palate for an augury of wonderful things to come, things he'd wished for with the single-mindedness of a long-buried seed seeking the unbearable beauty of a world drenched in light.

Tonight he wished only to read his newspaper at dinner without being distracted—or profoundly disturbed—by a bowl of soup.

But his fingers had already gripped the spoon again and skimmed the surface of the soup. His hand rose, lifting the spoon to his lips. He felt himself leaning forward a fraction of an inch.

He forced the spoon to return to the soup. It was too late. He was too old for this, too accustomed to being indifferent to his meals.

He resumed his perusal of the newspaper, though he was no longer certain whether he was reading of French bombings or American elections.

After an uneasy pause, Prior took away the soup.

❧

Dinner was a bloodbath of Romans-at-Carthage proportions.

Verity had been perplexed by Mr. Somerset's strident demand for only three courses, but not overly alarmed—if she was as good as she believed herself to be, then one course was enough. One mouthful was enough.

She did not learn about the soup immediately, for items carried away from the dinner table were returned to the scullery, rather than the kitchen itself. For the second course she served prawns that had been caught off the coast at dawn, creamy pink and bathed in a velvety white wine sauce. Along with the prawns she sent half a dozen small plates: lightly fried oysters, mussels in a curried broth, glazed chestnut, buttered peas, gratinéed potato, and braised leek.

After her initial diaster-laden months as Monsieur David's apprentice, in the Marquess of Londonderry's household, Verity had realized, to her own and everyone else's amazement, that she was talented before a stove. She had a sensitive nose, an unpolluted palate, and a manual dexterity rivaling that of a circus juggler's.

But she'd always cooked from instructions handed down to her—Monsieur David, having worked under the great Monsieur Soyer as well as at the court of Napoleon III, had a wealth of recipes that most cooks would give their knife arm to possess. That was, until she'd met *him*, a man who could find no pleasure in food, who only watched her wistfully as she ate and ate and ate.

Only then did she start thinking about the desires, fears, joys, and pains so inextricably intertwined in something as simple as a meal. Only then did she begin to cook purposefully, not merely to earn her wages and keep a roof over her head, but to satisfy hungers that extended beyond the needs of the stomach.

And everything she'd done, she did with him in mind, sometimes with memories of him like a print of fire in her head, sometimes with only a faint trace of longing seeping through her thoughts. But always, hovering just above the threshold of consciousness, was the constant refrain: if one day she had a chance to cook for him . . . if one day she had a chance to cook for him . . .

Her food became sensual—the tenderness of a kiss, the abandon of rolling down a grassy knoll on a summer afternoon, the intensity of a lover's gaze. She created new dishes—dishes both humble and extravagant—with but one goal in mind: to break through the barrier of the years and return him to a time before his losses had robbed him of this most primary of pleasures.

She wanted to give him happiness on a plate.

One bite, that was all she needed.

And one bite was apparently all she got. Mr. Prior himself came into the kitchen and took her aside to speak to her. The soup had been rejected after two sips, said Mr. Prior. And when the second course had been spread before Mr. Somerset, he'd sampled one of everything, chewed gravely, sat silent another minute, and risen from the table.

He was done with dinner. He did not even require the third course, the *petit pot de crème au chocolat* that the year before had had Monsieur du Gard, the Parisian industrialist, weep openly at the table because it made him remember his chocolate-loving sister, who'd given up school—and chocolate—so he could be educated.

Minutes passed before Verity realized that Mr. Prior was still speaking. She laid a hand on his sleeve to stop him from further apologies. "It's all right, Mr. Prior," she said, too numb to quite understand what had happened. "Gentlemen are what they are. Their preferences must prevail."

She troweled on her French accent. Everyone belowstairs knew that when her English approximated the slurriness of wet cement, she was done speaking.

Mr. Prior nodded and left. Verity turned back to her apprentices. "Well done," she said. "It was one of the best dinners we ever cooked."

And so it had been, abbreviated though it was. She'd thought it would be enough—it and all the blessings her heart could bestow—but she was wrong.

She had been entirely mistaken.

❧

At eleven o'clock at night, someone knocked on the library door. It was Prior.

"Would you be needing anything else, sir?" asked the butler.

As a matter of fact, Stuart would. Having had next to nothing at dinner, he was hungry.

Hunger rarely bothered him, as it merely signaled that mealtime was near. What he experienced now, however, was a different beast altogether. He didn't need food; he craved it.

It had been almost two hours since dinner had been removed from the library. He could still smell traces of it, fresh and voluptuous. Could still taste the miserly bites he'd allowed himself.

He'd made hardly a dent in the financial records before him. His mind, disciplined and focused otherwise, swam in images of food, luscious, pornographic images of the courses he'd ruthlessly sent away at dinner and the courses he'd forbidden from even arriving at the table.

"Yes. I'd like a sandwich."

At home he'd have gone to the kitchen himself, rather than summoning someone else. But on his first day as the new lord of the manor, he must be more lordly in his conduct, for as he judged his servants for their efficacy and character, they judged him too, for his worthiness.

"Certainly, sir," said Prior. "I will send someone to speak to Madame Durant."

The name was familiar. In another moment it all came back to Stuart.

The gossip had first reached him when he was on the march into Afghanistan to take part in one of the more stupid wars in history. What a laugh that had provided against the bleakness of the Khyber Pass: the image of Bertie shagging his cook—his *cook*, who was probably three times his girth and as ugly as the bottom of her favorite sauté pan. How the mighty had fallen.

"Madame Durant is still here?" The talebearers had been quiet on the matter a good many years. He'd assumed that Bertie had long ago come to his senses and sent Madame Durant packing.

"Yes, sir. We are pleased that she has stayed with us. Her skills are unparalleled."

Stuart paid little mind to the implicit rebuke in the butler's words. Madame Durant had to be one of the most infamous domestic servants in all of Britain, Bertie's insatiable lover who—some said—had introduced him to depravities involving pastry cream and rolling pins.

She cooked as if it were a prelude to a seduction, as if she'd bartered her soul to Lucifer to turn the humblest turnip to pure arousal for the tongue. Little wonder Bertie had not been able to resist her, Bertie who had loved the pleasures of the table since he was a boy, with a seriousness and a passion others reserved for hunting and horse racing—or law and politics.

"Is it quite necessary to disturb Madame Durant for a mere sandwich?"

"Once Madame Durant dismisses her staff for the night, all requests for the kitchen go directly to her, sir."

Stuart had meant to imply that Prior or one of the footmen could take care of the sandwich. Clearly the thought hadn't even occurred to Prior. It had been decades since Stuart was part of a household of such size; he'd forgotten the strict division of labor that marked the belowstairs hierarchy. A footman would be insulted and scandalized to be asked to perform the work of the kitchen, much as Madame Durant would be if she were asked to accompany the next Mrs. Somerset around town and carry the latter's purchases.

"Very well, then," he said, acquiescing, his tone marked by something that resembled anticipation far too much for his comfort.

Verity lived, as did most of the servants, in the higher reaches of the manor. As befitting an upper servant in a position of authority, her dwelling consisted of a parlor and a bedchamber. The rooms were small, but her sheets were not on display the moment she opened her door, and the parlor allowed her to accommodate the other upper servants for tea and an occasional game of cards.

In her thirteen years at Fairleigh Park, she'd made these rooms, spare and dowdy when she first arrived, into a comfortable, pretty home for herself. The rose silk-upholstered divan on which she sat, listening to Dickie relay Mr. Somerset's request, had come to her when Bertie had changed the decor in the solarium. His offer of the divan, along with two dainty end tables and a walnut escritoire, had flattered and fluttered her, presaging the day he would suddenly kiss her as they discussed the relative merits of sauce soubise and sauce béarnaise.

The rest of her parlor matched the furniture in gentility. The wallpaper, silver fleurs-de-lis on an expanse of azure, was good enough to grace the drawing room of a prosperous London merchant. Her carpet, a more profound blue than the wallpaper, had been weaved by Turkish girls who must now be in their dotage. On the console table by the door, beneath an oval antique mirror just big enough for her face, bloomed a vase of snowdrops that the head gardener had brought her in exchange for a batch of her madeleines, whispered to be as delicious as the first day of spring and twice as seductive.

She wanted Dickie to leave, so she could pluck all the petals from the flowers and crush everything to a black pulp with her bare hands.

She hadn't been so livid in years. She'd certainly never imagined it possible for her to be angry at *him*, she who'd only ever thought of him with the fervent devotion laid at the feet of a beautiful saint.

Perhaps she was more enraged at herself, for her abysmal failure, for believing that she'd achieved sorcery and enchantment enough to release him from the spell that bound him, and made him taste only in shades of gray.

She tried to take refuge in rationality. If he didn't like her food, then he didn't like it. It wasn't personal. None of this was personal. And of course he hadn't meant to saddle her with the making of a sandwich; the request only came to her because of her own long-standing insistence that she, and not her subordinates—many of whose working day started at half past six in the morning—took care of Bertie's late-night whims.

But *he* was not allowed to have human faults. Not when she'd held him in such esteem, such perfection of memory. Not when she'd lived chastely and reverently in deference to that memory. Not when she still—

She rose, went to the escritoire, and pulled out a piece of writing paper.

"Be so kind as to wait a minute," she said to Dickie as she unscrewed the cap of her fountain pen.

The footman who came into the library bore not a tray of foodstuff, but a folded note and a look on his face reminiscent of Prior's silent dismay earlier in the evening. Why was it that anything having to do with dining or the cook sent everyone in the house scrambling for their smelling salts?

The note, written in French, went a long way toward answering Stuart's question.

Dear Sir,

Dinnertime in this house is half past seven. When I have all my forces marshaled at Waterloo, I cannot be expected to wage a campaign in Leipzig at the drop of a hat.

The venue for dinner is the dining room. Generations of effort have gone into building, maintaining, and bettering the passage between the kitchen and the house. Years of training and practice are necessary before the house staff and the kitchen staff achieve such coordination that food arrives on the table piping hot and cooked to perfection. You may not, at will, decide that the library, at the opposite end of the house, serves your purpose better. It disrupts the entire process for everyone else involved.

My responsibilities in this house extend to producing breakfast, luncheon, and dinner. If you wish to dine at other times, your request must be made in advance. Mr. Bertram Somerset understood this. I'm surprised that you, sir, reputed to be a man of the people, have so little grasp of the consideration due those who labor on your behalf.

Yours humbly,
Verity Durant

P.S. The larder in the warming kitchen has bread, butter, and a meat pie, enough to hold you until breakfast.

Stuart was not unaccustomed to receiving irate letters. An MP never pleased all his constituents. And a barrister who won more cases than he ought to occasionally heard from incensed members of the opposing counsel.

This note, however, went beyond irate, evidenced by the violence of its writing. At several places on the page the nib of the fountain pen had torn through the paper, the letters not so much jotted down as slapped onto the page, the *t*'s and *i*'s barely crossed and dotted in the wrath of the one who wielded the pen.

He very seldom allowed himself anything other than a measured response. But he couldn't seem to think clearly. He was hungry. He was hungry because she'd served him food that had been the culinary equivalent of a siren song—he could no more eat it than a sailor of antiquity could relax and enjoy the music as he sailed into the rocky cliffs of Anthemusa. And now she would throw a tantrum because he wanted something as undemanding as a sandwich?

He pulled out a piece of his own stationery, and replied in French.

Dear Madame,

Are you trying to lose your position?
> *Your servant,*
> *Stuart Somerset*

Her return message came a few minutes later.

Dear Sir,

Are you hoping to be rid of me?
> *Yours humbly,*
> *Verity Durant*

No one would blame him if he did rid himself of her. Quite the contrary. He'd be applauded for his high standards and his gentlemanly consideration for his wife-to-be's delicate sensibilities.

Not to mention he'd never again be subject to the unwanted provocation of her cooking, the sybaritic beguilement of it. Never again covet her food with such inconvenient, hypocritical hunger.

Dear Madame,

Not yet. But I could easily change my mind.
> *Your servant,*
> *Stuart Somerset*

She watched him from just beyond the reach of the dim light, through the narrow opening of the door—

her archangel come to earth, his halo dented, his wings less than immaculate.

He stood over a loaf of bread, a knife in hand. On the chopping board there lay three, now four, rather beautifully sliced pieces of bread, each a precise quarter-inch in thickness. A kettle hissed, shrill and loud in the still air. He wrapped his hand in a towel, disappeared from her view for a moment, brought back the kettle, and poured the boiling water into a teapot that she also couldn't see.

The upper-crust gentlemen of this country were valiant in battle, decent to their inferiors, and passably competent in bed, but they were, almost without exception, helpless before the simplest of domestic tasks—and proud of it, taking it as a badge of their true gentility.

But he had been the illegitimate son of an impecunious woman. Had never stepped outside the slums of Ancoats before coming to Fairleigh Park. And had not forgotten how to take care of himself.

She'd come, teeth still gritted, to see to his sandwich, because it would have been a gross dereliction of duty otherwise: He had no obligation to appreciate her food; she, however, did have an obligation to feed him. But now she could no longer quite remember why she'd been so angry with him. She only wanted to gorge herself on the sight of him, the slash of shadow in the hollow of his cheek, the deep indentation of his philtrum, the slight part of his lips in concentration.

Mine, some utterly barmy part of her howled. *Mine. Mine. Mine.*

She remembered the marble-hard smoothness of his back. The way his hair had curled at his nape, the surprising softness of it against the inside of her wrist. The feel of his arm, wondrously heavy upon her as he slept, keeping her securely within the circle of his protection.

Suddenly he looked up, his eyes searching the crack of the door through which she spied on him. "Who's there?"

Between the mad urge to step forward into the light and the panic that would have her break into a run, she did nothing. He set the butter knife down on the rim of the butter crock. "Madame Durant, is that you?"

It's me. I'm here. Do you still love me?

She turned and walked away.

❦

Stuart lost his mind somewhere around the stroke of midnight.

Shortly after his nonencounter with Madame Durant, he'd discovered, set aside in a special holding cabinet in the warming kitchen, a silver dome-covered dish. Under the silver dome had been a small ramekin. He'd known instantly what it was, the dessert course that he had not allowed Prior to serve, despite—or was it because of—the latter's distressed protests that the chocolate custard was unique, sensational, and intolerably wonderful.

He'd had enough wherewithal then to cover the dish again and close the door of the holding cabinet. But now the chocolate custard was with him, alone, deep in the privacy of the master's apartment.

He didn't even have the excuse of hunger anymore. The bread and butter had been wholesome and filling. But he hadn't been able to stop thinking about the custard, its dark allure, its heady aroma that had made him want to stick his tongue inside then and there.

The chocolate custard sat on a small table, glossy, serene, entirely indifferent to his laughable internal struggle. He dug in the tip of a spoon, destroying its smooth surface—and released a coil of rich, dusky odor.

Chocolate. He'd never had chocolate before he came to live at Fairleigh Park, but when he was seven someone had given him a shred of paper that had once been wrapped around a piece of imported chocolate. He'd pressed the wrapper to his nose and inhaled as deeply as his lungs allowed, dreaming of chocolate enough to bury him.

Her custard smelled like that, a good smell made mythical by fervid imagination and true hunger. Suddenly he was famished again. He wolfed down the whole content of the ramekin in seconds, barely tasting anything as he ate.

Only as he slumped back into his chair did the residual flavors ambush his senses. For a moment the inside of his mouth tingled and luxuriated, a burst of glory. But the sensation faded just as quickly, leaving in its wake only the same obstinate, inexplicable craving.

A craving that was not limited to chocolate custard. He saw himself invading Madame Durant's kitchen and trapping her in a dark corner of her domain. He imagined her wordless consent, the urgency of her ungentle grip on his arms.

She would be thin and frail, with the heartbreaking strength of those too long accustomed to hard work. He'd cup her face between his hands and kiss her. She'd taste of whiskey freshly consumed, hot and pure. And all about them would billow the scent of high summer, strawberries ripened to the seduction of juicy red lips—

He came out of his chair. He was thinking of *her* again, when he'd already decided, most firmly, not to think of her anymore. A man could not set his life by the eclipses of the sun.

At least, try as he had, he could not.

❧

His bedchamber was dark and silent. A fire burned low in the grate, casting just enough of a glow for him to see his way to the window. He parted the curtains. The sky had largely disappeared. Between mounds of clouds flickered a few small, distant stars.

Something made him look down. A spark of reddish light glimmered on the terrace. The light quivered, stilled, then moved more languidly, and stilled again. He squinted.

A waning moon peeked out from behind a bank of clouds and illuminated a woman in a white cap, smoking a cigarette. She stood with her back to him, wrapped in a bulky shawl, her black dress melding into the shadows of the night.

Madame Durant.

The moon vanished. She became once more a dot of burning ash. Then even that sputter of light disappeared. When the moon emerged again, the terrace was empty, save for silvered granite and latticed shadows.

Chapter Five

July 1882

No one answered Verity's loud knock: no feet shuffling across floorboards, no surreptitious movement behind the curtains. Number 26 Cambury Lane remained as dark and silent as the inside of a mausoleum.

Verity could barely control her desire to kick the door. Would nothing cooperate this day?

She'd meant to depart Fairleigh Park first thing in the morning. But Mrs. Boyce had taken ill the night before and had asked Verity to supervise the jam-making—the strawberries were at their ripest and couldn't wait another day. She'd reluctantly agreed.

By the time the jam had gone into jars, the letter had come: a piece of paper in a neat handwriting that detailed Michael's doings and whereabouts for a week. The message was unmistakable. Her aunt knew who Michael was—Verity was never to embarrass her again.

When she'd burned the letter and stopped shaking, the skies had opened. What would normally have been a pleasant walk to the village had turned into a veritable slog, and she'd sat, for much of her train journey south, in stockings that had become drenched despite her galoshes.

And then, after she'd found a good place of lodging, put on dry clothes, and gone through much trouble to make herself presentable, did her luck improve? No. One'd think Stuart Somerset had a price on his head, the way he avoided his own residence. Not even a servant to answer the door and tell her the whereabouts of the master. What kind of a man bought a four-story house—six stories, if she counted the basement and the attic—without hiring a staff for it?

She'd knocked on his door at eight, retreated to a pub a quarter mile away, where she drew many inquisitive looks from the regulars, and returned at nine. And ten. And now eleven.

Ten o'clock was to have been her last try—the third time either the charm or an unmistakable sign that it was not to be. But she couldn't give up. Couldn't face the prospect of returning to Fairleigh Park without having accomplished a single one of her objectives.

She had it all thought out. First, she would become Stuart Somerset's cook. Then she would become his lover. Then, since it was her understanding that he was some sort of a lawyer and an MP, he could, as a favor to her, prove her identity. And once that was done, he would of course jump at the chance to marry her.

She would have loved to see Bertie's face at the wedding.

The letter from her aunt, however, took the wedding entirely off the table—Verity dared not contest the truth, not when Michael was exposed and vulnerable. And Stuart Somerset didn't get to where he was in life by marrying domestic servants with no known provenance. But with his help, she could still hurt Bertie.

Bertie had come to value her as a cook. And he was beginning to believe that he had in her a talent to rival that of any betoqued Parisian chef. It would be a blow to his gastronomic aspiration were she to defect to his greatest nemesis—and make his brother's table the most celebrated in all of England.

And then let him see his adventuress in bed with his brother. Oh, that would work wonders. On her own she could not hope to wound Bertie: She didn't matter enough, as she'd so belatedly learned. But in league with his brother, well, the least bit of nothing having to do with Stuart Somerset sent Bertie into a rage.

It was only fair that Bertie should know a little of the pain that blinded her. She hadn't been able to eat or sleep for weeks. Let *him* toss and turn. Let *him* lose his appetite for once.

But the door to 26 Cambury Lane did not open.

She kicked it. Still it did not open. Her big toe now throbbed awfully.

She hobbled onto the sidewalk and faced a choice of directions: toward the pub, to wait another hour in agitation, or toward Sloane Square, for a hack to take her back to her inn. A choice between folly and defeat.

Her feet started in the direction of the pub—

reckless, as her choices often were. Sense wasn't her strong suit. Had she more sense, she would not be here like this, a random caller with a recitation of brow-raising goals.

Instead, if she visited this particular house at all, it would be because the respectably married noble-woman she should have been had met Stuart Somerset at some soirée or another and decided to make him her piece on the side. She'd be fascinated by his unusual childhood and beg him to tell her titillating particu-lars—Had there been rats as big as cats in his house? Had he been illiterate? How had it felt to be hungry and poor?—then she'd whisper what details she'd gathered to her friends, tittering and perhaps shudder-ing delicately.

She made herself stop and turn around. Even the best neighborhoods in London were not entirely safe at night. She must leave now, or she'd be asking for trouble—her third stop at the pub had generated more than a few speculative looks, some from men she wouldn't want within fifty feet of her.

She'd walked no more than two minutes when she heard footsteps behind her—a man, approaching her fast. She spun around. Could it be Stuart Somerset, home at last and . . . coming after her? Of course it wasn't. She recognized the man—medium height, spindly, with bloodshot eyes and the smell of too much beer and inadequate soap. All night he'd loitered outside the pub with another man, the two of them raking her with interested stares, that interest multi-plying each time she returned and left.

The man was surprised by her sudden about-face. They stared at each other. His hands shot out toward her reticule. Without thinking, she clenched her fingers together, drew her right hand back, and socked him in the face.

In the side of his neck, rather, as he jerked his head away. It was still a solid hit. The man staggered a step, she noted with panicky satisfaction. She might be dressed the part of a lady tonight, but she was far stronger than any gentlewoman: She could lift stockpots half her height and carry a whole side of beef if necessary.

He swore and grabbed for her reticule again. He was not going to have it—her money was in her shoes, but in her reticule was the only photograph she had of her parents, brought along for luck.

She swung the reticule at him. Another solid hit. She'd stopped at a bookseller's and bought a Mary Elizabeth Braddon novel for her return trip. She hoped the book had wonderfully sharp corners.

"Bitch!" groaned the man, and seized her wrists.

She sank the heel of her right boot hard into his instep. He howled and slapped her. She barely felt the burning of her cheek and the snap of her neck, only the satisfaction of his next howl as she stomped his instep with her heel again, harder.

Her free hand spread open. She poked her fingers at the man's eyes. He screamed. She turned to run, hoping she'd hurt him enough to discourage him altogether—only to come face-to-face with his friend, an even more malodorous man.

"Get away." Her lips moved and words came out. "My husband will be here any minute."

The second man cackled. "You ain't 'ave a 'usband any more than you 'ave a willy."

A hand grabbed her hair from behind and yanked her head back. She kicked the shin of the man behind her and tried to brain the man in front of her with Mrs. Braddon's book. But she wasn't so lucky this time. He knocked her reticule aside. Then he caught her arm and twisted hard.

She yelped in pain and kicked his shin. He grunted and let go of her arm. She rammed her elbow into his rib cage. The other man pulled her toward him by her midsection, lifted her up in the air, and then threw her down. One of them jumped atop her; she was no longer sure who was who.

"Let's jus' take the bag an' go," the man standing to the side implored. "There be coppers soon eno'."

"I'll teach 'er a lesson first."

An enormous fist came at her. She shut her eyes and braced for the skull-shattering pain—and the loss of the only connection she had left to her former life.

❦

Stuart walked. It had been a long sitting in the House of Commons this day. He had the cabdriver drop him off some distance from his house, so he could have a little exercise.

He was tired. But the day wasn't over yet—he had an

invitation to a ball. And not just any ball, the Duchess of Arlington's ball.

His medals of valor, his new inheritance, his stature as one of the youngest members of Parliament—he'd won his seat in a by-election two months ago—those all counted. But the Arlingtons' ball tonight, *the* social event of the year, would cement his acceptance by Society, and stamp him with that particular cachet dispensed only by matrons of the highest standing.

Then the business of finding a wife would begin in earnest. He would leverage his current success. The young ladies would make their calculations concerning his future prospects. And he'd come to an agreement with one of them—a process of bargain and trade not essentially dissimilar from that which went on in a Delhi bazaar at all hours of the day.

So to the ball he would go. And dance. And talk of subjects that mattered no more to the course of history than a barnacle on the hull mattered to an ocean-liner. And then he would get up early in the morning for a meeting with the Lord Justice who'd sponsored him to Inner Temple.

He turned onto his street and stopped. There, not twenty paces from him, was a scene he did not associate with living in one of London's best districts: a street brawl. Worse, it was two men against one woman. The woman fought hard, but she was no match against her assailants.

He broke into a run.

The men threw the woman to the ground. One of them sat down on her and lifted his fist high. Stuart grabbed him from behind and heaved him away. He vaguely heard the man connect with a lamppost as he grabbed hold of the man's accomplice and hurled him in the same general direction.

The men groaned and scrambled to their feet. One of them reached for the reticule that had been dropped. Stuart put his foot on it. The men looked at the reticule, looked at Stuart, looked at each other, and ran as if their shirts had been set on fire.

The woman on the sidewalk slowly lifted herself to her elbows. Her hair had tumbled loose during the melee. A wild mass of curls concealed much of her dirt-smudged face. Her mouth was wide open in astonishment.

"Are you all right?" he asked.

And if she was, he'd return her reticule and get on with his own business. She was likely a prostitute whose healthy haul for the evening had lured her would-be muggers, and he owed her no more than a question of courtesy.

"I'm . . . I'm . . ." She looked about her person. "Oh, no!"

Her accent, all adamantine consonants and efficient vowels, did not sound like that of any street-walker he'd ever met. And he'd met plenty during his years in the slums of Ancoats.

"It's all right. I've your reticule."

He pulled her to her feet. Her scuffed and dirtied reticule, along with her crumpled hat, he pressed into her gloved hands. She curled her fingers tight about her belongings.

"Thank you," she said, her voice muffled. "Thank you, sir."

At some point within the past thirty seconds, she'd begun to weep, her tears as copious as seawater. She fumbled in her reticule. Her hands shook; she couldn't seem to find anything.

"Are you hurt?" He offered her his own handkerchief.

She shook her head and pressed his handkerchief to her eyes. But it was like trying to stop the Deluge.

No, not a prostitute, too soft for a life of streetwalking. He tried to place her. Her clothes, a good tailor-made jacket-and-skirt set, were less the choice of a tart than that of a respectable governess. Perhaps she was the employee of one of his neighbors, coming back from her evening off?

"Which house is yours, miss?"

She shook her head once more. "I don't live here," she said, her voice breaking. "I will see myself home, thank you. Please, don't let me keep you."

Again that accent, like the tapping of silver tines on a crystal goblet, more indisputably aristocratic than that of the viscountess with whom he'd conversed several days ago.

"I can hardly do that. You've already been set upon once," he said. "Come with me. I'll find you a hansom."

As soon as he made his offer he realized he couldn't very well walk with her while she was in such a state, disarrayed and sobbing. He took her by the elbow, turned her around, and guided her the short distance to his house. He unlocked the front door, stepped aside, and waited for her to precede him.

But the woman, who'd followed him with the docility of a spring lamb, did not do as he indicated. Instead, she drew back, alarmed at last. He could almost hear her jumbled thoughts. *He is a stranger. The other men had only wanted her money. He could do far worse to her.*

Good. So she wasn't altogether stupid.

She gasped. Her face swung to him. From behind her veil of hair, he almost made out her eyes. She stared at him as if he'd materialized out of thin air, her reaction something between shock and paralysis.

"Would you like to wash up a bit before we look for a hack?" he asked. "Have the use of a mirror?"

She stared at him one more second, then her hand went to her hair. She squeaked. After that, she followed him meekly into the house. He turned on the lamps in the vestibule and the main hall and pointed at the stairs. "The bath is two floors up. Second door to your left."

She ran for it.

And so her very well-justified mistrust of him had evaporated at the mention of the word *mirror*. Stuart shook his head. Perhaps she wasn't altogether stupid, but neither was she much smarter than a sack of turnips.

❧

Verity clung to the scalloped edge of the washbasin. Her hand hurt. Her back hurt. The outside of her thigh hurt where it had hit the ground when she'd been thrown down. But the pain was only a mute dissonance compared to the din in her head.

What should she do now?

When she'd been pinned down on the sidewalk, about to become a victim of London's criminality and her own stupidity, she'd sworn with the fervency of a new convert that she'd never again try to involve Bertie's brother in her pathetic affairs.

Her resolution had been followed by gallons of tears, brought on by an overwhelming relief that for once, it seemed, she would walk away from an act of immense idiocy unscathed.

And then she'd seen the number on the door: 26. 26 Cambury Lane. And it had stopped her tears cold: Her rescuer was none other than Stuart Somerset himself.

Was it preordained that they should meet this way? Did it mean that her scheme wasn't as harebrained as she'd thought? Should she, now that she'd cleaned up and repaired the worst of the damage to her hair, introduce herself and explain her purpose?

Except she couldn't see herself broaching the subject to Stuart Somerset. As brief as their exchanges had been, she'd been struck by his remoteness, the remoteness of the absolutely perfect. He was the kind of man who looked down upon follies like hers as she would regard an infestation of bedbugs.

Stuart Somerset would gravely tell her that he did not believe her story of woe and reprisal for a moment. That she'd been sent by Bertie out of some malicious mischief. That he certainly wasn't about to employ or sleep with a complete, not to mention dotty, stranger.

She could see herself belaboring the point, reminding him, in a manner both desperate and mean, of the pain they could cause Bertie. And he'd smile politely and show her the door. He had quite enough going on to cause Bertie any amount of pain. He didn't need *her* help.

Stupid, stupid, stupid; she mouthed the words at the woman in the mirror, at her hollow eyes and tearstained cheeks. Yes, it was stupid. Stupid to come to London, stupid to believe that Stuart Somerset could be her answer, and doubly stupid to never once think through her plan to the conclusion: Bertie's rage, her dismissal, her dismal chances of respectable employment elsewhere, given her now scabrous reputation, and Michael's tears, when she must once again give him up.

Perhaps her aunt had been right. Perhaps she was indeed weak, dim, ridiculous—a waste of her mother's womb—that after having already lost so much, she still stood ready to throw away everything else.

Well, she wouldn't. She'd go down, thank Stuart Somerset profusely, and leave in the first available hansom. Mr. Somerset and she would remain strangers, and that was that.

❧

Stuart left the morning room, where he'd finished the previous day's copy of the *Daily Mail*, to fetch the whiskey from his study. Something made him turn his head as he crossed the front hall. She was there at the top of the first flight of steps, standing still, her reticule and hat in hand, the hair that had been all over her face smoothed back and put away.

He had been to a few balls and had seen his share of pretty young girls descending grand staircases. His own stairs were quite plain. Her jacket-and-skirt set of gray wool was hardly ravishing. Nor was she even all that young—a good few years into her twenties, at least. And still she stopped him cold.

She was not classically beautiful—her mouth a bit too big for her thin, undernourished face, her chin a bit too strong. But such eyes she had, pre-Raphaelite eyes, deep and mesmerizing, the sort of eyes that inspired verse in the dullest man. And such lips, the sort of lips that incited sin in saints and angels.

"You were quick," he said.

"The damage was less substantial than I'd feared," she said, descending slowly. She had splendid vowels, pure sounds that sang of family trees with roots going as far back as the Battle of Hastings. Who was she?

Her eyes were still visibly red-rimmed. She held them slightly downcast, discreetly taking in his dwelling. Sir Francis had willed to Stuart everything that was not entailed. The Lords Justices of Appeal, before whom the case had eventually gone, had given Stuart the Somerset town house on Grosvenor Square. But without the rent-rich urban tracts that went to Bertie, the sheep land that Stuart received couldn't generate enough income for the upkeep of such a house.

So he'd sold the Somerset town house and much of its contents and bought the terrace house in Belgravia. The address was excellent. The house was more than adequate for a family of five, plus servants. And the furniture he'd retained from the other house—the best pieces—had been arranged with care and, he thought, some panache.

The console table near the foot of the stairs was a Chippendale. The mahogany longcase clock, by John Brown of Edinburgh, dated from the middle of the previous century. And the small oil of pastoral greenery set above the console table had been painted by none other than John Constable himself.

He had the strange sensation that she thought his house passable—nothing grand, but passable. In her swift glances there had been a certain familiarity. She recognized the pieces in the hall for what they were. And what they were merited the fleeting attention she directed their way and no more.

Her gaze returned to him. "Thank you," she said. "For coming to my aid."

Her eyes. When she looked at him full on, it gave him gooseflesh. "You shouldn't have been out alone this late," he said, more harshly than he intended.

"Yes, it was terribly asinine of me." Her face lowered. Her fingers twisted the rim of her hat. "I'm afraid I haven't the luxury of a footman."

"Why not?"

She looked and sounded highborn enough to have half a dozen footmen at her disposal. She was too old—

and too striking-looking—to not already be married. Had she slipped out for an adulterous rendezvous?

She lifted her head. Their eyes met. The skin just above his collarbone tingled. "Haven't got any lizards in my kitchen," she said, a trace of wistfulness beneath her matter-of-fact tone.

Her answer made no sense until he recalled that in Perrault's story of Cinderella—his and Bertie's governess had been an enthusiast of such tales—lizards were what the Fairy Godmother had turned into footmen, to accompany Cinderella on her nocturnal forays into Society.

"Not a pumpkin in your kitchen either?"

Her lips curved slightly. "Pumpkins aren't in season."

Her mouth was all expressive mobility when she spoke. It was a second or two before he realized that she was waiting for him to respond, and all he did was stare at her mouth, at its slightly uneasy twists and slants. Awareness flooded him: He was sexually attracted to her, in a manner he was not accustomed to—abrupt and primal.

"Would you . . . like some whiskey?" he heard himself ask.

"Well . . ." Her voice waffled with indecision. "If it's not too much trouble."

"No, no trouble at all," he said, in a tone he did not remember ever using with any woman who wasn't related to him—a gentle, careful tone, as if she were made of spun glass.

He held out his arm toward her. His gesture surprised her. She came within touching distance of him and gazed at his proffered arm a few heartbeats before placing her hand about his elbow, her touch so light that he wondered whether her fingers weren't simply floating above his sleeve.

Then her gloved hand settled a little more firmly, and his entire arm prickled. This close she smelled of strawberries at their ripest, the decadent scent of it rising from her like steam from a perfumed bath. He wanted to stick his nose in her hair and inhale until his lungs burst. He wanted to ingest her.

She let go of his arm as soon as they reached the study. He turned on the lamp, located the decanter of whiskey and two glasses. She again assessed his house, her head bent, her eyes busy. The study held a miscellany of incense holders and ivory carvings from his days in India, alongside the compilation of law books he'd been forced to accumulate to educate himself in the intricacies and precedents of English Common Law.

He poured them each a splash of whiskey.

"You extend such courtesy toward me," she said, accepting the glass. Did she take care that her fingers did not brush against his? "I could be your neighbor's scullery maid."

He could not see her as anyone's servant; she was singularly lacking in subservience. And he had not failed to notice the elegance of her motion, or the delicacy with which she held her glass. She had been raised in refinement, her physical grace effortless—thoughtless, almost, a habit too long ingrained for her even to notice. "Are you somebody's scullery maid?"

"No." She laughed, a sere, brittle sound. "Not currently, at least."

"What are you, then?"

"A nobody." She took a large swallow of her whiskey. "Most decidedly."

He tasted her bitterness on his tongue, like a trace of quinine. "Good," he said. "I was beginning to fear you were London's most celebrated courtesan, over whom I shall wreck my promising young political career."

What he said startled her. And pleased her. Her lips formed something that almost might pass for a genuine smile. "Well then, fear not. I'm no *La Dame aux Camelias*."

"No, you are only Cinderella," he said. "Tell me, what's Cinderella doing in town, without her coach, her footmen, or her ball gown?"

She glanced down at her glass, already almost empty. "It's obvious, isn't it? Something went terribly awry at the ball."

"What happened? Did her prince turn into a frog when she kissed him?"

"Oh, an absolutely fulsome toad."

Her tone was glib, but her words had a hard, disillusioned edge. He walked to where she stood and poured a generous amount of whiskey into her glass. "We must drown your devastation."

"Strong spirits only give Cinderella a hangover to go with her heartache," she said, even as she took a swallow of the whiskey. "It makes her terribly cross in the kitchen."

"I thought Cinderella was always gentle and kind and uncomplaining."

"Do you know why?" She looked up at him, her voice suddenly heated. "It's because these tales have been written by men, men who have never spent so much as an hour in the kitchen. The real Cinderella curses, smokes, and drinks a bit too much. Her feet hurt. Her back hurts. And she's resentful. She would like her pumpkin coach to run over the Wicked Stepmother. And Prince Toad too, if possible."

Her fury kindled a flame in him. He wanted to grab her and kiss her anger, her vehemence. He made himself move a few steps away. "Does she now?"

Her lips bent in girlish rue. She ran a finger down the side of her glass. "Did I ruin the fairy tale for you?"

"Hardly. The fairy tale was ruined for me well before you came along."

"Oh? How so?" She cocked her head, her eyes wide with interest, her own rage momentarily forgotten.

"The prince. A problematic character, don't you think? He always marries the most beautiful girl— Cinderella, Sleeping Beauty, Snow White. And of course he also inherits the castle and the kingdom. Makes you wonder what he has ever done to deserve such good fortune, except for having been born to the queen."

Now he was the one who said too much. And he never said too much.

She heard it, the undercurrent of resentment in his

words—her eyebrows raised. But she did not dig in that direction. "No wonder he turns into such a toad."

He exhaled in relief and raised his glass. "A toast to you, for having escaped your prince's amphibian clutch."

She regarded him, her eyes a clarity of infinite depth, so beautiful it hurt. Then she smiled, a smile at once despondent and hopeful. "A toast."

She poured the contents of the glass down her throat. Cinderella indeed drank a little too much. He was wary of overimbibing, either in a woman or in a man. But he'd build a distillery with his own hands and put it at her disposal if it were the only way to get her to smile again.

In the silence that followed, he belatedly remembered that he was supposed to get her a hack and send her home. He wished his man, Durbin, were around. So he could instruct Durbin to take his time— much time—before returning with the cab.

"Tell me a little of yourself, if you would," she said, not quite tipsy yet.

He should tense again. Such requests from women always put him on guard, because they invariably led, however circuitously, to questions about his childhood. He suspected that more than once he'd been seduced not for his looks or accomplishments, but because he'd once lived in a slum.

The women had all but begged for sordid anecdotes. *Tell me about pub fights. About shagging easy women in back alleys. Treat me as you would treat one of them.* They hungrily lapped up what aura of threat they perceived in him to appease the tedium of their existence, never mind that he'd been too young to shag anyone and never fought for the fun of it.

He didn't tense. He only took a sip of his whiskey. She didn't need him to tell her about the seedier side of life. "What would you like to know?"

She thought about it. "You seem to think you are not a prince. Then who are you?"

She was not asking for his name, but his story. If she was Cinderella, then who was he?

Just behind her on the bookshelves were all twelve volumes of Galland's *Les Mille et Une Nuits*. "Aladdin," he said.

"Aladdin," she said, her expression meditative. "A young man of humble origin who comes into control of a powerful djinn, who grants him riches and a beautiful, highborn wife."

"You can never control a powerful djinn," he said.

"No?"

"For every wish he grants you, he takes away something you love."

"What did you wish for?" she asked, naturally enough.

He could make something up, something fanciful and far from the truth. "A father," he said.

Her grip tightened around her empty glass. "And what did you have to give up?"

"My mother."

He wondered if the pain in her eyes was but a reflection of his own. Her face lowered. "My mother died when I was six. I miss her still."

"If she looked anything like you, she must have been very beautiful," he said impulsively.

Her eyes met his again, her aquamarine gaze a mixture of pleasure and wariness. "She *was* beautiful. But I don't think I am."

"Well, you are very much mistaken in that."

She smiled, a shy smile. Her pale cheeks colored. For a fleeting instant he thought she might let him kiss her. But then that gratifying moment passed and unease set in.

He saw his misstep. His inexperience in these matters served him ill. He shouldn't have made his interest in her so nakedly known. He should have offered her more whiskey instead. A cigarette even, for his vice-laden Cinderella. Or some of the biscuits Durbin kept in a tin somewhere—she looked as if the Wicked Stepmother had not been overly generous with food.

"I'll go for the hack," he said reluctantly.

He was a stranger to her. They were already in his house. She had no choice but to mistrust any express inclination on his part.

"Do you not have a carriage of your own?" she asked, her tone almost as reluctant as his own.

"No." Until he'd sold the Somerset town house, he hadn't even been able to pay Durbin for more than a year.

"And you have no servants to fetch a cab for you either?"

"My man is on holiday visiting his sister in Derbyshire this week. And my maid lives next door,

I've a third share of her. So I must do the cab-fetching myself, as lowering as it is."

"And leave me alone here?"

"You won't feel safe?"

"I meant, leave me alone with a very nice Constable painting in the house?"

"I think if Cinderella were to turn to thievery, she'd have done so already. Since she's elected to stay in the kitchen, I assume my possessions are safe," he said, moving toward the door. He was either an astute judge of character or dumber than the sack of turnips to which he'd compared her intelligence earlier.

Her words halted him. "You shouldn't trust me. You don't even know who I am."

"Then come with me. We'll take a stroll together. It's not every day a mere mortal meets Cinderella herself."

She almost smiled again. She opened her mouth to say something. Nothing emerged. Instead, she stared at the spot that he'd vacated.

He turned his head to look at the shelves before which he'd been standing. Books, his collection of mounted Hashshashin daggers, several small idols of Ganesh, the elephant god . . . and a little lower, the framed photograph of himself and Bertie.

"Is that you?" she said, her voice unnaturally flat.

"When I was much younger."

"May I?"

"Please."

She moved to the shelves and lifted the photograph. She was not very tall, but her arms were long and slender. As she bent her head, her hair gleamed in the light, a deep, burnished gold. Her thumb rubbed against the hammered silver frame as she gazed into the picture.

He took a few steps toward her, until he was standing nearly at her elbow, looking down at the lobe of her ear, the clean line of her neck, the tiny tendrils of hair at her nape that didn't quite make it into her chignon. Her scent of strawberry surged and teased. His lungs—and his head—were full of the smell of her.

She didn't say anything for almost a minute, her attention focused solely on the photograph. He wondered at this extraordinary, sustained interest.

"You look livid," she said at last.

"I was."

"Why?"

"My brother."

"Your brother the prince?"

He need not respond. She already knew.

"Do you still hate him?" She handed the photograph to him.

Did he? He studied the photograph. Some days he almost pitied Bertie, forcibly evicted from the town house he'd considered his birthright. Other days the pleasure he took in Bertie's humiliation was as strong and unmistakable as his own heartbeat.

He shrugged. "Sometimes."

"Then I don't like him either," she said, smiling oddly.

"Do you know him?" The question came out of nowhere.

"No. I don't know him at all," she said, decisively. She set aside her empty glass. "Shall we go now?"

"If we must," he said, shocking himself.

She cast a quick glance at him. "I really can't justify trespassing further on your hospitality."

Stay, he wanted to say. Make yourself at home. Trespass as much as you like.

"Let me find my hat," he said.

❧

"I'd always thought that particular household arrangement somewhat suspect," said Stuart, as they approached Sloane Street. "I remember asking our governess whether it would be quite all right if Snow White lived with seven shortish men."

They were in the midst of an improbable conversation on the private lives and thoughts of fairy tale characters. Only a minute ago, she'd declared that Cinderella would have little in common with Sleeping Beauty, who'd never done a day of hard work—sleeping for a hundred years, how idle and slovenly—but would welcome a chat with Snow White—keeping a house for seven was no mean feat.

She giggled. "And what did your governess say?"

"Fräulein Eisenmueller? She started shouting in German."

"I don't blame her. She was deliberately provoked," said Cinderella, smiling still.

"Yes, poor Fräulein Eisenmueller. I suppose I did provoke her. I didn't like the way she thought I was corrupt for my age, because I hadn't led a sheltered life." He felt himself grinning. "I dare say I knew more of what Snow White could conceivably do with all those shortish men than her spinster's mind could comprehend."

He shouldn't speak of such things to her. It was inappropriate. And he was never inappropriate, beyond that one frustrated instance with Fräulein Eisenmueller. Bertie, who loved all the pleasures of the senses with the abandon of a Georgian roué, had called Stuart a dried-up prig.

"Your poor governess," she murmured.

"Pity me instead. She made me think I was some sort of irredeemable degenerate until I got to Rugby, whereupon I immediately saw that the majority of boys were degenerates and I was but a year or ten ahead of my time."

What was it about her that made him disclose—with such alacrity—aspects of himself that others couldn't pry out of him with a crowbar and the patience of a Count de Monte Cristo?

She shot him a considering look. "What of men? Are they as much degenerates as boys?"

His heart beat faster. "They would like to be," he said, keeping his tone matter-of-fact. "But most of them lose what audacity and passion they once possessed as lads, so they think the thoughts but dare not do the deeds."

The distant clacking of hooves reminded him that despite his wishes otherwise, they weren't out for a pleasant stroll before returning to his house. His time with her was limited.

He stopped and raised his walking stick.

She looked a little surprised, almost as if she too had forgotten the business about the hansom cab. "What of you?" she asked.

"Pardon?"

"Have you lost *your* youthful audacity and passion? Or are you still a degenerate at heart?"

His heart now pounded. He wasn't so dense that he couldn't tell when a woman flirted with him. She was flirting with him.

"Would you like to find out?" he said. He wasn't a flirt. He could not take her question lightly.

Panic flashed in her eyes. The cab drew up next to them. The horse snorted. She let out a breath of relief. "Alas, we've no more time," she said, her voice high-pitched, her words a rush. "Thank you again for everything. Best of luck with your promising young political career. And good night."

He gazed at her a moment, then inclined his head. "Midnight comes. Godspeed, Cinderella."

❦

It wasn't until the carriage pulled away, with her waving from the window, her face wistful, that he realized he'd hoped to be in the cab. With her.

There had always been those who claimed that Stuart had not blood, but cold water running in his veins. He found it a strange assessment, except when it came to matters of the heart and the loins.

He seemed to have been born with a monkish temperament where women were concerned. He found the fate of nations to be of far more interest than trim ankles and pretty shoulders. Making love was like shooting grouse, an activity he indulged in when the occasion presented itself, not something he particularly sought.

What, then, was wrong with him tonight?

He wanted her. He wanted to stare at her, to smell her, to have his skin again crackle with electricity from her nearness. He wanted to devour her, to help her—and himself—find out exactly how much of a degenerate he could be when he put his mind to it.

England could declare a new war tonight and he wouldn't care.

"Where to, sir?" someone called out to him.

Another hansom cab had drawn up to the curb. The cabby looked at him expectantly. He forgot that he had not moved since she left, that he still stood at the edge of the street, as if he too were waiting for a carriage.

Wasn't he? Her voice had been quiet, but it had carried to him on a playful breeze. *Sumner House Inn, Balham Hill*. Balham Hill was in Clapham, a good three miles away. He'd need a carriage.

He meant to shake his head, to take himself home and change for Lady Arlington's ball. His life was Inner Temple, the Palace of Westminster, and the Season in full swing. There was no room for mysterious strangers and needless entanglements.

Besides, what innkeeper worth his salt would let him in at this hour? And what assurance had he that even if he could lie, cheat, and steal his way past the innkeeper, she'd allow his presence in her room for more than three seconds?

"Sumner House Inn, Balham Hill," he told the cabbie.

Chapter Six

November 1892

Dear Madame,

I'd like to review your menus for the day.
                                    Your servant,
                                    Stuart Somerset

Dear Sir,

For luncheon, a roast beef sandwich.
For dinner, four roast beef sandwiches.
                                    Yours humbly,
                                    Verity Durant

Dear Madame,

A roast beef sandwich for luncheon is fine.
For dinner, with the future Mrs. Somerset in

attendance, I need something more formal. I suggest one of your twelve-course dinners.

Your servant,
Stuart Somerset

Dear Sir,

Certainly. I will make sure that the future Mrs. Somerset is suitably impressed.
Many congratulations on your upcoming marriage.

Yours humbly,
Verity Durant

In accordance with the decision to delay the announcement of his engagement, Stuart had said nothing to Marsden as he dispatched his secretary to escort Lizzy and her father from London to Fairleigh Park. Nor anything to Mrs. Boyce or Mr. Prior.

He could have accomplished his objective with Madame Durant—a fancy dinner—without any mention of the future Mrs. Somerset either. And yet he'd wielded that name the way a Transylvanian caught abroad at night might brandish a braid of garlic.

Perhaps, in the end, it had only been a reminder to himself—that he was a betrothed man. That inexplicable surges of lust and curiosity where the cook was concerned were quite beneath him, however notorious and sexually rapacious the cook.

A reminder he shouldn't have needed in the first place.

Lizzy knitted. She would miss this week's meeting of the Ladies' Charitable Knitting Circle, but she still hoped to finish the muffler she'd started the previous week, before she was to leave for Bertram Somerset's funeral. It wasn't to be. The doorbell rang, signaling the arrival of Mr. Somerset's secretary. She grimaced, rolled up the muffler and the needles, and shoved everything into her knitting bag.

She'd turned on only the table lamp closest to her. In the drained light of a sunless November day, most of the drawing room was sunk in shadows. Before she could do something about it, the door opened, her butler announced Mr. William Marsden, and in came a man who could very well serve as the additional source of illumination the room needed.

Mr. Marsden was quite possibly the most gorgeous man alive—certainly Lizzy had met no one more beautiful. He had a thick head of gleaming golden curls, perfect eyebrows, long, expressive eyes, a strong nose, and lips that were really too sumptuous for a man, but somehow still managed to look chiseled and interesting on his face. And Lizzy loathed him with a passion that other women reserved for spiders that had crawled up their stockings.

She hated the showy and complicated knot of his necktie, the too fashionably snug cut of his coat, the sheen and luster of his hair that couldn't have been achieved without regular applications of lemon juice and egg yolk. She deplored that her dear Stuart trusted and depended on this peacock to the extent that he did. And it made her grit her teeth that as Mr. Marsden was no mere plebeian, but a son of the seventh Earl of Wyden, she couldn't very well ignore him and leave him waiting in the vestibule, but must receive him in her drawing room.

"Mr. Marsden, how good of you to come. Thank you for taking the trouble," she said, her words a winter's worth of ice under a thin gloss of politesse. She hadn't wanted Mr. Somerset's secretary to travel with them, but her father had been very much in favor of the idea.

"It's my honor and my pleasure," said Mr. Marsden, smiling slightly.

In her more lucid moments, she was somewhat alarmed at the intensity of her antipathy, given that Mr. Marsden had never done her any harm, nor even uttered an objectionable word in her presence. But then Mr. Marsden would smile, and her lucidity would find itself out in the back settlements of Australia.

Because it was a horrid smile, all filth and smut beneath a varnish of courtesy: a smile that said he knew something intolerable about her. And since it so happened that there was a wide swath of Lizzy's recent past that could not be known without getting her banished from Society, her loathing was contaminated with fear—and an almost nauseous awareness that she never found him more handsome than when he had on one of those reviled smiles.

Then his smile went away, and he looked at her with something that would have passed for genuine concern on the part of any other man. But on him, it only made her even more wary.

"Are you well, Miss Bessler?" he asked.

The quiet intimacy of his tone disconcerted her entirely. Though they'd been introduced two years ago, it had been shortly before she'd shut herself off from the outside world for the next seventeen months. Their acquaintance was of the most incidental variety and she saw no reason for him to care whether she was well.

Her father came into the drawing room. Mr. Marsden turned and greeted him. The men proclaimed their mutual pleasure at seeing each other again, while Lizzy silently breathed a thanksgiving that she was no longer alone with Mr. Marsden.

"Shall we get going, then, Papa?" she said brightly.

❦

Stuart had forgotten how beautiful Fairleigh Park was, even so late in the year. The gardens had been planned with the progression of the seasons in mind; the estate abounded in foliage the colors of wine and gold, warm and vivid against a backdrop of mossy evergreens.

Twenty years it had been, since he left for India at seventeen, furious at both his father and Bertie. But it felt even longer. The scent of Fairleigh Park in deep autumn—of falling leaves and the stillness of the countryside between the end of harvest and the bustle of yule—was one he associated with his earliest years in Yorkshire, before he started public school and came back home only during Christmas, Easter, and the months of summer.

He walked the mile from the gates of the estate to the village. The sun shed an anemic light, but it was still a clear, crisp day. The village had been built upon an incline, its biscuit-colored houses hugging the sides of a tributary to the Ure. A stone bridge from the sixteenth century spanned the fast-flowing brook.

As he passed through the village, curtains fluttered; curious faces appeared from around corners and behind drystone walls. The villagers had guessed his identity. He wondered what they thought of his seemingly triumphant return, at this once-illegitimate upstart having at last entirely supplanted Bertie.

Atop the bridge two young boys threw rocks and twigs into the stream below. Engrossed in their game, they paid no attention to him. He stopped and watched them.

See that leaf in the water, Stuart? If it's lucky, it will go all the way to the sea.

Will it really?

If it's lucky. My mum lived on a house by the sea, in the south. She died there. It was a pretty place. I want to go there again.

Even though your mum died there?

I wasn't there when she died. It will remind me of when she was alive. She used to sit on a chair and watch me when I sea-bathed.

He shook his head. That conversation had to be almost thirty years old. Amazing what random tidbits the mind uncovered at times, washing up on the shores of consciousness like jetsam after a storm.

He followed the market road out of the village and kept to it for another mile before setting out across the still green pastures to climb up the limestone ridge that defined the perimeter of the dale. From this vantage point it was easy to see that Fairleigh Park was a modestly scaled country house, more Petit Trianon than Château de Versailles. But once upon a time it had been grand to him, grand and spectacular, the closest thing he'd ever seen to a fairy tale castle.

I don't know where you live.

Somewhere in the shadow of the prince's castle.

He let the rocky paths take him the long way around to the woods behind the manor, in the direction of the gamekeeper's cottage. Bertie had left Fairleigh Park in sound shape: the estate supported itself and the urban properties were as lucrative as Stuart had supposed. Out of a four-foot stack of papers, only two items of expenditure had struck him as anomalies. One, Madame Durant's wages were notably less than what he'd expected. Two, Bertie paid for the public school fees of one Michael Robbins, the adopted son of Fairleigh Park's longtime gamekeeper.

Bertie had been generous in his charitable giving, but in every other instance his money had gone to churches, institutions, and committees—intermediaries, not individuals, except in the case of Michael Robbins. And Bertie didn't send the boy to some third-rate school, but to Rugby, one of the oldest and most prestigious public schools in the country and—ironically enough—Stuart's alma mater.

He wasn't certain how he felt about possibly having a nearly grown nephew. Old, perhaps. But if Michael Robbins were indeed Bertie's natural child, then Stuart would do right by the boy, as his own late father had done right by him—as well as he had known how.

The gamekeeper's cottage was squat and ordinary, its walls constructed from the same weathered white rock used in the miles of drystone walls that delineated fields and pastures in the dale. James Robbins, the gamekeeper, was in his early sixties, short, bald, and stout. He smiled widely as he realized who had come to call, his eyes nearly disappearing into the leathery folds of his face. Mrs. Robbins, as old as her husband, plain, and stooped, was visibly flustered as she welcomed Stuart into her unassuming home.

Stuart remembered her as the spinster daughter of the local curate, accompanying her father from time to time on his visits to Fairleigh Park. She'd married down considerably. The gamekeeper's cottage was shabby compared even to the curate's house, which had been no palace.

To Stuart's surprise, Michael Robbins was also at home—he'd been given a special dispensation to attend his sponsor's funeral. His parents presented him to Stuart with much pomp and pride: a young man of sixteen, tall, dark, and handsome, with undeniable intelligence in his eyes and a remarkable presence for an adolescent.

Stuart stayed a quarter hour. He drank tea, ate Mrs.

Robbins's lumpy seed cake, and engaged in small talk about the weather and the goings-on in the village. From time to time he addressed a question directly to Michael Robbins. The boy had acquired from his time at Rugby a startlingly pure upper-class accent. When he spoke, his parents listened in rapture, as if sonatas cascaded from his lips.

But it was more than his accent. It was his posture, his well-made clothes, his way of handling a tea-spoon—it had taken Stuart many raps to the knuckles from Fräulein Eisenmueller to achieve a similarly ele-gant grip. The boy looked entirely incongruous in the low-ceilinged, cramped parlor, a row of shotguns on the smoke-darkened wall behind him, a rusted snare under his chair.

As Stuart rose to take his leave, he sought a reasonable-sounding excuse to speak to the boy alone. But he needed not have taxed his brain. Michael Robbins shrugged into his own overcoat.

"I'll accompany Mr. Somerset back to the house," he said to his parents.

They left the gamekeeper's cottage together and spoke companionably about their Rugby experiences. They both belonged to School House and both played the eponymous sport—Michael did Stuart one better; he was the captain of the Running Eight.

Then a small silence took over. Stuart debated whether it was advisable to ask the boy outright about his true parentage and his possible connection to Bertie.

"Sir, please forgive me," said Michael. "But you

wouldn't happen to be related to me in any way, would you?"

Stuart had been struggling with an artful turn of phrase that would allow him to pose his question without shocking the boy. The boy, apparently, was beyond his powers to shock.

"You mean, as via my late brother?"

"No, sir. I mean, as in direct descent."

The question stopped Stuart in his tracks. Had Michael been six or seven years younger, he'd have wondered. But the boy was too old to be the result of his night with Cinderella.

"I do not believe so," he said.

Michael did not seem overly disappointed. He shrugged. "The odds were against it. But I thought I'd ask anyway."

"Does this mean that you are not related to my brother either?"

"I asked Mr. Bertram once, shortly after he told my parents he would pay my school fees," said Michael calmly. "He said no, that he'd made certain he did not sire any children out of wedlock."

Stuart was both relieved and strangely disappointed. But above all, he was astonished. Bertie had been paying for Michael's school fees since the latter was eleven. He himself at eleven would never have had the audacity to ask such a question.

"I hope you don't think that I'm not grateful to my adoptive parents, sir," said Robbins. "I love them dearly. But a man can't know who he is until he knows where he came from. And I've only half of the picture."

Half of the picture. Stuart resumed walking. "You know the identity of your natural mother?"

"I believe so, sir."

"Then why not ask her?"

"She denies it. But I know it's her." Michael kicked a pebble out of his way. "I hope I do not sound too deranged when I say this, but I remember my life as an infant—fragments of it, at least. I remember her face. The moment she came to Fairleigh Park, I knew she had come back for me."

And Stuart knew too. "Madame Durant."

Robbins's school fees were part of her recompense. Perhaps she feared that the Robbinses wouldn't accept such charity from her, so she routed it through Bertie instead, taking a cut in her in-hand wages.

Robbins did not deny it. "She always said you were a good example for me."

Madame Durant thought Stuart was a good example for her child—Madame Durant who wouldn't make him a sandwich?

"You are going to the house to call on her?" It was three o'clock in the afternoon, she wouldn't be needed in the kitchen yet.

"She would expect a visit from me, since I'm home," said Michael.

There was more obligation than anticipation in the boy's voice. Madame Durant's relationship with her child was not without complications.

"May I ask you a personal question?"

"Of course, sir."

"Your adoption is not a secret in these parts. You

are a promising young man and Madame Durant seems to have made an effort to stay close to you. Why do you suppose she denies that she is your mother?"

"I wish I knew. I ask myself the same question. All I can think is that she means to marry well someday, and it would not do to have a known bastard child about, adopted or not."

Stuart raised a brow at the boy's brutal cynicism.

"The world is an ugly place," said Michael, almost placidly. "People like me realize it sooner."

People like *them*. Illegitimacy tainted in different ways. For Stuart, it had been a deep-seated, constant fear that one wrong step, and it would all be taken from him. For Michael Robbins, it was a rage beneath the apparent blitheness.

"Tell me, young man," said Stuart, "what do you see as your place in this ugly world?"

❦

As much as Lizzy detested Mr. Marsden, she couldn't quite keep her eyes off him.

While regiments of grim-faced angels mass-manufactured most of humanity in some industrial division of Heaven—how could it be otherwise, given the relentless rise in population in England and everywhere else—Mr. Marsden could justifiably claim to have been created as a one-of-a-kind specimen, a pleasant afternoon's diversion for the Good Lord Himself.

He was, if anything, even more gorgeous upon closer inspection. In the tilt of his head and the carriage of his spine was beauty by the bushel and grace in ridiculously abundant spades.

After the second time he caught her looking at him, she turned her face and looked outside instead, into rain plastered against the streaked window, while the men talked politics, breaking down the likely Irish Home Rule votes constituency by constituency.

Somewhere north of Peterborough she realized that the compartment had gone quiet: Her father had drifted off to sleep. Mr. Marsden watched her, his lips curved into that hated smile that made her feel as if she had under her skirts a drunken lover who was liable at any moment to burst into a loudly slurred rendition of "God Save the Queen."

"Do you mind if I ask a personal question, Miss Bessler?" said Mr. Marsden.

She didn't bother to conceal her frown. "That quite depends on the question."

"You've beauty, poise, wit, and connections—everything a woman needs. Why haven't you married?"

It was a question that no one else had dared ask to her face. Beneath her carefully cultivated insouciance, her lack of a ring had chafed and incensed. To ask the question was to declare his intention to be a thorn at her side.

"You forgot to mention charm," she said coldly. "I'm generally acknowledged to have the charm of at least a Madame de Pompadour, if not outright that of a Josephine Bonaparte."

"Charm too, of course," he said, accompanied by a smile of irony. She'd never used her charm on him.

"Which boggles the mind even more that so many ordinary girls of your particular vintage of debutantes are comfortably settled in matrimony, while you remain unattached."

He was trying to get her to admit something. What did he want her to say? That she'd aimed too high in her youthful pride? That she'd believed that there was no one more qualified to be the wife of the country's richest peer or its leading intellectual? That she'd been sincerely convinced that anything less would be an insult to herself—to her beauty, poise, wit, connections, and charm?

"There is such a thing as luck in matters of matrimony, as in anything else," she said. "Those who admire me and those whom I admire have not coincided—until recently."

She wasn't supposed to refer to her three-day-old engagement until the announcement was in the papers, but she couldn't help it. Besides, as the person in charge of Stuart's calendar, Mr. Marsden had to know that she and his employer had been seeing a great deal of each other in recent months.

His reaction—a flicker of mordancy tangled with something she couldn't read—told her he quite understood. "I see," he said.

"My turn to ask a personal question," she said, though she, like he, was less interested in the answer than in the bloodletting of the questioning itself. "You come from one of our best families, sir. Why have you chosen a career as a lowly secretary?"

Everyone knew, of course, that he had been disowned and disinherited by his late father. That he didn't even have the dignity of a choice. He was forced to work.

"The life of idleness is not for me," he said, looking down at his hands, which were well-kept, except for what appeared to be a permanent smudge of ink at the edge of his right palm.

She twisted the knife she'd already stuck in him. "But surely, there are so many productive ways of passing time without becoming someone else's employee. You could have devoted yourself to the arts, the letters, the sciences. You could have helmed any number of charitable endeavors that would benefit from your skills of organization. You could have become a Member of Parliament."

"Alas, none of those noble pursuits pays a farthing," he said. "And it pains me, as I'm sure it pains you, to contemplate life without enough farthings in it."

Oh, had it ever pained and distressed her.

At her father's passing, the house would go to her eldest brother. Her father had never been a rich man. Her mother, certain that Lizzy would marry well, had distributed most of the money she'd brought to the marriage to Lizzy's two brothers. Were Lizzy to end up a spinster, she would have to subsist on the harshest of economies, a thought she'd carelessly dismissed for years before suddenly cowering under the looming shadow of its increasing likelihood.

But she wasn't about to admit any such thing to him.

"No, I'm afraid you are quite alone in your contemplation. Poverty is your lot, sir, not mine."

He glanced at her and she was struck by the starkness of it.

"Ah, Miss Bessler," he said lightly. "Your cruelty would break a heart less stalwart than mine."

❧

The scene was set in a manner identical to that of the previous evening: the big black brougham coming around the bend, its bell chiming softly in the evening air; the drive before the house awash in golden light that shimmered against the purple and crimson of dusk; the perfectly matched pair of footmen leaping off the carriage.

Except this time, Mr. Somerset was the one who greeted the arrivals, two gentlemen and a lady. The news that the lady was to be the next Mrs. Somerset had spread everywhere. The maids were excited by the thought of a grand wedding. Mrs. Boyce winced at the likelihood of unruly children in the near future.

From the solarium, Verity watched the young lady descend from the carriage. She was very tall, very beautiful, and very fashionably clad. Her coloring, like Mr. Somerset's, was dark and dramatic.

Their mutual affection was evident. When they greeted each other, their clasped hands remained linked a moment too long, even for a betrothed couple. As they walked arm in arm toward the house, they made a handsome pair—a breathtaking pair—their heads bent toward each other, speaking softly, listening closely.

Verity stamped down an urgent need for a fag. It was only the merest coincidence that he hadn't already married. He needed heirs. Fairleigh Park needed a mistress. He was doing everything he was supposed to do.

The master and his guests entered the manor; the servants carried in the luggage; the brougham drove off. She stared at the empty drive.

He had moved on. But she, she was a relic, a fossil, a fly caught in amber, unaware that eons had passed and the world had changed beyond recognition.

Now she had no choice but to leave.

❦

Dinner was a struggle from beginning to end.

Stuart did not know why, but he was vulnerable to Madame Durant's food in a way that defied all logic. While his guests reacted favorably to the courses—Marsden in particular was ecstatic—Stuart was in the middle of seismic shocks, a piece of himself coming undone with each mouthful.

But he could not walk away tonight as he had done the night before, nor could he refuse to be served while there were others at the table. He ate as little as he could, but a small serving of lightning was still lightning, and even the most modest of flames still burned.

Sometimes he didn't even know what he was eating—what was the taste of falling off a cliff?—he only knew he was eating because the rest of him swung between shock and dismay, unwilling to submit to, yet unable to impede this violent reawakening from taking place.

The sensuality of her cooking did strange things to him. He couldn't stop thinking of the woman in the kitchen who wielded such power and magic. Did she possess the alchemy to distill brutal longing and infuse her food with it? Or did she serve forth undiluted desire, disguised as nothing more alarming than a dish of crème caramel?

"In Paris, they speak of her as a goddess," said Marsden reverently.

No, not a goddess, a sorceress who exerted a dark enchantment. Who wooed him with decadent and impossible pleasures. Who made him forget that he was a most respectable middle-aged man about to become even more respectable with marriage and political ascent.

When he ate, there was only the food. And there was only the cook.

Chapter Seven

July 1882

Hunger made Verity panic.

Her appetite had been feeble for weeks. She hadn't eaten this whole day. But now, suddenly, she was starved.

With hunger came the stirring of old fears—dying in a gutter, languishing in a workhouse, becoming one of those women with rouged cheeks and hard eyes who blew kisses at passing men and took them upstairs.

She'd not had the foresight to purchase something on the way back to the inn. And she could expect no help from the innkeeper. He'd been quite put out with her for returning so late, after he'd already locked the front door—his was a respectable establishment, he'd grumbled, no comings and goings at all hours.

Her mind intervened, suppressing the grim dread of hunger, substituting in its place a different panic, one equally unnerving but lovely: the panic of Stuart Somerset.

Ah, yes, it was so much better to think about him, even if she could only do so rather incoherently, zigzagging between scraps of recalled conversation, fragments of Bertie's scathing commentary, and whole, long minutes of warm-cheeked euphoria.

Now that she put her mind to it, she realized that she knew quite a bit about Stuart Somerset, from Bertie and from the gossip she'd heard before she became Bertie's mistress. Mr. Somerset's mother had worked for Manchester's premier modiste. In the spring of 1854, Sir Francis had summoned the said modiste to Fairleigh Park as a rather desperate enticement to lure his wife, who'd refused to leave her bed since her confinement three months before, out of her invalidity. The modiste brought with her dozens of the shop's best bolts of fabric and two of her most capable seamstresses.

Lady Constance did not abandon her sickbed so easily. But Nelda Lamb, on the other hand, quite took leave of her good sense. Nearly ten years later, after Lady Constance was no more, Nelda Lamb returned to Fairleigh Park and brought with her the shameful result of her previous visit, a nine-year-old boy who was the spit and image of Sir Francis.

The boy, for all that he came from the gutters, quickly adapted to life at the mansion. Sir Francis raised brows when he sent the boy to Rugby, one of the nine great public schools singled out and named in the Public School Act of 1868. But the boy did not disappoint his father. He excelled at everything he did, quietly yet inexorably outshining his brother, who was a gifted athlete in his own right and no intellectual midget.

It's as if he were some sort of automaton, Bertie had said more than once. A windup mechanism that kept marching in one direction and one direction only—toward greater brilliance and distinction.

Boring. Dry. Moralistic. Wouldn't know how to have a good time if it rolled in crème anglaise and rubbed itself all over his lapels.

She'd giggled at this last. It had been a glorious day last summer. She'd made them a wonderful picnic, and they'd dined alfresco under a sky that was only a little less impossibly blue than her eyes—according to Bertie—and dotted with clouds of such pristine softness they could have been fluffs of eiderdown from God's own duvet.

I think everybody is boring and dry and moralistic next to you, her besotted self had told Bertie, Bertie with his generous capacity for pleasure, his golden good looks, and his assured handling of all the responsibilities that had been thrust upon him at such a young age.

But Bertie would turn out to be a horse's behind; and Stuart Somerset, not at all boring, dry, or moralistic. No, he was heroic, modest, discerning, perfectly behaved, and—her cheeks warmed again—not half so prudish as Bertie would have her believe.

If we must.

Would you like to find out?

Why had she said the name of the inn so loudly, enough to carry three streets over?

Because she desired him. She recognized all the

signs of impending infatuation: the awe, the yearning, the gathering of hopes.

As if her personal history hadn't yet taught her enough about hanging all her hopes on one man, she began to—driven by her mounting hunger—systematically imagine Mr. Somerset's arrival at her door, this very moment, an enormous tray floating magically before him.

On the tray—and because it was a magic tray after all—was everything that Verity could possibly want to eat. A plate of cold cuts. Vol-au-vent with a garniture of creamed seafood. Pâté baked in brioche. Fruits, both fresh from the orchard and incorporated into tarts, creams, and cakes.

Her mouth watered. Her stomach gnawed. From where she sat on the edge of the bed, her stockinged ankles crossed before her, she glanced at the door, unable to help herself.

Nothing.

She dropped her face into her hands and groaned at her hunger—she'd thought that by becoming a cook she'd at least never be hungry again—and at her untrammeled imagination—Mr. Somerset and the self-locomotive tray! What next, would he have a magic wand that made her clothes fly off too, so that she needn't feel any responsibility for sleeping with him, since she really, really couldn't help it?

Well, if her clothes had to fly off before a handsome stranger, tonight was not a bad time for it to happen: In her fluttered, disoriented state, she had yet to extract the sponge that she'd earlier lodged inside herself. She'd been mad to scheme on Mr. Somerset, but not so mad that she'd risk another pregnancy, no matter how remote the chance.

A knock came at her door. She looked up, almost sure it had been her mind playing tricks on her. The knock came again. This time every one of her muscles jumped at once.

"I've your tea, mum," said a woman's voice. The innkeeper's wife.

She had not ordered tea. But now that tea was miraculously here, she certainly wasn't about to turn it down. She scrambled off the bed, yanked her door open, and dropped her jaw in happy wonder.

It was a miracle indeed. The tray was huge and the tea service occupied only a third of it. The rest held roast beef, smoked salmon, toasted cheese, boiled eggs, bread and butter, and even a few slices of rich-smelling queen cake.

She followed the innkeeper's wife to the table, where the latter set down the tray. "How—" *How did you know I would have given a whole crown for high tea at this hour, kind woman?*

Then she noticed that the innkeeper's wife had brought two teacups and two sets of cutlery.

Her head swung around. Stuart Somerset stood just inside the door, his hair and eyes very black, his shirt very white against skin bronzed from nearly a decade on the Subcontinent.

He took in her modest room—mullioned window, bare floor, dark wainscoting that came to her shoulder. His gaze skimmed over her old valise, her muddy galoshes, and her nightgown spread over the rather surprisingly spacious bed.

Their eyes met. There was such a singular purpose to his that she had to look away almost immediately.

The innkeeper's wife curtsied to both of them—she hadn't curtsied to Verity before. He stepped aside to let the woman and her empty tray pass. The door closed softly behind her.

Her wistful, hearts-and-flowers fantasy withered in the harshness of reality. She might be a woman of ghastly moral turpitude, but she still knew a grave insult when she encountered one. For him to intrude upon her without permission, at this resolutely indecent hour . . . She owed him much, but not this much.

But because she did owe him, she held her silence, to give him a chance to apologize. Perhaps he did not realize the magnitude of his breach of etiquette. Perhaps.

He gave her nothing of the sort. "Won't you pour?" he said, inclining his head toward the tea service. She didn't move. He walked past her to the table, and poured for them both. "Sugar? Milk?"

She shook her head, turning down his offer of tea altogether, but he brought the black tea to her instead. "I won't make myself any more welcome than you'll permit me," he said.

She looked down at the cup and saucer that had somehow ended up between her hands—clutched in fingers prickling at the tips with a hot numbness. He returned to the table and began to load an empty plate.

"Why are you here?"

"I think we both know why I'm here." He glanced at her. "The question is, rather, how long you'll let me stay and what liberties you might allow me."

"None. I should think that much is obvious," she said stiffly. Had she sunk so low that a virtual stranger would assume that she was his for the asking—and a tray of tea? "I'm afraid you have wasted your time and your bribes."

"This is not a bribe," he said. He crossed what little distance separated them, took away her untouched tea, and pressed the laden plate into her hands. "I don't like the way Wicked Stepmother has been feeding you. And I haven't wasted my time. I wanted to see you again and now I have."

There was a gravitas to him that made the most ridiculous declarations ring with truth and authority. "I'm not so easily persuaded by pretty words that you have likely scattered across the length and breadth of London."

"I'm sure you will not believe me, but I lead a somewhat spartan existence, as far as glib womanizing is concerned. I'm usually far more interested in work than in the fairer sex."

"Are you? And are you also a very convincing liar?" How else could he have achieved the innkeeper's acquiescence—indeed, cooperation?

He looked full at her. "When required, yes."

"I should like you to leave now."

She used her kitchen voice, the one in which she spoke to her subordinates during working hours, the one that had held firm through both the jubilation of love and the despair of it.

It was obvious that he had not expected such unremitting firmness from her. He was surprised and disappointed—more than disappointed; the emotion that shadowed his eyes was deeper, rawer.

It shouldn't matter to her that he was disappointed, or despondent even. But it did. Because of the swiftness with which he concealed it, the way one might hide a bruise that had been inflicted by a loved one.

"When you have eaten, I will leave," he said evenly.

Again she couldn't hold the weight of his gaze. "Do I have your word?" she managed.

"Of course."

She began to eat. Her mouth was dry, her throat had closed. The food that she'd craved was hard to chew and even harder to swallow.

He broke off a piece of cake and studied it. "My mother worked in a mill when I was a child. We couldn't always make ends meet. She was adamant that we must pay the rent and keep our room, so we forwent food sometimes—never for very long, never more than a day and a half for me, though I think sometimes she went for longer without."

She stared at him. He did not look at her. "It was such a joy to eat then. The smells from pubs and chop shops would drive me into a frenzy. I would pass hours in a daze, dreaming of meat pies and a pudding bigger than my head."

Is he a gastronome like yourself?

Who, Stuart? God, no. He hasn't got a sense of taste any more than the Pygmies have a navy.

"Then I went to live with my father. From the day I entered his house, I never knew another moment of hunger. And never much cared for food again."

"Never?" She couldn't help her question, out of professional curiosity.

"Not once. The last time I had something good was the day my mother took me to my father. We got off at the village. She went into the general merchandiser's and bought me a farthing of boiled sweet. I ate it all on the walk to my father's estate—it was like sucking on God's thumb.

"A few weeks later I went back to the same shop and bought a whole penny of the same thing. It was cloying, horrible—it tasted of anise. I couldn't believe it. It had been so wonderful before."

He shrugged. Something struck her in the chest, a blow, an arrow, a pain as lovely as a boiled sweet to a hungry child.

"I'm sure I sound ridiculous," he said.

"When I was seventeen, I was at the end of my rope," she said, her voice very distant, as if another person altogether was speaking, from miles away. "I had no money, no prospects, and no family, except a baby I loved desperately.

"One day, when he was four months old, I decided that I would take my baby to the zoo, because every child should have a trip to the zoo. And then I would take him to an orphanage and drown myself in the Thames."

She'd never spoken to anyone else of that day, of her most desperate hour. Mostly she tried to shut away the memory—her escape had been too near, too much a thing of blind chance.

"I took him to every exhibit. He smiled and smiled, then he fell asleep. With my last bit of coin, I bought some treacle rock, determined to leave this world on a sweet note.

"It was the most awful thing I'd ever tasted. I started to cry outside the reptile house. I couldn't face the thought of losing my baby. Or killing myself. Or becoming a common prostitute."

The memory was all too clear now. The cold stone at her back. The taste in her mouth, as if she'd been chewing tar. Michael's soft warmness against her chest. The blurred feet of the passersby. The children's whispers. The governesses' stern admonitions against staring—*Come along. Nothing to see here*—reducing her life's tragedy to little more than a minor blight on the landscape. The bobby's gruff voice, telling her to take her moaning elsewhere. And then, the voice of the girl, clear and cool as the water of an oasis. *Leave her be*, the girl said.

"A girl came to me. She couldn't have been more than fourteen years old. She took off her necklace—it was a gold-and-pearl necklace—and gave it to me."

Verity's amazement had not dimmed with the passing years—the weight of the necklace in her bare palm, the warmth it still retained of the girl's skin, the strong squeeze of the girl's gloved hand. She'd reminded Verity not to sell the necklace for less than ten pounds. Then she'd left, rejoining a disapproving-looking woman standing some distance away.

The necklace, Verity sold for ten pounds twelve shillings two pence. The money bought her time to think, time to get over her shame and squeamishness about work, time to locate Monsieur David and ask for his help. It bought the uniforms she needed to enter service and the beautiful baby clothes she'd sent along with Michael when Monsieur David found a good family for him on the estate where he'd last worked.

"The next morning, after I'd come out of the pawn-shop, I bought a whole shilling's worth of treacle rock to give to the children in the tenement house. There was a tiny bit of it left at the end and I put it into my mouth without thinking. It was the most marvelous thing I'd ever had. It tasted . . ." How did one describe the taste of a simple piece of confection that had been imbued with all the giddiness, incredulity, and grati-tude that had made her soles elevate a little off the curb? "It tasted like hope."

A smile slowly spread over his face, a smile of aston-ishing warmth for a man of his coolness. As if he, too, tasted hope. Her heart fluttered anew.

"I like your story," he said softly. "What happened to your baby?"

"He was adopted by wonderful people, but I still see him every day."

She'd worked hard to become expert enough to cook for the master of Fairleigh Park. And it had been worth it. On the fine May day she first set foot in Fairleigh Park, Michael had been running outside the gamekeeper's cottage, a sturdy, beautiful child of three-and-a-half, enthusiastically dragging a half-torn kite through his adoptive mother's much-abused flower bed. He'd stopped when he saw Verity watching him, and then, just as she'd hoped and been afraid to let herself hope, he'd come running toward her and hurled himself into her arms.

Three years had passed since she'd kissed him good-bye, weeping uncontrollably. He didn't remember her name, or anything else about her. But he'd known instantly that she loved him.

"Lucky boy," said Stuart Somerset.

He selected a boiled egg and rolled it against the plate, making spiderweb cracks in the shell with hardly a sound. His hands, she suddenly realized, very much resembled Bertie's—fine, long-fingered hands meant for holding engraved fountain pens and a few cards after dinner.

And tossing street thugs ten feet into the lamppost. And peeling a boiled egg with delicate swiftness. He sliced the boiled egg in two, set the halves on another plate, and dropped a pinch each of salt and pepper next to the egg halves. Then he held out the plate toward her.

She looked down and was surprised to see that she'd already eaten everything on her plate. They exchanged plates. The egg was still warm, the white firm, the yolks just barely set.

The French had five hundred ways of making eggs. But there was something in the wholesome goodness of a fresh egg respectfully boiled that held its own against the multitude of fanciful preparations. This egg was not as fresh as those from Fairleigh Park's own henhouse. And it was boiled fifteen seconds past optimum. But still, it was a pleasure on the tongue, the yolk rich and sensual, the white so smooth she could taste the individual grains of salt on it.

She tried to prolong the pleasure, but finished in no time at all. "That was a good egg."

"I'm glad you liked it," said her wouldn't-be lover, folding the handkerchief with which he'd carefully wiped his fingertips. "Have the rest for breakfast."

With a little start she realized he was about to leave, as he'd said he would, now that she'd eaten.

"Would you hand me a slice of cake?" she said.

He looked up sharply, as if she'd requested he kiss her instead. Their gaze held a long moment, until the air around her became too taut to breathe. She began to wonder if she had indeed issued an invitation of the carnal sort. He looked away and did as she asked, bringing her two slices of cake.

"The cake is good, too," she said, somewhat stupidly, after a bite.

"Do you like cake?"

She felt his eyes on her, his attention a palpable heat on her cheeks, as if she were standing in her kitchen, not far from a stove on full bore.

"I like everything. A full stomach is a luxury that never galls." She bit into the moist cake again, exploring the crenellations of a dried currant with the tip of her tongue. "Thank you for the food. I was quite starved after I came back. And the thought of spending a hungry night was agony."

"My pleasure," he said simply.

She bowed her head. "I'm sorry that I was quite rude earlier."

"There's nothing wrong in putting your own well-being ahead of my sensibilities. Let's not forget that I wanted much from you."

Her face flamed. She stuffed her mouth with cake so she didn't have to respond.

"It's getting late," he said after a minute. "I should go before the streets of London are no longer safe even for a man."

"Yes, of course."

"Good night, Cinderella."

She set her plate down. "Good night. And thank you again for everything."

His lips pulled into an expression that half resembled a smile. "Let me know when you have found your true prince."

He crossed the scant distance that separated the table and the door, lifted his hat from where he'd left it on the coat tree, and reached for the door.

"Wait!"

He waited, his hand on the door handle. She took a napkin from the table, wiped her hands, and approached him.

"I would like to shake your hand," she said.

She extended her hand. He turned around and glanced at it. For two full seconds he did nothing.

Then he leaned forward, grabbed hold of her shoulders, and kissed her.

His kiss was nothing like his precise formality, but exactly like his burst of violence. She felt as if she'd been picked up off the ground and thrown ten feet into a lamppost. Her head spun. All the breath was knocked out of her. Her arms fluttered by her sides like a pair of confused old ladies.

Then she put her arms to use. She clutched him to her, as if she were a grasshopper and he the last day of summer, and kissed him back.

Chapter Eight

Lizzy walked the smooth, even embankment that had been built along the Ure. The sun had just climbed above the horizon. The river was illumed in a fragile light the color of watered beer. The world seemed new, the air clear and cold, so pure after London's sooty vapors that it almost hurt to breathe.

There was a time when she would have found Fairleigh Park wanting, when she'd have overlooked its fresh loveliness because it did not possess the mass and grandeur to rival Lyndhurst Hall, the Arlingtons' ancestral manor, or Huntington, Lord Wrenworth's seat.

But that was so long ago, when she'd believed that a mere batting of her eyelashes could cause a tempest in a man's heart, any man's heart. The young Arlington heir had certainly seemed susceptible to her charms, but he had loved her less than he'd feared his mother, who didn't think Lizzy's connections quite good enough for her exalted family.

She'd next set her cap on the Marquess of Wrenworth, whose mother had been long dead and who had the greatest fortune among all the titled men of England, Scotland, Ireland, and Wales. The marquess, despite Lizzy's assiduous courting, would marry a woman of no connections whatsoever.

The twin failures and her mother's death from what everyone had thought a mere seasonal cold had plunged Lizzy into a state of rudderless misery that had led to the disaster with Henry. And *that* had led to a deep melancholia from which she'd thought she'd never emerge. But emerged she had, weak and uncertain, to find herself almost on the shelf, her prospects of a good marriage—of any kind of marriage—halving with each passing year.

It was better fortune than she deserved that Stuart had at last decided to marry—and that he'd been receptive to her overtures. As a girl, she'd entertained thoughts of marriage with him, until she'd realized that while he was handsome and well thought of by her father, he had neither the importance nor the wealth that she'd decided was her due.

In the years since, while she'd blindly chased after the impossible match to satisfy her vanity, he'd risen high in the world. There was talk that after the passage of the Irish Home Rule bill, he would be given the portfolio of the Home Secretary. A Great Office of the State at his age could augur only one thing: a career at 10 Downing Street.

And now this very fine, very beautiful estate.

She sighed. He could have chosen any woman. He

chose her. Years ago she'd have been smug and superior about it. Now she was only grateful. She was determined to be a perfect wife to him. She would make him happy, and make sure that he never had cause to regret his choice.

"Are you quite all right, Miss Bessler?"

She jerked around at Mr. Marsden's voice. He stood a few feet away, an expression of apparent concern on his face. "You stopped walking and you've been standing in place."

How long had he been there, watching her? Had he followed her from the house? And why must her first reaction to his presence be a quiver of excitement?

"I couldn't be better, thank you," she said coolly.

He had behaved himself last night, at dinner and afterward. He could be quite the charming guest when he tried, which made her resent him even more for his deliberate provocation on the train.

"I understand that congratulations are in order, even though the official word will not be in the papers for a few days yet," he said.

"And now you need not trouble yourself on why I haven't married, despite all my sterling qualities," she said.

She resumed walking in the direction of the house, for a lady did not stand and converse with a gentleman. He fell into step beside her. "Lovely weather, isn't it?"

"Quite," she said.

"And what a tremendous dinner last night. The best I've ever had."

"I can't agree more."

"And Madame Durant is beautiful, or so they say."

There was something prurient in his tone. Lizzy glanced at him. He again wore that speculative dirty look.

Enough was enough. She would be Mrs. Somerset in a matter of weeks. She did not have to put up with this insolence from a mere secretary. She halted. "The way you look at me makes me intensely uncomfortable, Mr. Marsden. I would be most obliged if you would desist."

The obsceneness receded from his eyes. He had gray eyes that matched the cashmere scarf about his neck—yet another example of his vanity. She would not be surprised at all to learn that he wore padded shoes so that they would stand at exactly the same height of five foot ten.

"I'm sorry. Have I been so obvious?" he said, sounding more amused than anything else. "So you've noticed that I couldn't stop looking at you."

His admission set off a strange thrill.

"I would appreciate it if you made an effort, since it would be best for us to remain on amicable terms for Mr. Somerset's sake," she said grandly.

"Perhaps we might not need to maintain amicable terms," he said. "I haven't decided whether I'll let Mr. Somerset marry a woman of your . . . unconventional ways, and I've still a few more days to make up my mind."

"I beg your pardon?" she cried.

But her indignation wasn't what it should be.

Instead it was lined and stuffed with fear. Did he know about Henry? In what other way could she be described as "unconventional," a label she'd assiduously avoided, as it usually referred only to suffragettes and bluestockings and women otherwise unfit for the upper echelons of Society?

And if Mr. Marsden chose to take it upon himself to inform Stuart, who was to say that he wouldn't see it as his further duty to inform the rest of the world? Once her conduct with Henry became common knowledge, she'd be banished to some bleak cottage in the moors to live out the rest of her life in disgrace and ostracism.

"Paris. Madame Belleau's house. The burgundy chamber with the mirrors," he said.

She stared at him, understanding nothing at first. Then she did.

"Deny it," he prompted her. "Laugh at me and tell me it was only my sordid imagination. That you would never, ever do such a thing. That you never even knew such a thing was possible. What an abomination!"

"Oh, please." She was almost giddy with relief. What Mr. Marsden had witnessed was the merest of trifles, something she and Stuart could laugh about were he to learn of it. "Let us not insult Mr. Somerset's intelligence. Do you think he would care that I once allowed an omnivorous Frenchwoman to kiss me? I assure you that far worse things happen at the best finishing schools on the Continent."

"I think he might care if his fiancée preferred his cook to himself."

"Which I most decidedly do not, or I would have eagerly participated in the goings-on at school. And Madame Belleau only caught me at a moment of great ennui. Believe me, when she disrobed and beckoned to me from her overly gilded bedstead, I had absolutely no intention or desire to ravish her."

Mr. Marsden looked at her a long time, as if trying to decide whether she was telling the truth, and as if that decision held some great personal significance to him. "A good thing," he said at last. "Since her husband walked in a minute later."

"A good thing indeed."

"I always thought it a masterly performance that you put on, holding her hand, wiping her brow, and telling him that she'd succumbed to a particularly virulent case of the vapors."

It *had* been a masterly performance, if Lizzy said so herself.

"A depraved couple," she said. "She acted shocked enough, diving under the bedspread and giving me all those panicky looks, but I'm not convinced that his arrival was an accident."

Mr. Marsden chortled, with what seemed to be surprised glee. There was still something enigmatic about his mirth, but compared to what she was used to from him, it was as guileless as a baby's burble.

"A pity, really, that your Sapphic inclinations weren't more overwhelming," he said. "For I do love a good melodrama."

"You must look for it elsewhere, sir," she said. "Now, if you are done blackmailing me, good day."

He nodded. "Until the funeral, Miss Bessler."

She walked off, but as she turned to climb up the steps that led toward the house, she saw that he'd remained in place, watching her, his scarf streaming in the morning breeze.

❧

"I was looking for you," said Stuart to Lizzy, who approached the house from the direction of the river.

He wanted to apologize to her. It was her first visit to their future home and he'd been barely adequate in his role as her host and husband-to-be. The effect of dinner had lasted the whole evening—and well into the night—and it had been all he could do to pretend to listen to Marsden and Mr. Bessler's conversation and nod at seemingly appropriate points.

"I took a long walk," answered his fiancée, not sounding at all as if she'd noticed his distraction. She turned around and looked back at the wide avenue leading down to the wrought-iron river gate and the formal gardens that flanked the passage on either side. "Fairleigh Park is beautiful."

"Can you see yourself spending time here?"

"Very easily. I love it already."

"I'm glad," he said. "I know you wanted a much greater place for yourself."

"Oh, no. Please, Stuart, you must not go on reminding me of my girlish arrogance. I'm thoroughly ashamed to have been so vain."

He smiled at her. "You were not vain, but ambitious. I understand a thing or two about ambition."

"Sir?" someone called him from behind.

He turned around. It was the housekeeper. "Yes, Mrs. Boyce?"

Mrs. Boyce handed him a brown envelope. "Sir, the maids found this. I thought I should bring it to your attention."

The envelope had *To be buried with me* written across it. The script was elaborate, formal. Bertie's, from the days when they'd written each other almost every day, before Bertie's handwriting transitioned to a loose, loopy cursive during his later years at Harrow.

"Where did the maids find it?"

"In Mr. Bertram's sketch collection," said Mrs. Boyce. The housekeeper had asked him what she ought to do with Bertie's extensive collection of sketches and he'd told her to put everything away. "I had them put tissue paper between the sketches. And they came across it in one of the earlier portfolios. Shall I have it placed in the casket?"

The envelope was light and unsealed—presumably when Bertie had been alive, no one ever went nosing in his sketches but himself. Stuart emptied the content of the envelope into his palm.

Photographs, two of them. The first was a family portrait of Bertie and his parents. Bertie would have been about five or six, small, blond, standing next to his mother, his hand in hers.

The second was a photograph of two young boys. One was Bertie. It took Stuart a moment to realize that the other was himself. They sat on a stone bench, two stiff, serious faces—one must hold oneself entirely still, or the photograph would be blurred.

Then he saw it, their clasped hands on the bench. For some reason, the sight stunned him. He quickly slid the photographs back into the envelope.

To be buried with me.

He gave it back. "Yes, you may have it placed in the casket."

🍃

> *Dearest Georgette,*
>
> *I wonder why I never asked you this before, but do you remember that hushed-up scandal about Mr. Marsden, the late Lord Wyden's second-youngest son? At the time you said—you horrible tease, you—that you knew the truth from eavesdropping on your mother's conversation with the distraught Lady Wyden, but that your mother caught you and made you swear not to say anything to anyone.*
>
> *And remember that you told me that you'd let me in on the secret after Lord and Lady Wyden had both passed on? They have, and I want to know what happened. Don't make me wait too long.*
>
> *Kisses to the twins,*
>
> *Love,*
> *Lizzy*

🍃

"I'm sorry, sir. Did you say Manchester South or Manchester South West?" asked Marsden.

"South West," Stuart answered.

This was the second time Marsden had asked Stuart to repeat something. But Stuart was little better. He kept losing his train of thought and once had to ask Marsden to recite back a paragraph so he'd know what he'd said.

"While I am sympathetic to your anxieties with regard to your constituents' strong feelings toward the Irish Home Rule bill," continued Stuart, "allow me to point out that these same constituents voted you into office knowing full well that electoral success for the Liberals would return as Prime Minister Mr. William Ewart Gladstone, who has made it abundantly clear during his years in opposition that Irish Home Rule is a matter of moral imperative, that he stands fast by his commitment to the Irish and will reintroduce the bill in the upcoming parliamentary session."

He paused, waiting to see if Marsden would need any further clarification. But Marsden only looked up expectantly.

"With the support of the electorate, and with Mr. Gladstone's skills and persuasion, it is fully expected that the bill will pass in both Houses. I understand, having been a young MP myself, that you would not wish to be left out of this historic vote. Furthermore, I believe you would not wish to bypass the opportunity for an early and speedy passage of certain private bills near and dear to your heart."

"Corporate charter?" asked Marsden, his pen scratching furiously.

"Railroad," said Stuart.

Now that the threats had been laid, Stuart engaged

in two paragraphs of cordiality. It was the last letter for the morning. Marsden closed his notebook and rose. "I'll have these ready for you tomorrow, sir."

"Thank you," said Stuart.

They were ahead of schedule; it would be another five minutes before the carriage pulled up in front of the manor to take Stuart to the funeral.

"I've been meaning to ask, sir, do you think it wise for Mr. Gladstone to push for Irish Home Rule again? It cost him the government last time," said Marsden.

"It very well could this time also," said Stuart, shuffling through a pile of letters Prior had brought in a quarter hour ago. Privately, he wasn't quite as confident of the bill's passage as he projected in his letters to hesitant backbenchers. The Conservatives still held the House of Lords. The Liberals had only a forty-seat majority in the House of Commons. And the courage to do the right thing was a rare quality in any politician.

"Yet you have thrown your support behind him," said Marsden.

"The Irish grow restless. But they are still willing to work with us. Do we really wish to procrastinate until the day they decide to take up arms?"

"Haven't they already taken up arms, in a way?"

"If you speak of the bombings in the eighties, those were the action of an overwhelming minority. I would prefer that we act before the sentiment for violence finds favor with a greater part of the population," said Stuart.

He was a pragmatic man who saw the best course of

action as the one that did the least damage over time. Set that time horizon far enough and the best course of action from a pragmatic point of view matched well with the right thing to do on principle. It was one of the reasons that Mr. Gladstone had come to value him: His levelheaded approach to governing complemented the Grand Old Man's passionate moral commitment.

"Let's hope our MPs see it as you do."

"They will," said Stuart. There was nothing he could do about the outcome in the House of Lords, but he did not intend to fail in his role in the lower house. That vote he would deliver to Mr. Gladstone if he had to browbeat, bludgeon, and blackmail every last Liberal MP into line.

"I might have some useful information on a few MPs, sir," said Marsden.

"Excellent," said Stuart. Any intelligence Marsden supplied was certain to be something no MP would ever want publicly known. "We might yet make a back-stabbing, blackhearted tactician out of you."

Despite a letter of character from the mayor of Paris himself, Stuart had been reluctant to take on as his secretary an aristocratic young man who'd spent five years in Paris, rubbing shoulders with writers and artists—and anarchists, for all Stuart knew. Will Marsden, however, had turned out to be an extremely pleasant surprise. He was exactly as the mayor had said: competent, meticulous, and unfailingly reliable.

"I understand from the servants that you are to be married, sir," said Marsden.

"The servants are always the first to know everything," answered Stuart. Though in this instance the servants' excessive knowledge was entirely his doing—after he'd informed Madame Durant, he'd gone ahead and told his own valet, with the understanding that it was not news that the latter needed to keep to himself. "Yes, Miss Bessler has accepted my suit."

"Congratulations, sir."

Marsden did not sound overly enthusiastic. Stuart wondered whether he reciprocated Lizzy's antagonism in some way.

"Thank you," he said. "The wedding will take place mid-January—much too soon really, but I want it done before Parliament opens. It is rather an unfair burden to place on Miss Bessler's shoulders alone, so I have pledged your assistance in the matter. I trust you will prove as invaluable to Miss Bessler as you are to me?"

Marsden lifted the cover of his notebook halfway. He didn't look at Stuart. "Are you certain that I would be able to do justice to your wedding, sir? I've no experience in the staging of weddings."

"I understand that as part of your duties at the *mairie* you undertook social events of a similar scale and brought them off successfully. You'll do fine."

Marsden let the notebook cover drop. He tapped his pen twice against it. "Thank you for your confidence, sir. I shall strive to make it a most worthy event."

❦

Stuart arrived at the church ahead of everyone else. The vicar, a kindly man, asked him if he wished to spend a private moment with Bertie. It was a sincere, if routine, offer for a minute of seclusion with the dearly departed. Yet Stuart found himself paralyzed, as if he'd been thrust before a monumental decision.

"Yes, thank you," he said, because it was expected of him.

Bertie's casket rested on a catafalque at the end of the nave, before a wall of wreaths. It was a beautiful casket, the best mahogany money could buy. As Stuart approached, his reflection walked toward him in the glossy varnish, his face distorted by the curve and angle of the coffin.

A large spray of white lilies adorned the top of the casket. Stuart ran his finger along a cool green stem.

Do you like flowers? Bertie had asked. It had been a bright June morning, a few days after Stuart's arrival.

Stuart had nodded. He'd never seen so many flowers in bloom. Roses, roses, and more roses. The garden had been a fairy tale.

I'm going to make new varietals of roses. Dozens of them. Do you want to have a rose named after you?

Stuart had smiled. It was the first time he'd smiled since his mother had left. *If you are sure it's a boy rose.*

Ever since his return to Fairleigh Park, old memories he didn't even know he still retained had crowded just beneath the surface of his mind, waiting for only the slightest trigger to break into his consciousness.

He and Bertie had played hide-and-seek in this very church. Afterward, Bertie had taken Stuart to High Street and introduced him to old Mrs. Tate, whose dusty shop sold books and bizarre odds and ends, and whispered in his ear that he'd heard Mrs. Tate had been a naughty woman in her youth. On their way home it had rained. And Bertie had talked of his mother, because his face was already wet.

That boy would grow up to be jealous and fearful of him, Stuart reminded himself. He would tell Stuart that Sir Francis had prayed for Nelda Lamb to die, when it seemed she might recover from her illness. And whip an army of lawyers before him, driving Stuart to the brink of bankruptcy.

But *those* memories rang hollow before the lily-covered casket. They'd spurred Stuart for so long, their venomous potency had diminished to a fraction of their former power.

Stuart lifted the spray of lilies and set it aside. The lid of the casket was heavy, but it rose smoothly. Inside the elaborately padded coffin, Bertie lay in formal repose. He wore his hair swept back, in the same style Stuart remembered from his late adolescence. That hair, however, had thinned in the twenty intervening years. Where it was brushed away from his forehead, Stuart could see the edge of Bertie's scalp, a congealed shade of bluish-white.

Until this moment, he had only understood Bertie's death intellectually.

He stared at Bertie's throat—surely the collar had been pulled too tight. A fresh boutonniere of red rose had been pinned to Bertie's lapel. Bertie's hands—so alike to his own, when the brothers otherwise bore little physical resemblance to each other—were folded together across his abdomen. And next to his hands, the envelope marked "To be buried with me."

From outside came the sound of carriage wheels crunching on the gravel drive. Mourners were arriving in front of the church. Soon they would populate the pews. Stuart lowered the lid of the casket.

There were voices. The first mourners were already walking up the steps of the church. But they sounded very far away.

That photograph. It had been May, hadn't it? And they'd been in a part of the gardens that had later been dug up and completely rearranged. It had been during Sir Francis's brief passion for photography. And they'd had trouble holding still, lapsing again and again into giggles. And—

Stuart opened the casket, opened the envelope, and removed the photograph of Bertie and himself. He barely had time to slip it into his breast pocket and put back the lilies before the vicar returned.

The vicar smiled at him, brimming with incurious good nature. "All right, sir?"

Verity wept.

She had not expected to cry. She'd thought of Bertie only in passing since his death. But as the organist struck the last quivering notes of "End of the Road," and six of Bertie's Harrow classmates hoisted his casket onto their shoulders, the tears came, as if they'd been there all along.

He hadn't loved her the way she'd hoped he would, but she'd been able to make a good life for herself here, under his aegis. In the ten years since the end of their affair, he'd never once made inappropriate advances toward her, never unleashed groundless criticism against her work, never withheld a raise when she'd earned one.

Around him, the estate—and her kitchen—had revolved with a steadfast, comforting regularity. His habits gave rhythm to her life. His palate guided her gifts. Her true North he hadn't been, but he'd been a solid path that had not led into murky woods, nor shifted uncertainly underfoot.

And she'd scarcely realized how much she'd appreciated it, until this moment, when he would be packed under six feet of earth, when it was too late to tell him that she was grateful for his decency and consideration.

❧

After the funeral, Michael located Verity in the kitchen. She was alone. Luncheon, a cold buffet, had been prepared in advance so that all the servants could attend the service.

He inhaled the air. "Madeleines?"

"Madeleines," she answered. The first batch had already come out of the oven, little golden shells cooling on the rack.

"In memory of the late Mr. Somerset?"

She sighed softly. "A tribute."

After the end of their affair, she'd never made madeleines again for Bertie, her one lone revenge. A petty gesture, now that she thought of it. She loved nothing more than that her food should bring people pleasure. And Bertie had adored her madeleines to bits.

"A farewell tribute?"

"I suppose you could say so."

"No, I meant—is it a farewell to us? Are you leaving?"

She looked about her beloved kitchen. She would have to leave its familiar odors and textures behind too. And her rooms, her sweet home and shelter. The grounds of Fairleigh Park. The gardens that rivaled earthly Eden come the first month of summer.

"I saw you cry at the funeral," said Michael. "You stayed because you loved him. And now he's gone."

No, I stayed because I love you.

Love had once been such an easy subject. When he'd been a child, they'd made the expression of love a game of hyperbole. *My love for you is deeper than the tunnel to China. My love for you is enough to melt all the steel in Damascus. My love for you is more constant than* π (this after Michael had learned about the circle at school).

But somewhere along the way they'd lost that camaraderie, especially after she'd told him that no, she wasn't his mother, and that she had no idea who his parents were.

"Mr. Bertram Somerset was once very dear to me," said Verity. "But he is not the reason why I stayed. Nor the reason why I may leave."

Part of her wanted to hand in her resignation that very afternoon, while a different part of her begged for another day, another dinner, another chance. She wasn't ready to completely give up. She still thought she had magic enough.

"You'll go work for Monsieur du Gard, then?"

Monsieur du Gard was one of the wealthiest members of Bertie's gastronomic circle, the one who consistently offered her the highest wages to cook for him.

"Possibly," she said. "Isn't it what you've always wanted for me, fame and glory in Paris?"

"Isn't that what you've always assured me you don't want?" said Michael.

"People change, don't they?"

He stood close enough that she smelled the toilette water she'd made for him last summer, with pine oil she'd purchased from an old Hungarian émigré in Manchester. Her room had smelled like a forest for days on end.

Michael gave her a chill look. "They certainly do."

❦

From the hothouse, Verity had her first look at Mr. Somerset in good light.

She'd avoided him, of course. But even without any measure of evasion, in the absence of a direct summons, the cook and the master of the house—one who wasn't fanatically devoted to the art and science of gastronomy—could pass months without catching sight of each other.

At the church she'd mostly had a view of the back of his head, a view that had been further obstructed by an inconveniently placed pillar. He'd sat at the foot of the pulpit, while she'd stood at the very back, in a huddle with the other servants—the distance between them sixteen rows of pews and the whole structure of the British class system.

The hothouse was located behind the manor, in a cluster of other utilitarian structures—the kitchen complex, the brewery, the dovecote—and separated from the rear gardens by a boxwood hedge almost ten foot high. Not the sort of place where one expected to see the master of the house loitering.

But when she looked up from the spread of potted herbs set on propped-up planks, he was only a few feet away, on the other side of the glass panes, walking slowly, a cigarette between the index and middle fingers of his left hand.

He came to a stop, his profile to her. He was thinner than she remembered, and older than he'd looked in the photograph that had been in the newspaper, which now she judged to have been taken at least half a decade ago. Faint shadows darkened the underside of his eye. His forehead was creased. A groove carved from the side of his nose to the corner of his mouth.

Some lovers were fortunate enough to grow old together. They'd grown old apart. She did not think him any less handsome. She only wished that she'd been there when the first line on his face had appeared, so that she could have stroked and kissed and cherished it.

He was to depart Fairleigh Park within the hour, not to return until after the New Year. But she would not be here when he came again. She'd be settled down in Paris, on her way to gastronomic immortality.

She suddenly realized that she was exposed to his view, with nothing between them but clear glass panes that had been wiped down just two days ago. She sidled toward a tall trellis overgrown with cucumber leaves. Her movement caught his eye. He looked in her direction just as she slid behind the trellis.

Her heart pounded. Through the gaps in the leaves she could still see him. He stared at the spot where she stood behind the trellis. Then he took a step toward the greenhouse. Then another step. Then another.

She recognized the look on his face for what it was: desire, beneath all the outward paddings of respectability. Not quite the roiling desire she'd sensed when he'd come into her room that night at the inn, but desire all the same, fully formed and intent.

Her breath was in tatters. Her heart hurtled itself every which way, an occupant of Bedlam hell-bent on breaking out. The handles of the snippers dug into tender places between her fingers, so tightly did she clutch them.

She didn't want it, she thought rebelliously, almost angrily. She didn't want him to be the kind of man who fancied his cook. With Bertie it had been different—they'd had the love of food in common. But Stuart Somerset was indifferent to her food. And all *he* knew of Madame Durant was that she'd slept with his brother: an easy woman.

His gaze swept the hothouse—and located the door. No, please, not this way, not discovered because he wanted to see the slutty cook.

He stared at her again. What could he see of her? The hem of her dress? The frill of her apron? The tip of her fingers hooked over the trellis to keep herself steady? And why, for God's sake, did he want anything of Bertie's cook?

His hand lifted. He took a hard drag of the cigarette. When he expelled the smoke, it was from between his teeth. He threw down what remained of the cigarette and ground his heel over it, a gesture that was almost as agitated as the beat of her heart.

His eyes remained on the ground for a few seconds. When he lifted his head again, the glance that came her way was shuttered, like shop windows after a riot. And then he was gone.

❧

Why had she hidden herself from him?

He could think of a variety of reasons, none of which made any sense, except perhaps she really was as ugly as the bottom of her favorite sauté pan and skittish about strangers. But it really didn't matter why she'd acted the way she had. Why had *he* come all this way in the hope of seeing her?

He had not meandered into the vicinity of the hothouse by accident. She'd been on his mind ever since the end of the funeral, when he'd realized with a lurch, outside the church, that the weeping female servant he'd passed on his way out—even with the handkerchief pressed to her face he'd seen the sheen of tears on her cheek—had been none other than Madame Durant herself.

She'd worn a white cap and a black dress, a uniform nearly identical to those of the other servants. Yet there had been something different about her: in the placement of her shoulders, the gloves she'd worn.

He'd have gone into the hothouse. As they'd faced each other on two sides of the cucumber trellis, he'd felt an overwhelming stirring of excitement. It was only what he'd wanted that had stopped him cold.

He'd wanted to touch her. To pin her against the trellis with his body, the smell of crushed green leaves in his nostrils. To hold her face and examine her features, to see what had seduced his brother, and what, sight unseen, had disturbed his thoughts and his hours of repose.

There in the humid warmth of the hothouse, shielded from prying eyes by climbing cucumbers and ripening tomatoes, he would have run his fingers along her jaw, over her lips. He would have wanted to insert his thumb into her mouth, to see if the inside of it was as succulent as the scallops she'd served the night before.

And then he would have wanted to taste her. Would she taste warm and sweet like the crème anglaise in which she'd floated isles of *blanc et neige*? Cool and subtle like the champagne jelly he'd had for luncheon? Or would she taste like chocolate, to someone who'd never known the mystery and guile of the aphrodisiac of the Aztecs?

He'd overlooked his desire for Madame Durant the first time, because she'd been a mere proxy, a vehicle for him to think of *her*. This time he had no such excuse. He had not been thinking of Cinderella, but only of the woman behind the trellis, the one whose food had unleashed beastly things in him, the toe of whose lavishly polished black boot fascinated him because it had been an unexpectedly soigné touch in an otherwise humble ensemble.

He reminded himself that such lust had no place in his life. He was to be married in two months. And even if he had no fiancée, and no plans for marriage at all, fraternization with the cook would still have broken every principle he had for himself. He had not forgotten where he'd come from, or the harshness of life that had befallen his mother because his father had felt free to indulge himself with a social inferior.

He'd nearly reached the house when Lizzy came out, already in her traveling dress.

She smiled. "Oh, good, you are here. Now we can finally have our tea."

❧

Tea came almost as soon as he'd sat down in the drawing room. And with tea came plates of small, golden tea cakes in the shape of shells. Even from across the drawing room, Stuart smelled them—the same smell from Bertie's handkerchief, he realized instantly, but in full force, as if he'd been hearing a faint strain of music in his mind, only to suddenly encounter it in all its symphonic splendor.

The odor went straight to his head, resurrecting more long-dead memories—sun, warmth, laughter that rang clear under blue skies, he and Bertie swimming in the trout stream, Bertie sketching under a tree while he sat up in the tree, reading the latest copy of Bertie's *Boy's World* magazine.

"Ah, madeleines," said Marsden. "My favorite."

"Were they also my brother's favorite?" Stuart asked the second footman.

"I'm sure I don't know, sir. I've been here eight years and this is the first time I've served these."

"Hmm," Marsden sighed. "My compliments to Mrs. Boyce, all the same."

"These didn't come from the stillroom, sir," said the footman. "They came from the kitchen."

Stuart already knew. Only Madame Durant's cooking had such power. And they *had* been Bertie's favorite, and had meant for him something beyond a combination of common kitchen ingredients. Had evoked a lost era, a better time.

Stuart thought of the boys in the photograph, their hands held tight. Seven years later they would despise each other. For the next twenty years they would communicate only through intermediaries, sustaining the hostilities as if the bonds of brotherhood had never meant a thing.

And now Bertie was dead. Too late for weddings, births of children, or sheer old age to bring them together, the overheated spite of yesteryear forgotten in the bright joy of the occasion, or simply because too many years had passed and they could no longer remember their trespasses against each other.

He wanted to tell someone about them, about the boys in a garden that no longer existed, the brothers who had discussed death and life on an old stone bridge, the sibling who was going to name a rose after him—and he could only think of one person who might understand the intensity and ambivalence of his sentiments.

He'd wondered why she'd wept at Bertie's funeral. Bertie had made no provisions for her in his will. He hadn't even ever set her up properly as a mistress—she'd worked for him all throughout their affair. Perhaps they too had ended their association on a bitter note. And only now could she recall him without lingering resentment distorting her memories.

He needed that, needed the past she and Bertie had shared, their long, complicated history an echo of his own twisted chronicle with Bertie.

But he'd just walked away from her, the soles of his feet tingling as if he'd stepped back from the edge of a precipice.

He left his seat and went to the window that overlooked the gravel drive leading away from the house. It came down to a question of potency. What did he want more, to put Bertie's ghost to rest or to avoid Madame Durant?

It seemed almost a rhetorical question. Of course Bertie was more important. Yet he hesitated for another full minute. He would need to conduct himself with excruciating care. And watch every thought and impulse. And not let his guard down.

And never trust himself.

❧

Verity watched the carriages depart, the brougham carrying the master of the house, his guests, and his secretary, the wagonette with the one maid and two valets that had accompanied them on their visit. Her gaze followed the brougham until it was entirely obscured by the trees that grew most thoughtlessly along the drive.

And they did not live happily ever after.

The end.

It was all expected, all run-to-course, all predetermined even. And yet it was a furious pain unfurling, its dark tentacles strangling her heart.

The end.

She closed her eyes.

The knocks on her door she ignored. The kitchen could do without her for a few minutes. She didn't know how much time passed before she turned around and saw the note that had been slipped under her door.

Dear Madame,

I require your presence in London.

     Your servant,

     Stuart Somerset

She read the brief message three times before she understood it. Then the words burned.

Why did he want her in London? To gratify those curtailed desires that had been writ plain on his face? To have her someplace private so that he wouldn't be deterred by the fear of exposure should he want to explore his improper curiosity again?

It went against everything she knew of him. But what other reason could there be for the summons to come so abruptly, almost immediately after their near-encounter in the greenhouse, when it had been decided well in advance that no servant from Fairleigh Park was to follow him to London until after the New Year?

Well, she wouldn't go. She was a servant, not a slave. She was free to leave his employ at any time.

She sat down at her desk and began her resignation letter.

Chapter Nine

July 1882

Stuart could not believe what he was doing, nor the vehemence with which he did it. He all but ravaged her mouth, unable to stop himself for fear that she would stop him first.

Her lips were the opulence of *Arabian Nights*. She tasted of cake and whiskey—sweetness and fire, like the first sunrise after the Deluge. His fingers dug into the thin calico of her blouse, hungry for her skin, her everything.

Let me. Only let me. Please.

Then she did—she kissed him back. The floor tilted, stars fell, and he was entirely vanquished. He was a stranger to her. And yet in her kiss there was an enormous trust. He was humbled; he was grateful beyond words. He couldn't remember the last time he felt such affinity for another person, such willingness to yield everything of himself.

He pulled back. He was no longer accustomed to emotions of such intensity. His heart couldn't seem to handle it. He didn't know whether to rejoice or be frightened witless.

She looked at him, her eyes full of dismay. Because he'd kissed her? Or because he'd stopped?

He wanted her too much. And he knew, better than anyone else, what happened when he wanted anything too much. There was a price to be paid. There was always a price.

"You can still send me away," he said.

But even as the rational coward in him looked for a way out, the rest of him would have none of it. Whatever the price this time, he would pay it, for the sanctuary he would find with her—for the sanctuary he had already found with her.

"I can't," she said softly.

And he knew then that he was hers, for as long as she would have him. He cupped her face in his hands and kissed her again. The mad urgency was still there in him, but a great tenderness had overcome him. And he wanted not to overwhelm, but to cherish.

She was even more delicious this time—like boiled sweets and treacle rocks, for all the promises she held. A pulse at the top of her neck throbbed against his ring finger, a hot, fast rhythm in synchronicity with his own heartbeat.

He was a fighter, not a lover. He'd always left the particulars of lovemaking to the women who took him to bed. And so he'd feared that he would be clumsy and awkward with her. But tonight he was in grace. As his hands slipped lower to work at the buttons of her blouse, his fingers moved with an unhurried dexterity.

Her skirts melted away. Even her stays presented little challenge.

When she was left only in her chemise, he sat her at the edge of the bed and continued to kiss her as he took off his coat and waistcoat. She helped him pull his shirt over his head.

He kissed her throat, her shoulders, her arms. When he bit her slightly at the base of her neck, she emitted a whimper of pleasure, a tiny sound that exploded in his veins—he wanted only to please her, and now she was pleased.

Everything he did seemed to please her. She shivered when he kissed her behind her ears. Nibbles at the inside of her elbows produced little sighs that made him dizzy. And when he licked her breasts through the thin lawn of her chemise, she all but heaved him off the bed.

He pushed up the chemise to worship her unhindered, her strawberry-scented skin, her perfectly round navel, her nipples that were like satin upon his tongue. She yanked off the chemise, wrapped her limbs tightly about him, and with the undulation of her body, let him know that she was ready for him.

It was like the first time. No, it was far better than his first time, during which he was half-drunk, still recovering from his first bout of malaria, and not altogether certain whether he'd have consented to the act if he hadn't been so inebriated.

She scorched him. He was in torment, the sweetest, purest torment of his entire life. With every thrust he wanted to let blessed release wash over him. With every labored breath he held back, prolonging the pleasure, the tremors at the edge of the eruption.

Then she cried out and shuddered. And he could not have stopped himself had the fate of nations and the lives of millions depended upon it. His climax gripped and struck him. He shook and convulsed from the violent pleasures that tore him apart and tore him apart some more.

He let go, gave in, and fell over the edge.

❦

He was sleepy, but he was also suffused with a splendid sense of well-being, a euphoric elation.

He rolled onto his side, pulling her with him, keeping her close. She was flushed, her hair a messy, unruly tumble, her breaths still short and uneven, like his own.

He stole a quick kiss: She looked too adorable.

"It's after midnight, Cinderella," he said. "You are still here."

She smiled shyly and pulled a sheet up to her clavicle. "The modern-day Cinderella mostly understands that crime is rampant in our fair cities and that it makes no sense to run out of perfectly safe buildings into nighttime streets."

He caressed the top of her shoulder. Her collarbone was prominent. Without the padding of her clothes she was even thinner than he'd supposed. "I'm glad the modern-day Cinderella is so prudent."

"The modern-day Cinderella disappears at dawn instead," she said. "When the trains begin running."

"Prudent and logistically literate, the modern-day Cinderella is a marvel of womanhood." He leaned forward and kissed her on the lips again. "Wait here."

She had her head propped up when he returned to bed with another plate of cake. "You are hungry?"

"It's for you," he said, setting it down next to her. "You need to eat some more."

Her gaze dropped. "Thank you," she said. "Nobody thinks to feed me nowadays."

"That is a crime." He broke off a piece of cake and offered it to her. "Now eat, young lady."

"You sound like my old governess."

"Did you not eat properly as a child?"

"Not at all. I had to be chased and pinned down and threatened with dire consequences to touch my supper."

"I find that hard to believe."

"I didn't particularly care for food until I left home and meals no longer appeared with tedious predictability on the table." She accepted another piece of cake from him. "Nothing like hunger to focus the mind on what's really important."

"A full stomach?"

"A full stomach."

He smiled. "What did you think was important before?"

"Clothes."

"Clothes?"

"Yes, gowns, and frocks, and blouses, and bonnets,

and gloves, and shoes, and—" She glanced at him. "Do you want me to go on?"

He'd like her to go on simply to hear words fall from her lips—like pearls dropping onto a silver plate. "I had no idea Cinderella was ever so shallow."

"Oh, but she was." A pause. "And is. In fact, I've always suspected that she'd gone to the ball less to snag a prince than to prance about in a new ball gown: the former is an unlikely prospect; the latter, an assured pleasure."

"You mean to tell me gowns are more exciting than princes?"

"Oh, by far." Her teasing expression turned rueful. "And did she not tell you? The modern-day Cinderella has recently announced a moratorium on princes, especially the amphibian sort."

"But not on bastard brothers to amphibian princes?"

She flushed furiously. "Well, she is quite shocked about it. The brother must think very ill of her, seeing that she is obviously rather loose and easy."

He was shocked about it too. And ecstatic. And grateful. "Easy? My God, I've never done so much begging in my life," he said truthfully, stroking her hair.

And he'd been a nervous wreck. All the years of practice in concealing fears and anxieties had been the only thing that kept him from acting the blathering idiot. And she'd held herself so stiffly and had been so insulted. He'd marveled that she hadn't realized that *he* was at *her* mercy, not the other way around. She had nothing to fear from him. He was the one who had broken a lifelong rule—never impose, never importune—to court rejection and abuse.

And yet, when her refusal came, instead of leaving immediately, as he'd promised himself, he'd parried shamelessly, buying a minute here, another minute there, stealing a few more glimpses of her at the risk of exhausting all her goodwill, arming her with knowledge that she could potentially use to bludgeon him.

He'd given her such power over him.

But she hadn't made fun of him. She'd gifted him with her own story, a story that had made the hairs on the back of his neck rise, because it was a close thing. And when she'd described the taste of the treacle rock, her lips hovering on the edge of a smile, her eyes illuminated with the light of a long-vanished London morning, she'd been as beautiful as Hope itself.

"I believe you are as chaste as a nun, but even such virtue as yours cannot withstand the irresistible force that is my virility and charm," he teased.

Her lips twitched, not quite allowing herself to laugh, not quite able to subdue all impulses of mirth. He couldn't help but kiss her again, softly, making a thorough study of the contour of those lips. *She* was the irresistible one here. He'd never had it in him for playfulness, or for remaining abed after the deed was done, just to look at her, and to talk to her of nothing at all. Already he felt the stirring of fresh desire.

"I wouldn't have guessed you were the kind of man given to kisses and sweet speech," she murmured.

"And you would have been right," he admitted. "I

think kisses are a waste of time—if I ever think about them at all. And usually I find it a strain to talk to women. They are not interested in anything I find useful or important."

"What do you find useful or important?" She cocked her head at a coquettish angle.

"Electoral reform. Working conditions in factories and mines. State schools. Foreign policy, especially toward central Asia." He'd resigned from the army in disgust at the way the war had been handled. And Mr. Gladstone would always have his loyalty for having been a staunch, principled opponent of the war from the very beginning.

"I'm not sure I can find Afghanistan on a map," she said, her eyes twinkling.

He laughed. "I could care less. Or I could show you, if you are ever interested."

God, he was mad for her.

She cast him a quick glance and reached for the cake, chewing it slowly. He watched her. It was easy to tell when she enjoyed her food, as in the case of the boiled egg. She'd pressed the egg white against her lower lip, so that a few grains of salt and pepper stuck to its softness, then she'd licked her lip, seasoning the tip of her tongue, before biting into the egg itself. He'd heard the sighs she made, sensed the motion of her tongue inside her mouth, and it had been all he could do to not knock the plate aside and shove her into bed.

But now her mind wasn't on the cake. She was eating for something to do. So she didn't have to respond to his offer, perhaps. He let the silence elongate, until the cake had disappeared.

"Tell me your name," he said.

"I thought we knew my name already," she said.

"Your real name. It's only fair. You know where I live. You can find out anything you want about me."

"You already know everything you need to know about me," she said.

"I don't know where you live."

"Somewhere in the shadow of the prince's castle."

"And where is that?" he asked, even though he already knew she would not answer.

"North of here."

That was more than he'd thought she'd say. "How far?"

"Not quite as far as Scotland."

That left half of Great Britain and hundreds, if not thousands, of manor houses that could qualify as a *château*, the French word that was usually mistranslated as "castle" in English. Good Lord, he was seriously trying to wrest clues out of thin air.

"Give me a little more."

She hesitated. "It's a place you'd have no trouble finding on a map."

And how was that supposed to help him? He never had trouble locating anything on or off a map.

"Have mercy." What was a little more begging? It had already been conclusively proven that he had no pride where she was concerned.

"I've said too much already."

Her voice had a faint unsteadiness to it. She really

believed it, that she'd said too much, when she'd given him a haystack the size of the Pennines.

"All right, then I won't ask anymore where you live." He would simply have to keep her in his sight. Though how he could do that *and* meet with the Lord Justice in the morning he didn't quite know yet. "Tell me what brought you to London."

She rested a cheek on her palm. "You, of course."

"Me?"

"It had to have been you. Or why would we be here together, when we were perfect strangers only hours ago?"

Indeed, what other explanation could there be? They had to have been destined to meet—and to love. "Stay with me, then," he said. "I will take care of you."

She smiled a little. "You are too kind."

She didn't believe him. She thought it was an impulsive offer he would regret at sunrise. She didn't know him very well, did she?

"You've seen my house. I also have some sheep land in North Yorkshire. Within the next twelve months I should be called to the bar. But for now I'm subsisting mostly on interest, so you'll have to wait a bit—maybe quite a bit—before splurging on a Worth wardrobe. But whatever else you want, I'll be happy to supply."

"A carte blanche from a poor man. Now I've heard everything."

"I never said I was offering a carte blanche." And he wasn't exactly a poor man—he had quite a bit in his bank account from the sale of the Somerset town house. But fear of renewed penury ran deep. He would not touch the principal unless he absolutely could not get by otherwise. "I should hope that as my wife, you would wish to manage our household budget wisely. A carte blanche defeats the purpose."

Her indulgent expression vanished, replaced by an astonishment that bordered on incomprehension. "You are offering *marriage*?"

"Yes."

"*To an absolute stranger?*"

Her shock surprised him. There was an intimate connection between them, as if they'd known each other always. They were not strangers; they'd merely never met before. "I know you far better than I do any of the young ladies from whom I'm expected to select a spouse based on the acquaintance of a few dances and half a dozen insipid conversations."

"At least you know who they are. You don't even know my name."

"Certainly not for a lack of trying. So you may not hold it against me."

She shook her head. "I don't hold it against you, but against myself. You are a gentleman. But I'm not a lady."

"By marrying me you'll *be* a lady."

"I'm not a virgin either."

"I believe I've noticed that already."

She shook her head some more. "Why? You've everything ahead of you. Why would you wish to burden yourself with someone like me?"

"Are you London's most celebrated courtesan after all?"

"No, of course not."

"Do you have a history of crimes and misde-
meanors?"

"No."

"Are you married?"

"God, no."

"Then you won't be a burden to me, but an asset."

He had his cynical observations on marriage. But he
had a healthy respect for its institutional power in le-
gitimizing and sanctifying the illegitimate and un-
sanctified. And as a man, he had a certain leeway in his
choice of a wife. A woman who spoke and looked as
she did, who had that indefinable essence that separated a spellbinding woman from the merely comely—
he had no doubt that after an initial period of cautious
reservation on the part of his friends and colleagues,
she would be a smashing success.

"I can't. You can't. You won't." She sighed, a sound
of wretched resignation. "It can't be."

"Then have the courtesy and compassion to tell me
what exactly is the impediment." He grew a little impatient with her. Why all this mystery and secrecy? What
was she afraid of?

Her eyes dimmed. He was instantly contrite.
"Forgive me. I didn't mean to be cross with you."

"No, don't ask for forgiveness," she said. "You do
me such honor."

She touched the back of her hand to his cheek. He
brought her palm to his lips. For a moment he thought
he was kissing the hand of a bricklayer. He turned her

hand toward the light to better study it. She yanked. He did not let go.

On her hand was writ a record of ravage and hardship. Scars, faded and thin, marked her index and middle fingers. On the back of her hand and the base of her palm were a half-dozen blemishes, burns severe enough to have permanently discolored her skin—skin as rough as his mother's had once been.

"My God," he murmured. So she did work in a kitchen. And he'd been so incinerated by desire he hadn't even noticed until now.

In his distraction, she managed to snatch her hand away. He reached for it again, but she'd already clenched it: her thumb buried deep in the enclosure of her fingers.

"Let me see your hand."

"I don't want you to see it."

"There's no need to be ashamed over honest work."

"More pretty words," she said.

"Yes, I sense myself in severe danger of becoming a lyrical poet."

He made a slow, detailed tour of the ridges and dips of her knuckles, traced each finger down to the first joint, and turned her tightly fisted hand over.

The mound of her palm, the edge of it, her fingernails—he caressed everything that was not expressly denied him. Worshipped her as if she were Aphrodite of Milos freshly unearthed and he the humble excavator struck dumb by her beauty.

When she eased the slightest bit, he pounced and unclamped her hand. She sucked in a breath as he ruthlessly exposed every part of her palm and her fingers. She made a move as if to close her hand over his.

"Don't," he said. "I want to touch your calluses."

"Why?" Her voice was low and plaintive. "Why would you want to touch them?"

"Because they are yours."

She sank her teeth into her lower lip and acquiesced. He raised her hand and pressed a kiss against an old burn mark. He kissed her knuckles, one by one, learning their angularity, savoring the feel of her skin against his lips.

Then he licked a callus. She gasped—a sound that ignited his blood—and tried to close her hand again. He permitted no such thing but ran his tongue over her callus once more.

Her reaction was so acute—and she was so stunned by it—that it all but made him break a piece off the headboard in a surge of lust. Her work-toughened palms were sensitive beyond belief. A simple nibble produced moans; his teeth raked gently across the center of it, shudders.

Her other hand gripped him behind his back. Her body molded into his. He understood what she sought. She wanted him inside her. It made him weak. It made him hard as a mace.

He yanked back the sheet and invaded her fully in one long, hard thrust. He linked their fingers together, so that every part of her hands touched every part of his, and kissed her on the mouth. He did not stop kissing her as he filled her, searing in her heat, buckling under the pleasure, until he had to jerk his head back for breath as his orgasm pummeled and slammed into him, breaking him into pieces again and again.

*

Verity stared at her hands in wonder. She hadn't taken care of them in weeks. They were rough as salt, the joints of the fingers knobby, the skin red and splotchy from too much immersion in water—the symbol of all the costly mistakes of her life. If anyone had told her that she could be seduced merely by having these hands fondled and stroked, she would have snickered in derision and replied that her chopping board would sprout leaves first.

But such huge sensations he had invoked, making love to her hands. Such pleasure, downright frightful in its intensity. She wanted to weep for the wonder and joy of it.

From behind her Mr. Somerset held her snugly. "I'd like to do this every night," he mumbled.

She heard the sleepy smile in his voice. Her heart broke clean in two.

"Promise me you'll think about it," he said, as if she could *not* think about it.

"You are mad," she told him.

"Mad in general, no. Mad for you, granted," he said, his speech slow with the onset of slumber.

"You are mad," she repeated.

But no response came from him, other than a squeeze of his arm about her.

"Mad. Mad. Mad. Mad," she said, to no one in particular.

A monstrous hope threatened to lay waste to her. Already it was telling her to believe Mr. Somerset entirely—in his honor, his sincerity, and his sanity. Here was a man, said the perfidious hope, who was not only persuasive and clever—and handsome, of course—but also wise, judicious, true-seeing, a man whose gaze pierced past her present lowly stature and her past sexual peccadilloes directly into the beauty of her soul.

Marriage. God, marriage. He *was* mad.

What would they tell others about her? Where was she from? Who were her family? What had she done with herself until this point?

And how would she even begin to tell him that he'd proposed marriage to the tarnished cook who'd slept with Bertie and had been deemed not nearly good enough to be *Bertie's* wife?

He would not want to marry her if he knew. He would not even want to look at her. Worse, he would be livid that she'd strung him along this far, knowing full well who she was, who he was, and all the bad blood between the brothers.

But he loves you, said the plaintive voice of her romantic idealism, from the frowzy cell that she had dragged it into after Bertie had beaten it comatose.

Would love pacify his anger when he learned her identity—the only identity she had left, now that she could never breathe a word of Lady Vera to anyone again? Would love save him from bitterness and disappointment when he became all England's laughingstock, and his promising young political career foundered on her notoriety as surely as if he'd chosen to ruin himself over London's premiere courtesan?

She wanted to believe, believe that his love—their love—was a wonder for the ages, as patient as the humble currents that sculpted deep canyons, as enduring as the pattern of seasons.

Perhaps it was not completely outside the realm of possibility for them to find a measure of happiness together. Perhaps he could practice law in some quiet provincial town. And they could have a small, neat house, with a garden and a sunny nursery for the children they would have—

Her tears spilled again. She wanted the life he promised her—wanted, wanted, and wanted, with the frenzy of a lost caravanist crawling toward a distant mirage.

But she could not deceive herself. Beyond this room, beyond this night, were norms and unspoken rules enough to crush any rebellion in the heart of a sensible man.

He'd fought for respect and respectability all his life. She'd done nothing but destroy her own. She could not in good conscience destroy his, even if he allowed it, even if he encouraged it.

In the morning, when his common sense returned, he'd be grateful to find her gone, to know that he would not be held to words of folly spoken in moments of high passion. That he still had all his future ahead of him.

And she, she would have the memories, and the consolation that he still had all his future ahead of him, because she'd walked away, taking with her only her valise and the last of the cake.

Chapter Ten

Mr. Somerset's house was in the middle of a terrace of identical stucco town houses. A portico, set on Roman Doric columns and supporting a balustraded balcony above, shielded the entrance.

Number 26 Cambury Lane.

Verity yanked her gaze away from the front door. Before the house, to the left of the portico, a space had been created between street and house to provide for a service entrance to the basement. The space was surrounded by a shoulder-high wrought-iron railing for the protection of pedestrians. A gate in the railing opened to a set of steps leading down.

The plain, sturdy service door was opened by an equally plain, sturdy housekeeper, who introduced herself as Mrs. Abercromby. Verity gave her own name and the names of the subordinates she'd brought, Becky Porter and Marjorie Flotty, a slow-witted but dedicated scullery maid.

The basement contained the kitchen, the pantry, a

water closet, something Mrs. Abercromby called the boiler room, and the servants' hall. The servants' hall was a tidy room, with wallpaper that might once have been the color of freshly kilned bricks but had since darkened to the reddish brown of roasted barley malt.

They'd arrived at teatime, and the other servants of the house were all present in the servants' hall, seated on benches to either side of a long table. There were two maids, Ellen and Mavis, as well as Mr. Durbin, Mr. Somerset's valet, and Wallace, who lived upstairs in the mews and took care of Mr. Somerset's brougham and two black Friesians.

Ellen and Mavis shared cooking duties, and both looked relieved, rather than peeved, that a professed cook with her own kitchen crew was now among them. They were intrigued by Verity's apparent Frenchness— and seemed not to know much about her past with Bertie, for their interest was mild and benign.

Verity accepted the offer of tea and Mrs. Abercromby's hard biscuits and tried not to remind herself that the last time she was in this house, she hadn't needed to come in through the service entrance.

Why had she come at all?

She'd composed her resignation letter and a polite, if terse, response to Mr. Somerset, regretting that she could not go to London, as she would be in Paris instead. Then, letters in pocket, she'd gone down to Mrs. Boyce's office. But when Mrs. Boyce had asked what she could do for Verity, instead of handing in the letters, she had made a request for jars of preserved vegetables and fruits from Mrs. Boyce's stillroom to be crated and shipped to Mr. Somerset's town house.

She'd spent the next day directing her underlings in packing the pots, pans, knives, and other tools she needed to cook in an unfamiliar kitchen—never once, somehow, breathing a word to Letty Briggs, her lead apprentice, that Letty would be the one to head the kitchen in Mr. Somerset's town house. She made arrangements with the head gardener for the fresh hothouse produce that he would send four times a week to London, a city notorious for its problematic supply of greengrocery. She also informed Becky and Marjorie that they would decamp to London, not trusting that Becky would successfully resist Tim Cartwright in her absence, or that some of the friskier undergardeners wouldn't take advantage of Marjorie's limited understanding of the ways of the world.

She'd believed, almost to the end, that Letty would go in her stead. And then, at five o'clock in the morning, mere hours before they were to board their train, she realized, as she opened her valise and tossed in her things, that she had no intention of letting anyone go in her stead.

She was a moth drawn to flame, except the lucky moth didn't know any better. She did. And she couldn't stop herself.

"At what time does Mr. Somerset like his dinner?" she asked.

The world was better behaved when she cooked. In the kitchen she was the mistress of her own fate—or at least it was easier to pretend so.

"I can't remember the last time Mr. Somerset dined at home," said Mrs. Abercromby, sounding faintly embarrassed. "He takes his dinners at his club. But I'm sure he means to dine at home more now that he has a proper cook."

"He will be dining out tonight also?"

"I asked him this morning before he left," answered Mrs. Abercromby. "He said you should have some time to settle in."

Settle in. How could she ever settle in here, in the house he would share with another? But Verity said nothing else. When teacups had been drained and biscuits swallowed, she followed Mrs. Abercromby up the service stairs to the attic.

Her room was small, papered in dark brown to better hide the notorious effects of London's air, and cold despite the fire already burning in the grate. Opposite the door, the bed lay against the far wall, where the roof leaned in too close to do anything but lie down beneath the four-pane window. To her left was a desk and a chair. To her right, under a speckled mirror, stood a wash cabinet, with a pitcher and a basin on top of it and a chamber pot likely concealed inside.

It was no worse than what she'd expected. She'd shared a smaller room with two other girls when she'd worked under Monsieur David. But she did not want to live in *his* attic, did not want to be *his* servant, did not want reality to further chisel away at her hallowed memories.

And yet here she was. How long would she stay? Until Christmas? Until the wedding? Until he and his new wife had filled their nursery with beautiful, dark-haired infants?

She opened her valise and fumbled for her work dress. She had a pressing need to be in the kitchen.

"I'm sure Mr. Somerset is most kind. But I'm here already and I might as well cook," she said to Mrs. Abercromby. "At what time does the staff dine?"

Instead of taking his dinner at the Reform Club, as he usually did, Stuart dined at the splendid Belgrave Square town house of the Duke of Arlington, more familiarly addressed as Tin by his friends—from the years when he'd borne the courtesy title of the Marquess of Tinckham.

Stuart had run into Tin at the bathing pool—they belonged to the same swimming club. After a friendly half-mile race, Tin had mentioned that his mother wished to see Stuart; would Stuart mind coming over for dinner?

The Arlingtons, having produced two prime ministers in the last one hundred fifty years, were one of the country's most politically prominent families. Tin's late father, the tenth duke, had been a man of enormous persuasion, by virtue of both his oratorical prowess and his unimpeachable personal rectitude. Tin, however, lacked the gift. His heart was in the right place, but he had neither the nerve nor the charisma to herd others to his point of view.

Many a time Stuart wished that the late duke had

lived to see the Liberals return to power, and that he was on hand to prevail against his more reluctant colleagues in the House of Lords. Failing that, he wished that the late duke's seat in the House of Lords, instead of passing to his son, had gone to his widow instead, for the Dowager Duchess of Arlington was—and had always been—the shrewdest politician in the entire clan.

"What is this I hear about Mr. Gladstone refusing to let his cabinet participate in the drafting of the Home Rule bill?" asked the dowager duchess.

She was a matron of the most distinguished appearance, her hair a perfect silver, her black dinner gown the best Japanese silk, and her diamond necklace worth possibly the price of Stuart's entire house. She was also that rare woman who became more handsome as she aged. The uncharitable might attribute that to her having never been a beauty, but Stuart, who admired the dowager duchess, felt it to be due to her fine intellect, her iron will, and her leonine grace, qualities too often overlooked in a younger woman in favor of a pair of sparkling eyes and a smooth pink cheek.

"I'm afraid your intelligence is as good as mine, Madame," said Stuart. "And it's not only the cabinet that has been excluded, but the Irish MPs too."

Tin shook his head. "Has he learned nothing from the debacle of eighty-six?"

Stuart voiced no judgment. The opening of parliament was still two months in the future, the first reading of the Irish Home Rule bill even further away, but already dissent brewed in the ranks—hardly an auspicious sign.

"What does the cabinet propose to do?" asked the dowager duchess.

"Persuade Mr. Gladstone to agree to a consultation, if we could. And if we cannot, then get our hands on the finished bill as soon as possible."

The dowager duchess accepted a dish of Bavarian cream from her footman. "Anything that concerns you particularly?"

The entire matter concerned Stuart deeply, for it was his responsibility to shepherd the bill through the lower house. Serious flaws in the bill would make its passage an even greater uphill battle than it already promised to be.

"The money, Madame, always the money," he said.

How much would everything cost? What was to be Ireland's contribution to the Imperial Exchequer? Dared he hope that Mr. Gladstone's calculations contained no mistakes when there was no one to check the Grand Old Man's work?

The dowager duchess smiled slightly. "Of course, the money."

Stuart took a spoonful of his serving of Bavarian cream. Like the rest of the meal, it was good, but far from divine. The dowager duchess prided herself on having the best of everything. He wondered how she'd react when she realized that Stuart now had the best private cook in England.

Almost as if she'd heard his thought, Her Grace

said, "There is word in town that you've inherited your late brother's cook, Mr. Somerset."

"I have."

"A problematic woman, from what I've heard."

It didn't surprise Stuart that the dowager duchess would know about Madame Durant. But it did surprise him that she'd speak of her. The dowager duchess was not a loquacious woman and rarely conversed on frivolous topics. He'd have thought the subject of Bertie's cook to be quite beneath her. "She is not the perfect servant, but her food is good enough for the queen and the pope. For that I'm willing to tolerate an artistic temperament."

The dowager duchess took a sip of her sauterne. When she spoke again, it was to ask him about legislative matters that he planned to have out of the way before the first reading of the Irish Home Rule bill.

But later, at the conclusion of dinner, as she rose to withdraw, she called Stuart to follow her. He glanced at Tin. Tin shrugged. His mother did as she pleased. Stuart caught up with the dowager duchess outside the dining room—she was waiting for him.

"There is something you should know about your cook," she said.

Again his cook? "You speak of Madame Durant, Madame?"

"Ten years ago, your brother came close to marrying her."

Stuart said nothing. He was shocked.

"I cannot divulge my source, but you may trust me that it is reliable." The duchess had a brief, ironic smile that faded into a moment of harsh void. Then her expression was once again astute and elegant.

"I see," said Stuart.

"Your brother had one of the best tables in all of England. So I understand that you've come into quite an asset in acquiring his cook. But I advise you to be leery of having such a woman in your household."

"Thank you, Madame. I shall proceed with extreme prejudice."

She nodded and withdrew.

For most of his trip home, Stuart was preoccupied with the dowager duchess's revelation, that Bertie had come close to marrying Madame Durant. It was only as the carriage turned onto Cambury Lane that he began to assess what precisely Her Grace had been trying to warn *him* away from. It was not as if *he* would marry Madame Durant, under any circumstances.

He was not Bertie. Bertie's ancestry could not be challenged. Bertie could marry down and remain every inch the gentleman. Stuart, who must prove at each turn that all the commonness of his mother's blood had been eradicated from him, could only marry up—as in the case of Lizzy, whose maternal grandfather had been a viscount.

He didn't bother to add "except for *her*"—because she had been the exception to every rule in his life.

As he alit before his house, he realized just how strange the exchange with the dowager duchess had been. His engagement had been announced in the papers earlier in the day; he couldn't offer to marry

Madame Durant if he tried. Furthermore, Her Grace had all but acknowledged that a cook of Madame Durant's caliber was a most useful asset—not only for him, but for Lizzy in establishing her position as a hostess. And yet she still exhorted him to get rid of Madame Durant, in a manner that was almost urgent for the cool, laconic duchess.

He wondered what Madame Durant would think were she to know that there was such interest in her humble person in the highest spheres of Society.

Dearest Lizzy,

My goodness me, what a long memory you have. All right, you naughty girl, here it is—though I really shouldn't even mention any such thing to an unmarried young lady.

Mr. Marsden was caught with his professor. In flagrante delicto.

Oh, dear, merely writing those words makes me a bit light-headed. I don't know if you've met him—why are you interested all of a sudden?—but what a darling, beautiful boy he was in those days. I was a bit in love with him myself. Imagine my shock when I learned the truth!

There, now I've discharged my oath. You must write me back soon and tell me all about the engagement, or I shall never forgive you for making me find out in the papers first.

The twins won't stop coshing each other with

handy objects. I can only hope they'll be able to tolerate as much pain when they grow up.

Love,
Georgette

Lizzy whistled. *In flagrante delicto.* With his *professor.* Oh, dear indeed. This was much worse—and much better—than anything she could have imagined.

Would people living in glass houses never stop throwing rocks? For him to try to endanger her engagement because he thought she had Sapphic inclinations! Truly, she'd have expected some solidarity instead.

But now she knew his dark little secret. A rich, delicious secret. She smiled and imagined how she would amuse herself when he arrived at her house on the morrow to help with her nuptial campaign. Imagined his surprise, dismay, and fear, because now she had the absolute upper hand.

No wonder he used to regard her with such dirty glee. She was quite in the mood to rake him over with that same knowing, salacious look.

But as she practiced the perfect arch sneer, she was aware of a different and more disturbing response. She felt let down. Disappointed. She supposed that she had implicitly assumed Mr. Marsden's antagonism to be fueled at least in part by a frustrated attraction to *her.*

Old habits died hard. Some part of her—the part that used to be able to ferry a man from across a ballroom with one look—still persisted in thinking of herself as irresistible, her glances and smiles as perilous as daggers and quicksands.

Oh, well. Oh, the vanity.

❦

Stuart's town house, like any other self-respecting urban domicile in Britain, did its very best not to smell of food, even though it did not have the luxury of separating the kitchen from the main dwelling, an advantage of the country house. Instead, the kitchen was relegated to the basement, with both the kitchen door and the green baize door that led to the basement shut tight at all times. Food served to the master was never carried about in the open, but only via the service stairs or the dumbwaiter that connected the kitchen with the dining room.

So it was impossible for Stuart, sitting in the tranquillity of his study, to smell anything other than the still-drying ink on his notes and the cup of cold coffee sitting on his desk. But he did, and had been for hours.

Fried sole, golden and perfect. Roasted venison, tender and gamy. A dish of potato, rich with butter and cream. And, of course, a tremendous dessert, something dramatic, bourbon flames over forbidden fruit.

He'd managed to work, but he'd been on the edge of outright restlessness. As the clock struck quarter past one, he capped his pen, blotted his notes one last time, and rose.

But instead of climbing up two stories to bed, he

pushed open the heavy green baize door and went down into the basement. He made this trip often enough, a candlestick in hand, for a quick bite of something to eat when he worked late and the rest of the household was long abed.

Usually his kitchen smelled of dampness and inexpertly roasted joints. Tonight it smelled like a hungry beggar's dream: yeast, herbs and aromatics, simmering meaty broth, and a curl of sweetness around the edge of the warm humidity.

He set down the candlestick and switched on the gas lamp. The small kitchen was more or less the same, yet altogether different. Someone had cracked a hard whip, for he'd never seen the place so spotless; even the narrow slats of usually blurry windows, set high in the wall and looking out to the surface of the road, glistened like a newborn's eyes.

The disheveled collection of pots and pans on the dresser had been replaced by heavy cast-iron skillets and gleaming copper molds. The stoves, otherwise cold at this hour of the night, heated not one but two stockpots of broth. On the narrow worktable at the center of the kitchen rested a large round bowl, containing a spongy-looking piece of rising dough covered by a moist towel—Mrs. Abercromby, an admittedly weak baker, preferred to purchase bread from a nearby bakery.

In the holding cabinet where leftovers from the servants' dinner were kept, there was no fried sole, no roasted venison, no gratinéed potatoes or flambéed fruit. His imagination had indeed been getting the better of him. Instead, there was a small beef pie baked in its own ramekin, stewed celery, and a modest portion of apple suet pudding—humble foods, and emphatically not French.

He broke off a piece of the beef pie's crust. It melted in his mouth, crispy, flaky, its underside moist with flecks of a perfect gravy that made all the other gravies he'd ever had in his life seem either as heavy as macadam or as thin and listless as the heroine of a gothic novel.

He closed his eyes as the flavors rippled. Before Madame Durant, he couldn't remember the last time sensual enjoyment so overtook him, and so powerfully focused his attention on the corporeal side of his existence.

Trying a piece of the stewed celery, he sighed again. She had a marvelous touch with vegetables.

He ate half of the beef pie, most of the stewed celery, and all of the suet pudding—it was simple, homey, and welcome, like the sight of a cottage with smoke rising from its chimney to a traveler who'd been lost days in the wilds.

And therein lay the danger of Madame Durant and her cooking—not that it was delectable, but that it was evocative, and made him think far beyond food. The rediscovery of taste was as perilous as he'd feared it would be, rousing other dormant, dangerous longings for everything he did not have, everything he'd hoped to hold dear and could not.

Her, of course; her always. His mother, who promised him that she would visit often and never did. His brother, who'd once been a brother, not an enemy. All loved, all lost, all gone, leaving only him to remember them in the dead of the night, hungry no matter how much he ate.

Chapter Eleven

As Lizzy's afternoon would be taken up receiving calls of congratulations, Mr. Marsden came in the morning. She took great care with her toilette and selected an especially fetching gown. She told herself it was because she always felt more powerful when she looked more beautiful—only to be peeved when he sat down to business with scarcely a glance at her.

"I'd like for us to divide the tasks today," said he. On the index finger of his right hand, he wore a heavy gold ring in the shape of a lion's head. The lion had rubies for eyes. "I'm sure the last thing either of us wanted is to work in duplicate."

"Certainly not," Lizzy said.

No, the last thing either of them wanted was to be revealed for who they were beneath the facades they presented.

"I've made a preliminary list of items needing attention." He pulled out a longish list. "I assume that you'll wish to take in hand matters pertaining to your gown, your trousseau, and your personal ornamentation."

"Quite so."

"And I assume you'll want to delegate the wedding breakfast to Madame Durant? There is no other cook to rival her in all of England, unless it is Monsieur Escoffier of the Savoy perhaps."

Did she hear an odd inflection in his voice? The last time he'd mentioned Madame Durant, it had been in conjunction with the innuendo that Lizzy might like to bed the somewhat notorious woman.

"I'm amenable to the idea, but I will need to approve of the menu."

"I will make your wishes known to Madame Durant. And ask whether she can take on the wedding cake too." He uncapped a pen and jotted down a few words. The ruby eyes of the golden lion glittered as he scratched away. "St. George, Hanover Square for the wedding?"

"Yes."

The church was just down St. George Street, a stone's throw away. Her family had been in attendance for generations.

"I'll have a date reserved. Banns or license?"

"License, of course." Everyone who was anyone married by special license.

Mr. Marsden made further notations.

From the public gallery, she'd watched Stuart give speeches in the House of Commons—Stuart at work was very much the same man he was at leisure, thoughtful and measured. Mr. Marsden, however, was a different man altogether.

There was nothing here that would hint at either the dirty smiles of her antagonist or the charming chattiness of the young aristocrat so well embraced by her father. Even his awareness of her, otherwise a suffocating constant like a corset laced overtight, had been subsumed in his absolute concentration.

"I will take care of that," he said. "You will prefer to choose the stationery and the flowers?"

His face was smooth, perfectly shaven, no missed patches, no nicks or cuts. He couldn't possibly afford a gentleman's gentleman on his wages, so he must have shaved himself, standing before a mirror in his undershirt.

With something that was almost a shudder she realized that she had no problem at all imagining him in *dishabille*.

"Miss Bessler?"

"I'm sorry. What did you say again?"

The glance he cast her was one of faint disapproval, much as a schoolmaster would look upon an absent-minded pupil. "The flowers and—"

"Yes, I would. The flowers and the stationery, that is."

And so they went down the list, Lizzy now fully alert and vigilant against any unruly caprices of her mind.

"That is everything I have," he said, at the end of forty-five minutes.

They'd been extremely efficient. He was thorough and thoroughly organized. But she was not in the habit of ceding anything to him. "I'm surprised you've made no mention of the decorations. Surely something more than a few floral arrangements is required."

"I've thought about it," he said.

"And?"

He looked at her for the first time since they sat down. "And I've produced some sketches."

She raised a brow. "Indeed?"

He dug into the document case he'd brought with him, pulled out a portfolio, and handed it to her with no more care than he'd have passed along a week-old newspaper. "They were a pleasant diversion," he said.

Inside the portfolio were a dozen or so drawings, mostly done in pencil, a few in watercolor. The first was of the front steps of a church. Small topiary trees trimmed to perfect spheres graced the ends of each step; the ribbons tied to their slender trunks fluttering prettily in the breeze. The next drawing depicted pews of a church, as viewed from the nave. A gauzy fabric—tulle or organza—had been gathered into a long garland that draped from pew to pew, pinned with bouquets of cool white gardenias.

The church took up two more drawings. Then came several sheets of smaller images, three or four to a sheet—details on a wreath that would hang over the church door, engraving on a silver cake knife, a boutonniere of lily of the valley blossoms laid against a feathery leaf of fern. Then two views of the bridal carriage and, to finish off the collection, an arch of flowers set behind the head table at the wedding breakfast.

The drawings were exquisite. She blinked and shuffled through them again. No, alas, her eyes had not played a trick on her. "They are—they are beautiful," she was forced to admit.

She thought she sensed an easing of tension in him—but was that her imagination? Had he been tense at all? Was it even possible that he of all people would wait with bated breath to see whether she approved of his efforts?

"Keep them if you'd like," he said, nothing but politeness in his voice. "The wedding is yours."

"Thank you," she said. Then, with more reluctance, "You've gone quite above and beyond the call of duty."

He rose. "It was a tremendous honor for Mr. Somerset to entrust the planning of his wedding to me. I've every intention of making it one that will be remembered for years to come."

There was something strange to his expression. A random thought flicked through her mind and quite stupefied her. Could Mr. Marsden be in love with Stuart? Could that be the reason behind his dislike of her?

She'd been waiting for their consultation to finish before bringing up the matter of Mr. Marsden's past scandal. But now she was too astonished to do anything but rise and shake his hand as he took his leave of her.

When Mr. Marsden was gone, she sat down and reexamined the drawings. She wasn't always in agreement with his choices of colors and flowers, but she was continually charmed by his use of familiar elements to conjure something fresh and original.

The designs would have taken hours, many hours. It had been only a few days ago that Stuart had officially assigned Mr. Marsden to help her. He would have had to work deep into the night to draft, alter, then finalize the details. Had he done it for the love of his employer?

It would have been a greater love than she'd ever known.

She dismissed the thought. She was already too fortunate; she did not deserve to want more. The solid affection she shared with Stuart would only deepen with the passage of time. Their marriage would be the envy of many.

The drawing of the wedding breakfast still remained in her hand. She set it down. Something caught her eye. Her thumb had covered an orange-blossom wreath placed at an odd angle. For a moment she thought it a whimsy, floating tilted above the wedding party's table. Then she saw that, no, it didn't float, but rested atop a filmy heap of bridal veil.

She went to the window for better light. The veil was translucent against the more opaque white of the tablecloth. And unlike other parts of the drawing, it had no faint pencil outline underneath, as if Mr. Marsden had painted it on impulse. And yet, near-invisible as the veil was, he'd done it in exquisite detail. There were diaphanous lumps and creases in the carelessly crumpled veil. Two orange blossoms had been caught underneath a sheer fold. And one corner of the veil had fallen over the edge of the table, casting a transparent shadow against the tablecloth.

It was a piece of art in and of itself, this trifle of an unnecessary detail. She shook her head. Why had he bothered? Why had he taken the better part of a day—a night—to produce something so delicately beautiful and so easily overlooked?

And it certainly did not seem to be what one'd paint when one's heart was breaking for the want of the groom. No, she'd have said that it had been painted out of an intense longing for the bride.

For her, Lizzy, who didn't know what to think anymore.

Verity had been puzzled by the small size of the staff at 26 Cambury Lane. She'd thought it was because there was no mistress—no need to finish all the work by noon to impress the house's orderliness and cleanliness upon the callers who began arriving soon after luncheon. Then Mrs. Abercromby explained to her the significance of the boiler room: central heating.

Except for the attic and the basement, the house was heated by a system of hot-water radiators. No climbing up and down the staircase with heavy baskets of coal all day long to replenish the coal shuttles in the abovestairs rooms. No sweeping out a dozen fireplaces and relighting as many fires every morning. No coal dust and cinders getting everywhere despite one's best efforts otherwise.

Furthermore, as Mavis informed a fascinated Becky, the boiler also served as a conduit of hot water to Mr. Somerset's plumbed bath.

"No haulin' water up or down—they rigged somefink fancy when they done the heat. The water's fast up there. I tell you, Becky, it's the grandest tub in London. You can make tea for an army in it."

Becky sighed. "I'd like to soak in a tub like that once in me life."

"I think 'bout it every time I clean it. But I know the missus will catch me at it," said Mavis, referring to the housekeeper. She lowered her voice. "Or worse, the master!"

Mavis and Becky both giggled. Marjorie, elbow deep in dishes, remained oblivious to the human interaction around her. Verity permitted no chatter when she was in the middle of cooking. But times like this—cleaning up after luncheon—she did not strictly ban silly talk between the maids, knowing how lonely a life in service often was for young women far away from family and not allowed followers.

Mavis lowered her voice even more. "Might be fun, though, if the master did catch me."

"Mademoiselle Dunn," Verity said coldly.

"Beg yer pardon, mum," said Mavis hastily. Then she and Becky took a look at each other and burst into fresh giggles.

They were in high spirits—it was half day for the servants. Mavis was eager to go out dancing and she'd invited Becky. Becky was tempted, but turned down the invitation, as she'd already promised her aunt she'd come round for a visit, Marjorie in tow.

Listening to young women scarcely half her age planning their diversion made Verity feel old. She couldn't remember the last time she'd visited a dancing pub—her feet and knees would quite kill her in the morning. She no longer had any desire to flirt with men she didn't already know. And her idea of an evening of fun was trouncing Mrs. Boyce at Russian whist.

But she did go out, in the end: She visited a conveyer of specialty foods to secure a supply of truffles and took a short stroll on Regent Street.

When she'd joined Monsieur David's kitchen sixteen years ago, she'd wept from fatigue every night, too tired to even think of Michael. In those days she used to take herself on her half days to Regent Street, to look into the windows of all the fashionable dressmakers. It was no doubt a reflection of her shallowness— that in her moments of despair she turned not to the church or to improving books, but to frivolities of satin and brocade in a modiste's shopfront. But turned to them she had, religiously.

Later, she'd understood that it hadn't been so much the dresses themselves that had sustained her through those long days and dark nights, but the shining hopes that they'd embodied, hopes of not only the day when she'd be able to own a piece of gorgeous frippery again, but of the day when she'd be together with Michael, when she could afford a decent future for him too.

Hope. Hope had brought her to London, when

Sense would have had her depart for Paris. Hope that burned in her like an altar lamp, a flame of a prayer for him, for them, for a miracle.

She sighed. All this, even after she'd written his secretary and accepted the honor and responsibility for his wedding breakfast and his wedding cake. When would she ever learn?

❧

When Verity returned to 26 Cambury Lane at half past four, night had already fallen. She was the only one in the house: Mr. Durbin had plans to meet friends at a pub and then attend a music hall show; Ellen and Mavis, she had the feeling, would try to stay out as late as possible without sending Mrs. Abercromby into a rage; Mrs. Abercromby had said she'd be back at eight, the same time Verity had told Becky and Marjorie to return, to make a favorable impression upon the housekeeper.

In the kitchen she filled a kettle, intending to boil water to carry to her attic room for a sponge bath. Then she remembered what Mavis had said earlier about the lovely plumbed tub in Mr. Somerset's bath.

She hadn't known such a luxury in years, not since she stopped sharing Bertie's bed. The thought of lowering herself neck-deep into hot water was almost too delicious to contemplate. She glanced at the man's pocketwatch she always carried—those made for women kept shoddy time. Quarter 'til five. If she was in the tub by quarter past, she would have finished her soak, dressed, and wiped down the tub by six, two hours before anyone returned.

What a mad idea.

Oh, why the hell not? He would have wanted Cinderella to have a proper bath at his house, wouldn't he?

🍃

The hot water brought back memories, first of Bertie, of the time when he'd accused her, smilingly, of loving him only for his tub. And then it dredged up far older memories—of the baths she'd suffered through as a child, the dozens of dresses she'd had at her disposal when she emerged from those baths, and the lovely woods and streams she could see from her vanity as her maid untangled her wet hair. Except in those days, she never looked *at* the woods and streams of her ancestral estate, she'd always looked *beyond* them, intent only on the world outside.

The world outside would turn out to be thrilling, heartbreaking, and difficult at every step—it had certainly taught her to jump at the chance of a hot bath, however illicit and risky.

She'd been in this bath before, of course—it was here that she'd cleaned herself up after Mr. Somerset had rescued her from the footpads—but she remembered little of the room. It was small, with dark blue walls, an oval-backed chair on which she'd laid her clothes and her towel, and a waist-high chest of drawers.

A large radiator to one side of the tub kept the bath

toasty—God bless these newfangled modernities—and dried her drawers, which she'd washed earlier when she laundered herself before the soak. On the other side of the tub was a stool on which she'd set a glass of cold water. She wetted a handkerchief with the cold water and smoothed the handkerchief over her face so that she wouldn't become light-headed in all the hot water and steam.

She leaned her head back and sighed as the knotty muscles of her lower back slowly relaxed. This was just what she needed. Not until she had completely immersed herself did she realize how tense she'd been for the past few days.

She'd expected to have dealt with a summons from him already, and had waited, all edges and nerves, to rebuff him, not knowing how he would react to her refusal to meet with him, or how she would respond should he resort to an ultimatum.

But so far, nothing. Four days she'd been in London, and the only interaction they'd had was through her food: She personally cooked him his breakfast, if toasting and buttering bread could be called cooking, and he always finished most of what she left in the holding cabinet for him at night. No summons, no notes, and only one directive conveyed through Mrs. Abercromby about a dinner that he'd host the week after. It was as if he'd submitted to some mad impulse by ordering her to come to London and, once that was done, forgot her entirely.

While she went about on pins and needles, ate too much pudding, and slept ill. While her awareness of him built and built. Every morning from the kitchen window she watched him leave, her eyes fastened to the cuffs of his trousers and the swing of his frock coat, her heart as hungry as a London stray. His valet liked to iron his shirts in the servants' hall; the scent of clean linen and generous starch filled her with lascivious thoughts of stripping those same shirts off him. And even when she strictly minded her own business, a silly maid like Mavis would bring up the naughty notion of being found by the master in his bathtub.

A frightening, problematic, and awfully arousing thought.

She sank a little deeper into the tub. In her younger years she'd desired kisses and sweet words of endearment. These days what she wouldn't give for a jolly good shag, a sweaty, screaming, bed-shaking—

Her hand found its way to the troublesome place between her legs and stroked herself. She really shouldn't be so lustful—she'd pleasured herself as recently as the night before. But lustful she was and her body begged for relief.

Oh, well, if she were to do it, she might as well do it properly. Without lifting the handkerchief from her face, she raised one foot out of the tub and felt for the hot water faucet. There, that would be the one that was still warm. She turned on the faucet with her toes. Wouldn't want the water to grow cold and distract her, would she?

Stuart returned to a dark and empty house.

He needed some papers from his study. On a different day, a telephone call would have sufficed. But it was a half day and there was no one home to answer the telephone or deliver the papers.

He pulled off his gloves and warmed his hands over the radiator in the study. By habit, he poured himself a measure of whiskey. But a few sips later, he realized that it was not whiskey that he wanted, but a good, sturdy tea, which he'd declined at the office.

He hadn't eaten much for luncheon. Nor would he have had much dinner at the Reform Club. Between breakfast and midnight, he ate only enough to not be distracted by hunger, saving himself—in a manner that he could only ironically describe as chaste—for when he could be alone with her food again.

The biscuits for tea were kept not in the kitchen, but on the sideboard in the servants' hall. Mrs. Abercromby's valiant but ultimately doomed rock biscuits—more rock than biscuits—had been replaced by a small quantity of shortbread. And little wonder the quantity was so limited. The foundations of Heaven must be built of this fresh, buttery sweetness that was a greater testament to the glory and mercy of the Almighty than any cold marble or vulgar gold.

He had the uncivilized urge to eat everything right there in the servants' hall. But he controlled himself. He would enjoy it more if he were to have the shortbread with a cup of tea, in some comfortable lounging clothes. He set a kettle to boil in the kitchen, and went up the stairs to change.

As he reached his floor, he heard the unmistakable sound of water running in the bath at the far end of the corridor—the one shortcoming of the plumbing in the house was that when the water ran, it ran loud, the pipes groaning and squealing, a duet between a defective organ and a tone-deaf bassoon.

But why would the water turn on by itself? Was there a leak? He walked faster. The bath was only for his use and had no lock. The door opened at his touch.

Steam rushed at him, a foggy roomful of it. For a moment he couldn't see anything. Then, the shock. There was someone in his tub, a woman. In the rising mist, she sat neck-deep in water, her head tilted back, her face covered by a wet handkerchief, her hair a damp, darkish knot. The tops of her knees barely emerged from the water; her left arm, long and prettily rounded, rested along the rim of the tub.

It could only be Madame Durant, in the flesh. He leaned back against the door, speechless at her transgression.

And her nakedness.

A foot lifted out of the tub, along with a good length of shapely calf. Her skin glistened in the honeyed light, faintly steaming with the heat of the water. His heart instantly beat twice as fast.

He'd never before been susceptible to the general male mania over the female foot, the pathetic longing for a peek of a trim ankle, or the breathlessness generated by a saucy boot with bits of leather cut away to reveal the stocking underneath. But now he, too, ran the risk of being enslaved by a beautiful high arch and clean pink toes.

She shut off the faucet with those clean, pink toes and lowered her foot. Given the respite, he tried to collect himself and think beyond his immediate reaction of marvel and lust. She was a servant who had intruded upon his privacy and used facilities reserved for him without so much as a by-your-leave—a grave infraction by any measure.

Had it been anyone else, he'd have a word with Mrs. Abercromby, who would in turn give the woman whatfor, or perhaps even let her go if she had been unsatisfactory in other tasks. But the offender here was the mysterious, salacious, sublime Madame Durant, whose food he couldn't stop eating, and whose unseen presence was a silent hunger that smoldered within him, a hunger made greater by every bite of her food—so much so that he'd postponed summoning her time and again, for fear that he might be blind to his own weakness, that though on the surface of his mind his reason was Bertie, underneath swam a beast of lust that awaited only the most meager of opportunities to snap him in its jaws.

It was best that he left immediately. He was already staring too hard at her throat, her arm, and those knees that hovered just beneath the water. What action he would take in light of her offense, he could decide later—after his mental faculties had a chance to recover from their current stunned ineptitude.

He reached behind him for the door handle. She emitted a small sigh and it was a lick to his groin. He stilled abruptly. What was it? The sound came again and it was another hot, hungry lick.

He looked back at her. The right arm that was submerged, to which he'd given no thought other than that it blocked what could have been a delightful view of her breasts . . . there was the barest motion at the top of her right arm. She whimpered again. And he was as hard as a bobby's nightstick.

At last his mind registered what his body had instinctively known: Her whimpers were whimpers of pleasure. And she was—she was—

Perhaps Bertie had been right about him being a prude. He could scarcely bring himself to even think of that word in connection with a woman, though he understood perfectly well now what she was doing, without a stitch, without a shred of shame.

What was he about to do? Leave? He couldn't move a single muscle.

Well, he could, but in the wrong direction—*toward* her, his footfalls muffled by the thick rug that had been laid down for winter.

The water hid little beneath its clear ripples, not her skin, not her pink nipples, not her hand, placed directly over her pudenda. He couldn't see exactly what she was doing—damn the shadows cast by the edge of the tub and her raised knee. Why, oh, why had he never installed a chandelier directly over the tub?

She raised one foot out of the water, and then another, and braced the balls of her feet against the edge of the tub. And suddenly he saw much better, so well that he was light-headed with incredulity and lust.

Long fingers stroked pretty pink parts—stroked, rubbed, petted. Her toes flexed. Beneath the handkerchief, her lips parted in another sigh. Her motion quickened. There was now a new tension to her arm and her wrist. Her fingers pressed hard. He was afraid she would hurt herself, but her pleasure only seemed to heighten: her hips gyrated, the fingers of her other hand splayed open, the moans that emerged from her throat became louder, more blatant.

He wanted to rip off the handkerchief and feast on the sensuality of her face. He wanted to use his hand for a small measure of relief—he hurt, intensely, with the force of his desire. He wanted to launch himself into the tub and replace her hand with some part of himself—any part of himself. But he dared not move. He dared not even breathe.

Don't stop. For God's sake, don't stop.

She didn't. She pushed herself farther and farther up that steep slope of pleasure. Her feet slid back into the tub to brace against where the tub curved up. Her left hand gripped the edge of the tub. Her pelvis lifted—her entire torso lifted. Water lapped at her pointed nipples.

His heart hammered. The rest of him was on fire—perhaps he'd already burned to cinders, he wouldn't know. And didn't care.

Her breath caught. And caught again. She expelled air in fits and gasps, her torso stretched taut. A bit of the handkerchief caught between her clenched teeth.

He grasped on to the chest of drawers, his knees weak, all the blood in his body now pooled in one place and one place only.

He wanted her. He had to have her. Now. *Now!*

He tasted blood on his lip. His hands shook. His will broke piece by piece as she writhed and panted in the final throes of her self-induced passion.

Then she cried out—and he very nearly lost control. Her ardor, her flushed skin, her peaked nipples lifting high with the arch of her back. God, what had he done to deserve such temptation?

God.

In her fantasy, Verity was in Mr. Somerset's bed, her legs splayed wide, her person thoroughly impaled.

It had started in the tub, of course. Imagining him coming through the lockless door of the bath had been a fearsome thrill, so much so she almost lifted the handkerchief from her face to make sure that he hadn't really come.

But she'd resisted, because that would have been a silly thing to do—and because the sight of an empty bath would have drained her fantasy of much of its startling power. Instead, she shut her eyes tighter.

Yes, he was there in the bath. His gaze, hot and shocked, swept her body, lingering in all the most inappropriate places, feeding the hopeless, rampant desires in her.

Because this was *her* fantasy, he would never do anything improper with his cook—he was not that kind of man. He would leave her to her privacy. But then her handkerchief would slide off and he would see her face.

In reality she could not begin to conceive of his re-action. Would he be glad? Would he be angry? Would he perhaps not recognize her at all? But no, this was not reality, so they could skip over the thorny, compli-cated parts and proceed straight to a wild, crazed cou-pling.

With her gasping in mortified arousal, he'd fish her out of the tub, throw a towel around her, and carry her to his bed. His kiss would be rough and impatient. His end-of-the-day stubble would scratch her chin and throat—and she would not get enough of it. She would not get enough of him.

The imagined climax in his bed would happen as soon as he came into her. The real climax in the tub was a peak to rival Mont Blanc. She hadn't come so hard and furious in a while. And if it hadn't been for the long practice of keeping quiet and still while she pleasured herself—the walls between the servants' rooms at Fairleigh Park were thin and her bed there creaked abominably—she'd have shattered the mirror with her screams and made a lake of the bath.

Her ungoverned breathing was loud and promi-nent in the quiet of the room. Then she heard some-thing that made her whole body seize—the breathing of another person, harsh and shaky. For a moment her mind went entirely blank. Then she prayed feverishly that it was anyone but him. Mr. Durbin, Wallace, the coalman, it didn't matter.

Anyone but him.

"Madame, you will present yourself in my study in half an hour," said Mr. Somerset, in perfect French, his tone only slightly uneven.

God.

❧

She couldn't move for several minutes after he'd closed the door behind him, except to rip off the handkerchief and stare at the door, both of her hands over her open mouth.

Then she leapt into frenzied action, drying herself, throwing on her clothes, wiping down the tub, wiping off the water that had splashed onto the floor. She ran back to her room and, with mostly useless hands, tried to do something with her hair.

He'd called her beautiful once, when she'd been still young. Alas, the wild-looking woman in the mirror was neither young nor very beautiful. Her profession dictated that she spent the preponderance of her waking hours in a milieu entirely hostile to smooth skin and soft hands. She fought back against the travails of the kitchen and the encroachment of time with an array of homemade creams and emollients, but she couldn't banish the fine lines that already webbed the corners of her eyes, nor could she reverse the slack that she'd begun to notice under her chin.

She shaped her hair into a tight bun at the nape of

her neck, tied on a clean apron, and pinned a cameo brooch at her throat. The person who stared back at her in the mirror looked almost respectable, like a governess, or a Salvation Army lieutenant. Not at all the sort of woman who'd be caught touching herself in unspeakable places.

She covered her face and groaned.

The door to the study was ajar. The light was on. She heard him moving about inside, his physical restlessness an echo to the jangling of her nerves.

So this was it, the moment of truth. Three thousand and more days and nights—hopes and dreams, delusions and illusions.

And they did not live happily ever after.
The end.

Chapter Twelve

She knocked when exactly half an hour had passed. He'd been waiting—he'd known the moment she'd arrived in the corridor, three minutes ago—and still the knock made his pulse lurch.

"Come in," he said.

He'd miraculously remembered the kettle he'd set to boil in the kitchen before heading upstairs. So he'd made tea and brought it to the study, along with her shortbread biscuits. But he hadn't been able to touch either. Instead, it had taken two inches of whiskey and three cigarettes to steady his hands and calm his shattered nerves.

Even now he saw her in his mind, all pretty tits and wicked fingers. He wanted to suck on those fingers, lick clean every last dram of her essence. He wanted to spread her open and fuck her until he went blind.

It was the long abstinence, he tried to tell himself: Such was life that if he remained chaste for ten years, someone entirely unthinkable must come along and make a bonfire of his virtues. But he knew better. There was something about Madame Durant that drew him toward her, an enigmatic pull like that which kept the moon in orbit around the Earth.

He prayed that the power of this heretic hold she had over him derived solely from her mystery, a mystery that would unravel at first sight. He drew in a long breath, moved away from the window, where he'd kept his forehead pressed to the cool glass—he really needed to plunge into a bathing pool and swim a hundred laps—and took his seat behind the desk.

But she did not come in. At the edge of the door peeked a fold of her dress. And if he listened very, very carefully, amid the drone of the evening traffic and the overenthusiastic blare of street musicians on Buckingham Palace Road, he could sieve out the sound of her unquiet breathing.

He rose. Etiquette and decorum be damned.

He was nearly at the door when she spoke. *"Monsieur, éteignez la lumière, s'il vous plaît."*

She wanted him to extinguish the light.

"Why?"

"Because . . . I've too much shame to face you." Her voice was not the sultry seduction he'd expected, but uncertain and awkward. "If it pleases you, sir."

He didn't want to be alone with her in the dark. It was not done. It was highly improper. And it would do nothing to dispel her mystery.

"Sir, please."

There was more than embarrassment in her voice. There was desperation. He waffled, sighed, and gave in.

He returned to his seat and turned off the desk lamp. For a moment he couldn't see anything. Her dress soughed, woolen skirt on flannel petticoats. Her footsteps, at first clear, the heels of her shoes clicking against the floorboards, became muted as she crossed the Khotan carpet he'd brought back from India.

His eyes adjusted to the darkness. In the meager light that meandered through the window, he perceived her outline, a solid blackness against the more insubstantial shadows of the air.

He regretted his moment of gallantry already. The entire point of his summons was to see her face, not to further whet his curiosity. He felt along the edge of the desk for the whiskey glass and tipped the remainder of its contents down his throat.

The silence stretched. He let it. He could think of nothing to say that wasn't either stupid or blatantly prurient.

Do it again. Let me watch. Let me see your face when you come.

"You wanted to see—to speak to me, sir?"

Her voice came from the farther reaches of the room—she'd put as much space as possible between them. The darkness and the distance were no doubt meant to salvage her respectability, but all he could think of was the sweet shadow between her thighs.

"My dinner party," he said, amazed at the seeming coolness of his tone. "Mrs. Abercromby spoke to you of it?"

She didn't respond immediately. Was she as surprised as he by the perfect propriety of his end of the conversation? "The dinner for eighteen next week?"

"Yes. You had enough notice?"

"Yes, sir."

"Good," he said.

Silence burgeoned again. Perversely, he refused to dismiss her. It was a poor gratification to sit fifteen feet from her in the dark, but it was better than nothing.

She broke the silence first. "Would you care to see the menu, sir?"

"No, that will be unnecessary."

"Would you—" Her voice dropped. "Would you like me to cook something for your dinner?"

His fingers latched on to one of her shortbread biscuits. He bit into it. The sensation was dizzying. Pagan. He imagined crumbling the biscuit over her and licking the crumbs from her skin.

"No. I do not wish to inconvenience you on your half day," he said.

He couldn't handle a full meal from her tonight. He would incinerate.

They lapsed into silence once again. Her feet shuffled against the carpet. He broke off another piece of shortbread and let it melt on his tongue, despairing in its divine sweetness.

"Sir, may I—may I be dismissed?"

"I've one question and then you may go."

"Yes, sir?"

He meant to ask whether she needed to send for more kitchen help from Fairleigh Park. It wouldn't do to be shorthanded for the dinner.

"Tell me, when you were in the tub, what was on your mind," he said. "What were you thinking of?"

She made a sound that was a choked gasp. Her breaths were fast and shallow. He closed his eyes and tortured himself with another biscuit, the divine sweetness spreading through his veins like hot poison.

How the mighty had fallen. Was it only thirteen years ago that he'd laughed at Bertie for succumbing to the spell of his cook? Now he was the one caught in her allure, an allure that could not be described with any economy of words.

She said something. He barely heard her. It sounded like "New."

"I beg your pardon?"

"You."

"What?"

"I said I was thinking of you," she said. "*You*, sir. Good evening, sir."

❧

This time Mr. Marsden wore a silver ring in the shape of a serpent. The serpent had tiny, emerald eyes, and wound itself twice about the middle finger of his left hand.

Lizzy couldn't stop looking at the ring. She wanted to touch it—and perhaps Mr. Marsden's hand, too—to see his naked reaction in that first fraction of a second, before self-preservation could intervene.

She'd spent what little spare time she'd had in the past few days staring at his drawings, because she couldn't get enough of them—or rather, couldn't get enough of the secret thrill that ran amok in her when she gazed upon their painstaking lines and fragile colors. Couldn't get past the idea that he'd done them for her and her alone.

She knew it to be a stupid and possibly harmful preoccupation. She knew that it was the vanity in her, yearning to be the object of *somebody's* grand passion. She knew that Georgette was never wrong in her gossip. And still she kept at it.

"What do you think?" asked Mr. Marsden.

She retracted her gaze from his hand and pretended to study the sheets on the *secrétaire* some more. They'd spoken on the telephone two days ago. She'd informed him that she'd decided to use a calligraphist to hand-letter the invitation, and he'd said he'd bring her some samples from a calligraphist he knew.

"I think it's superb," she said. She wrote a very fine hand herself, but the calligraphist was an artist. "Is it the work of a man or a woman?"

"A man."

A man, was it? "And how do you know him?"

He'd stood by the writing desk while she perused the calligraphist's samples. Her gaze once again slid across the papers to his hand, laid lightly at the edge of the desk. His cuff link was silver too, but without ornamentation, a rarity for him. And good Lord—she hadn't noticed this until now—his shirt was not white, but the palest shade of green.

"We share a house."

"A particular friend of yours?"

"We exchange books from time to time."

She decided that this was as good a time as any. "Only books. You haven't exchanged anything more significant?"

His fingers splayed and dug into the rosewood top of the *secrétaire*. Then he removed his hand altogether. "I beg your pardon?"

Oh, good. He was on the defensive already. She leaned her shoulders back and tilted her face up. Watchful eyes. Compressed lips. And was that a quickened pulse she detected, throbbing the veins of his jugular?

"I know why you had to leave England," she said, drawing out her words, savoring the power they gave her. "So you need not pretend otherwise."

"I'm sorry, I've always believed that I left England for an adventure abroad. Please enlighten me as to the true reason."

He was guarded, but not nervous enough. She had a moment of doubt. To counter it, she rose and looked him straight in the eye. "And not because you were discovered doing the unspeakable with an Oxford don?"

She sensed the shock in him. A long pause of silence. He looked down. "It was hushed up. How do *you* know?"

She smiled a little, almost as much in disappointment as in triumph—at least now her obsession with the drawings would cease. "Nothing is ever completely hushed up. And I have my sources."

He tilted his face and glanced at her from beneath

his lashes. Her heart skipped a beat. It was a beautiful, almost seductive look. "Is that so?"

"You needn't worry," she said, trying to regain her upper hand—not that she'd ever lost it. "I won't breathe a word to Mr. Somerset. I know how important it is to him to have a reliable staff . . . and how important it is to you to retain your livelihood."

"Why, thank you, Miss Bessler."

She did not fail to notice the sarcasm in his words. Her upper hand seemed not to have properly subdued him. "I shall expect you to conduct yourself with suitable decorum. It would not do to have Mr. Somerset's reputation besmirched by association."

"Could you elucidate as to what the proper decorum entails? Do I need to live in complete abstinence, or would you be satisfied with discretion on my part?"

"I wouldn't be satisfied with anything less than absolute discretion," she said haughtily.

"You've any suggestions as to how I am to accomplish that?"

"There are places, are there not, for men such as yourself? Places where everyone allowed entrance has a stake in the discretion of everyone else."

"I'm sorry to say I gave up those places years ago. The last time I went to one, I caused quite a scene." He smiled. "Have you ever had two men fight over you, Miss Bessler? It's not pretty—bleeding noses and dislocated jaws abound."

"Two men fought over *you*?"

He flicked a speck of invisible dust from his cuff.

"Two drunken fools. I prefer my courtship more civilized."

She swallowed. She supposed she could see how he might rouse such passions. He was beyond comely. And there was something deeply wicked about him.

"But to return to your point, Miss Bessler, you may rely on me to be discreet. Not only because of my admiration for Mr. Somerset, but also because I've a passionate concern for my own hide and no desire to see the inside of a gaol."

"No, I'd imagine not," she said, shivering a bit. She'd not thought of the ghastly consequences of a possible prosecution against him.

"And to reciprocate your magnanimity..." He paused, as if considering. Then he smiled, and it was *that* smile again. "To reciprocate your magnanimity I'll let Mr. Somerset discover for himself that your maidenhead is as lost as the Ark of the Covenant. I won't breathe a word."

She took an involuntary step back. "That is slander."

"That is derogatory. But truth can never be slander, no matter how derogatory," he said. "I work for a barrister, I should know."

She bit back the panicky *How do you know?* quivering at the tip of her tongue and cast a glance toward the door of the drawing room. She'd left it ajar, but there was no one about. "Do you care to explain yourself, sir? Such is a strong accusation indeed."

"What is there to explain? You've been afraid of me for a long time, for something that you thought I knew. And yet what I knew in truth did not worry you at all. So it stood to reason that it hadn't been a woman, but a man, that it had gone too far, and that Mr. Somerset has no knowledge of it."

She'd struggled with it, the fact that she'd likely contracted a marriage under false pretenses. She'd decided that Stuart was too sophisticated a man and too kind a friend to take her to task for it, and that she'd make up for her lack of a hymen by being the best possible wife under the sun. But Mr. Marsden's provocation again placed that moral dilemma front and center, forcing her yearning for worldly security to war with her conscience.

"You've no proof," she said.

"And neither do you."

He was referencing her breached maidenhead again. She almost snarled at the double entendre, but limited herself to a deep frown. "Well, this is a pretty impasse."

In the silence that followed, he collected the sheets of calligraphy samples into a neat stack and slid them into his document case. He strapped and buckled the case shut, lifted it, then set it down again, as if he couldn't decide whether to walk away or to stay. Then he glanced at her. "Perhaps we could learn to be friends."

She snickered. Friends with this popinjay who wanted nothing more than to take her down? "And we will base our beautiful friendship upon . . . ?"

"Our mutual knowledge of each other's darkest secrets—and that it would cost us too dear to be enemies."

"That is not enough," she said flatly.

He twisted the serpent ring once around his finger. "Would it offer additional inducement if I said I liked you?"

At the beginning of their meeting she would have instantly believed it, but now she only frowned deeper. "My goodness, what do you do to people you *don't* like?"

"I'm somewhat doubtful as to whether you will be good for Mr. Somerset. But that doesn't mean I cannot appreciate you for what you are: a beautiful, clever, witty woman, cool under fire and persistent."

Something in her ached. He'd described her precisely as she wanted to see herself, but increasingly could no longer. "Can a man such as yourself truly appreciate a woman?"

"As well as you can appreciate another woman."

She said nothing.

He came close, took her hand, and brought it close to his lips. "What do you have to lose?"

Much, she was sure, though she could not name what her loss would be.

She thought he'd kiss the air above her wrist or some such, but he pressed his lips into the knuckles of her middle and ring fingers, and the contact was an electrical experiment gone awry. The nerves in her arm nearly snapped with the shock—and the thick pleasure—of it.

She yanked her hand back. He raised a brow.

"Good day, Mr. Marsden," she said.

"Good day, Miss Bessler," he replied. "And think of my offer."

❧

"Oh, Stuart, it's beautiful," exclaimed Lizzy.

They were in her drawing room and Stuart had come to present her engagement ring. He'd spared no expense. The ring he'd had in mind at first had been an ordinary engagement ring with a row of gems that spelled *regards* acrostically. The ring he'd been determined to buy when he returned from Fairleigh Park would have featured a large single sapphire—her birthstone. The ring that was on her finger now, purchased in the morning, after he'd spent a fitful night dreaming of Madame Durant, was a spectacular diamond, burning with white fire.

"You shouldn't have," she scolded him. "Why, this could have paid for our servants for years to come."

"I want you to be pleased," he said. "That's far more important. And—"

"But I am pleased," she said, almost vehemently. "I couldn't be more pleased with you."

"And I want you to know how happy I am that we've made this commitment to each other," he finished, hoping his words conveyed all of his sincerity and none of his desperation.

He *was* happy. He couldn't be happier. Lizzy had so many qualities to recommend her. *And* she was beautiful, her face flawless, her figure straight out of a fashion plate.

Yet even as he gazed fully upon her loveliness, it was Madame Durant he saw in his mind's eye—Madame Durant, who most emphatically did not have a nineteen-inch waist, or the slender arms that Lizzy showed to such advantage in her evening gowns.

In reality, his cook was likely short and dumpy. But he had trouble thinking realistically of Madame Durant. Instead, he thought *voluptuous, shapely, erotic*—and hungered after her body as he hungered after her food.

He lifted Lizzy's left hand and kissed her just above where the ring glittered. She looked at him, her dark eyes wide and intense, as if waiting for lightning to strike. Then she averted her eyes.

"Are you all right?" he asked, not sure what to make of her countenance. "Are the wedding preparations coming along?"

"They are coming along. And I'm very well." She flexed her fingers and coaxed an even greater sparkle from the diamond. "How can I not be? My dearest one has just given me the ring of any woman's dream."

There was something in her tone that wasn't quite all right. He should ask more questions, massage the problem out of her, and put her mind at ease—it was not too early for him to give her comfort and succor. But the guilt in him chose to latch on to her words. She *said* she was very well, didn't she? Then all must be well, and he could console himself that his unfaithful thoughts were entirely without significance in the greater scheme of things.

"Will you stay for dinner?" she asked.

"I'd love to, but I can't tonight," he said, rising. "I've called a meeting at the club over dinner. May I have the pleasure of taking you for a drive tomorrow afternoon instead?"

"Of course. I shall look forward to it."

"As shall I."

He kissed her on her cheek and took his leave, departing her house with a sense of escape: he need not face his fiancée—or his conscience—for another twenty-four hours.

He had not done anything wrong, but God did he want to, and the list of wrongs he wanted to commit with Madame Durant rivaled a Dickens novel in length. It didn't seem to matter at all that she was a woman of questionable character and ill-considered judgment; he wanted her as a caught fish craved the sea.

He wouldn't touch her. And he would send her away after the wedding. But for now he allowed himself to crave, and to dream of an existence without fiancées, rigid social classes, old fears of the taint in his blood, or anything else that would hold him back from joining her in that warm, deep tub.

I was thinking of you. You, *sir.*

❧

Verity stood on the outside steps leading down to the service entrance and waited for Mr. Somerset to return home.

A London fog was always an unwelcome visitor. It smelled of slop and had the wet fingers of a horny drunk, poking into tender parts where a fully clothed woman didn't think mere weather could penetrate.

But the fogs she'd known in her years in London were gentle mists compared to the *thing* that had materialized this evening. While she'd cooked dinner, traffic in the street above had moved as if underwater—slink and slither of darker forms in a soupy opacity. As the evening wore on, visibility had reduced further. Light from the nearest street lamp was now a dim orange halo that illuminated only itself. And she could barely see her own hand when she held her arm out straight.

She was worried. He should be back already. Had Wallace become hopelessly lost? The fog was the color and consistency of a cheese soufflé, the kind of atmospheric obliteration that had pedestrians walk open-eyed into the Thames. It would be all too easy to misjudge the distance and miss a turning.

The vapors kissed her cheeks with icy lips. She pulled her shawl tighter about her person and lit a cigarette, preferring the harsh acridness of tobacco to the softer smother of the miasma.

She didn't hear his steps until he was almost directly above her, the fog curling thick and yellow around the edge of his frock coat. Though he couldn't see her—didn't even know she was there—her heart pounded as if he'd caught her naked again, her hand between her thighs.

The entire day she'd passed in a daze, interrupted now and then by bouts of severe anxiety—not that he would want his cook, but that he wouldn't. Now that they'd met—after a manner—and that she'd professed her desire for him, it would be intolerable if he didn't return it in some measure.

Keys jangled. Then stopped. Then the tinny sound of something metallic brushing against stone—the buttons of his frock coat on the half wall at either side of the front steps?

"Who's there?" he asked. In *French*.

Fear needled her, until she realized that it was only the cigarette that had given away her presence, the lit end of it far more visible than her black-clad person.

"Bonsoir, Monsieur," she answered. Her voice sounded different to her ears when she spoke the Provençal French of Monsieur David—lower, scratchier, more vigorous than refined.

The keys jangled again, this time against the top of the half wall. "Madame Durant," he acknowledged her, calmly, courteously. "You received my message?"

"Yes, sir." The meeting that he'd scheduled for the evening had to be canceled due to the fog. And instead of rescheduling it at the Reform Club, he'd invited six ministers and MPs to his house the day after next to confer over breakfast. "I'll have everything ready."

"See that you do."

His keys lifted, jingle and clatter. They'd come to the end of the conversation. He would see himself into the house now.

But she couldn't bear to let him go yet. Their encounter had shaken her, but it had also unchained an appalling need to be closer to him—she'd missed him so. And no matter how much she reminded herself that he was engaged to marry another, there was a part of her that insisted that, no, he was hers. All hers, always.

"Sir, Wallace didn't come back with you?" she asked.

The keys stilled. "I had him put himself and the carriage up some place closer to Inner Temple. It was too dangerous to drive."

"Then how did you come back?"

"By tram. And on foot."

"And that, that was not dangerous?"

"It was." His walking stick tapped. Once, twice. "But if I were to take a hotel room, I would be deprived of your food."

He'd come more than three miles in this weather, facing very real risks of getting lost and getting injured, for her food? "I didn't know you liked my cooking this much."

"You didn't?" He chuckled softly. "Well, now you do."

"But the first time I cooked for you, you sent the food back to the kitchen without touching it."

Silence. The fog twisted and slithered. Then the sound of a match being struck, a small burst of orange flame—he'd lit a cigarette. The reddish light at the end of the cigarette glowed with his inhalation.

"Do you know, Madame, what happens to a man who spends decades in the dark, then steps suddenly into full sunlight?"

"No, sir."

She heard him expel a breath. She smelled the

smoke, a warm pungency that swirled about them both.

"He is blinded by the light," said Stuart Somerset. "And I didn't want to be blinded. Good night, Madame."

Chapter Thirteen

Michael's letter came on the afternoon post, a short missive, not even quite one page. He acknowledged the two letters Verity had sent, but made no apologies for not replying sooner. He'd been busy: He'd taken over as the editor of a student journal and his team had just defeated the Cotton House team at rugby.

Verity sighed, in pride and frustration. He let her in on so little of his life these days; she hardly knew him anymore. Had she been wrong to send him to an elite school? Was it the snobbery of his classmates that had made him chill and distant?

But she didn't think the snobbery of the middle-class boys at a more ordinary public school would have been preferable. And the thought of sending him to a mere state school had never occurred to her. No, she'd always been determined that it would be Rugby and Cambridge, as it had been for the men in her family for generations.

Well, perhaps not always. And certainly not before that chilling letter from her aunt ten years ago. Until then she'd have been happy to see him grow to manhood, be he a farmer, a clerk, or a gamekeeper, like his adoptive father. After that she'd pushed him as hard as she pushed herself—she'd never managed to impress her aunt in all her years at Lyndhurst Hall, but now that her aunt's eyes were on her again, she couldn't stop herself from trying.

She instructed Michael in elocution, eradicating from his speech every last trace of Mr. Robbins's broad Yorkshire vernacular. She taught him all the foreign languages with which her governesses had tortured *her*. She initiated him into the myriad and mysterious rules of etiquette that governed the deportment of the upper echelon. By the time he was ten he spoke English like a royal duke, acquitted himself in French, Italian, and German, and knew that a gentleman removed his glove before shaking a lady's hand and that should he be present for a luncheon, the last thing he should do was offer a lady his arm—that was how one spotted parvenus and pretenders from a furlong away.

But all the courtly manners in the world weren't enough for the adopted son of a gamekeeper. So she'd drummed into him that he did not want a life like hers, that he owed it to himself—to her—to be the best at everything he did, because it was the only way he'd ever be treated as an equal of those to the manor born.

She opened the locket she wore around her neck and gazed at the picture inside—Michael and herself, her hand draped possessively over his shoulder. It had been close to the start of term his first year at Rugby. She'd taken him to Manchester and bought him all new clothes of the best material and workmanship, from hats to linens and stockings.

On that trip they'd had their portrait taken at a photographic studio, their lips clenched tight to prevent overly broad smiles not suited to the solemn occasion. They'd been drunk on possibilities then—both of them seeing Michael's future through nothing but rose-tinted glasses.

She closed the locket and reread Michael's terse letter twice before putting it away. There was another letter, the envelope addressed to her by an unfamiliar hand. Mr. Somerset's secretary had said that Miss Bessler might have instructions for her concerning either the wedding breakfast or the wedding cake. She stared at the envelope for some time, then sliced it open with one hard flick of her letter knife.

The piece of paper inside contained no instructions either on the wedding breakfast or the wedding cake. Nor was it even a letter. There were dates listed, and underneath each date, a few brief words.

> *21 November*
> *Unwell. Could not keep down his supper.*

> *22 November*
> *Still unwell. But attended his classes and met with the journal staff.*

23 November
Played in the match against Cotton House against
the advice of many. His team won.

She started shaking. Michael. The observations were again about Michael. Her aunt had a minion at Rugby, with easy access to Michael.

She added coal to the grate and made herself a cup of tea. The tea calmed her down some. Perhaps her aunt thought Verity would try her luck again with Bertie's brother. Perhaps she believed that the warning needed to be renewed every decade or so. It didn't really matter why her aunt chose to do what she did. As long as Verity kept her mouth shut about her origins, Michael was safe. And keep her mouth shut she would, for the rest of her life.

For now, the important thing was that Michael was unwell. She couldn't see him, couldn't nurse him, couldn't even berate him for his neglect of his health without making him ask questions.

So she must cook for him.

❧

Stuart smelled the madeleines the moment he walked past the front door. But when he asked Durbin and Mrs. Abercromby about the sweet, haunting scent, they only looked puzzled and said that they did not detect a thing.

It was impossible to work, so he went to bed at the unheard-of hour of eleven o'clock. But an hour later he could stand it no more. The scent of the madeleines was everywhere in the house. And faint as it was, nothing else could overpower it, not the soap with which he'd washed his hands, the lavender water in which his sheets had been laundered, or even the cigarette he'd lit and extinguished without quite realizing either.

At least this time he had not imagined things. Had the scent of the madeleines in the basement been any stronger, it would have tyrannized the senses. As such, it was only maddening in its beauty, as if spring had arrived overnight.

He blew out his taper and let the scent slowly saturate him. Memories surfaced like a creature of the sea, leaping above the waves. It had been a rainy day, long ago. Cooped up inside, he and Bertie had played hide-and-seek. For his turn, Stuart had tucked himself into a particularly snug spot in the wardrobe in Bertie's room. And his hiding place had proved so clever that Bertie had gone by twice, even poked his head inside the wardrobe, without seeing Stuart.

But there, alone in the dark, a desperate homesickness had assaulted him. He missed the friends he'd left behind in Ancoats, the pub owner who'd taught him to read from the *Manchester Guardian,* and the Catholic prostitute who'd watched him after school and done her best to convert him to Papism.

And he missed his mother, who had disappeared off the face of the earth after their good-byes the previous June.

He worried constantly about her. Could she make her own tea and toast? Would she remember where she'd kept the key to the door? And why hadn't she sent news to let him know that she was all right?

He didn't even realize he'd been crying until Bertie had climbed inside the wardrobe, found a place for himself, and handed Stuart a handkerchief.

"I miss my mum too," Bertie had said.

And that was all Bertie had said in the half hour and more he'd stayed with Stuart, until Stuart was sufficiently himself again to leave the wardrobe.

What had happened to them?

You may be legitimized, but you will never be one of us.

But that hadn't been the cause, only the final sundering of a bond that had been attenuating a long time. Bertie, secure in his parentage, had seen school and sports as little more than rituals to which he must give a nod. To Stuart, everything that he was asked to undertake—new subjects at school, new sports, new hobbies that Sir Francis wanted to share with him— had been a test, a test he couldn't afford to fail, lest he be shamefully ejected from his new life.

Bertie had never understood why Stuart would spend his holidays reading all the extant volumes of *Controversiae* in the original Latin, translating *Candide* into English when perfectly good English editions already existed, or running miles every day across the thirty thousand acres of moors that belonged to the estate—never, that was, until the idea occurred to him that Stuart was deliberately trying to win a greater portion of their father's love, an idea bolstered by Sir Francis's increasing pride in this younger, illegitimate brother.

It seemed implausible, in retrospect, that their bond should have been susceptible to such gross misunderstandings. Yet like a shining blade rusting to dust, it had happened gradually, sometimes imperceptibly, until it was too late.

To Stuart's left a door opened. A narrow swath of light swung into the basement. He shifted in surprise and knocked over the candlestick he'd set down next to him.

The opening door—it was the door to the service stairs—reversed its motion.

"Madeleines," he said, as the door was about to close. "They were Bertie's favorite."

For a long time no one responded. He'd spoken in French. He wondered now if he'd confounded a peckish maid braving the cold stairs for a bite of something to eat.

Then her voice came, careful and low. "Yes, they were."

Giddiness flooded him, a reaction better suited to an adolescent given to a secret rendezvous than a respectable middle-aged man who would rather draft parliamentary bills than make love.

"Was he happy?"

"Bertie?" His question surprised her. "I think so."

"Tell me why you think so."

He moved to gain a direct line of sight to the service stair door. It was slightly ajar. The stairwell was dark except for a flickering orangish light, and the only thing visible of her was, as always, a bit of her black dress.

"The people of the parish thought well of him: The gentlemen liked him, and so did their widows." Was that a note of slyness to her voice? "He busied himself with the composition of a local history and the expansion of the gardens. And he ate better than anyone else in Britain."

He smiled. Dinners obviously mattered a great deal to both Bertie and his cook. "Good," he said.

Bertie had never returned to London after he'd lost the town house to Stuart. It cheered Stuart that Bertie had settled into his life in the country, that he'd been surrounded by people and food he enjoyed in his last years.

"Were you—" she stopped.

"Yes?"

"Were you close once, the two of you?"

His heart swerved. "Did he tell you that?"

"No. He usually spoke of you as if you were a horseman of the Apocalypse. I thought he must have cared greatly for you at some point, to have become so embittered," she said.

Stuart, in return, had never spoken of Bertie to anyone, had pretended that Bertie was something that could be excised entirely from his existence.

"Yes, we were close once." The admission, after all these years, was as sweet as it was terrible.

"What happened?" she asked softly.

He didn't want to talk about their estrangement, the slow choking of affection, the uneasy drifting apart, the sudden, sinking realization one day that coolness had turned into hostility, that he had no concrete understanding of how they'd arrived there, and therefore no notion at all how to return things to the way they'd once been.

"Do you know the first thing Bertie ever said to me?" he asked instead.

He'd said his good-byes to his mother in the midst of the bewildering elegance of the manor. Or rather, she had talked and he'd stood dumb and mute, stunned from her revelation that she would not remain at Fairleigh Park with him. The more she reassured him that he would be all right, the queasier he'd become, until his silence had drained her of her power of speech altogether. In the end, she'd only embraced him and walked away.

And when he'd turned around, there had been Bertie, gesturing from behind a door.

"What did he say?"

"He said, 'They say the French eat snails. I want to try. Will you help me find some?'"

The woman in the service stairwell chuckled. "Did you?"

"Not immediately."

His father had come into the drawing room instead and given him a stern talk. Stuart was to be a gentleman now. He must forget everything he'd ever seen, heard, or learned on the streets—never mind that Stuart had never lived a day on the streets, and had only been taught what all English children ought to be taught at the charity school he'd attended.

Then he'd been hauled upstairs to be scoured raw, the clothes he'd brought with him burned, his small tin of prized possessions—a pencil he'd received at Christmas, the pin he'd won at school for being the best speller, and the crucifix that Lydia, the Catholic prostitute, had pressed into his palm the night before—thrown away while he was in the bath.

"We did look for snails the next morning, but it was a disappointing hunt. I was no use at all in the woods and Bertie could only find tiny ones that wouldn't be worth the trouble."

But then they'd sat down on a log and Bertie had given Stuart the essentials he needed to survive his new life.

Do not say "legs" in front of Fräulein Eisenmueller.

Do not disturb Father when he reads his paper.

Do not ask about the women who sometimes come to the house late at night.

Do not ever let servants, not even the frightful housekeeper who's been at the house since time began, forget that you are the master's son and they are entirely replaceable.

Bertie had been his lifeline in those days. He'd taught Stuart how to speak, how to behave at the table, and how to extract proper respect—respect that Stuart had been sure he didn't deserve—from servants, villagers, and the children of guests.

"Did you love him?" he asked her.

"I did. Very much," she said.

The calm goodwill of her answer moved him, the way children walking down the street holding hands still moved him.

"I loved him too. Very much," he said. "I wish I hadn't waited until he died to remember that."

She made no response. Her silence drew him closer to the service stairs. When she spoke again, her voice was near, so near that it gave him gooseflesh.

"Once Bertie and I shared some madeleines on a picnic—it was some months before the Court of Appeal's decision came down—and he said, 'When we were small, I tried and tried to find something that Stuart would actually like to eat. I never succeeded. But I think he would have liked this.'"

Stuart smiled. So that was what Bertie had been trying to do, all those years that he'd placed one exotic item after another before Stuart and peered at him with anxious hope.

Suddenly there were tears in his eyes. He tilted his face up. He should not have allowed anything to come between them. He should not have taken Bertie for granted. And he should not have persisted in thinking that Bertie would never understand him and so it was useless to try to explain himself.

The corridor went dark.

It took him a moment to realize that she'd extinguished the light she'd carried with her. The hinges squeaked slightly, and then he smelled her, a stir of butter and flour in the still air.

Her hand brushed him at an odd angle across his torso, as if she held out her arm in search.

"Can you see, Madame?" he said.

She came up to him and wrapped her arms about him. He seized with shock, then embarrassment at this unsolicited contact, this assumption on her part that he needed to be comforted by a servant.

Physical contact in his life was largely limited to handshakes and an elbow offered to the ladies. Even with Lizzy the extent of their intimacy had never gone beyond anything greater than handholds and kisses on the cheek. He couldn't remember the last time anyone had embraced him, fully, solidly, and sustained it for more than a fraction of a second.

But he did not disentangle himself from her. After a few seconds, it didn't seem quite so appalling. Her warmth seeped into him along his torso—he hadn't realized that he was cold, standing in the basement in nothing more than his pajamas and his dressing gown.

And she wasn't short—the top of her head came to just under his nose, making her about medium height for a woman. Her cap smelled of starch; the fringe of it tickled his chin ever so slightly.

"I'm all right," he said. "Thank you."

She moved, but only slightly. The edge of her cap caressed him from his jaw to the lobe of his ear. Riots erupted along his nerves. She breathed deeply and he realized that she was inhaling *him*, the odor of his skin. His pulse accelerated.

"What do I smell of?" he murmured.

"A fastidiously clean man who uses French soap for his bath."

She spoke with her lips almost touching him—her breath soft and moist against his skin. Then she pressed those lips *into* his skin, and kissed his neck. The entire surface of his body smoldered, so much so he could barely tell where her kiss had landed.

She pressed another kiss into his neck. No, it was

more than a kiss: a nibble. She tasted him, the touch of her tongue a white-hot blaze.

He flung her away from him: literally picked her up and threw her. Her body thudded heavily against the opposite wall of the corridor. She yelped.

"Don't!" He sounded at once distant and furious. "I'm to be married."

He would not succumb to it. He would not.

"I'm sorry," she said, her voice small and distraught. "I'm very sorry."

Pride called for him to storm out of the basement in a show of his moral superiority. He obviously lacked sufficient pride, for he stayed exactly where he was, his breath ragged, his hands flat against the wall behind him.

"I'm sorry," he said. "It's not your fault."

Everything was his fault. She would not have done it had he not wanted it. And of course she knew that he wanted it—lust steamed from him like the scent of blood from an abattoir. During the day his mind turned to her with an obscene frequency. At night he dreamed incessantly of her.

She made no response. His ears caught the tremble of a sob. She was weeping. He was instantly at her side. "Did I hurt you? Are you all right?"

He felt her shake her head, but he didn't know which one of his questions she'd answered. He caught hold of her face—both of her cheeks were wet and cold—and tried to wipe away her tears.

"Don't cry. Please don't cry."

Fresh tears rolled down her cheeks, warm rivulets

against his thumbs. Before he knew what he was doing, he'd leaned down and kissed her tears, tasting the salt and faint bitterness of it.

Her skin was not flawless softness, but that was on a par with saying that Helen of Troy did not excel at embroidery. It simply did not matter. It was *her*, her jaw, her cheek, her eyelashes fluttering against the corner of his lips, her hair and clothes and skin that retained the lingering scent of the madeleines.

She tilted her face a little and suddenly their lips were only a fraction of an inch apart. He imagined he could see her exhalation as little puffs of ghostly vapor. She was breathing fast; her breath smelled of warm apple pudding. And he was hot all over, hard and hungry and impatient for his downfall.

He wanted to sink his mouth against hers, lick the inside of her lips, and stroke her moist, mobile tongue. He wanted to roll her gorgeous nipples between his fingers and feel them engorge. He wanted to push up her skirts and take all the liberties that she would allow him—many, he was sure, for her breath shook and trembled in anticipation.

It would be simple and sweet to take her right here, to ease the ache of desire that had never subsided since the moment her chocolate custard had first touched his lips. A quick, mindless fuck, to wean himself from this irrational lust that had gone on too long already. A quick, mindless, explosive, luscious, incendiary, staggering—

With his last iota of control he took a step back, and another. He was to be married, to a dear girl with whom he'd chatted warmly only hours ago as they took their round in the park, a dear girl who did not deserve the disgrace of a fiancé who shagged the help seven weeks before the wedding.

And even if he'd never proposed to Lizzy, his reputation could ill survive this. No one had forgotten his origin; they but refrained from mentioning it when they could find no fault with his conduct. The moment he started consorting with undesirables, the gossipmongers would nod at each other and concur that it had always been only a matter of time before he revealed his true heritage.

"You are all right, I take it?" he said, making sure that his voice was free from inflections.

"I'm perfectly well. Pray do not let me keep you," she said, her breathing under control.

There was something commanding, even imperial to her formal answer. It astonished him. Somehow he'd never noticed before that despite her strong accent—she spoke the throaty French of the South—her grammar was impeccable and her verbs, from past pluperfect to *futur antérieur,* perfectly conjugated.

He wasn't aware that French cooks were culled from a higher social stratum than English ones. Where had she come by her educated speech? From Bertie? He could see Bertie helping her with her English perhaps, but teaching a Frenchwoman to speak better French?

In the end, it was she, not he, who first walked away, her footsteps echoing on the damp stone floor. She did not go up the service stairs, but entered the kitchen, shutting the door behind her before turning on the light.

He listened for a few minutes to her quiet, purposeful motion in the kitchen. And then he and his still heavy loins fumbled in the dark until he found the beginning of the steps that would take him up to the green baize door and out, back to his world, a world that had no tolerance for passionate mistakes—at least not for a man like him.

Chapter Fourteen

Lizzy loved a good dance, but it must have been two years, at least, since she'd last attended one. Mrs. Mortimer's dance was her reward for herself, an evening of fun and frolic to bid good riddance to her overlong stay on the shelf. And during the first hour, she enjoyed herself thoroughly. She talked; she laughed; she showed off her engagement ring and danced every set.

Then, in between dances, Mrs. Douglas, a junior minister's wife, approached her. Lizzy did not care for Mrs. Douglas, an avid gossip and busybody who never met a rumor she couldn't spread like so much manure. But she pasted a smile on her face and received Mrs. Douglas's congratulations in good grace.

"And we shall see you at Mr. Somerset's dinner next week, shan't we?"

"But of course," said Lizzy. "Come prepared to marvel, my dear Mrs. Douglas, for Mr. Somerset has inherited the most astonishing cook."

"Oh, I wouldn't miss it for the world. But . . ." Mrs. Mortimer looked about them, leaned in, and spoke from beneath her fan. "A piece of advice, my dear Miss Bessler. Sack the cook as soon as you are married."

"Mrs. Douglas, I must have misunderstood you," Lizzy said coolly. "Have reliable cooks become so easy to replace these days?"

"No, of course not. Goodness knows, mine is a nightmare and still I dare not let her go." Mrs. Douglas giggled nervously. "But you know what people have said about that woman and Mr. Somerset's brother."

And you know what people have said about your *brother and that governess,* Lizzy was tempted to retort. But she was to be a politician's wife and such open skirmishes were best avoided.

"I will keep that in mind," she said.

That encounter wasn't enough to spoil Lizzy's mood on its own, but she turned around only to be confronted with the sight of Henry and his new wife, a sweet young thing who looked as if she'd stepped out of a beauty soap advertisement, arriving at the dance.

Word was that it had been love at first sight. He'd proposed to her within a month of their first meeting and three months later they were married, ten days before Sweet Young Thing's eighteenth birthday.

"Are you an admirer of the great philosopher, Miss Bessler?"

Lizzy started. Mr. Marsden stood at her elbow, watching her. He tilted his chin in Henry's direction.

"No," she said. Her gaze returned to the happy couple.

"Allow me to phrase it better. *Were* you an admirer?"

Had she been? It was difficult to say. To this day she couldn't adequately explain to herself why she had taken Henry Franklin as a lover. Because life as a failed debutante was one of unending tedium? Because she meant to destroy herself in a fiery act of nihilism? Because since she couldn't have either the highest title or the greatest wealth, what use was her virginity?

Henry had been a married man from the beginning of their acquaintance, but he never concealed his distaste for his wife, a pale, limp woman who spent her days as a semi-invalid. His honesty and brutal intelligence had intrigued Lizzy, as well as his reputation as the most esteemed philosopher of his generation.

She'd thought herself an intellectual equal to Henry, the sort of woman who fascinated a man. And perhaps she was his intellectual equal, but she was no match for him in callousness or manipulation, for Henry's fine mind and voracious sexual appetite both paled in comparison to his effortless disregard for others.

When his first wife had unexpectedly passed away of pneumonia, Lizzy had thought Henry would propose to her, only to have him laugh and tell her that she was but one of his mistresses, and that while she was a fine diversion when he was in the mood, he married only virgins.

She'd been speechless. He was the one who'd taken her virginity, or did he not remember? He did, he assured her. But since she had so little regard for it, why should he value it more? And what evidence did he have that she hadn't slept with other men since then?

It might have been all right had that been the end of it. After all, a man so publicly dismissive of his wife probably had it in him to be devoted to no one but himself. But then Henry had fallen in love, hard, and Society talked of nothing but the vast romance of his courtship, his endless tenderness to the young woman who'd captured his heart, and what a changed man he'd become.

And *that* had nearly destroyed what remained of Lizzy's confidence.

"Do you think, Mr. Marsden, that had I been an admirer of Mr. Franklin's, I would choose to tell you, of all people, about it?"

He chuckled. "I would never have told Mr. Somerset anything, you do realize?"

She turned her face to him, paying attention now. He was in dark evening formals, the tails of his jacket cut long, his features perfect as always—Cupid grown up and out to wreak havoc.

"And how do you suppose I should have realized such goodwill and restraint on your part?" she said sharply.

Their eyes met. He smiled, a small, rueful smile, and raised a punch glass to his lips. "I beg your pardon. Of course you've no way of knowing."

The musicians struck up a new waltz. He surveyed the landscape about them. "I see no one rushing this way to claim you. May I have this dance?"

The refusal was on the tip of her tongue. But then

Henry glanced in her direction and her answer changed. "You may, sir."

He set down his punch and swept her onto the dance floor without another word. She expected him to be a good dancer, light-footed and graceful. He was better than good; he was divine. His build had seemed so slender, almost willowy. Yet this close, with their bodies braced together at every turn, he was stronger and more solid than she'd imagined.

"What, precisely, are you doing at a gathering for mostly impressionable young people, sir?" she demanded.

"I was invited. A gentleman who is willing to dance is always a prized commodity—and no doubt I'd make some sweet young thing a suitable husband."

"You?"

"Why not? I'm generally considered a sensible, reliable man. And even you must acknowledge: I turn heads wherever I go."

She wasn't about to acknowledge that, even though she saw, out of the periphery of her spinning vision, young women gawking at them—at him. "Are you not living in dire poverty?"

"Do I look it?"

She had to admit he didn't. His clothes, if anything, were on the extravagant side. "Impressionable young women have less impressionable mamas who are better informed about your pennilessness. And even if some foolish matron thinks you'll do for a son-in-law, why would *you* want to do it? Isn't it a bit like going to a symphonic concert when you are deaf?"

"No, more like taking someone who prefers music hall to a symphonic concert. It's not my cup of tea. But should all the music halls in England burn down, and I'm desperate for music, I will make do with a symphonic concert."

Meaning he was quite capable of going to bed with a woman. Somehow she managed not to step on his toes while the significance of his words sank in.

"And since you demand absolute discretion from me, a married man is less likely to be suspect, no?"

"I should dearly pity the young woman on whom you choose to spring this deception," she said severely.

"Now that is harsh, Miss Bessler."

"No more than you deserve."

"I believe I deserve better from you, but that's a different topic altogether." He wheeled her out of the way of an inept couple careening around the ballroom. "Do you think there is not one grown-up, sophisticated young lady in all of London who would find marriage to me an acceptable bargain?"

"What is in the bargain for her, other than your penury and your certain-to-come philandering?"

"I've been to quite a few symphonic concerts on both sides of the Channel, for one thing, so I'm well at ease with . . . symphonic concerts. I'll be a suitably attentive husband, as I've no ambition that would keep me at the Palace of Westminster six months out of the year. And she would be the only woman for me—my heart, my anchor, my day, and my night."

He spoke with an unwavering gaze and a sardonic

smile, all the while steering a perfectly elliptical path around the ballroom.

Her heart beat fast, and not from the dancing. "What of music hall?"

"What's a little music hall in a marriage with much mutual affection and a great deal of symphonic concerts?"

She heated in places that should never heat for *him*. Valiantly she ignored the sensations. "Why have you been to so many symphonic concerts when your natural inclination is for music hall?"

"Convenience. Availability. Acquired taste. Who knows?" He shrugged with one shoulder. "And who cares?"

"I do," she said tightly. "The last thing I want is a promiscuous man who goes on a boudoir rampage while hungering for what a woman cannot give him."

"But you and I will not be attending symphonic concerts together anytime soon, will we, Miss Bessler?" He gave her a look that was as arch as any she'd ever doled out to cloddish suitors. "And as long as my wife is well pleasured and happy, I can't think why you would have cause to complain."

She took a deep breath and let it out. "You are a very trying man, Mr. Marsden."

"You are a very prejudiced woman, Miss Bessler."

"You've earned my prejudice, Mr. Marsden."

"True enough. Allow me to apologize. I never meant to distress you in any way and I'm sorry that I did." He looked into her eyes. "Forgive me."

She did step on his toes this time—his apology was

even more unexpected than his offer of friendship had been. The music came to an end. He let go of her, offered her his arm, and walked her back to the periphery of the ballroom.

She eyed him, not sure how much she could believe of his sincerity.

"Marsden, haven't seen you in a while. You've kept yourself out of trouble, I hope?"

Lizzy froze. Henry. She hadn't thought of him since she'd stepped onto the ballroom floor with Mr. Marsden.

"Henry, how do you do?" Mr. Marsden smiled most pleasantly. "And how do *you* do, Mrs. Franklin? You are more beautiful every time I see you."

"Mr. Marsden, you are too much," Sweet Young Thing protested—sweetly.

"No indeed. What I am is too trite. I'm sure Henry finds new and original ways to immortalize your beauty with every passing day."

Sweet Young Thing giggled in delight and placed her hand on Henry's arm. "Mr. Marsden, you'll embarrass Henry."

Mr. Marsden was not at all repentant. "For having the wisdom and foresight to marry you, Mrs. Franklin? I hardly think so."

Lizzy had thought that face-to-face with Henry and Sweet Young Thing she'd be paralyzed in stiff awkwardness. Instead she was entirely caught up in Mr. Marsden's flirtation—he must have attended a great number of symphonic concerts indeed, to achieve this degree of deftness with the ladies. Sweet Young Thing was aglow with pleasure. Henry, on the other hand, looked as if he'd caught a whiff of some pease porridge, nine days old.

"Have you met Miss Bessler?" asked Mr. Marsden of Sweet Young Thing. "Allow me to present the lovely Miss Bessler. Miss Bessler, Mrs. Franklin. Miss Bessler, you already know Henry, I believe."

"Mr. Franklin and I have met on several occasions," Lizzy said.

"Oh, Henry, you never told me," said Mrs. Franklin innocently. "And I was just admiring Miss Bessler's figure on the dance floor."

"My oversight, my dear," said Henry.

"I dare say you would cut quite a dashing figure on the dance floor yourself, Mrs. Franklin," said Mr. Marsden easily. "I hear a polonaise starting. Shall we have a merry stomp?"

He really was a superb dancer. It was easy for a man to look frantic in a polonaise, all arms and legs and tripping feet, trying to catch up to the relentlessly swift rhythm. But he managed to look as smooth as if he were in the middle of a quadrille, while flying across the room, spinning himself and Sweet Young Thing three hundred and sixty degrees every two seconds.

"Congratulations on your upcoming marriage," said Henry.

Lizzy turned her head. She'd forgotten Henry again, this time with him standing right next to her.

"Thank you, Mr. Franklin," she said.

"A word of caution from an old friend," said Henry. He glanced about them—most of the young people had joined in the polonaise, leaving only a few chaperones engaged in rapt conversation. "I know you have strong needs, but you must be wary of men like Marsden."

Lizzy raised an eyebrow. "Mr. Marsden is my fiancé's secretary."

"How convenient," said Henry. "But Marsden is not to be trusted. He will use you and discard you."

She didn't think she'd ever come across a finer example of the pot calling the kettle black. "Thank you, Mr. Franklin. I'll be most cautious."

"Now that I know what it is like to be in love, I don't wish your heart broken again," said Henry, in an earnestness that was more unconscious pomposity than sincerity.

Lizzy wanted to roll her eyes. Henry in love was still the same self-centered oaf. How blind and stupid she'd been. "How good of you, sir. If you'll excuse me, I'm suffering from a tremendous thirst."

She was stopped on her way to the punch bowl several times by remote acquaintances offering felicitations on her engagement. By the time she reached the refreshments table, the polonaise had finished and Mr. Marsden was already there, helping himself to a piece of iced cake.

"Would you care for a little turn on the gallery, Miss Bessler?" he asked, once she had a glass of punch in hand.

It was exactly what she wanted. The gallery overlooked the ballroom, where a *minuet de la cour* had started. The ladies' flared skirts in shades of pale sun and pastel skies twirled and swished in time to the music.

Lizzy sipped her punch. "How did you survive being cast out by your family?"

Mr. Marsden shot her a glance. She did not look back at him, knowing that she'd asked a far more personal question than their acquaintance granted.

"I'd like to say with élan and insouciance," he said. "But that would probably not be an accurate answer."

"What did you do, precisely?"

"Matthew painted portraits for tourists on the Pont Neuf. I learned shorthand and found work as a secretary."

"Who is Matthew?" His lover?

"My brother. We were together in Paris. He's still there."

She didn't know there had been two banished Marsden brothers. "And you generated enough funds by painting portraits and taking dictations?"

"Enough to keep a roof over our heads and buy bread, but not enough for anything else." He turned his back to the railing. "I went to a great many symphonic concerts with the rich ladies of Paris in those early years, to have a proper dinner and sleep in a room that wasn't freezing."

She was both horrified and intrigued. "You sold yourself cheap."

The corner of his mouth lifted. "Beggars could not be choosers. Though I did my best to find women with whom I would go to symphonic concerts even without the inducement of wine and beefsteak."

The heat in her returned. What did it mean that he'd sleep with women without the incentive of a warm bed and a full stomach?

"Was it really true, that story about two men fighting over you?" she asked. "Or did you make it up to shock me?"

"It happened in Paris, seven years ago, in front of dozens of witnesses—none of whom would admit to being there, of course. But should you ever meet Matthew, he would gladly give you a highly embroidered version of it, and tell you that it was a battle royal between a Bourbon and a Bonaparte."

So much for her secret hopes that Georgette was dead wrong about him. "But it was not between a Bourbon and a Bonaparte?"

"No, they were a banker and a poet."

"Was it . . . was it gratifying for you to watch?"

"Gratifying?" He glanced at her as if she'd lost her mind. "No, I was terrified. I was twenty years old. I'd been in Paris only weeks. And I'd thought the . . . the French a cheese-mad lot of weaklings. The men were both well over six feet in height, barrel-chested, and savage. I'm not ashamed to say that I fled that night and would flee again if I saw either of them today."

A chuckle escaped her. They stood for a few minutes in a silence that, though not precisely companionable, brooded no dark, uneasy currents.

"I've been there," he said. "It was a harsh life. No matter what I know or think I know about you, I would never subject you to the same."

The *minuet de la cour* ended. The dancers drew apart.

The center of the ballroom emptied in an exodus of soft laughter and elaborate trains.

He'd faced her nightmare—poverty and alienation—and lived to tell about it. There was a curious strength to him, a resilience not immediately obvious and probably easily overlooked by most people, including herself.

"If you are not rushing to a symphonic concert, or the music hall, perhaps you'd like to escort me to supper, Mr. Marsden?" she heard herself say.

He looked at her a moment, the way one might gaze upon a much-changed old friend. Then he smiled. "For that privilege I'll give up music altogether."

Chapter Fifteen

Verity spent much of her Sunday cooking at the soup kitchen on Euston Road that handed out thin stew and bread in the cold months. She preferred that to attending church, where she usually fidgeted during the service. She didn't think God minded that she was off feeding the poor—if He did, then she was doomed anyway, church attendance or not.

She'd taken Marjorie with her—she and Becky divided the task of looking after Marjorie when the latter wasn't in the kitchen, with Becky responsible for the half days, and Verity taking the full day on Sundays. They returned to the house in the middle of the afternoon. She made Marjorie an omelet—the girl needed more substantial food than what the soup kitchen had to offer—set Marjorie in the servants' hall to eat, and climbed up to the attic to wash her face and take off her dress for a good brush, so that it didn't smell permanently of turnip.

She grabbed her stockings and drawers from the

back and arms of the chair where she'd hung them to dry and put them back in her valise. Then she rebuilt the fire in the grate, changed, and ruthlessly scoured the hem of the dress she'd worn. More ruthlessly than either the soil or the fabric of the dress called for, no doubt, but the agitation inside her made greater gentleness impossible.

She could forgive herself for rushing out of her hiding place to embrace him—it wasn't always easy to remember that he knew her only as Bertie's former cook and paramour. But why, oh, why had she given into the impulse to taste him, when he'd already, mostly politely, told her that she should let go of him?

Every time she remembered the way he'd thrown her, she had to close her eyes and wince in mortification. To be rejected with such unequivocal force. To have to be told that he would not lower himself to hobnob with her—if only she hadn't been so vain as to want to impress his breakfast guests with her croissants, for which she had to make midnight trips down to the kitchen to turn the dough.

But then he had held her face and kissed her tears. And his lips had lingered close to hers for so long she had been convinced he'd kiss her any moment, only to pull away and leave her completely alone.

She was confused. As much by his enigmatic intentions as by what *she* wanted from *him*. There had been so much that was impossible that what little remained in the realm of plausibility had all seemed tawdry. But things had gone in unpredictable directions. And sometimes, when she let her guard down, she could almost believe that he loved her.

Mr. Darcy's love it wasn't: This was no bright, honorable admiration for a pair of fine eyes and a lively wit. If anything, it was like a love for the bottle: full of guilt, shame, troubled dreams, and dark compulsions.

And she both hated it and thrilled to it: It made her vulnerable, miserable, and strangely happy all at once.

She brushed the dress one more time, shook it, and went to hang it on a hook on the wall. That was when she saw the package on the rickety desk, laid down before Michael's photograph like an offering.

The package was wrapped in brown paper and tied in brown twine. She undid the twine, peeled back the paper, and looked upon an oil painting that was no bigger than her two hands put together.

It was a still life of someone's midday meal. On a silver platter atop a still-creased white tablecloth, a helping of pink, caper-sprinkled salmon beckoned. A plate of lemons—one whole, one half-peeled—had been helpfully provided. There was also a ramekin of olives, golden wine in thick-bottomed glasses, a knife only the ebony handle of which could be seen, a salt shaker, and to the side, a large pewter jug so beautifully polished it gleamed like black pearls.

Rich details teemed on the tiny canvas: the light caught and held by an individual caper; the long, dapper curl of bright yellow lemon peel hanging off the side of a plate; the presence of a half-eaten olive that she imagined had been the long-dead painter's appetite getting the better of his artistic patience.

A present from Mr. Somerset. Or was it an apology? Highly—no, hugely—improper. Not only in the present itself, but also in the manner of the giving—he had stepped inside her room while she was at the soup kitchen, her valise wide open, her washing drying on the chair.

She wished he hadn't: Not because she was ashamed that he'd seen her old drawers and her not-so-new stockings, but because the too beautiful painting set her heart soaring, like Icarus high in the sky.

The world hadn't changed, nor had their places in it. If they were to allow something beautiful to come to be, then it would only make the inevitable that much harder, that much more unbearable.

Don't, she thought. *He is to be married.*

Don't.

But she knew, as surely as Icarus had been doomed to plunge and tumble from the beginning, that she would ignore her own excellent advice. And that she, too, would risk flying as close to the sun as her wings of wax could lift her.

❦

"Do you have anyone specific next to whom you wish to seat the Arlingtons?" asked Mr. Marsden.

Lizzy was sick of seating charts. Or rather, she had trouble concentrating on them. Instead, she couldn't stop looking at him. He had on a real cravat in blue silk, beautifully knotted, such as she hadn't seen in ages—most valets couldn't manage anything more complicated than an octagon tie these days.

"Seat them next to whomever you please," she said, reckless. "I want a reprieve from seating people. Tell me about music hall."

He dropped his pen.

He picked it up and blotted the droplets of ink that had splattered onto the seating chart. "It's an amusing way to spend an evening."

"You know what I mean," she insisted.

He flashed her a smile that was as bright as a theatrical footlight. "Music hall is an actionable offense in this country. I'll need an inducement to expound upon it."

She glanced at him from underneath her lashes. "What inducement?"

"Symphonic concerts."

Her heart bounded high enough to knock against her palate. "I beg your pardon?"

He looked at her steadily and the air around her thickened into pudding. At last he said, "I want to hear about your experience at symphonic concerts. Did you like it?"

She dragged the *Debrett's* from across the desk and opened it to a random page. They hadn't had to use it. He seemed to know everyone's pedigree and precedence by heart. "What would you say if I said I did?"

"I've been asking myself that very same thing," he said. "I decided that I hoped you liked it."

"Why?"

"Because you could have been ruined over it, you

stupid woman. At least you should have enjoyed it while you were at it."

No one had ever called her a stupid woman. But he said it with such resigned tenderness that she couldn't even begin to protest. It was almost as if he'd called her his sweetheart.

He tilted his head. "Well, did you?"

"I thought I did," she said, finally admitting her transgressions. "But the memories offend me now."

"Henry Franklin is a remarkable ass," he said firmly. "I'm glad you didn't marry him."

She smiled a little. It was, of course, very childish and unsophisticated of her that she should feel this deep sense of kinship upon his unsparing denouncement of Henry. Ah, but what a splendid feeling.

"Are you still displeased that I'm marrying Mr. Somerset?" she asked, not sure she wasn't flirting at least a little.

He capped his fountain pen. "*Displeased* is not the right word."

"What is, then?"

"Mr. Somerset regards you as a favorite young cousin, a dearly loved niece even. And as such he is apt to be very, very indulgent of you. While he's busy working for the betterment of the common man, you'll be free to do whatever you wish."

"And that is a terrible thing?"

"Perhaps not. But we all could use someone to tell us, from time to time, that our action is ill-advised. Mr. Somerset is not that person for you, nor do I see you as that person for him—you are too grateful, too determined that he should never hear a harsh word or an adverse opinion from you."

He startled her. How did he know? How had he sensed the little flutters of anxiety that had characterized her interaction with Stuart of late—the cost she must bear to maintain a false perfection?

"You seem to have thought more about my marriage than I have," she murmured.

"Perhaps I have," he said.

Her heart was once again in her throat. "Because you are a student of human nature?" she said, her voice full of forced levity.

"Because—" He stopped.

"Because?" She hoped she didn't sound too curious, or breathless. She was both.

He pulled the *Debrett's* toward himself, and turned the pages purposefully, as if looking for something. "You remember your question about music hall?" he asked, without glancing at her.

"Yes?"

"I have never been to music hall. All my life I've only ever been interested in symphonic concerts."

She thought she heard distant artillery, but it was only the slow explosion of his words against her eardrums.

"That time in Paris, Madame Belleau was hoping to seduce me with a tableau of two entertwined women— I was to join you if everything went according to her plans."

"But—"

He slid *Debrett's Peerage and Baronetage* toward her. It

was open to the page on the Earldom of Wyden. The book was a slightly older edition, from before the passing of the seventh earl. Five sons were listed for the titleholder. Her attention immediately went to the fourth one: His given name was not William.

Do you remember that hushed-up scandal about Mr. Marsden, the late Lord Wyden's second-youngest son? Georgette's answer had been correct. But Lizzy's question had been wrong.

"You are thinking of my brother Matthew," said Mr. Marsden. "He is the fourth; I'm the middle one. I left home because I disagreed with my father's decision to disown Matthew, who was too young and too naïve to survive on his own."

"Why did you not say so sooner?"

When she first brought it up, for instance. It would have been embarrassing then. It was ten times so now. She cringed to think how she'd tried to intimidate him with sins not his own.

"I thought perhaps you'd be less wary of me," he said, "if you believed me to be inclined solely toward music hall."

"You would tolerate this level of misconception for me to be less wary of you?"

He smiled, a weary smile. "I did, didn't I?"

She rose, too agitated to remain sitting. "Why?"

He rose also. "Do you not know already?"

She said nothing. He collected his things. Then he came and kissed her just below her ear, an intimate and entirely inappropriate place. And while his kiss burned, he saw himself out.

❦

Her Grace Sarah, the Dowager Duchess of Arlington.

Verity's vision blurred. "We've a duchess coming to dine here?" she asked weakly.

"Oh, yes. The master calls at the Arlington house. He's been a guest at Lyndhurst Hall—that's the Arlingtons' country seat, don't you know—a good dozen times since I came to work for him," said Mrs. Abercromby with staunch pride. The middle class might very well despise the aristocracy in this day and age. Those in service, however, preferred the old elite, who on the whole treated their staff much more liberally than did the suspicious and tight-fisted middle class. "But it's the first time Her Grace will be dining here. The master is moving up in the world, I tell you, Madame Durant."

The world was a small place. Verity had no idea Mr. Somerset was acquainted with the Arlingtons at all, let alone that the acquaintance was of such standing.

She did not dread cooking for dignitaries. Among the guests who had dined at Bertie's table had been literary luminaries of the age, tycoons wealthier than entire cities, and even a former president of *la Troisième République*. But the thought of cooking for the Dowager Duchess of Arlington made her tremble: It would be like cooking for a stone statue of Hera.

She drove herself and everyone else hard, so much so that she was annoyed to realize that it was a half day again, the day before the dinner. It was on the tip of her tongue to inform the girls that they would remain and work. But as she looked about her, she realized that most of what could be done at this point had already been done, that her girls waited with bated breaths for luncheon to finish and their short-lived freedom to begin.

She let them go. Alone in the kitchen, she made her pâté, a mixture of goose breast and pork ground very fine, which must cook for three hours and be stirred nonstop. Normally, the stirring was split between several people, in half-hour shifts. She was forcefully reminded soon after she began why that was the case, but by then she had no choice except to go on.

At the end of the three hours, her arms felt only marginally attached to the rest of her. But the pâté had turned out quite well, so she could not be entirely unhappy. She set the pâté aside to cool and checked her watch: a minute past five o'clock. She would shape the batch of sugar paste she'd made the day before with the molds that had arrived from Fairleigh Park that morning.

She did not look up at the sound of horse hooves. But she did when a hack came to a stop in front of 26 Cambury Lane. A man's black city pumps, his striped day trousers, and his walking stick emerged from the hack. The vehicle departed. The man disappeared from her view. And then she heard the opening and closing of the front door on the floor above.

Mr. Somerset had come home.

The bath was dark and empty.

Stuart had been saved from himself, or so it would seem. He'd expected her to be in his tub, waiting, veils of steam writhing about her.

He'd warned himself most severely that he was likely to do something he'd regret should he return home when no one else was there except her. He'd carried a photograph of Lizzy with him all day as a reminder. And he'd left his office at two o'clock in the afternoon and visited both the bathing pool *and* the gymnasium, in an attempt to replace concupiscence with exhaustion.

All for naught. He'd come home at this most dangerous hour and headed straight for the bath—only to stare into an empty tub that gleamed a cold white in the light of the gas lamp, a lamp that he'd turned on because the darkness and the lack of steam in the bath hadn't been enough to convince him of her absence.

He had ascribed *his* hunger and *his* covetousness to her. Had imagined that she'd be in the tub because *he* wanted her to be in it. Had berated himself entirely for show—his self-reproach as ritualistic and useless as the search for Guy Fawkes before the State Opening of Parliament.

And now he was exposed for the fraud that he was. Because he wasn't relieved by her absence. Not at all. In fact, he couldn't remember being so disappointed since the first anniversary of that night, when he'd stayed up 'til dawn, convinced that Cinderella would return.

He didn't know why—perhaps because he couldn't

stand the emptiness of the tub—he reached out and turned on the faucets. The pipes moaned and trembled. Water came, first a trickle, then a gush that shook the plumbing even harder. He plugged the tub and watched it fill. He should be using cold water—wasn't that the traditional prescription for overamorous men? But steam undulated from the rising water. He dipped his fingertips in the water and it was hot, as hot as he imagined she must be, in places he longed to touch.

He remembered the kitchen light he'd seen from the street. She was home—close at hand and accessible. He wanted to see her. He needed to see her.

He would see her.

Verity slapped sugar paste into the mold, thankful for the mindless work, for she certainly could not concentrate on any subtle, delicate cooking now, not with the pipes groaning and the boiler in the room down the corridor rasping and rattling.

The plumbing had made just such noises last week, when she'd filled the tub for her use.

She closed the mold for the centerpiece, turned around, and saw that the little window on the dumbwaiter showed red: It was needed upstairs. What did *he* want with the dumbwaiter?

She dispatched the dumbwaiter upward and it came down with a note.

Madame, your bath awaits.

She flushed. Underneath the note was a piece of black cloth. When she picked it up, the cloth resolved itself to be a soft mask that would cover her from her brows to just above her upper lip.

This was unlike him. He was as reckless as she had been the other night, when she'd kissed him under his jaw and got herself tossed across the corridor for her trouble.

It was wrong—and they both knew it. To happen upon each other by chance was one thing, to intentionally orchestrate a tryst quite another. And for him to run a bath for her, and for her to accept—they might as well meet unclothed in his bedchamber instead.

But try as she did, she could not find dishonor enough in his invitation to refuse. Because she would agree to meet unclothed in his bedchamber too. Because there was nothing he wanted that she didn't also want.

She felt for the stubby pencil she always carried in her pocket, wrote her reply on the note, and sent it to him.

In the dining room two floors above, the dumbwaiter clicked into place. At first Stuart thought she'd returned his note as a refusal, then he saw her swiftly penciled response.

Merci. Je viens.

She was on her way.

He folded the note and put it in the inside pocket of

his waistcoat. Later he'd place it in a locked drawer of the desk in his study, along with other notes she'd directed his way. Not that he needed anything by which to remember her—he remembered every word, every touch, every tear. No, they were merely to reassure him that it had really happened, that there had been such a woman, and that with her, he had been that man.

Chapter Sixteen

She knocked on the door to the bath. Absolute silence. Then, *"Entrez."*

She entered, a candlestick in hand. The candlestick was his. He'd left it behind in the basement the other night, and she'd picked it up and carefully concealed it: Trust a gentleman to never wonder what his servants would think to find his source of illumination lying drunkenly across the basement floor, the taper broken in several pieces.

Her back to him, she set the candlestick atop the chest of drawers. Then she turned off the gas flame in the sconce affixed to the wall. The candlestick held only the stub end of a taper, its wick trimmed almost bare. The bath dimmed. Her own shadow loomed large. A tracery of fire gilded the curves of the tub. The water inside took on a glow like that of the final throes of a sunset.

"Will I ever see you in good light?" he asked, his

voice too serious to be teasing, too wistful to be entirely serious.

She had to resist the urge to tug at her mask—it was quite secure already, tight and snug against her features. In her mirror she had looked rather dashing, as if at any moment she might pull out a rapier and execute a fancy flourish à la *Three Musketeers*.

"And what purpose would it accomplish for you to see me in good light, sir?" she countered.

She turned toward him—and realized that it was the first time she'd seen *him* in any kind of light since Fairleigh Park. She'd forgotten how strikingly handsome he was, his hair inky, his irises as dark as mine shafts.

He sat in the oval-backed chair, his posture beautifully upright, his hands loosely braced under his chin. He looked a little tired, a little melancholy, like a man at the end of a long revelry who did not want to go home yet. But as he leaned back and regarded her, she caught a glimpse of the coiled vitality and undisguised desire in his eyes—

Be still my heart.

"You speak as if there is still good sense to be had here," he said.

"I haven't let go of mine," she said. It wasn't completely a lie, only largely one.

"Then I shall rely on you. I left mine at the office. Perhaps at Fairleigh Park itself."

She ducked her head. The bath was small, and they were close. She couldn't be sure the light was quite as muted as it needed to be.

"Well, Madame, your bath awaits," he said, without further preliminary.

She swallowed. She'd gone back to her room, used the water with which she was about to make tea to quickly sponge herself, and then, in a decision that no doubt revealed the full extent of her amorality, slipped on only her dressing robe. Now her hand closed around the ends of the robe's sash. She dipped a finger in the water—it was hot, just the way she liked it. She swallowed again, opened the robe, and let it drop.

The breath he sucked in reverberated in the steam. She leaned forward, braced her hands on the edge of the tub, raised one foot, and stepped into the water. She had her side to him, but she was quite aware that he still saw everything: her breasts, her buttocks, her sex.

Once both of her feet were inside the tub, she sat down and stared at the wall, not quite bold or wicked enough to look at him.

"You overwhelm me," he mumbled.

A small smile relaxed her tense lips. "You certainly know how to make a middle-aged woman feel appealing."

"How middle-aged are you?" he asked, after a few seconds.

"Thirty-three."

"Not that old."

"Not at all young."

"Your body is beautiful."

She suppressed the leap of her heart and turned her

face toward him. "Only because you haven't slept with a nineteen-year-old woman in a while."

For a moment he seemed shocked at her forwardness, then he laughed softly. "No, not in a while. Perhaps not ever."

Then the laughter disappeared from his eyes. "Let me see your face."

"No," she said.

A look of bittersweet longing came over him. He quickly looked away, but the damage—to her—was done.

She'd come to realize that the man in her heart had become less Stuart Somerset than an ideal man she'd invented and reinvented over the years. The real Stuart Somerset was a mystery to her and, more than once, a disappointment: He was nothing of the fearless lover she remembered, but a man very much ruled by—and in thrall to—the conventions of Society.

Sometimes she wondered whether she still gravitated toward him simply because she could not face the fact that her faithful love might have been a mistake—a beautiful mistake, but a mistake enormous and pervasive all the same.

But now as she gazed upon him, her heart did something strange, a twist, a clench, a fracture—she didn't know what precisely, but yes, the damage was done. She was falling in love with *this* man, this man who wouldn't touch her, kiss her, or marry her.

"Do you mind if I smoke?" he asked.

She shook her head.

He rose, and lit his cigarette on the taper. Their eyes

met. He was much closer to her now and could probably see most of her, despite the dusky air and the ripples of reflected candlelight on the water. She drew her knees in and circled her arms about her shins. His reaction was a smile as knowing as it was resigned.

He knocked the cigarette against the bowl of the candlestick, using it for an ashtray. "Where did you learn to cook as you do?"

"At the Marquess of Londonderry's household," she said—and instantly realized her mistake.

He caught it. "Not in a Parisian establishment?"

She might as well go with the truth now. "No, in the Londonderry kitchen, under a great, but unsung, chef named Monsieur Algernon David."

He nodded. "How did you come to work for Bertie?"

"Monsieur David had worked for Bertie for some years, until the Marchioness of Londonderry poached him away—at least that was how Bertie told it. He recommended me for Fairleigh Park."

"And Bertie took you on this recommendation?"

"No. Bertie was quite convinced that while women might make adequate farmhouse cooks, only men could be acolytes in the temple of cuisine. Finally I bought a train ticket, went up to Fairleigh Park, and insisted that he gave me a fighting chance: I would cook a meal for him, and if he rejected me after that, I'd leave."

Mr. Somerset exhaled a cloud of smoke. "And he couldn't say no afterward?"

"I suspect he could have said no. He compiled a

long list of my shortcomings as a cook—he was knowl-
edgeable and critical about his food. Most French
cooks do not care to be told by an Englishman how to
cook, but I was quite humble and said that I valued his
opinions."

He smiled. "Did you?"

"No. I thought then that he was unbearably fussy,
but I wanted the position."

"Did you resent having to resort to such humility to
secure the position?"

She chuckled. He'd been too long away from
Ancoats. "You must understand, sir, to become the
cook at an estate like Fairleigh Park was a tremendous
step up in the world for me. I would have a room of my
own, far better wages, and a kitchen maid to bring me
my breakfast every morning. Bertie could have made a
list of my faults twice as long and I'd have gladly nodded to it."

"And yet you flew into a rage when you thought *I*
had insulted your food."

Ah, he caught her there. She rested her chin on her
knee, looked up at him, and allowed her inner co-
quette to give the answer. "It would seem, sir, that you
are destined to provoke a passionate response in me
no matter what you do."

His hand, the one holding the cigarette, tightened
into a fist, nearly crushing the cigarette. He looked
away, and then back at her. "I'm trying very hard to not
join you in that tub, Madame. Please don't make it any
more difficult for me."

She was hot, so hot. "Why make me sit here in

exhibition, then, when you are determined that you cannot, must not, have anything to do with me?"

"I don't know," he said. "If I did, I'd have put a stop to it a long time ago."

She lowered her gaze. "Would you like me to leave?"

"No!"

He said it with such force that it startled both of them. Their eyes met. He laughed without humor. "I like to torture myself, if you can't tell yet."

He snubbed out the cigarette and took a step closer to the tub, his eyes obsidian. "Torture me some more, Madame. Do what you did last time."

Her cheeks were fiery enough to toast bread. But the tease in her would not rest. "Sir, I spent three hours this afternoon stirring a batch of pâté without rest. I can barely lift my arms."

In his eyes was a lust of biblical proportions, the sort that would call down sulfur and brimstone upon an entire city. "I'm tempted to order you to do it, tired arms or not."

She raised her hand and, with water dripping from her fingers, smoothed the hair at her temple. "Why don't you then?" she said softly.

❧

He cast a shadow over her. Despite this, her eyes glittered faintly, their color a mutable sheen like that of dragon scales. When she smiled, as she did now, he could see the lovely curvature of her lower lip, generous and full.

She was beautiful.

"I have a better idea," Stuart heard himself say. "Let me do it for you."

Her smile disappeared. "You are mad."

Vous êtes fou.

"Yes, quite," he said. "Will you let me?"

She looked away from him. "You know there is nothing I wouldn't let you do."

If ever mere words could bring him to his knees, those were the words. He wanted to sink down before the tub, hold her face in his hands, and kiss her, mask and all. He turned around and looked for a towel in the drawers instead.

He opened one and held it out, as he'd seen Durbin do countless times. "Come."

Slowly she rose, water cascading from her, her skin flushed, her body as beautiful as that of Cabanel's Venus: dainty breasts, a deep navel, and hips so voluptuous they melted his vision.

She leaned forward to climb out of the tub. He couldn't look away from her nipples—erect and the most erotic shade of muted pink.

She wrapped the towel around her person. As she dried herself, he retrieved her robe and held it out for her. She turned around and dropped the towel. He had a fleeting view of her back and her round bottom before she shrugged into the robe.

The robe was of a shade too deep to distinguish in the scant illumination, of a material that glistened darkly, the shimmer of new moon on swift water. She pulled the sash tight. No, no nineteen-inch waist here.

But she had delicate shoulders and an elegant neck. And there was nothing he wouldn't do for her.

"Are you cold?"

She shook her head. The bath was small and the radiator large. He himself was far too warm in his clothes.

He blew out the candle. "Take off your mask."

He'd bought the mask the same day he'd bought the painting—and had nearly given both to her together. Then he'd come to his senses and swore he'd throw the mask away. But he never did.

"What for?" she murmured, even as he heard the soft shush of her sleeves against her hair, her fingers working on the knot behind her head. "You can't see me."

He didn't answer that. He turned her around by her shoulders and cupped her face in his hands. With his fingers, he explored her features, as if she were virgin territory and he a captivated cartographer.

"I don't need to see you," he said.

He only wanted to remember the texture of her skin, flaws and all. To know the warmth of her cheek and the pulse at her temple. To etch the topography of her face upon his memory—the sweep of a brow, the softness of an earlobe, the slightly chapped fullness of a lower lip.

"Kiss me," she murmured.

"Only in my dreams."

He felt his way to the chair and sat down. "Come here. Sit on me."

Utter silence greeted his blatant words. Then she let

out a slow breath. "You seem to know exactly what you are doing. Have you done this before?"

He braced his feet apart. "No. But I've imagined it."

And imagined it. And imagined it.

She emitted a faint, strained sound. He heard her move in the dark. As she groped for the chair, her hand landed on his forearm. She immediately let go. She turned around and sat down on the edge of the chair, between his legs, almost not touching him at all except for one hip at his right knee.

"Move back until you are against me."

She complied. He ground his teeth at the sensation of her barely clad backside pressing into him—he was as hard as a bludgeon.

"I won't touch you anywhere else," he said, less a promise to her than a reminder to himself.

"I wish you would," she said.

"Shhh. Not another word out of you." Or he'd lose his mind.

He parted her robe. His fingers encountered soft, still-damp curls. She obligingly opened her thighs. His heart pounded like a caught thief's. His hand reached farther.

She was damp there too—but not from the bath. He expelled a shaky breath. So soft, silky, and sleek. So impossibly arousing. *I wish you would.* He could. There was nothing to stop him.

He closed his eyes. No, he'd made a deal with his conscience. He would touch her only to pleasure her, not himself.

Gingerly he caressed her where she was most moist. She sighed, a sound that made his ears burn.

"Show me what to do," he said. Or perhaps he begged.

She pressed her hand over his and guided his fingers, sliding his index and middle fingers around plump, lovely flesh. She leaned back and rested her head on his shoulder. The sensation of her hair brushing his jaw and cheek was almost more than he could stand. He was in Heaven. He was in Hell. He was hot and hard and dying for relief, and she, without a care in the world, whimpered and moaned, her breath fluttering against his earlobe.

"Harder," she said. "Do it harder."

"I don't want to hurt you," he said. He sounded desperate.

"You won't. Do it harder."

He did it harder. Her hips tilted up to meet the motion of his hand. Up, lowered, up, lowered—impossibly exquisite friction against his erection. Her other hand clamped over his forearm. She turned her face and kissed him just above his collar—wet, hungry kisses that shot straight to his testes.

All her muscles tensed. She cried out. He felt the tremors beneath his fingers. It was too much. He dipped his head and bit into her shoulders—no, he would allow nothing for himself. The pressure of his teeth only made her climax more violent. He almost wept, in awe of the beauty of her pleasure, in pity for himself.

Her tremors subsided. His near-crisis faded into the

usual insistent, painful need she aroused. Then she kissed him again above the collar, and parts of him leapt in response.

"Don't," he said.

"Let me return the favor for you," she said earnestly.

It was a marvel he didn't ejaculate upon those words. "No."

"Why not?"

"Because that would be wrong."

"More wrong than what we just did?"

"That wasn't wrong. That was . . ." Sublime, breathtaking, and so intense it would monopolize his dreams for years. He could only repeat himself. "That wasn't wrong."

She exhaled, a sigh of Shakespearean complexity. Her arm lifted and hooked behind his neck. She snuggled closer to him, her cheek against his jaw. He banded his arms about her middle, unwilling—and unable—to let go.

"Thank you," she said. Her breath was sweet, sweeter than apples—she'd eaten a perfectly ripe medlar.

For the pleasure, he supposed. "No, thank *you*," he said.

"What for?"

For this wordless embrace. For the warmth, comfort, and substance of it.

"For all the memories, old and new. For the madeleines. For having loved Bertie. For—"

She twisted in his arms. Suddenly her lips were upon his and he was too weak and too glad to resist. She kissed him solemnly, urgently, deeply, as if he were a sweetheart at last returned from a long, long war, and she'd waited until her youth had fled and her hair turned white.

When they finally pulled apart, her cheeks were wet. And so were his, he realized with a jolt.

"I love you," she said. "Always."

✦

After she left—Mrs. Abercromby would return early today, she'd explained, because of the dinner on the morrow—Stuart remained a long time in the bath, in the dark, thinking of her.

There were ways he could hold on to her, and still remain faithful to Lizzy. As much as he burned for it, he would survive not making love to her—as long as he could have her in his arms once in a while.

It wasn't enough, of course. In their predicament, they could never have enough, only bits and scraps, stolen encounters of powerful pleasure and equally powerful anguish.

But to give her up altogether now was unthinkable. He would keep her close, for as long as she would let him, and live as did those natives of rainy climes who spent the vast majority of their days under an overcast sky and made the most of their rare, glorious glimpses of the sun.

Chapter Seventeen

Stuart's hopes died abruptly twenty-four hours later, as his fiancée was shown into his drawing room.

"Sorry I'm late." She squeezed his hand briefly. "I didn't mean to be. When you are prime minister, you will do something about the logjams, won't you?"

She smiled at him, looking very young and very stylish in a dinner gown the color of evergreens in winter.

"Of course, I shall banish them all," he said, as his heart sank without a trace.

He had betrayed her. There was no other word for what he had done. In the confines of the bath, it had been easy to pretend otherwise, to believe that what he had done and what he wanted to do were both beyond the judgment of the simplistic sexual mores of his time.

It was not the simplistic sexual mores of his time that he faced now, but the trust in Lizzy's eyes. It didn't matter that he never had taken and never would take any pleasure with Madame Durant, not even when he was alone. He had touched her and kissed her and held on to her as if he were a beggar and she his last shining penny.

He loved her—in ways he understood only marginally, an emotion too powerful, too primal for a civilized man. And *that* was the ultimate betrayal, far worse than furtive touches in the dark, far worse than even outright fornication.

"Banish them all, eh? Now, that will indeed make me the most popular hostess in London," said Lizzy, her smile widening.

Her smile was a corrosion of acid upon his conscience.

"Anything to make you the most popular hostess in London, my lady," he said.

She replied, a witty observation on the current spate of popular hostesses. He probably heard and understood her just fine, because he said something in return and she laughed rather brightly. But he had no idea what either of them had said.

His guests arrived on the Besslers' heels. Stuart gave dinner parties often enough, usually catered by a capable woman named Mrs. Godfrey, whose cooks took over his kitchen for a day and whose height-matched footmen served in the evening alongside Durbin. The hired footmen were present, circulating trays of amontillado sherry and vermouth. The usual collection of tails-clad men and bejeweled women occupied his drawing room, chatting genteelly with one another.

But tonight it felt utterly unreal, as if he'd walked into the middle of an elaborate tableau and must play along. All the while the woman he loved slaved below-stairs, with no idea that their time together would come to an abrupt end.

His heart struggled and pleaded like a wrongly accused man. *Don't do this. Don't do this.* But he had no other choice. Love was a thing of no consequence to a man in his position—only duty counted, duty alone, duty above all.

She was mounting a production aimed to dazzle. He had been informed that the menu was her interpretation of the best-known feast in recent history, the meal enjoyed by Czar Alexander II, the then-future Czar Alexander III, and the King of Prussia at the Café Anglais in 1867—otherwise known as the Dinner of the Three Emperors.

He had not asked her who she thought needed such impressing, and now he would never have the chance. The kind of dinner she used to produce daily for Bertie would have quite sufficiently amazed his guests. Such elegance as she intended for tonight was beyond the experience of most of his guests, with the possible exception of the Arlingtons.

The arrival of the Dowager Duchess of Arlington and her son, the current duke, caused a stir. As Mr. Gladstone's deputy, Stuart had various dealings with the peers of the realm who took their seats in the House of Lords. He also occasionally attended politics-centered country house gatherings. But on a purely social level, he did not quite move in the same rarefied spheres. The invitation issued to the Arlingtons had been more a whim on his part than anything else, since the dowager duchess had seemed so particularly aware of Madame Durant. He'd been more than a bit surprised that she had accepted.

Lizzy, to her credit, betrayed no sign of discomfort as she greeted the Arlingtons, despite having once been told by the dowager duchess not to look to her son for a husband. Stuart, on the other hand, could only wish that he'd not invited the too-sharp duchess. If she breathed one word of his Verity, his facade of normality would crumble.

At the appointed hour, Durbin announced dinner. Stuart offered his arm to the dowager duchess, and they proceeded to the dining room, where murmurs of "Oh, my" and "Good gracious" immediately broke out.

Stuart had epergnes and vases and candelabra enough. But they remained in storage tonight. Instead, pairs of Corinthian columns marched down the center of the dining table. Between the columns were four-foot-tall reproductions of classical statues. There was Artemis the Hunter, alert and confident, her left hand in the antlers of a young buck, her right hand reaching toward her quiver. There was Venus de Milo, beautiful and sensuous. And nearest to the head of the table there was the Winged Victory of Samothrace, marred and maimed, but triumphant all the same.

He'd seen many an elaborate table in his time, the majority pompous and misguided, a few with a genuine spark of artistry. But he'd never encountered what felt to be a defiant table. True, she was French, and what she used were some well-known pieces from the Louvre. Nevertheless, it was a statement on herself— her reputation, her sensuality, her fearlessness.

The gentlemen waited for the ladies to take their seats. The ladies waited upon the dowager duchess. The dowager duchess stood unmoving, staring at the sugar paste reproductions that mimicked the quality of marble quite uncannily.

When she at last took her seat to his right, Stuart thought he heard her murmur, "She hasn't changed."

"I beg your pardon, Madame?" asked Stuart.

The dowager duchess shook her head. "It was nothing."

The meal commenced with potage *imperatrice* and potage *fontanges*. In all fairness, Stuart thought perhaps he should have attached a note of warning to the invitations: beware the food. But who would have paid him any mind? To his guests, the only perils of dinner were indigestion and weight gain.

The conversation that had reached a steady hum as the soups were brought in faltered abruptly when the first spoonfuls reached unsuspecting lips. Potage *imperatrice* was a thickened bouillon. Potage *fontanges* was, if one must be blunt about it, a soup made from pureed peas. But the looks of amazement on his guests' faces would have one believe that they'd been given sips from the Fountain of Youth.

She'd outdone herself. He didn't know how it was possible, but the flavors of the soups were more fierce and more seductive than anything he'd ever tasted. He was robbed of speech, almost of thoughts altogether.

The only thing left to him was a hot, brutal grief, and a relentless wish that it didn't need to end this way—swift and merciless.

His guests' silence was the one small mercy of the evening. Beside him the dowager duchess ate carefully, soundlessly, the expression on her face halfway between pain and bliss.

Toward the end of the course, the conversation tentatively resumed. No one spoke of the food—the experience was too strange, too unnerving for a roomful of good, solid Englishmen and -women who'd never had their attention commandeered by mere dinner. Instead, they murmured distractedly of the weather and the deteriorating congestion of the roads.

That fledgling conversation ground to a halt each time a new course landed on the table. The hush that descended was half-astounded, half-reverent. There were startled gasps when the *pâté chaud* came around. Even something as mundane as an ice to clear the palate between the courses received solemn, undivided attention.

By the time Madame Durant's variation of the *bombe glacée* arrived on the table, layered, in deference to the weather, not with ice creams but with vanilla custard, chestnut cream, and chocolate mousse, all the good breeding and restraint represented at Stuart's table were barely enough to hold back his guests from launching themselves face-first into their desserts.

He held himself together only with the training of a lifetime.

When they had demolished the *bombe glacée*, Lizzy,

at the far end of the table, came to her feet. One by one, the other ladies left their seats, slow and dazed. The last person to follow Lizzy's lead was the dowager duchess. She remained where she was and gazed into her empty plate. For a shocked moment, Stuart thought there were tears in her eyes.

Then she rose, straight and regal, and departed the table.

In the drawing room, while she waited for the gentlemen to join them, Lizzy had to dance attendance on the dowager duchess.

She'd once tried to ingratiate herself with the duchess—then not yet dowager, as her husband still had been alive. To say she was unsuccessful was to call the Thames somewhat muddled. The duchess had let her have it with an icy majesty that had infuriated, humiliated, and impressed her all at once.

The duchess was not a chatty woman. After scant minutes, Lizzy had already exhausted her own limited capacity for monologues. Since she'd received countless unsolicited advice concerning her married life from women who barely knew her, she thought perhaps the duchess might warm up to a request for instructions.

"I'm to be married soon, Madame. I should dearly love to hear your wisdom on the subject of marriage—and husbands," she said.

"You are not me, Miss Bessler, and you are not

marrying my late husband," said the dowager duchess. "I do not see how my experience could be of any relevance to you."

"No, indeed," Lizzy murmured. At least let it be said that she was dressed down by the best.

But then the dowager duchess regarded her a minute. "I have not congratulated you on your impending marriage, have I?"

It was the first time the duchess had ever expressed any kind of interest in Lizzy's person. She was flustered in spite of—or precisely because of—her fear and awe of the old woman. "No, Madame, I do not believe so."

"Since you accepted Mr. Somerset's proposal before his brother passed away and left him Fairleigh Park, I see you've finally gained enough sense to appreciate a good man for what he is."

"I certainly hope so," said Lizzy, not quite sure whether she'd been praised or insulted by the peeress.

The dowager duchess smiled. "You still believe that I refused to let my son marry you because your father had no title."

"That was what you yourself told me, Madame."

"That was a reason you could understand. I forbade the match because you did not care enough for my son. He is kind and gentle. And as such, he deserves a woman who loves him, rather than one who merely sees him as a means to an end."

Lizzy could say nothing in her own defense. It was exactly how she'd seen Tin, a sweet, malleable chap and the perfect conduit of her own ambitions.

"I imagine I'd have done the same were I his mother," she said.

The door to the living room opened. The gentlemen had arrived. Her fiancé, after a moment of almost obvious hesitation, came toward them.

"Mr. Somerset," said the dowager duchess, "I was just about to tender my felicitations to Miss Bessler. I do not believe either of you has ever told me how you decided to marry. It has been a friendship of long standing between you, has it not? What prompted the change?"

Stuart looked almost riled by the question. Lizzy knew, of course, that he wouldn't blurt out such frank answers as that she'd hounded him with invitations to dinner and her almost continual presence at the Palace of Westminster at teatime. But she panicked nonetheless—the dowager duchess had that effect on her.

"I was unwell for quite a long time," she said. "Mr. Somerset sent me a beautiful arrangement of flowers every month. They were the one bright spot in an otherwise dreary time."

Stuart slanted her an astonished look. She supposed that as private a man as he was, he preferred that such details of his life not be shared with others.

"Indeed," said the dowager duchess. "I did not take you for the kind of man who communed via buds and blooms, Mr. Somerset."

"I am not, by and large. But a man must make exceptions for an exceptional woman," he answered.

Lizzy wished he'd continued with the exceptions after her recovery. She missed the flowers, missed the lift they gave to her heart and the sense of kinship they brought her.

"Charming," said the dowager duchess coolly. "Now, Mr. Somerset, won't you be so kind as to fetch me Sir Randolph Beresford?"

Stuart tried to avoid both Lizzy and the dowager duchess. With Lizzy it was easier, as the host and hostess were not expected to socialize with each other. He also had hopes where the dowager duchess was concerned, thinking his interview with her had come and gone. He was mistaken: He was summoned back to her later that evening.

The dowager duchess rarely participated in, let alone initiated, small talk. But with him sitting next to her, she prated on about her plans for Christmas, her charities, her grandchildren—torrent upon torrent of inconsequential details. He had the sensation of having been fed too much laudanum, his awareness woolly, reluctant, his smiles stiff and hollow.

Then all of a sudden, she said, "I never knew anyone could cook like that."

And it was as if someone had thrown him overboard as he slept, the return of alertness abrupt and full of dread. He sat frozen, too stunned to gather himself properly, his reaction plainly exposed.

But the dowager duchess did not look at him. Her gaze was solely upon the sculpted handle of her walking stick. "It was ... it was as if my entire life, I'd never dined on anything but air and water until tonight."

Don't say anything, Stuart warned himself. *Don't say anything.* "I believe I felt the same the first time she cooked for me," he said.

The dowager duchess rubbed her thumb against the ebony of her walking stick's handle. It was shaped like the head of a dragon. "It made me remember—how it made me remember—all the best and worst days of my life. The day I met the late duke, the day of his funeral, the birth of my children, the ones who did not survive."

He did not believe he'd ever heard her speak of such personal matters. His astonishment served him well, for she looked at him, and smiled wryly at his expression.

"Do you know, Mr. Somerset, that my late husband's elder brother—the ninth duke—was married to my sister?"

Stuart shook his head. The ninth duke and his wife were long dead.

"She was much younger than me, beautiful, and clever. I'd always adored her. And my husband had a fierce admiration for his brother. For a time they were the most handsome and magnetic couple in Society— that was, for as long as they lived. They perished at sea together."

There was the beginning of a crack in her voice.

"They had three children, but only one who survived them—she and her governess had been traveling on a different vessel. My husband and I became her guardians and raised her with our own children, who loved her as much as we did."

Her voice now faltered audibly. "But we lost her when she was sixteen—and it devastated us. It devastates me to this day."

"I'm sorry," said Stuart. And he was, grief-stricken. Was life nothing but a continual bereavement, with a few moments of misguided happiness thrown in to keep hopes alive and the days bearable?

In another uncharacteristic move for her, the dowager duchess laid her gloved hand over his and gave a small squeeze. "I will take my leave of you now, Mr. Somerset," she said, rising. "It has been an evening I will not forget."

Lizzy thought it had gone well. And she said so to Stuart, after the drawing room emptied. "Although you must have a word with your cook. She simply cannot cow the guests into silence every time. I want my dinner table to be known as much for the conversation as for the food."

She flashed him a teasing smile. The smile he returned her was drained. "I'll let Madame Durant know."

Her father had gone to use the water closet; the two of them were alone in the drawing room. She went up to him and embraced him, laying her cheek against his lapel.

"Why did you stop sending me flowers?" she murmured.

"Now I'll have to remember that I sent you flowers," he said, his voice wooden. "I'm not sure that Her Grace quite believed it."

Her heart tightened. What did he mean by it?

"Why wouldn't Her Grace believe it?"

"She knows me too well."

"To think that you'd ever send flowers to me?"

"To think that I'd send flowers—and on such consistent basis—to a young lady before I'd decided to pursue her hand," he said. "But I'll be sure to send you flowers from now on, since they please you so well. Do you like roses? We've some interesting varietals at Fairleigh Park."

Her heart sank. There had not been a single rose in all the flowers she'd received in seventeen months. But the card that had accompanied the very first bouquet had said *The Office of Stuart Somerset, Esq.*, and so she'd assumed that the subsequent bouquets, which had no cards but which all came from the same florist, had been sent by order from his office too.

There were other people who worked in that office: three law clerks and Mr. Marsden.

I believe I deserve better from you.

But when she'd thanked Stuart in person for everything he'd sent her, he'd graciously acknowledged her gratitude. He certainly hadn't protested that he hadn't sent her anything.

Because he had. He'd sent a box of books on philosophy (she'd boasted to him of her new philosophical inclination during her affair with Henry), sundry tonics for listlessness and wasting (most of which sat in a cupboard, unopened), and some sheet music for the latest French songs, which he'd acquired when he'd visited Paris—considerate, proper gifts that would raise no one's brow coming from a gentleman friend of long acquaintance.

But she'd believed that he'd sent the flowers. And had made her decision to marry him based in no small part on that very assumption.

At the sound of her father's approaching footsteps in the corridor, she pulled away. "It's late. I should be going."

"You forgot to tell me whether you like roses," he reminded her, with an elaborate gentleness, so elaborate it was almost as if they were playing parts on a stage.

"Don't insist on it. We are almost married; we don't need such superfluous gestures."

"But you said only now you wished for flowers."

Not anymore. And not from him. So she pretended that she didn't hear him. "Ah, Papa, there you are. We must hurry before we wear out our welcome here."

Stuart looked at her oddly. But she'd already set her departure in motion. He shook hands with her father and, ever proper, bowed to her. He always adhered to the strictest rules of conduct before her father, but tonight his bow seemed to symbolize the distance between them, a distance that increasingly felt unbridgeable—and filled with everything she dared not, could not, and would not say to this man with whom she'd made the commitment of a lifetime.

The summons surprised Verity. She thanked Mr. Durbin and changed out of her nightgown into a clean dress, one that didn't smell too much of dinner. Her hair she pushed under a cap. She opened a jar of face cream that she'd made from beeswax and spermaceti and dabbed it across her cheeks, stopping only when she remembered that she'd already applied some earlier in the evening—and that she wasn't quite ready to show Mr. Somerset her face yet.

Her heart beat fast as she knocked on the door to the study. She couldn't imagine that it was merely a desire for conversation that had led to the summons. But what could he have wanted badly enough to send Mr. Durbin after her at this hour?

"Come in."

"La lumière, Monsieur," she reminded him.

"It would look odd," he replied.

Neither Mrs. Abercromby nor Mr. Durbin had gone up to bed yet and both might stop by the study to see if he had any needs before they retired for the night.

"I will stay by the window," he said. "I won't turn around."

Perhaps you should, she thought.

And perhaps she shouldn't have said "I love you" so precipitously. She did not regret it, for it was true. But things hardly needed to become more complicated between them.

She entered the study. The curtains were open. He stood with his back to her, in his shirtsleeves, his hands in the pockets of his dark evening trousers—a man two inches over six feet, wide-shouldered, and whipcord lean. She remembered the sinewed tightness of his body from their embrace in the basement and from their lovemaking the day before.

Lovemaking, she repeated the word in her head. The memory of the pleasure he'd brought her was a hot jolt in her abdomen.

"Why did you and Bertie never marry?"

The question came out of nowhere and disoriented her. "Gentlemen don't marry their cooks, sir."

"I was told he came close to marrying you."

Her heart stilled. "And who would tell you such a thing, sir?"

"The Dowager Duchess of Arlington," he said. "She was here tonight."

She swallowed. "I'm—I'm surprised that Her Grace would even know that I exist."

"Well, she does. And I've never known her to speak frivolously on any subject," he said.

He admired the dowager duchess, she suddenly realized. Of course he did. So did she, to this day. The dowager duchess had no flaws and no weaknesses. Her husband had worshipped her. Her children were paragons one and all. And though she'd never been beautiful, she had the presence and fierce handsomeness of a falcon.

"Was it true, then, that Bertie meant to marry you?"

She supposed Bertie had considered it seriously enough to undertake the trip to Lyndhurst Hall—without telling her where he was going. He would have gladly married the Lady Vera Drake and allied himself with the Arlingtons: a very satisfying nose-thumping at his brother, who had no hope of ever joining such a fine family.

"No," she said. "He never meant to marry me. He would not dream of marrying his cook, certainly not when Society and his brother would derive such amusement from it."

For a moment she thought he'd turn around. She tensed. But that moment passed and he stayed where he was. And said nothing. She clasped her hands in front of herself, behind herself, then finally wiped her perspiring palms on her dress.

When the silence distended too much, she blurted out, "I would like to thank you for the painting, sir. It is exquisite."

"No, it is I who should thank you. My breakfast meeting went swimmingly thanks to your croissants. I've never accomplished so much in so short a time with this particular collection of colleagues."

Her lips curved in pleasure. She became bolder. "And the dinner tonight, sir, did it go well also?"

She heard a low chuckle. "Yes, it went very well. My guests were speechless with wonder. In fact, Miss Bessler requests that they not be made quite so speechless in the future. She likes a bit of intelligent conversation to go with her dinner."

Her smile died. Frightful how easy it was for her to forget that he was pledged to another. When they were alone, the world seemed to begin and end with the two of them.

"I will see what I can do," she said carefully.

"Thank you," he said.

There was a byzantine pause, then he took a deep breath. "I asked you to come tonight because I wanted you to know that I've invited Michael Robbins to London. I expect him to arrive Saturday in time for dinner. We'll dine at home."

"Michael?" she blinked. "Michael will be here?"

"For a day or so, yes."

"I didn't know you knew him."

"We met while we were both at Fairleigh Park for Bertie's funeral."

"I see," she said. Michael had said nothing of it.

"There was a photograph of him in your room. I hope you'll be pleased to see him."

"You invited him . . . for me?"

"In my letter to him I told him that I'm considering assuming my late brother's role as his sponsor and would like to know him better," he said. "But yes, it was for you."

"Thank you," she said, half-stunned. "It's been a long time since anyone has taken so much trouble on my behalf."

"I want to do more for you. I want to lay the world at your feet."

Her heart pounded. *Turn around*, she wanted to say. *Turn around*. Instead, she was the one who couldn't bear the intensity of her emotions. She turned her back to him, afraid she would do something irredeemably stupid.

On the shelves before her was the frame that had

held the photograph of the Somerset brothers. But *that* photograph was no longer there. It had been replaced by another, also an old photograph, of two young boys gazing solemnly at the camera. Her eyes were immediately drawn to the boys' clasped hands, a gesture of such trust and solidarity that the passage of time had only amplified, not lessened, its power and intensity. And so it took her a long moment to realize that the boys in the frame were none other than the Somerset brothers.

An almost intolerable joy pierced her. If ever she sought a sign of forgiveness and renewal—it was here, right before her eyes. There was hope for them. There was.

"Why don't you, then?" she said. "Lay the world at my feet, that is."

❦

It had started to rain, wet threads that glinted a dull, ephemeral ocher in the light of a distant street lamp. A clarence rolled past, the coachman hunched under his coat. Rain streaked over the day's deposit of soot on the windowpanes, a watery distortion of Stuart's view.

The force of her hope was a knife in his chest. After all that had happened with Bertie, how could she still be so naïve, so unabashedly, heedlessly optimistic? And yet he wanted to hold on to her hope and carry it next to his heart. He wanted to do as she asked, and offer her everything that he'd waited so long to give.

"Michael departs Sunday afternoon. You will leave

London no later than Monday morning," he said. "You may take what time you need to collect and transfer your belongings from Fairleigh Park. But I expect you to have vacated your post before the end of the year."

The dead silence burned. He stared empty-eyed at the rain. *Remember this.* This was what happened when he chose to indulge himself at her expense. It was she who lost her position, her home, and her hard-won proximity to her son.

He forced himself to continue. "I understand you have been asked to contribute the wedding breakfast and the wedding cake. I will make your excuses to Miss Bessler."

"You are disgusted with me," she said, her voice pale, disembodied.

He shook his head. "No, I am in love with you. And it is wrong."

"It is not."

"It is. And you know it is. Were you Miss Bessler, would you tolerate it?"

"Were I Miss Bessler, I'd prefer a husband who isn't in love with someone else."

He sighed, his heart bound and shackled. "Miss Bessler and I have made a commitment to each other, a commitment that I cannot break without severe repercussions. But beyond that, we are also friends of long standing. And I will not hurt her to please myself."

She said nothing.

"I'm sorry." He had no defense against the accusations of his own conscience. "I will assume responsibility for Michael's education. I will provide opportunities for advancement when he is finished with university. I will—"

"No, thank you," she said quietly. "That will not be necessary."

"Let me help, please."

"You don't owe me anything. There were two of us in this delusion. You did nothing to me without my eager consent. I'm only sorry that—" She took a long breath. "No, I'm not sorry for anything. Such is love. And such is what happens to a cook who wants too much."

He turned around. But she had her back to him, her fingers clutched tight around the photograph of himself and Bertie. She seemed very small, her head bent, her shoulders heavy, her neck so vulnerable he could barely stop himself from taking her in his arms.

"I'm sorry, Verity."

"As am I," she said. She let go of the photograph and wiped her hand across her face. "Good-bye, Stuart."

Chapter Eighteen

On Saturday evening, after she finished cooking dinner, Verity carried a kettle of water up to the attic. She already had a tea service set out on her desk, and a tiered cake stand that she'd borrowed from Mrs. Abercromby. She stoked the fire and set the kettle to heat. Then she lifted the cloth she'd draped over the cake stand, to fuss some more with the display.

On the bottom tier were rectangles of mille-feuilles and rounds of bite-sized walnut tartlets. The next tier held chocolate-robed macaroons and small cream puffs. And at the very top, instead of the usual madeleines, she had a miniature quartet of boat-shaped coffee tarts.

It was a very pretty array, if she said so herself. She wondered if Michael would perceive it as a transparent effort on her part to cook her way into his heart again. On any other day he would have been right. But not to-day. Today she'd made one thing after another to keep herself in the kitchen—because when she was in the kitchen, she could clear her head and focus only on the task before her.

It was a dangerous panacea. To forget for a while her ruined heart was to shatter it anew each time she remembered. And each time she remembered, the pain was such that she scrambled for a way to get back into the kitchen, to cook something, anything, to forget it again, even if only for a few minutes, a quarter of an hour.

The water boiled. She made a cup of tea for herself. She hoped Michael came soon, or he would find her crying into her tea towel.

Such is love. And such is what happens to a cook who wants too much. Brave, serene, wise words, when she was anything but. She alternated between a longing to do Stuart bodily harm and an equally fierce desire to kidnap him and run off to some unknown country where they would never be found.

Her things she'd already packed. It was, she supposed, the best way to break the news to Michael. She wished she knew how he would react—he was unpredictable these days. She hoped for warmth and closeness, but she would settle for anything that wasn't undiluted apathy.

Footsteps in the corridor. She was at the door before she could tell herself to remain calm and wait inside. But it was only Mrs. Abercromby, a tallow in hand, yawning.

"Mrs. Abercromby, you are retiring for the night?" she said, as she was already standing outside her room.

"Yes, Madame."

"Mr. Somerset and the young man have retired too?"

"No, they have gone out—the young man said he wished to see London at night. Mr. Somerset told me and Mr. Durbin not to wait for them."

Gone out. Michael had *gone out*. But she'd made all his favorites. And he must know that she'd made all his favorites and would wait for him.

She bid good night to Mrs. Abercromby, returned to her room, and closed the door behind her. She supposed she should have known better. He was sixteen, not six, and petits fours and her company were no match against what London's nightlife had to offer.

She sat down and stared at the cake stand. Now she'd have to eat everything by herself. The first streaks of inevitable tears tumbled down her face. She reached for a coffee tart.

❧

Sometime in the middle of the night she opened her eyes. She'd heard a noise. But she closed her eyes and drifted back to sleep.

She didn't know how much more time passed before she bolted upright in her bed. She stuffed her feet into her house slippers and grabbed the robe she always kept by her side. In the dark she fumbled for a match to light her lantern.

The door to the room shared by Becky and Marjorie was wide open. Becky Porter was curled tight, cold from the draft despite her layers of blankets. She mumbled and shielded her eyes against the intrusion of light. The other cot in the room was empty.

"Is it morning, Madame?" Becky asked sleepily.

"Go back to sleep," said Verity. There was no need for both of them to look for Marjorie; at least, not until she was sure Marjorie had left the house.

At irregular intervals—sometimes days in a row, sometimes not for weeks or even months—the maids who shared Marjorie's room at Fairleigh Park would find mud or grass stains on the hem of Marjorie's nightgown. As Marjorie rarely injured herself, and seemed no worse for wear the next day, no one paid her sleepwalking much attention.

But in London Marjorie could disappear and never find her way back. It had been a worry at the back of Verity's mind. But she had refrained from locking Marjorie's door from the outside at night, for fear that the girl, thwarted, might open the window and leave that way instead.

She'd been told that sleepwalkers tended to do the same thing in their sleep as they did during the day. She quite doubted the accuracy of that—Marjorie's days at Fairleigh Park did not allow for leisurely strolls through the grounds, which seemed to be all she ever did in her night episodes—but in this instance, she hoped Dr. Sergeant was right.

Marjorie was not in the kitchen, nor was she in the servants' hall, or any other place in the basement. Verity's heart sank, until she remembered to check the service door. It was bolted from the inside—thank goodness.

There was still the possibility that Marjorie had let herself out through the front door. Verity went up to the ground floor, but she stopped long before she was in sight of the front door.

Michael's voice came from the morning parlor. He was singing. Or rather, crooning. "They walked 'til they reached his cottage and there they settled down, Young Willie of the royal blue and the lass of Swansea town."

The song was slightly off tune, but sweet and tender.

"Do you remember? You always liked that one," said Michael. "You are smiling. You do."

Verity stormed into the morning parlor. Michael, in his nightshirt and dressing gown, sat on a sofa. On that sofa with him, in nothing but her nightgown, her hair a loose braid falling over one shoulder, was Marjorie Flotty, her head resting against Michael's shoulder, one of her hands in his.

"What do you think you are doing?" Verity demanded.

Michael looked up, not at all surprised to see her—he must have heard her come up the steps and across the main hall. He placed a finger over his lips. "She's asleep."

Verity lowered her voice, but not the vehemence of her tone. "That is no excuse for you to lay so much as a finger on her. Or to keep her with you in an indecent state. You should have called either myself or the housekeeper when you realized she was up and about.

Now remove your hands from her person. I'm taking her back to her room."

Michael did nothing. If anything, his grip on Marjorie's hand tightened. "I've seen her like this many times."

Verity's jaw clenched. "What do you mean?"

"I found her one night, wandering in the woods behind the cottage. I took her back to the manor. Ever since then she's come to see me from time to time, when I'm on holiday from school. We are friends."

"Friends." There was a note of horror in her voice. Michael had just told her that he had been with Marjorie alone at night, *repeatedly*.

"It's not what you think," Michael said pointedly. "I care for her like a sister. There has never been anything inappropriate between us."

"I would not characterize your current intimacy as appropriate."

"And you would be an authority on proper conduct, Madame?" Michael said tightly.

Verity was speechless. As if to further incense her, Michael raised Marjorie's hand and rubbed her knuckles against his cheek. To Verity's astonishment, Marjorie smiled. In her waking hours, the girl's expression was invariably as blank as an unpainted wall, her eyes without even the sometimes intelligent look of a cow.

But now, with that smile on her face, with her eyes lowered, her lashes so long that they cast shadows on her cheeks, there was something almost wondrous about the sight of Marjorie, as if she'd been kissed by an angel, her whole person aglow in grace.

Michael gazed at her. "She is so beautiful when she smiles," he said wistfully.

Verity could scarcely conceive of it, her gorgeous, talented, eloquent Michael loving—even if it was only a brotherly love—Marjorie Flotty, the thick-witted scullery maid born and raised in the parish workhouse.

The same workhouse to which she used to take stews and buns from Fairleigh Park, Michael in tow. And wasn't it Michael who had first asked if she needed another scullery maid in her kitchen? The next day the workhouse had sent her Marjorie, and she hadn't had the heart to send the poor girl back.

Marjorie's smile suddenly vanished, like a candle flame blown out by the draft. The light on her face dimmed, and Verity was once again looking at the dull, uncomprehending serf from her kitchen.

"They told me she wasn't born this way. Something happened to her in that workhouse and wrecked her. And she had a stillborn baby when she was thirteen—they never found out who did it to her," Michael said. "She is my age. If my parents hadn't adopted me, they might have adopted her instead. And then none of these things would have happened to her."

Verity bit her lip, hard. "You mustn't think like this. You are not responsible for what happened to her."

"I know," he said. "But I can't help it."

Verity sighed. He was breaking her heart and she didn't know if her heart could take any more breaking.

"We'd better get her back to her room," she said. "It's awfully late and if she doesn't return soon, Becky might get up and start looking."

Michael touched Marjorie's hand to his cheek again, but this time she did not smile. "Come, Marjorie," he said gently. "You must go to your room now."

He pulled Marjorie to her feet and relinquished her hand to Verity, but he preceded them up the service stairs and waited in the corridor as Verity tucked an unresisting Marjorie into her cot.

Verity closed the door behind her and stood there, turning the handle of her lantern in her fingers. Shadow-faceted orange light churned across the walls.

"You want some tea?" she asked.

"I'd better go back to bed now," he said at the same time.

The silence was long and uneasy.

"Well," she said, "good night, then."

"Thank you for the madeleines you sent," he said. Then he turned and left.

❦

"You do Rugby great credit," said Stuart.

They stood on the platform of Euston Station, a few yards back from the track, where Michael's train already awaited, intermittently bellowing steam. Earlier in the day they'd attended church together, then dined at the Savoy Hotel, and Michael had impressed Stuart with his extraordinary grasp of the finer points of etiquette.

"Thank you, sir," said Michael, his satchel in hand. "I do hope that the good people to whom you introduced me will not resent you for it later, when they find out who I am."

Stuart had introduced Michael as the son of a very fine family from the vicinity of Fairleigh Park, on leave from Rugby to visit Stuart. At the worthy name of Rugby, the other worshippers simply assumed that "fine" meant old and established.

"I'm sure you noticed that I presented you only to those who asked that you be presented to them," he said.

Even so, there might be repercussions somewhere down the road. But that Michael did not need to know.

Michael shook his head slightly. "I did not notice that."

"Our situations are somewhat analogous in that I, too, must be careful of how I conduct myself," said Stuart.

The waiting train whistled, its long hiss forcing a pause in the conversation.

"Your mother has done well in her instruction of you," said Stuart, when the train had quieted to a more even rumble. "You will have no difficulties moving in Society."

"My mother has indeed done very well by me. But deportment I learned from Madame Durant," said Michael.

Each syllable of that name was a twist of pain. It took Stuart a little while to grasp what Michael had actually said.

"You learned how to present yourself in English Society from a French cook?"

Even as he spoke he saw that the only thing particularly French about her was her accent, an accent the authenticity of which he, a non-native speaker who had spent very little time south of Paris, could ill judge.

"Perhaps she is French—she's never admitted otherwise," said Michael. "But given that I learned to speak the Queen's English from her, I don't believe so."

"Madame Durant speaks the Queen's English," Stuart said slowly, almost dumbly.

"Better than—" Michael paused. "Better than I."

He'd meant to say "Better than you or I."

For some strange reason, Stuart thought of his Cinderella of that long-lost night, her syllables as polished as the facets of a diamond.

Haven't got any lizards in my kitchen.

Cinderella, too, had worked in a kitchen.

No, impossible. He would have known. He would have known her anywhere, under any conditions.

Would he really? From one night's acquaintance, after a span of more than ten years, in the dark, while they spoke in a different language?

"What else did you learn from Madame Durant, besides the Queen's English?" he asked, his tone suitably casual, even as his fingers clenched over his walking stick.

"Continental languages. And how to behave myself in every imaginable scenario involving a member of the peerage, his wife, and his daughters." Michael chortled. "I believe she once taught me how to give the direct cut. I used to call her the Duchess of Fairleigh Park."

She had splendid vowels, pure sounds that sang of family trees with roots going as far back as the Battle of Hastings.

No, he was fashioning similarities from thin air. Their bodies were entirely different. The colors of their hair were dissimilar.

Bodies changed. So did hair color. Bertie's hair had bleached lighter in the summer months and turned more brown than blond over winter.

She always said you were a good example for me.

That comment had always struck Stuart as odd. Now it was surpassing strange, in light of what she herself had said. *He usually spoke of you as if you were a horseman of the Apocalypse.* How had she managed to form such an elevated opinion of him in the face of *that*?

"Cinderella."

"Beg your pardon, sir?"

Stuart had no idea he'd spoken the name aloud. "Cinderella," he said. "A highborn young woman who ends up in the kitchen, subjected to menial tasks."

"I think I know that story," said Michael. "I imagine Mr. Bertram wasn't quite the prince she'd hoped for."

Tell me, what's Cinderella doing in town, without her coach, her footmen, or her ball gown?

It's obvious, isn't it? Something went terribly awry at the ball.

Ten years ago, according to the Dowager Duchess of Arlington, Bertie had come close to marrying Madame Durant, but never did. Ten years ago, his Cinderella materialized outside his town house, with a story of a prince turned to toad.

"Have you never asked her for her true identity?"

"More times than I can count. But she wouldn't tell me anything. And she never speaks of her life before she was seventeen."

When I was seventeen, I was at the end of my ropes. I had no money, no prospects, and no family, except a baby I loved desperately.

A loud gong went off in Stuart's head.

What happened to your baby?

He was adopted by wonderful people.

Stuart stared at the young man beside him. The resemblance was not great. But that meant little. He himself had not resembled his mother at all. "Before you left for Rugby, did you see Madame Durant on a regular basis?"

"Yes, sir. Almost every day."

He was adopted by wonderful people, but I still see him every day.

His heart slowed to a dull thud. What little blood reached his brain pulsed heavy and sluggish in his ears.

"If you don't mind, Robbins, may I ask you where were you born?"

Michael looked perturbed. Stuart realized that he'd thrown aside all pretense of casualness. He now treated Michael as if the boy were a key witness in the trial of the century.

"In London, sir, I was told."

"And how old were you when you were adopted?"

"When I was about six months old."

"You once told me that you remember fragments of your infancy. Do you perhaps recall a trip to the zoological garden?"

Michael jerked visibly. "No. But my mother keeps a box of mementos from when I was a baby. There is an admission ticket to the London Zoo in that box—and neither of my parents has ever visited London."

Stuart didn't know whether he was hot or cold. He seemed to have lost all sensation in his extremities. The train whistled, snapping him out of his paralysis. "That is a call for you to board," he said to Michael.

But Michael now stared at him as if he were the Ghost of Christmas Future. "Sir, could you tell me how you know about the zoo?"

Stuart shook his head. He didn't want to talk about it.

"Sir, please!" said Michael. "Please, I beg you."

Stuart turned his face away. "It was a story told to me by a woman I met many years ago. She took her infant son to the zoo and later gave him up for adoption."

"That was Madame Durant?"

"She did not give me her name."

"Would you recognize her if you saw her, sir?"

Stuart did not reply.

"That's her."

Stuart looked down to see an open locket thrust his way. A sudden, overwhelming reluctance seized him. He wanted to push the locket back. He'd built a Taj Mahal of a shrine around the memories of his Cinderella, and he liked it just fine. And so much time had passed. And sometimes truth did no one any good at all. And—

He looked; he couldn't help it. There were two photographs in the locket. One was of Michael and his parents. The other photograph was of Michael, four or five years younger than he was now, and a woman in her late twenties who wore a jaunty straw boater trimmed with a pair of Mercury wings.

He didn't recognize her immediately. Perhaps because her cheeks were no longer hollow, her chin less pointed. Perhaps because the image was in sepia and his memories of her were saturated in color—her eyes, blue as the shallow water surrounding a Maldives atoll; her lips, a rose in full bloom; her hair, the gold of the Incas. Perhaps because he'd always thought of her as infinitely vulnerable, whereas the woman in the photograph brimmed with confidence, her gaze direct and strong.

It was her eyes that broke the last of his resistance. He did not want to recognize her. He did not want to find out, at this too-late juncture, that Cinderella and Madame Durant were one and the same. But it was no use. He knew those eyes, knew them and loved them too well.

He handed the locket back to Michael. A perspiring porter, shoulders strained, pushed a cart of steamer trunks past them. A weary-looking young matron hurried two beribboned little girls along, promising puddings and new dollies at the end of the journey. An elegant older couple strolled by, the wife's hand on the husband's arm.

Stuart slowly realized that Michael was watching him, waiting for him to say something. What could he say? That for half of his adult life he'd been in love with a figment of his own imagination? That she could have found him and told him the truth at any point during the past ten years but chose not to? That once wasn't enough, she had to break him one more time?

"That's her," he said.

❦

"Here, Mademoiselle Porter, let me do it," said Verity.

She hadn't been able to sleep after the encounter with Michael and Marjorie. So she'd taken Marjorie's hat from her room, opened the package of the ribbons she'd bought for her girls for Christmas, and re-trimmed Marjorie's tatty hat. And then, to be fair, she'd done the same for Becky.

She took the hat ribbons, tied them smartly under Becky's chin, and turned Becky around to the mirror. Becky gave a delighted squeal. "Oh, thank you, Madame."

Marjorie, on the other hand, stared at her altered hat in bewilderment. "Where'd my hat go?"

"That *is* your hat, Marjorie," Becky said impatiently.

They'd gone over the point a dozen times already. "Madame made it pretty for you."

"It's not my hat," Marjorie said stubbornly.

Verity sighed. How could she have been so stupid? She should have known Marjorie would be distressed rather than pleased to find that a familiar belonging had mutated without warning. "You are right, Mademoiselle Flotty. It is a different hat. Your old one is at home. We are going home now; we'll find it there. Now put on the new hat so we may leave."

They'd already said their good-byes to the other servants earlier in the day, before the latter left to enjoy their Sunday off. Now they descended the service stairs and exited the empty house via the service entrance.

"Will we take the tube today, Madame?" asked Becky, as they climbed the steps that led up to Cambury Lane.

"The tube will have your dress and your hair smelling of motor grease, Mademoiselle Porter," said Verity. "We are better off taking th—"

Stuart. He was crossing the street, coming toward the house. Verity turned on the step, but Marjorie and Becky crowded the way down. She glanced back at him. He looked directly at her.

The contact of their eyes was a shock that crackled all the way to the soles of her feet. But the paralysis was hers and hers alone. He continued his stroll, the motion of his walking stick fluid and unhurried. There was no surprise on his face. There was nothing whatsoever.

Perhaps he hadn't recognized her. But even so, he should have inferred her identity—how many middle-aged women were likely to emerge from the service entrance to his house?

"Madame?" came Becky's hesitant voice.

Verity was blocking their way. She moved, on feet that felt like wet plaster, and reached the curb at the same time he did. Behind her, Becky curtsied, hissing at Marjorie to do the same.

"Madame, a minute of your time, if you would," he said without stopping.

In the next moment he had the door open and was waiting for her. She had no choice but to turn to her subordinates. "Wait here."

The last thing she saw was Becky's wide-open mouth as she entered the house through the door reserved for the master and his guests.

Chapter Nineteen

ait here," he said, the exact same words in the exact same tone as she'd used with Becky and Marjorie.

He climbed up the stairs and left her alone in the main hall. She set down her valise and took off her gloves—her palms perspired, she didn't want to ruin her best pair.

The longcase clock was still there, as was the Constable painting, which had been joined by a small, unsigned watercolor. Next to the Chippendale console table, there was now an upholstered Hepplewhite chair. She sat down on it. She shouldn't, of course, but her limbs didn't seem to want to continue to support her weight.

Time ticked away on the longcase clock, an otherwise pleasant, homey sound that made her heart palpitate. She wiped her palms on her skirt and thirsted after a good, stiff drink.

Would you like some whiskey? She wished he would offer her some.

She jumped to her feet when she heard him coming down the stairs. He arrived carrying a large, ornate box, the kind in which bespoke boots were delivered to the homes of prized patrons.

"This belongs to you," he said, in English.

"To me?" she replied uncertainly, in the same language.

She thought he clenched his teeth at the sound of her speech. He pushed the box toward her. "You may leave now."

The box was practically shoved into her chest. She took it and stumbled a step back. "Sir, what is it?"

"Something of yours," he said. "Good day, Madame."

She watched in disbelief as he turned and left the main hall. Somewhere beyond her view, the door to his study closed softly. Only scant days ago, he'd said he was in love with her. He'd once wanted to marry her. Did any of it count? Did their history not merit a few more words at their final farewell?

She set the box down on the console table and lifted the lid. Beneath a great undulation of gray tissue paper, she found not handsome bespoke boots, but a pair of rubber galoshes. They were not new—she could see places where the rubber had hardened and cracked in fine lines—but they were clean, the last speck of mud eradicated through laborious brushing. Though why anyone in his right mind would want a spotless pair of galoshes when come the next downpour they'd only—

She emitted a shriek, then clamped her hand over

her mouth. The galoshes were hers! Well, not really hers, since she'd borrowed them from Mr. Simmons, the head gardener—who had been then a new arrival at Fairleigh Park and not as disdainful toward her as many of the other servants had been after she stopped sharing Bertie's bed—and she'd had to buy him another pair when she'd forgotten his at Sumner House Inn.

But to Stuart the galoshes had been hers.

There were sachets of dried lemon peel and lavender inside them. Mr. Simmons would die laughing if he knew that his nasty old overboots had been so ardently venerated. She, too, had the urge to giggle—even as a drop of abrupt tear fell on the back of her hand.

She replaced the box lid, bent down, and kissed the box. Then she went to look for Stuart in his study.

❧

She didn't knock. One minute he was staring at the whiskey decanter, wondering if he had enough to render him comatose. The next minute she was there beside him, the hem of her skirt nearly brushing the side of his shoe.

"May I have some whiskey?" she asked.

The weight of her angular, sculptural English syllables made him shiver, as if a ghost had passed through him. He poured. He was a well-mannered man and it was not in him to refuse a politely worded request. His knuckles around the neck of the decanter, however, were quite white. He wondered if she noticed.

She didn't. She had stars in her eyes, eyes like the sky in paradise. He could scarcely look at her—she was exactly as he remembered and nothing as he remembered. Her eyes and her lips were every bit as extraordinary as his memories had insisted. But she was neither delicate nor frangible—a woman made not of porcelain but of steel.

"Thank you," she said. She took a sip. "It's the same whiskey, isn't it?"

He said nothing. He was caught between the two versions of the same woman, trying to reconcile the distant perfection of Cinderella to the robust reality of his cook. He couldn't.

"I've missed you so much," she murmured.

"Have you?"

"Every day. Every night."

He'd never thought of her eyes as seductive, but they were, God, they were. And she was far more sexually ripe than he was prepared to think of her. He turned his gaze away, and poured some whiskey for himself.

"You could have found me anytime."

"I didn't know how I would be received."

"That is a lie and you know it."

She shook her head. "How was I to know that you really loved me? That you didn't wake up in the morning and regret everything?"

He raised a full glass to his lips and finished half of it in one long swallow. The whiskey spilled down his chin. He wiped his jaw on his sleeve—a vulgar gesture that he never would even contemplate otherwise, but he was beyond caring. "That is not what I'm talking about. You deliberately withheld your identity from me. And you never came to me because you knew precisely how you would be received were you to tell the truth."

She blinked. "And how would I have been received?"

"As you were today," he said coldly. "I believe I've shown you the door already."

"Because I was Bertie's cook? I told you that I was a nobody."

"No, *I* was a nobody. You were known far and wide. The only British domestic servant more infamous was the queen's Scotsman."

"Really?" she said, her eyes downcast. "I didn't know my notoriety reached quite that extent."

"Believe me, it did." He downed what remained in his glass. "It did. Even people who didn't know Bertie from the Duke of Wellington thought you must be the best fuck since the invention of the mattress."

She blanched at his language.

"Ten years I squandered on you, ten years of faithful devotion. I spent money I swore I'd never touch on three sets of detectives, looking for you. I could have married. I could have had children. I needed not to have worshipped your sham idol. But I did, because you never had the decency to let me go. You let me cling to false memories and false hopes."

She had been leaning toward him, but now she leaned away, as if trying to accommodate the size of his anger. "I thought you would regret your offer in the morning," she said, her eyes sincere. "I thought you wouldn't want anything to do with me once the sun rose."

"You were right. I wouldn't have—*if only I knew*. And that was why you hid it from me, wasn't it? You wanted to preserve an illusion. You knew I wouldn't touch Verity Durant with a ten-foot pole, so you didn't give me a chance to repudiate her. Then you took that illusion home and left me to pick up the pieces."

"That's not true. I never meant to—"

"It doesn't matter what you meant or did not mean to do. I'm sure you concocted all sorts of lovely and noble excuses and I'm sure you wholeheartedly believe in each one of them. But this is *what you did*—you took that illusion home and left me to pick up the pieces."

"I'm sorry!"

"*You* are sorry? Ten years I waited for you to come back. I revered your galoshes as if they were splinters of the One True Cross. I dropped good money into every church coffer I ever came across on the off chance that there is a God and that he could be bribed into protecting you. And when I finally moved on, you had the gall to come and make me fall in love with you again, knowing perfectly well that there was never any other possible outcome except more misery!"

"I'm sorry. I didn't mean to—"

He didn't know what happened. But suddenly the whiskey glass was no longer in his hand. It hurtled across the room and shattered against the mantel. She flinched at the sound, her face as colorless as skimmed milk.

He dragged in a harsh breath. "If you didn't mean

to, you'd have left right after Bertie's funeral. If you didn't mean to, you'd have shown yourself. If you didn't mean to, you wouldn't have in the end. Now please leave. And go far away."

"Stuart—"

"I don't recall ever giving you permission to use my Christian name. Refrain from such liberties."

She gazed at him a long time, with stubborn hope. And then that hope began to die little by little, until he could stand it no more. He turned away. "Go."

She moved, then paused by the door, still waiting for him to change his mind. He did not look her way. She let herself out of the study. Her footfalls in the corridor were agonizingly slow, as if she were the Little Mermaid emerged from the sea, and every step was walking on knives.

At long last the front door opened and closed. He shut his eyes. He'd always associated her return with an extravagant happiness, the kind promised by fairy tales to keep children from despairing before life's indiscriminate hardships. But he'd believed it, moondust and starlight and all.

It was not to be.

They did not live happily ever after.

The end.

❦

31 Baker Street was an unprepossessing two-bay, brown-brick house, with dormant window boxes affixed to each of its six windows. The six windows were

evenly divided in number between the three upper stories, in size they became progressively more squat as Lizzy tilted her head back farther.

She took a deep breath and knocked on the front door, the paint of which had faded from black to a darkish gray. Ever since the night of Stuart's dinner she'd been desperate to see Mr. Marsden in person, but they had no more meetings scheduled, and this—Sunday afternoon, with her father napping and the servants away from the house—was the earliest opportunity she had to visit him.

Five weeks and scant days to her wedding—what an awful time to be thinking that she might have made a grave mistake.

The door opened with surprising speed, and out spilled a muted but still hearty burst of masculine laughter. Lizzy froze—or she might have turned around and fled.

"Good afternoon, miss," said the small, neat woman who had opened the door, her voice calm and friendly. "Mr. Todd is not home this afternoon. But I will give your card to him if you leave one with me."

Mr. Todd was the calligraphist who shared the house with Mr. Marsden. And it was from his card that she knew their address. "I'm not here to see Mr. Todd, but Mr. Marsden."

The woman, presumably the landlady, looked faintly surprised. "Certainly, miss. Mr. Marsden is home. I will take your card to him."

The landlady went up a set of narrow, squeaky stairs. Lizzy looked about her. She supposed the inside of the house could still be described as respectable, but genteel it wasn't. The bits of plaster braids on the ceiling showed signs of a diligent and ongoing battle against London's soot and grime, a battle that promised no eventual victory. The air smelled of linseed oil and boot black. Through a door that had been left ajar, Lizzy had a view into the landlady's cramped sitting room, where a skinny tabby napped on a rocking chair upholstered in faded pink chintz.

On the next floor the hum of conversation subsided. She felt a bigger knot forming in her belly. She'd come at a bad time, but she must speak to him, and she'd already waited too long.

The landlady reappeared. "Follow me, please."

She was led into a small but surprisingly bright and cheerful drawing room, cheerful because of the pale cornsilk wallpaper on which floated whimsical balloons and airships. There were three men in the room. Mr. Marsden, pleasure writ plain on his face, immediatley came forward to shake her hand, alleviating her fears of an awkward entry.

"Miss Bessler, what a delight to see you. Allow me to present Mr. Matthew Marsden, my brother, and Mr. Moore, a good friend of ours. Gentlemen, this is Miss Bessler, the most beautiful lady in all of London."

Matthew Marsden was an inch or so taller than his brother, and would have been startlingly handsome had he been standing next to anyone but Will Marsden. Mr. Moore wasn't anywhere near as striking as the Marsden brothers, but he had a good-natured face.

"Mr. Marsden, you are too kind," she protested. "By most accounts, I'm only the third most beautiful woman in London."

Mr. Marsden laughed. "Well then, 'most accounts' must be sensationally misguided. Please, Miss Bessler, have a seat."

She did, with a surge of renewed anxiety that he would now politely inquire into what had brought her to his house. He did nothing of the sort.

"We have been gossiping, Miss Bessler," he said. "Or at least trying to. My brother and Mr. Moore are in England after a two-year absence and hungry for all the latest and naughtiest stories. Alas, they have been quite disappointed with my store of knowledge—I no longer move in Society as I used to. Dare we turn to you for a better supply of anecdotes?"

"Well," she said, relaxing. "I did run into Ladies Avery and Somersby week before last."

Lady Avery and Lady Somersby were the leading chroniclers of Society's passions and follies. They would not dream of sharing anything too juicy with an unmarried young woman, but Lizzy had received information on the courtship-in-progress of several gentlemen known to the Marsden brothers and Mr. Moore and for the next half hour they discussed the pursuits of lucre, power, and privilege that occurred along the path to the altar.

"Oh, and I almost forgot, the younger Mr. Fonteyn is courting Lady Barnaby," added Lizzy.

"Lady Barnaby, as in Sir Evelyn Barnaby's widow?"

cried Mr. Moore. "But she must be twenty years Fonteyn's senior."

"And twenty thousand pounds richer too," said Lizzy. "There is no such thing as a wealthy woman who is too old."

"I think you would fare far better with Sir Evelyn's widow than Fonteyn," said Matthew Marsden to his brother.

"What, and give up poverty?" Mr. Marsden laughed. "Never!"

"Well, there is something to be said about being poor but independent and obliged to no one," said Mr. Moore.

"Then again, after one's elderly bride gives up the ghost, one can be rich *and* independent and obliged to no one," Lizzy pointed out.

"An enviable state of being," Mr. Marsden said. "But it is my firm belief that a man should whore himself out only for necessities, never luxuries."

Matthew Marsden and Mr. Moore both whistled. Lizzy raised an arch brow. "And what do you consider necessities, Mr. Marsden?"

"Coal, Camembert, wine, books, and"—he tossed her a mischievous look—"occasional tickets to symphonic concerts."

"Oh, yes," said Matthew Marsden earnestly. "I agree wholeheartedly. Symphonic concerts are an absolute necessity in life. There were years when I pined daily for the chance of one."

Lizzy spat out her tea, laughing. Three sets of handkerchiefs immediately appeared before her, along with puzzled glances from Matthew Marsden and Mr. Moore. Mr. Marsden laughed silently, his shoulders shaking. She took his handkerchief and wiped herself, her mirth too great to be embarrassed.

"What's so funny?" demanded Matthew Marsden.

"I'll tell you later," said his elder brother. "Now the two of you had best hurry or you'll be late for tea at Miss Moore's."

Mr. Moore jumped up. "My aunt does hate unpunctuality. Quickly, for the sake of my place in her will."

Everyone laughed. Matthew Marsden and Mr. Moore shook hands warmly with Lizzy and then ran down the steps like a stampede of buffalos.

She remained on her feet after the leave-taking. Mr. Marsden, after casting a quiet glance at her, moved to the window. The afternoon's sun was about to sink beneath the roof of the opposite houses. One last ray managed the angle, penetrated the panes, and embraced him in a blaze of light. His hair shone as if it had been painted by Vermeer, strand by strand.

"I like your brother. He seems a very good sort of man," Lizzy said, her voice tentative now that she was alone with him. She had been alone with him on other occasions, but somehow, in his drawing room, alone felt more completely alone.

"Matthew is an angel," he answered.

"And is Mr. Moore . . . ?"

"No, Mr. Moore is a friend. The one Matthew loved passed away three months ago—he is still in mourning."

"Oh. I didn't realize."

"Matthew is a very private person. On a par with Mr. Somerset, I would say."

The mention of her fiancé's name brought back reality—and the purpose of her visit. She'd better get to it—on Sunday afternoons the servants had leave and absented themselves from the house, but her father would wake up from his nap soon enough and wonder where she'd gone unaccompanied.

"Should I ring for more tea?" asked Mr. Marsden.

She shook her head. Since nothing could serve as a proper preliminary to the sort of questions she intended to ask, she skipped the preamble altogether. "Was it you who sent me flowers when I was unwell?"

He walked to the table and poured cold tea into a cup, the clear, umber fluid arcing silver in the light that seemed to have followed him. "It took you this long to realize?"

"It did. Your demeanor did not lead me to suspect you."

"It's always easier to pretend not to care."

Then it meant he did care. Her heart soared—and crashed at the same time. God, five weeks to her wedding. "I thought it was Mr. Somerset."

"You are blind, Miss Bessler."

"Yes, I was." His wet handkerchief she'd wadded and discarded on the tea table. Now she opened it and pulled the corners straight. "So . . . you have formed an attachment to me."

"Is that what the English call the desire for symphonic concerts at all hours of the day with someone?"

She reached for the cold tea he'd poured and drank it. "You are English yourself. You know very well that is indeed what we call it."

"All right, then. I have formed an attachment to you that has lasted beyond all reasonable expectations to the contrary. It is extraordinarily unruly and bothersome. Have you any advice on how this condition may be ameliorated?"

She didn't want it ameliorated. "Why didn't you come to me sooner?"

"When I thought that you'd have more interest in a bosom friend than a man?"

"You are not very careful in choosing to whom you form your attachments, are you, Mr. Marsden?"

"Attachments are what they are. We but find reasons to justify them."

"What was your reason, then, all the while you still thought that I was a follower of Sappho?"

"That Madame Belleau could be wrong."

"Why didn't you ask me?"

"I didn't want to find out that she was right. But then, when it seemed that you might marry Mr. Somerset, I couldn't stop myself—an impulse I've regretted very much since."

She looked up sharply. "Why? You wanted her to be wrong. You know now that she was wrong."

"Yes, but it would have been easier to accept your marriage to Mr. Somerset had I believed otherwise."

"So that's why you declared yourself at last. Because you could no longer stand the thought of my marrying Mr. Somerset."

He picked up a coconut biscuit and then set it down again. A fraction of a second later he was standing before her, as close as if they were about to start a waltz—which was far too close for any kind of normal interaction. But she did not move away.

Instead she studied his silver stick pin, which she'd first thought entirely plain, but which at this proximity resolved itself to be hammered in the shape of a tulip. She was beginning to like the way he dressed, with little fancies and eccentricities. Or sometimes with a big splash of whimsy, like the sail-rigged airships on his wallpaper.

He touched a thumb to her cheek, the sensation like that of coming into contact with a creature of the wilderness—a stag perhaps—nothing fearful, but unfamiliar and unpredictable. "Does your presence here mean what I think it means?"

His hand slid down, and now nestled next to her lips, as if waiting for her to speak to feel the vibration. Her breath came in shallower.

"I'm not sure what you think it means. I came to find out about the flowers."

"For that you could have sent me a note. You needn't risk coming here by yourself."

His other hand settled behind her neck, warm and strong and intent.

"It's not that risky coming here," she said, her voice reduced to a whisper.

"No?"

At last he kissed her.

The moment their lips touched she suddenly had a

better understanding of attachment, of what it meant to desire symphonic concerts at all hours of the day with someone. It wasn't his hunger that surprised her—she'd sensed it all along, she supposed—but her own. She had enjoyed the intimate act with Henry, but she had never wanted it to this extent. She wanted Mr. Marsden—Will. She wanted to yank out his beautiful antique silver stick pin and toss it across the room because it was in the way. She wanted to use him, to astonish him, to own him.

She pulled away.

"I can't do this to Mr. Somerset."

"Then tell him you cannot marry him."

"And then what? Marry you?"

"It would be a challenge—you are not the easiest of women, as I'm sure you know. But I'm game."

"*You* are game?" she cried. "You've nothing to lose. I don't want poverty to be my lot. My pride may not survive it."

"Then you must do what's best for your pride."

She was startled. "Pardon?"

"I won't always be a secretary, but most likely I will not have a country seat in this lifetime. And I may not ever have a house in Belgravia. So if your pride is the most important thing to you, you should marry Mr. Somerset and enjoy everything that he can give you," he said, his tone perfectly serious.

"You are supposed to persuade me to see things from *your* perspective."

"I don't want you to be persuaded. I want the decision to come from you and you alone."

She walked away to the far corner of the room—not very far—and turned around before her knees hit a canterbury full of books and periodicals. "You understand that my other choice is to do nothing: I only need to follow the course that has already been laid out and paid for."

He smiled slightly. "I was there planning your wedding, if you'll recall. It promises to be exceptional. Much time, effort, and money would be wasted were you to walk away from it. Moreover, Mr. Somerset could very well become prime minister someday: There will be women lined up to take your place, should you choose to vacate it."

Her hands lifted in a gesture of futility. "You are not helping at all."

"I'm not helping *me* at all. I'm helping you as well as I know how." He approached her in her corner and traced her eyebrow with the tip of a finger, a touch that shocked her with its intimacy. "You are a hardheaded woman, Lizzy. You want all that glitters. You want London at your feet. And yet in here," he rested the back of his hand briefly against her heart, "are the inconvenient desires of a romantic."

"I thought I was a cynic."

"As am I. And there is no worse fate than for a cynic to fall in love and realize that while cynicism is a fine shield against shallower emotions, it is no use at all against love."

"I don't know that I'm capable of such love," she said mutinously.

"I don't know that you are either, which makes me worried for myself."

She gasped. "That is a very fine thing to say to the woman you love."

"It's not an insult. Marrying down goes against the instinct of most women of our class. I cannot promise you perfect happiness: It doesn't exist. We'll find each other and our life together unsatisfactory at times. There will be days when you'll envy the new Mrs. Somerset and wish you'd chosen differently. And I don't know whether you've depth and wisdom enough to get past the inevitable second thoughts that will arise—possibly again and again."

She shook her head in exasperation. "You are literally pushing me back into the arms of my fiancé. Do you have anything to say for yourself, any enticement for me at all? Would it be nothing but doom and gloom if I were to marry you?"

"Enticements: Hmm." His thumb indented her lower lip. "Well, many symphonic concerts, to start. And that is something you will not get from Mr. Somerset—I don't think his mind leans much toward matters of the flesh."

"Perhaps mine does not either, after Henry Franklin."

He tilted his head toward her and licked her where his thumb had been, and it felt like a lick between her thighs. Her exhalation was startled—and plainly pleasured.

"Are you sure about that?" he murmured.

She chuckled, to let out some of the tension building in her body. "Perhaps not. But I don't think a marriage can be based on carnal desires alone. What else do you have to offer me?"

He kissed her on the lips. "A respect for your mind." He kissed her again. "As much freedom as I would give myself." He kissed her one more time. "And a surpassing interest in the lovely, fascinating old woman you will become one day."

Her heart shook at both his kisses and his words. She was suddenly afraid that she might tell him right this moment that she'd forsake all for him. She turned around and left running.

❧

Stuart drank steadily. He hadn't moved since she left, except to replenish his glass again and again.

He'd always disdained the numbness that came from a bottle—his mother in a drunken stupor in Torquay had been one of his least cherished memories—but today that numbness couldn't come fast enough. How many glasses had he downed? Five? Seven? Why, then, when he breathed, did it still feel as if his lungs had been punctured?

The doorbell rang. The glass slipped from his hand and broke at his feet.

How long had she been gone? How did one keep track of time in Hell? He might have been in the study for days already, drinking himself into a state. But his servants hadn't returned to gaze aghast upon him yet, so it couldn't have been too long.

He reached for another glass and poured it half full. The doorbell rang again. He almost dropped the glass again.

Was it her? And what would he do if it was her? Banishing her once had cost him everything he had. He had not honor, righteousness, or strength enough to do it again. He had not even enough rage left—the bleakness in his head had drained him of the mental vigor required for the care and feeding of anger.

He raised the glass and tossed back its contents. He wouldn't answer the door. She needed to understand that it wasn't some passing consternation on his part that had led to her exile, but a carefully considered decision of principle. There was no place for her in his life. There had never been any place for her in his life. Why couldn't she see it? Why couldn't she leave him alone so that his insides could die in peace?

He crossed the room, tripping and nearly falling on the shard-strewn carpet, to stare at the clock on the mantel—he could no longer make out the hands on his watch. The second hand of the mantel clock moved at the speed of a crippled snail. It crawled. It shuffled. He could swear at one point it took a nap. Bright-eyed infants could have grown up, married, and aged into witless dotards in the time it took to circumnavigate the clock; hell, dynasties could have risen and collapsed.

There now, he made it through one minute without rushing out to open the door for her—he no longer needed to grip the mantel so tightly. He'd make it through another minute, and then another. She would get the point eventually, that his mind was firmly made up, that nothing could dissuade him from his set course.

The bell clanged again. His heart seized. He spun around—and fell, onto a splinter of agony. He got to his feet, pulled a piece of glass from his knee, and ran. He banged his shoulder on the doorjamb of the study, banged his other shoulder on the longcase clock, and almost smacked his face into the door.

Just remember, close the door before you kiss her.

He yanked open the door, then slammed it shut in the next instant, his heart as shattered as the broken glasses in his study.

It was not her, but Mrs. Abercromby, who must have forgotten her keys. And he had just put the lie to all his principles, every last one of them.

Chapter Twenty

Verity found Michael smoking on the front stoop of the gamekeeper's cottage. He wore an old tweed jacket that was both too loose and too short for him, mud-splattered boots, and a wool cap that rode low on his brow. He smoked not with a gentleman's elegance, but with a laborer's impatience, the cigarette pinched between his thumb and index finger, its tip reddening with each restless inhalation.

Michael usually returned to Fairleigh Park by the middle of December. But this time he had been invited to a classmate's home for a week after the end of term. And had arrived only the evening before.

"Been out working?"

Michael looked up, surprised—he must have been distracted; she'd walked up to him and he'd not seen her. "Shot some vermin," he answered. He did not try to hide the cigarette. Instead, he reached into his pocket and offered her one.

She took it. She'd never smoked in front of him, but

she wasn't surprised that he knew her little vice. "Thank you. I'll have it later."

He took one last deep suck. Getting off the stoop, he dropped the fag end where he'd dropped the ashes, and kicked some fresh snow on top of it. He climbed back up and held open the door for her. "Come inside?"

She preceded him into the parlor. "Your parents resting?"

The Robbinses took naps early in the afternoon. She preferred to visit Michael at that time, to have him to herself, rather than interacting under his parents' somewhat uneasy watch. The Robbinses were wonderful people. But Verity baffled and alarmed them. They weren't sure what to make of her or what seemed to them their son's continued closeness to her.

"They won't be down for another three quarters of an hour," Michael answered. "Have a seat. I'll get us some water."

She cleared newspapers and a pile of Mrs. Robbins's knitting from the table. He returned with a small steel kettle—ducking his head so as not to conk it on the low lintel—and set the kettle over a spirit lamp.

"I brought some tuiles—almond biscuits. You'll like them," said Verity.

Madeleines were his favorites but she couldn't bear to make madeleines now, not even for him. It had been a fortnight and a day since she left London, but the pain hadn't let up at all—pain and regret and occasional outbreaks of angry, insensate hope that made everything even worse.

"Thank you," he said. He took off his cap and hung it on a coat tree by the door. "I like everything you cook except liver."

She arched an eyebrow. "Insulting my foie gras again, aren't you?"

Wisely he did not respond to that. Instead, they spoke of her back, his chores, and Mrs. Robbins's most recent bout of culinary disaster. Michael toyed with his pocketknife as he answered her questions. She observed his hands, as she always did. No bruises, no scrapes—no recent fights.

When the kettle sang she made tea and served the tuiles on a plate. Michael ate a dozen in a row, one after another. She watched him eat. She used to watch him for hours on end, as he played and read and talked himself through games he'd invented with sticks and rocks.

He glanced at her. She looked away. When he'd been a child, she'd badly wanted him to grow up and be the kind of man she hadn't had the good fortune to marry. Now she wished time hadn't gone by so fast, that he still reached only to her waist, and that she could hold him close and he would be content to remain in her embrace.

"I heard you were invited to a classmate's place. Did you enjoy your visit?"

He shrugged. "You don't refuse an invitation to Buckingham Palace, even if you'd rather have your tonsils removed than sit down with the queen for tea."

"Was it that bad? I thought the Baldwins were a good lot."

"I didn't go to the Baldwins'. I went to the Cove-Radcliffs'."

The tuile in Verity's hands broke in two. The Countess of Cove-Radcliff was the Dowager Duchess of Arlington's eldest daughter. "I didn't know you were acquainted with anyone from that clan."

"Nigel Granville worked with me on the newspaper this year. To be sure, I didn't expect an invitation from him and he seemed almost embarrassed to be inviting me. But he did, and I went."

"His sisters, did they treat you well?"

"How do you know he has sisters?"

"They always do, don't they?"

Michael shrugged again. "They were perfectly decent to me. But enough about me, what is going on between you and Mr. Somerset?"

Miraculously she did not spill her tea all over the small table. That was another trouble with such elderly children. They saw and heard far too much. She looked to make sure the door to the parlor was firmly closed before taking refuge in the present tense he'd employed.

"Nothing."

She half despised herself for not having left yet. She'd handed in her resignation letter but had put her last day as the thirty-first of December—as much time as he'd allowed her. She wanted to spend these last ten or so days she had with Michael. But that wasn't the only reason: If she was no longer at Fairleigh Park, how could she stomp all over Stuart and heave him to the curb as he'd done to her, should he turn up begging for forgiveness?

"Nothing now, or nothing ever?" asked the boy. "I showed him a photograph of you and he turned the color of death."

So that was what had happened. By the time Stuart came back to 26 Cambury Lane, he'd already known what he was going to do with her.

"Mr. Somerset and I met once before, ten years ago. I was set upon in London and he came to my rescue."

"Really? I'd have thought, judging by his reaction, that there was more to it than that," Michael said, coolly alleging scandalous behavior on her part.

"Well, one thing led to another and before I knew it, Mr. Somerset proposed to me."

Michael choked on his tea. "He did what?"

Verity smiled a little and shook her head inwardly: Michael wasn't surprised that she might have slept with yet another employer, but he was shocked that someone had offered her marriage.

"He asked me to marry him."

"Then why in the name of all that's sane and proper didn't you marry him then?"

"He didn't know that I was his brother's cook," she said. "I left without telling him. And when he found out—when you showed him my photograph—he was very displeased about it. He threw me out of his town house and discontinued my employment. I am to evacuate Fairleigh Park by the end of the year."

Michael's expression changed. "You are really leaving?"

"I should have left after Mr. Bertram's funeral. But yes, I'm leaving."

Michael poured himself another cup of tea. He drank it, sip by sip, until there was nothing left. "Is there any chance you would grace me with the truth before you left?" he said.

Between them, there was only one truth that mattered.

She looked down into her palms, a broken piece of tuile in each one. "Must we go through this again?"

"I remember you, you know, from when I was a baby. I remember you feeding me from a bottle. And you used to wear a white brooch on your bodice. I would always try to pull at it when I was drinking from the bottle. And one day the brooch was gone, and I was terribly upset about it. I wouldn't drink from the bottle. I kept trying to find the brooch. You cried and cried."

She stared at him. He had described a day several weeks before she took him to the zoo. The brooch had belonged to her mother, a cameo brooch which she'd had to sell, for far less than it was worth, because she had been frightened and witless and had not known the first thing about bargaining.

He couldn't have been more than four months old at the time.

"Why did you never tell me this?" she whispered.

"There are things I do not tell you, just as there are things you do not tell me." He looked at her. "Would you admit it now? Would you at least admit it?"

She shook her head, still in shock.

His face hardened. "Even Mr. Somerset's story confirmed it. He said that you'd once taken me to the zoo, and there is that zoo ticket in Mum's box that has never been accounted for. How can you still deny it?"

"I told you already, Michael, the last time you asked. There was nothing I could tell you about your birth mother then. There is nothing I can tell you about her now."

His eyes simmered in anger. "Then at least have the decency to tell me why you won't acknowledge me. It's not as if I turned out ugly, or stupid, or disgusting."

"Michael, please keep your voice down. You'll wake up your parents." She kept her own voice to a hoarse whisper.

"I don't care. You owe me this. If Mr. Somerset won't marry you, then why must you still keep me a secret?"

"Mr. Somerset has nothing to do with any of this."

"Then tell me why!"

The cottage practically shook with his bellow. Verity stared at him, shocked at his vehemence, at the possibility, no matter how remote, of violence inside him.

"I can't."

He smashed the heel of his fist against the parlor door. And then took two startled steps back when a gentle, almost timid knock came at the door.

Mrs. Robbins entered the parlor and suddenly it was very crowded.

"I'm sorry, ma'am," Michael immediately said. "Did I wake you up?"

Whenever she saw Michael with Mrs. Robbins, Verity was always filled with envy. He treated his adoptive mother with a care that was now almost entirely absent from his dealings with her. She rose to her feet. "Mrs. Robbins, I apologize for the ruckus we made. I'll see myself out now."

"No, please don't go." Mrs. Robbins turned to Michael. "I was the one who made Madame promise that she would not tell you the truth."

Michael paled. He stared at Mrs. Robbins as if he did not know her.

Mrs. Robbins blinked rapidly, her face lined and gaunt. "We are elderly, homely, and unsophisticated, whereas Madame is young, beautiful, and refined. I was afraid you would not want us as your parents if you knew. I didn't realize that by keeping the truth from you I'd cause you such pain. I'm sorry."

Michael said nothing.

Mrs. Robbins patted him gingerly on the arm. "I'll go up and give you two some privacy."

There was a long silence after the door closed behind Mrs. Robbins.

"How did she know?" Michael finally asked.

"She suspected, not long after I came here—in those days, as soon as she turned her back, you'd come to visit me." Verity sighed. "I don't think she expected her suspicion to be quite so accurate, though. She was shocked when I admitted to it—and a bit panicked. She loved you so, and she was terrified I might take you away from her."

"I'm sorry," said Michael blankly. "I was quite rude."

"Yes, you were. I'm hurt that you'd think I would ever deny you the truth so I could marry better, when—" When all of her life's choices had revolved around him. "But it's all right. In your place, I would want to know too."

"I'm sorry," Michael said again. He plucked at a loose thread on his sleeve. "So you *are* my mother?"

He sounded shocked, for all that he'd insisted he knew all along.

"For a very short while, for as long as I could hold on to you."

He went to the cabinet where Mr. Robbins kept a bottle of gin and poured directly into his teacup.

"Can you tell me anything about my father?" He turned around.

She sat down again. "His name was Benjamin Applewood. He was a groom who worked in the stables at the house where I grew up. A very sweet, unassuming man."

"*Was.*" Michael took a gulp from the teacup. "He is dead?"

"He died shortly before you were born, from a fever of the blood."

They had gone to Southampton to buy passages to America. But Ben's savings had been stolen almost as soon as they got off the train—he'd never been farther afield than Tonbridge, and the chaos and criminality of the city had been beyond him. Neither of them had

had any notion that money needed to be sewn into undergarments or concealed underfoot in their shoes.

Third-class train tickets cost only pennies. They sold the ivory buttons from her dress, bought two tickets, and went to London, where Ben said his foster brother lived. They never located the foster brother, but Ben found work at a place that hired out carriages. They lived at Jacob's Island, an unsavory rookery south of the Thames, hoping to save up enough money, with Verity doing her utmost to pretend that it was just the scary part of the fairy tale she was living through—that her happily-ever-after was but another day, another week, another kiss away.

Ben's death had stripped the last bit of romance from life in the outside world. As long as he had been there, she could ignore that she lived at the edge of a slum in a mice-infested room. But bereft of his income and his protection, she became utterly alone, without a single skill that could earn her a legitimate penny.

"Were you married?"

The trace of hope in Michael's voice made her heart hurt. "I'm sorry. We didn't have the money to marry. We thought we'd have a proper wedding once we were settled and prosperous in America."

Michael took more from the teacup. "My father's family, do they know about me?"

She shook her head. "He was an orphan who was fostered with a clergyman for a while. He came into my family's employ when he was thirteen, after the clergyman passed away."

"What about your family, do *they* know about me?"

He must have seen the darkening of her expression. "They do, don't they?"

"Some of them," she said.

"Was it because of me that you had to leave your family?"

"Yes and no. Once it was discovered that I was with child, I was taken away and told that I'd spend the rest of my life under lock and key. It was a future that gave me nightmares. So when your father came to rescue me, I went quite willingly."

He looked at her. Then he drained his cup and reached toward the bottle of gin again.

"Michael, that's enough."

To her shock, after a moment of hesitation, he put the bottle of gin back in the cupboard. "At school the rumor has always been that I'm a Very Important Man's bastard—that's why they tolerate me, I suppose. I wonder what people would say if they knew the truth."

"I don't believe the worth of a man lies solely in his parentage, or even mostly. Of course it is enviable to know with perfect confidence where you belong from the very beginning, but it's not so terrible to find your own place."

"You say that because you know where *you* came from."

"A place that I can never go back to. I'm still searching for my place, like you."

He made no response for long seconds. Then he nodded slowly.

She rose. It was time for her to leave: Mrs. Robbins

would be anxious to talk to him. "Come to the Servants' Ball tonight. I'll have a good cold supper buffet laid out. It will be a good time."

"I don't know. Some of the servants look at me funny."

"Some of the servants have always looked at me funny, doesn't stop me from going every year. Come and bring your mum. She'll enjoy playing on a proper piano—Mr. Somerset gave one to the staff for Christmas, they uncrated it just this morning."

"I'll ask her if she wants to go."

"And I'll need someone to help me keep an eye on Marjorie, of course. I'm going to be too busy dancing and flirting."

"Don't talk like that. You are too old for it."

She gave him a hard whack across the chest. "We'll see how ancient you feel when you are thirty-three."

He caught her hand and held it. She looked at him and her chest tightened. Such a hard life she had chosen for him, pushing him always to rise above his humble station, to find a place among people who'd rather not give him a place. And he'd never complained.

She embraced him. In her arms he was all skeleton, long, strong bones under worsted wool. "Come and see me sometime in the evenings, before I go."

"I will," he said. And hugged her back.

❦

The panic was sudden and complete.

One minute Stuart was calmly discussing the

proposed Customs and Inland Revenue Act with the Chancellor of the Exchequer, the next minute every last bit of his logic and rationality had deserted him.

Perhaps things would have come to a head sooner had he seen more of Lizzy. But Lizzy had become something of a hermit in the past two weeks. And Stuart, existing in a strange limbo, away from both the woman he loved and the woman to whom he was promised, postponed his final decision again and again—because he knew Verity wouldn't leave without seeing Michael one more time and because he knew from his conversation with Michael that the boy wouldn't return to Fairleigh Park until a week before Christmas.

A week before Christmas was yesterday.

What if she'd met Michael and left already? What if she did not want to be found? The false sense of security that came from knowing where she was evaporated in a second.

He was, all at once, frantic to leave London. But one did not quit the Chancellor of the Exchequer abruptly and without reason. Worse, on his way out of 9 Downing Street, where he maintained his Chief Whip's office, he had to settle squabbles between MPs, adjust the legislative schedule, and reassure everyone and his son-in-law—who were all worried sick over what Mr. Gladstone was doing with the Irish Home Rule bill—that everything was under control.

By the time he flagged down a hansom he'd become hopelessly unnerved, convinced he was too late for everything, even though logic told him that she hadn't left yet, that her resignation became effective only at the end of the month.

Outside the train station he bought a penny's worth of treacle rock for luck. But it, like everything else he'd eaten in a fortnight, tasted like so much peat: When he'd cast Verity out, he'd lost his newly redis-covered sense of taste, too. And he missed it. God, he missed it.

He wanted to love food again. He wanted to be sur-prised, bewildered, or even assailed by his dinner. He wanted to be vulnerably, pleasurably, and dangerously alive.

He wanted *her*.

He'd tried to get on with his life, tried to pretend that everything would be all right if he simply carried on as before. But it was impossible when she was both Cinderella and Verity Durant; when he seemed des-tined to fall in love with her, no matter what little frac-tion of her he knew.

London raced by outside his first-class compart-ment. He lit a cigarette and stared, unseeing. He had no idea what he would do were he to see her this day. What if she wanted nothing to do with him? And, al-most as terrifying, what if she did want something to do with him?

If he truly lost her again, he would lose the best part of himself. On the other hand, he'd spent decades building up his reputation and his career, neither of which would escape unscathed were he to take up with her.

He exhaled and watched the smoke obscure the air

before him. It didn't matter. He would cross that bridge when he came to it. Only let her be there. Let her still be there.

❧

Since Stuart hadn't sent a cable ahead—he was half-afraid that if she knew he was coming, she might leave—he walked the mile from the village to his estate. As he approached the manor, he heard the piano that he'd given to his staff as a Christmas present.

For a few short months when he was five, or perhaps four, with his mother claiming to be a respectable widow, he'd lived in a lodging house for women. The place, kept by a pinched-face spinster, had been dark and glum, except during the evenings, when the parlor came alive with music and singing, around an ancient spinet that had first seen service in the reign of the Mad King.

His mother had bartered the stitching of new curtains for the entire house for music lessons from the spinster and soon she was playing for him and the other women who lived at the lodging house. She played ballads she'd known in her youth and the latest songs she'd learned from the other women at the mill.

The melodic evenings came to an abrupt end when his mother was discovered with her new beau in her room. They had to move to a frightful new place. The beau disappeared and she cried often. And whenever Stuart put his arms around her and asked her to tell him what was wrong, she'd say, her voice breaking, that she missed the spinet, she missed the music.

The front door of the manor was locked, but the service entrance in the rear wasn't. He followed the music to the servants' hall. Before its door he closed his eyes a moment.

Let her be there.

The servants' hall was festive—there were garlands of evergreen and swags of holly and a Christmas tree full of candles—and crowded: Stuart had stumbled upon the Servants' Ball.

The indoor servants were in their dress uniforms, the outdoor servants in their Sunday best. A footman played the piano. Mrs. Boyce and Mr. Prior, in the absence of the master of the house, had led off the Grand March—a procession around the hall in a pattern of straight and serpentine lines. The Robbinses were all there, Michael with a sprig of holly at his lapel, walking with a maid who looked as if she didn't quite know what was going on. Two pairs of giggling maids—the women outnumbered the men—brought up the tail end of the procession.

But *she* was not among the servants.

Someone saw him. Soon everyone saw him. So he danced the quadrille with Mrs. Boyce—the highest-ranked female servant—while Mr. Prior partnered Mrs. Robbins, who, despite her marriage to the gamekeeper, was still considered a lady around these parts.

It was the longest dance of his life. All he could think was how stupid he had been, to not come for her sooner. He'd been a wiser man at twenty-seven: He'd known then that she was everything he ever wanted, that the two of them were meant to be each other's comfort and refuge. But now, at thirty-seven, he was a fool. He'd pushed her away and she might never return again.

At the end of the quadrille, everyone clapped. Stuart pasted on a smile and did likewise. Then the door to the servants' hall opened and in walked Verity Durant.

She was bareheaded, her dark golden hair pinned up in a simple top knot. Unlike the other servants, she wore neither her dress uniform nor her Sunday best, but an honest-to-goodness evening gown of cobalt blue velvet.

The gown was a decade out of fashion, its bodice and hems unadorned, its neckline so modest—baring only an inch of skin below her collarbone—that it could have garnered approval from the Puritans. But with the blue velvet choker at her throat and the long white gloves that reached past her elbow, the gown was nothing less than ravishing. *She* was nothing less than ravishing.

After all these years, Cinderella had arrived at the ball.

And suddenly Stuart could breathe again.

Conversation halted; mugs of beer raised toward lips went still in midair. Simmons, the head gardener, leaped up to intercept her. Prior, who outranked Simmons, cut into the latter's path. When Stuart rose, however, all the other men backed down.

She'd been walking toward Michael. But when

Michael glanced Stuart's way, she did too, and stopped dead. Stuart did something he'd never done to a servant: He bowed. After a moment of unresponsiveness on her part, she curtsied to him.

"Let us have a waltz," Stuart said to the footman at the piano. "Do you know one?"

The footman didn't. But Mrs. Robbins did. As the first strains of a Strauss waltz wafted from the piano, Stuart held out his hand toward Verity. She didn't move. He didn't care. She was still here—it was the only thing that mattered. He would gladly keep his hand extended all night if that was what it took.

She stepped into his arms only when it would have caused a scene otherwise.

"What are you doing here?" she said in French, without the Provencal accent. Her voice was tight, her expression tight, her entire person taut as a pulled bow.

"I have come to apologize and ask for your forgiveness."

"So you may go to your wedding with a clear conscience?"

"I won't marry Miss Bessler," he said. Strange how a choice that had so agonized him earlier now seemed so clear, so inevitable. "I want to be with you—if you will have me—for the rest of my days."

"It sounds very pretty," she said, an edge of what sounded like anxious anticipation to her otherwise flat tone. "But what are you offering me exactly?"

"An arrangement that I hope will suit both of us."

They spun halfway around the servants hall before

she spoke again. "You want me to be your mistress, in other words."

"I know I offered marriage last time. I—"

"You don't need to tell me why you can't marry me," she said brusquely. "I know. Last time I did not accept your offer for precisely those reasons."

She smelled wonderful, of freshly peeled oranges and simmered cream. With a start, he realized that he was hungry—for the first time in two weeks. Marvelously hungry and ready to demolish the entire cold buffet.

"I could have compelled you to marry me then," she went on. "You swore up and down that you would marry me no matter what."

"Yes, you could have." And he'd have honored his words if she'd held him to them. But the outcome of such a marriage—with resentment on all sides—would have been disastrous and they both knew it. "This time it will be a marriage in everything but name."

Except there was no such thing as a marriage in everything but name. Without the blessing of the Church and the sanction of the Law, any other arrangement was illicit. He could not appear in public with her and she would have none of the rights and privileges conferred upon a spouse.

"For what it's worth, I love you," he said, not knowing whether it was enough to make up for everything he didn't offer her. "And I will do everything in my power to make you happy."

She looked away. "You asked me to leave, so I have made plans. And now you change your mind and ask me to abandon my plans. How do I know you will not regret this in a few weeks, when gossip reaches everyone's ears and your respectability tarnishes?"

"Because the tarnishing of my respectability is nothing compared to the pain of losing you," he said. "I will deal with the consequences as they come—I can bear almost anything, as long as we are together."

She pressed her lips together. "I really don't want to say yes."

His heart floated on clouds. "But you will?"

She didn't answer directly. "You look terrible," she said.

"Middle-aged and lonely," he answered. "We've wasted ten good years."

She was silent for an entire minute. "We have, haven't we?" she said.

And he knew then that she'd said yes. And it scarcely mattered at all that his good name would be bandied about and laughed at all over London, perhaps all over the country. Let the gossips have their day. They could not take away his happiness.

He had to relinquish her at the end of the dance. He danced next with Mrs. Robbins, and then with his other female employees, even the youngest scullery maid who hardly came up to his middle—a few minutes of personal contact to make up for the rest of the year, during which their existence would register only most tenuously among the demands of his daily life.

And in between the dancing he ate, solidly, almost lecherously. And the hunger in his heart, too, was fed and fed well.

She also danced and ate. She was born to dance; her gracefulness made Prior's stiff steps look fluid, and even Simmons's duckish lead look dashing. And she flirted, not so much with Prior, the two of them maintaining the dignity of a pair of uppers but with everyone else—the footmen, the undergardeners, the groundskeepers, even the stable hands.

He kept his distance, until he'd danced once with all the women present. Then, in true genteel fashion, he made known his preference by dancing with her another time, cutting in during her second dance with Simmons. "May I?"

Simmons bowed with Elizabethan flourish and yielded his place.

"He told me that Bertie used to pay him to weasel madeleines out of me. I was just debating whether to tell him that you kept his galoshes on an altar for ten years." She smiled, speaking in a coquettish, French-accented English, flirting with *him* now.

"And hullo yourself, Cinderella," he murmured. "You never told me she was a flirt."

"Oh, she's an awful tart, that one. Messieurs Grimms almost exhausted their household's supply of washing soda scouring her story clean."

He chuckled. "And did the Fairy Godmother come for a visit today?"

"I wish. Then I wouldn't have had to spend an extra hour letting out all the seams so I could get into my frock."

"It's a beautiful gown."

"This ratty old rag? Why, thank you. I had it made for eating out in Paris with Bertie."

"Sounds like it was a fun affair."

"It was, while it lasted."

He felt inadequate. "I'm not as much fun as Bertie."

"Maybe not—I don't know yet—so you'd better love me more."

"I will." It was an easy promise to make.

They had the floor to themselves now. The other servants watched them dance, with varying degrees of curiosity and astonishment on their faces.

"But what about Miss Bessler?" she asked.

"I will speak with Miss Bessler."

"What changed your mind?" she asked. "Earlier you were adamant about not derailing your engagement."

"Once I realized that I couldn't live without you, all other things fell into their proper places."

She glanced down a second. "Will Miss Bessler be all right?"

"I don't know yet. But she is better off knowing everything in the open. Then she can decide for herself what she wants."

"Thank you," she said. "For taking such trouble on my behalf."

"On our behalf."

"Our behalf, I like the sound of it." She gazed into his eyes. "Shall I come to your apartment tonight?"

"I wish you could. But I've spoken to Bumbry just now and he is readying a carriage for me. I will take the late train and go back to London tonight."

"Why such a hurry?"

"So I may reach Lyndhurst Hall first thing tomor-row morning and—"

She stopped abruptly. It was a few seconds before they could find the beat of the music again. "I'm sorry. You said you were going to Lyndhurst Hall. What for?"

"To speak to Miss Bessler. She and her father are there as the Arlingtons' guests—Mr. Bessler and the late duke were close friends. In fact, I've been invited to spend Christmas there myself, but I much prefer spending it with you."

"Would the Dowager Duchess of Arlington let you?" she asked, her voice tight again.

It was an odd question. Then again it had been equally odd for the Dowager Duchess of Arlington to have exhibited the degree of interest she had in Verity Durant. But he did not believe that the dowager duchess would actively interfere in his private life.

Before he could reassure Verity, however, Michael cut in, and whisked her away.

Chapter Twenty-one

I'm fine, Papa," Lizzy said to her father.

Mr. Bessler was studying her yet again for signs of listlessness and apathy—for him, the specter of her melancholia always hovered in the background. She was ashamed to still be worrying him at her age, when she should be providing him with the comfort and joy of a daughter well settled. "Truly, I am, Papa."

Arm in arm they climbed up the grand staircase. They were spending the week at Lyndhurst Hall and her fiancé, too, would shortly join them.

Lizzy said good night, kissed her father on the cheek, and went to her chamber. Once there, she dismissed her maid almost right away: She wanted only solitude.

Three weeks before her wedding.

She'd not seen either Stuart or Will Marsden in the past fortnight, and it should tell her something that she missed Will far, far more. Indeed, at least once a day she wanted to rush out of wherever she was, find him, and tell him that she would marry him. Right away.

But then she would doubt herself. What if she were indeed as shallow as he feared? Certainly nothing in her recent past indicated the sort of strength of character required in such a situation. And it was not only her own unhappiness she dreaded, but his—she desperately did not want to become an embittered old woman and make him miserable to the end of his days.

Someone knocked at her door. The sound startled her. She looked at the clock: five minutes past midnight. "Who is it?"

A card slid in under her door. She belted her dressing gown and went to pick it up. *Mr. Wm. Marsden*.

Her heart hammered. When had he arrived at Lyndhurst Hall? "How do I know it's really you?"

Another card slid into the chamber. On it was written *Music hall*.

She chuckled despite her nervousness. She opened the door a crack. He slipped in and carefully closed the door behind him, turning the key in the lock—an act that made her heart hammer even harder.

"What are you doing here?" she said in a whisper.

For him to visit her in her chamber at this hour— and for her to permit him entrance—was beyond scandalous. If they were discovered, her reputation would certainly fall into a richly deserved ruin.

"I'm a desperate man," he said. "And so I've decided to resort to desperate tactics."

"And?"

"And I'm going to seduce you."

She didn't think she'd ever been so deliciously offended in her life. "And you think that will make me marry you?"

"I don't know. You are the most heartless woman," he said. "If not, at least I'll have the satisfaction of knowing that you will spend the rest of your life wishing you could shag me again."

"Oh, my. Arrogant, aren't we?"

"Not humble perhaps, but we speak only the unvarnished truth."

He came up to her and, without another word, kissed her. Her head spun. Desire invaded like a horde of Mongols. She pulled away, gasping.

"Well, that was most inappropriate of you, sir." She wasn't going to give in so easily.

"Really? Then perhaps you'll like this better."

He kissed her again and, as he did so, untied her dressing robe and pushed it off her person. She again pulled away and mock-sputtered. "Sir, have you no shame?"

"None at all," he said. "Watch."

He undid the tiny hooks on her nightgown one by one, exposing her skin in a long narrow V from throat to belly. "Now watch this," he said, as he pulled apart the top of the nightgown, exposing her breasts in their entirety.

She stopped breathing. He closed his eyes, opened them again, and slowly exhaled, all the playfulness in his expression gone. And suddenly she was as nervous as she'd ever been. Was she ready for this, for everything it implied?

He sank to one knee in front of her. Her eyes widened. Was he going to propose to her formally? No, he pulled the sash out of her robe. He straightened and placed one end of the sash over her nipples.

"Thank you for thinking of my modesty," she murmured.

"Say nothing of it," he said, gazing into her eyes.

He slid the six-foot-long strip of silk across her front. The sensation was indescribable, like being licked, but cooler and smoother. She gasped. He reversed the slide of the sash, and it was that sleek, keen pleasure all over again.

"I always feel such a sense of anticipation when the orchestra tunes up before a symphonic concert," he leaned forward and whispered into her ear.

"You mean it hasn't started yet?" she managed to say.

"No. But now we proceed to the overture."

He lifted her and set her bottom on the bed—a bed that was almost as tall as a hedge—lifted her nightgown up by the hem, and kissed her knees and up her thighs. She instinctively clamped her legs together. But he easily pried her open and continued with his upward—inward—exploration.

"This . . . this is very shocking." She knew what he intended, but she'd never experienced it, and it seemed wicked even to her rather jaded soul.

He laughed softly. "What? Have you attended only third-rate symphonic concerts in your life, Lizzy?"

And then he put his mouth on her and showed her exactly how one went about giving a first-rate symphonic concert. Oh, but he was clever and knowing and adaptable: Within a minute his strokes and nibbles were exactly those that gave her the most scorching pleasure.

She watched him; she couldn't help herself. She'd never felt so exposed, and yet so queenly and worshipped. She loved what he did to her. But even more than the physical pleasure, she loved the feeling of being so at ease with someone that she could enjoy such a dreadfully intimate act.

And then she could think no more lucid thoughts, but only of what he did to her. Her eyes shut. The sensations—like warm cream poured over her—became hotter and sharper in the darkness behind her eyelids. She writhed. She bit her lower lip to keep quiet. She gripped him by the soft curls of his hair.

She crescendoed like a Beethoven symphony, the kind that roused a whole concert hall of genteelly dozing patrons in the very last minute with its cymbals and percussions.

But he did not stop. With his lips and tongue he reminded her that they were only on the overture, and much was still to come. Her second climax exploded almost right after the first one, and the third on the heel of that.

She pulled him into bed. He was hard and burning against her. But he refused to enter her. "No, it's too risky. It was a last-minute idea—I don't have any precautions with me."

"I thought you meant to marry me."

"Yes, but what if something should happen to me before we could marry?"

He was right: She did have a hard heart. But her heart melted now. Henry had always insisted on precautions too, but it had been for the sake of his standing and reputation, not hers. But this man, oh, *this* wonderful man.

"Will, my sweet Will," she murmured, her heart full of love.

She slid lower and took him into her mouth. She'd done the same for Henry and had not particularly cared for it. But with Will it was entirely different. She loved everything about it, the texture, the heat, the way he expelled ragged breaths at her greediness—and, ultimately, the hot, unchaste taste of him as she swallowed every last drop.

"My God, Lizzy," he rasped weakly as she returned at last to enfold him in a tight embrace.

"Yes," she said with a fully satisfied smile. "I will marry you."

❦

Lizzy was still abed when her maid delivered a note from Stuart: He'd arrived at Lyndhurst Hall and wished to speak to her. She dressed, ate a quick bite for breakfast, and sent a return note that she would wait for him on the interior balcony that overlooked Lyndhurst Park's orangerie.

It was a fitting place, she supposed, to bid adieu to her conceited quest, because here was where it had started. Not that she hadn't always been a bit vain and more than a bit ambitious, even as a child, but prestige and wealth hadn't been her only goals then, or even her primary goals.

She'd had a fierce pride in her intellectual capacity and planned to read both classics and mathematics at Girton College. But then, she'd accompanied her parents to Lyndhurst Hall and was awed into speechlessness by the beauty and grandeur of the place. She especially fell in love with the lush orangerie, a spectacular two-story glass structure that ran the entire length of one wing of the house, full of rare species from the tropics that luxuriated a deep green even in the full of winter. After that, there was nothing to do but become the next mistress of this majestic place, and be accorded the same reverence that greeted the Duchess of Arlington wherever the latter went.

Today she paid no mind to the orangerie. She missed her Will already—he'd left Lyndhurst Hall at the break of dawn to arrange for a marriage license from the Bishop of London, so they could get married on the day she was originally to marry Stuart and enjoy the wedding that they'd planned together. She paced on the balcony, full of energy and excitement, though she'd had barely an hour of sleep—she and Will had stayed up much of the night whispering to each other and giggling like children.

A great deal of it was gossiping, the kind of juicy, no-holds-barred gossip that could only be enjoyed with someone one trusted completely. But they also submitted to a few serious minutes of planning for their married life.

As it turned out, Stuart had been about to sponsor

Will to Inner Temple—Will had started as a secretary, but had quickly caught on to the intricacies of law.

"But we can't in good conscience have him be your sponsor anymore," she'd pointed out anxiously.

"Not to worry. I'm sure the dowager duchess will strong-arm someone else to sponsor me—she was the one who found employment for me when I returned to England."

"Why would she take such interest in you?" she'd asked. "And come to think of it, what are you doing here and why did she allow someone of your womanizing ways to set foot in her house?"

"Visiting her, of course. She's Matthew's godmother and she has turned a blind eye to my womanizing ways ever since I allowed myself to fall into poverty and disgrace for Matthew's sake."

Lizzy had shaken her head. "Why is every man I know indebted to that woman?"

"That's why you want to be her; so you too can lord it over all the men in England," he'd said with a teasing affection.

"How true," she'd admitted. "Now I will have to find a different way to harvest wonder and admiration from the general populace. I think I will attend Girton and become a fearsome scholar after all, one of the finest minds of my generation."

"I think that is a splendid idea." He smiled. "Besides, there's nothing like shagging on Plato."

"Or Pythagorus."

"Or Pythagorus. How could I have forgotten good old Pythagorus?"

She inhaled the mossy scent of the orangerie and smiled hugely at the memories.

"Have I caught you in a good mood?"

It was Stuart, standing at the door.

She cleared her throat and pulled herself into a semblance of serenity. "Yes, you have."

"Sorry I kept you waiting. I passed Her Grace on my way and she wanted to speak to me." He came to where she stood and kissed her on the cheek. "I've been worried about you—you haven't left your house for a while. I hope I'm not to blame, for overwhelming you with wedding preparations."

"I'm quite completely and perfectly fine now. I have never been better, in fact." Except for her nagging concern about him. He deserved much better from her. And now he would go into another frantic session of the Parliament without a wife to look after him. If only she could be sure that he would be as happily settled as she, then—

"Good," he said. "Because there is something I need to tell you."

His tone caught her attention. There was something unsettling about it. And the way he looked— she'd seen that particular look on him only when he conferred with his colleagues in the House of Commons on intractably thorny issues. "Yes?"

He took a deep breath. "I have fallen in love with someone."

She wasn't sure she understood him. She stared at him. "With whom?"

"With Madame Durant," he said, his tone clear, without hesitation or shame.

Her ears rang a little. "Madame Durant. You mean your cook?"

"Yes."

"Are you absolutely certain?" It was an asinine question, but she did not see it at all of her very proper, very straitlaced Stuart.

"Quite."

"This is . . ." She could not conceive that a man such as he would even take notice of his cook, let alone spend any time with her. Let alone fall in love.

In love.

"My God," she murmured. "Some stupid woman at your dinner party told me I should sack your cook as soon as I became Mrs. Somerset. I never imagined that there'd be any truth to her insinuations."

"I'm sorry. That is one of the reasons I wanted to speak to you, so that you need not be subject to such unpleasantness in the future."

She resumed her pacing, her motion propelled more by sheer astonishment than anything else. She stopped at the railing of the balcony. "Do you mean to marry *her*?"

Now, that would be truly mind-boggling. He would destroy everything he'd built of himself if he did so—he wasn't placed so high in the world that he could marry whomever he pleased, and there was always his illegitimate birth that people would pounce on, given half a chance.

"You know very well I cannot marry her." It seemed

to pain him to say that. "But I plan to spend as much of the rest of my life with her as possible."

"So you are crying off our engagement."

"If you will let me go, I will be humbly grateful." He gazed at her and his eyes were wistful. "I'm sorry, Lizzy. My heart belongs to her."

She shook her head. She really did not know him, did she? A clandestine love affair with the most unsuitable woman. And yet it did not diminish her opinion of him. To love as he did—with passionate commitment—was the only way to love.

"I wish you both the very best then," she said.

And it was the answer she would have given had there been no Will Marsden in her life. She was not so set on her own prerogatives that she was willing to chain the lives of others to accomplish them.

"Thank you," he said. He closed the distance between them, took her hands, and kissed both of them. "Thank you. I did not plan on this. I cannot stop loving her, and it is not fair to keep you in the dark. Otherwise I would never choose to hurt you."

She kissed his hands in return. "You didn't hurt anything other than my vanity—and that's only because I want to believe that every man in the world is secretly in love with me. And your decision does make it much, much easier for me to tell you that I've come to doubt the wisdom of our union as well."

He smiled ruefully. "I'm not surprised that you have, what with my distraction."

"Yes, but I would be lying if I didn't admit that I've been distracted too."

He was startled. "Is there someone else?"

She could not stop the smile that rose to her lips. "I'm going to marry your secretary, Stuart."

His expression of disbelief was probably an exact facsimile of her own look of stupefaction earlier.

"I thought you couldn't stand Marsden."

"I've changed my mind."

They stared at each other a minute, then broke into laughter. "We have been a fine, mischievous pair, haven't we?" he said, still chuckling.

Then, for the first time in their long acquaintance and without her prompting, he embraced her. "I cannot tell you how this puts my mind at ease. Marsden is a good man. I am already in the process of sponsoring him to Inner Temple. He will make a fine barrister and make you an excellent husband. And when he inherits, you will be very comfortably off—far better than if you'd married me without my brother's estate."

When he inherits? What could Will possibly inherit? He'd been cut out of both of his parents' wills. And since those parents were already dead, there was no possibility of his being restored to said wills.

"I didn't choose him for his inheritance," she said dumbly.

"Of course not. But it's always reassuring, is it not, to know that there is ease and plenty in your future? I acted as Marsden's counsel in the matter, so I speak on good authority."

Lizzy was more flabbergasted than she'd been at Stuart's declaration of love for his less-than-respectable cook. Will was not a poor man. And yet he'd allowed her to think that he was. Why? Did he really think her so shallow that he had to test her? But she'd agreed to marry him, believing that he was penniless. Was this all but a game, then? Did he have any true intention of marrying her? Had he really gone to arrange for a special license, or was he laughing all the way back to London at how he'd gulled her?

Stuart kissed her on the cheek in parting. "Don't forget to invite me to your wedding."

Wedding? What wedding?

❧

Verity had half-fretted that Miss Bessler would not let go of Stuart so easily. But her worries turned out to be quite unfounded. He cabled her to tell her that he was a free man and asked her to join him in London—since he'd planned to be away at Lyndhurst Hall, he'd given his servants a week of holiday, and the town house was conveniently and discreetly empty.

Michael took Verity to the train station.

"I am not sure how I feel about this," said her son. "Are you aware that you are not setting a good example for me? Can't Mr. Somerset marry you instead?"

She shrugged. "Not when we both want him to retain his position in Society."

"Then I hope he knows you are forsaking fame and fortune in Paris for him," said Michael as she hugged him good-bye.

She chortled. "I'll make sure that he never forgets

my sacrifice." She kissed Michael, then waved at him from her compartment.

She wished that Stuart, in his haste, hadn't sent the telegram from the post office nearest Lyndhurst Hall. Not that they could keep their arrangement a secret for long—discretion was the best they could achieve— but she did not want it known to the Dowager Duchess of Arlington so soon.

The dowager duchess had ways to track Verity's movement—how else could she know to deliver a letter to 26 Cambury Lane within days after Verity had moved there? If the dowager duchess learned that Verity had returned to London again, and that Stuart, too, had cut short his stay at Lyndhurst Hall in favor of London, would she not infer that something was going on between the two of them? More importantly, would she interpret it as another attempt by Verity to reclaim her old identity?

Verity arrived in London in a strangely uneasy mood. But Stuart had left her a key to his town house before he departed Fairleigh Park, and the feeling of unlocking his front door and gliding inside quite buoyed her. At last, no more service entrances for her where he was concerned.

But her pleasure fizzled a little when the house turned out to be empty. Where could he be? She'd thought he'd be waiting for her. She lifted her valise— the rest of her things would be sent along later—and trudged up the stairs.

She used the water closet and washed her face in the washbasin in the bath. It was when she contemplated re-

peating history yet again—waiting for him in the tub—
that she heard the front door open and close below.

She rushed down and quite knocked him into the
wall on the first-floor landing. Without a word, she
threw her arms around him and kissed him until
she was completely out of breath.

Only then did she bother to ask, "Where were you?"

Before he answered, he took her face between his
hands and kissed her back with a hunger that made
her whimper. "Out on a heroic quest."

"For dragons?"

"No, for something that apparently doesn't exist in
England."

"What is it?"

He pulled up her skirts, his hand blazing a trail of
fire up her thighs. Then she gasped, for he went directly for the ribbons of her drawers. The drawers fluttered to a heap around her ankles.

His hand found her and toyed with her, his touches
barely there, yet etching paths of fire. "Would you like
me to show you?"

"Yes," she panted.

At her fervent affirmative, however, his hand left
her. She gripped him by the arms, her body pulsing in
stark need. He returned shortly, and touched something round, soft, and smooth to her inner thigh.

"I went out and bought it today. You can't begin to
guess the trouble I had." He braced her legs farther
apart and stroked her with the silky cover of the
sponge. "Every place I went to assured me that they
carried nothing of the sort—why, they were a proper,

decent, God-fearing establishment. Every shopkeeper assumed that I was there to land him in hot water with *somebody*, because a dried-up prig such as myself couldn't possibly have a personal use for something so nefarious."

He twirled that nefarious something slowly, against a most sensitive point. She gripped his arms even harder, this time to help her remain standing.

"It was a woman, in the end, who took one look at me and promptly emptied my pocketbook. I think she sold me all the sponges in the sea."

The travels of the silk-wrapped sponge continued. She bit down on his lapel, tasting warm wool, hungrily inhaling the scent of the clean, starched linen of his shirt.

Now he pushed the sponge against her. It resisted, then slipped in suddenly, his finger sinking inside her all the way. They both gasped.

"God, I hope I bought enough," he said.

For a moment, reality intruded and her heart wrenched. She'd brought along a supply of sea sponges herself. But the length to which he'd gone forcefully reminded her that as much as he loved her, he could never go for a stroll in the park with her, never mention her in polite company, and certainly never give her any children—because any children they produced would be illegitimate, and he was the last man to willingly contribute to the creation of illegitimate children.

But then he freed himself from his trousers and entered her. And she forgot everything else. She shuddered and convulsed almost right away, her pleasure-starved body releasing—and releasing and releasing—years of pent-up desire in one sustained, glorious peak after another.

❦

"I adore this room," she said. "But I didn't expect you'd sleep in a place like this."

The room was done up entirely in shades of white. Chairs and stools were upholstered in ivory brocade. Counterpanes were the color of a distant clipper's sails. And the curtains were an inner layer of translucent muslin and an outer layer of sugar-white grosgrain, with pipings of airy blue.

"My mum always pined for whites. So for me white was—is—the color of luxury."

After their lightning-like lovemaking on the stairs, the doorbell had rung, and it had been the delivery of the substantial tea that he had ordered from the Savoy Hotel. They'd eaten, and made love on the dining table. Afterward, Stuart had gone down to the basement and packed the boiler with enough coal to last the evening. Then they'd taken a bath together, and only finally made it to his bedchamber minutes ago.

In her dressing gown, she climbed on top of the bed and stood on her knees to study the seascape that hung above the headboard. "Who painted this? It reminds me of the little piece in the main hall—not the Constable, the new one."

He hesitated only briefly. "You've a good eye. They were both painted by my mum."

His answer surprised her. She looked closer. "She was talented. Her technique wasn't perfect, but she had a good understanding of color and composition." She turned toward him. "I didn't know you ever visited with your mum after your relocation to Fairleigh Park."

"I didn't," he said. "Except once."

His father had forbidden his mother to ever contact him, in person or by post. But Stuart hadn't known it. For years he'd assumed she'd abandoned him. But when he'd been sixteen, he'd accidentally found out that Sir Francis paid Nelda Lamb a quarterly allowance—which quite put the lie to what his father had always claimed, that he didn't know where she was.

Sir Francis had put her in his house in Torquay, where Bertie's mum had lived out the last years of her life. It had been a brilliant move: It took Nelda away from Manchester, where Stuart might more easily find her, and also gave her something greater to lose should she renege on her promise to Sir Francis and contact Stuart.

Quietly Stuart dug up the address of the house in Torquay. At the end of his Easter holiday, he left two days early, ostensibly to return to Rugby. On the way he switched trains and headed farther south, to the Devon coast.

He arrived in the middle of a balmy spring afternoon. The entire coastline was in bloom, the bay as blue as a rain-washed sky. He left his luggage in storage at the train station, inquired for directions, and made his way up the hill behind the Strand.

His heart thrashed in his chest like a bagged weasel. He imagined her standing before her window, watching the road, the way he used to climb to the top of Fairleigh Park's wrought-iron gates and look out to the country lane beyond, hoping to see her arrival. Or perhaps she would be at devout prayer for him, tears streaming from her eyes. Or writing to him, loving letters that she'd preserved, hundreds of them, for the day when he would come.

He broke into a run at the sight of the house, white and demure. The green door opened. A maid, her apron askew, looked him up and down, disappointed. "You are not my Bobby!"

His heart sank. Such an untidy and insolent maid would have been sent packing from Fairleigh Park without a character. A mistress who tolerated such a maid was at best of questionable respectability.

Hysterical laughter exploded inside the house, laughter both female and male, laughter that would have been considered too shrill and uncontained even for the servants' hall at home.

"Is this Mrs. Lamb's house?" he asked, hoping for a negating answer.

"If you've a card, I'll take it to her," said the maid.

He pushed past the maid into the front hall. The laughter still hadn't subsided. Through a half-open door, he saw a man in a brown day coat and a woman wearing a yellow-on-blue polka-dot frock, sitting on his lap.

When he reached the parlor, he saw that the woman in polka dots wasn't the only one on a man's lap. A woman in a shade of scarlet far too provocative for daytime wear wriggled and giggled on another man's lap. The third woman, a kohled, rouged hag, had a hookah in hand. And at barely four o'clock in the afternoon there were already half a dozen empty wine bottles all about the parlor.

"Mrs. Lamb, who's your darling young friend, and where have you been keeping him?" gurgled the woman in scarlet.

Only then did he see a fourth woman, clad almost entirely in white, seated on a bench before the piano and slumped over the lowered lid that covered the keys, an empty wineglass at her elbow.

He didn't recognize her. He remembered his mother as a weary, fading woman, aged before her years, her hair thin, her face haggard, her skin always splotchy either from the cold or from some dermatological ailment. The woman with her face down on the piano lid seemed hardly older than himself, beautiful, creamy, languorous.

She didn't recognize him either. Not immediately. Nor after a good long, dazed look. He realized to his disgust that she'd overimbibed as much as the woman in scarlet, only her reaction was torpor instead of lasciviousness.

Suddenly she leapt off the bench and lurched at him, tripping over one of the bottles on the floor. He barely caught her.

"Stu! My God, it's you." She clutched him so hard he thought she would break his left humerus. "It's my son, everyone. My son!"

Stuart coldly endured the awkward introduction to her friends. The men were no more lecturers and artists than he was a Druid priest. And if the two women supposedly married to them didn't belong to a brothel—and if the hookah-smoking hag wasn't their madam—then the trip south must have wreaked havoc with his powers of perception indeed.

He'd always thought his mother a lady, despite her poverty. He'd remembered a gentleness to her, and she'd spoken with more refinement than everyone else. But now he heard her hopeless accent, saw the coarse way she waved her spoon in the air when tea had been brought in, heard her laughter, as loud and shrill as that of any of her guests.

All he could think was how right his father had been to insist on a complete severing between mother and son. She was not a lady. She wasn't even half so respectable as Fairleigh Park's housekeeper.

He rose to go, citing a tight schedule that did not permit him more time for visiting. She ran after him out of the house.

"What's the matter, Stuart? Why are you leaving?"

"I already told you, I have to go."

"But you've only just come. Stay for dinner at least."

"I don't think I will."

Tears rolled down her face. "I was afraid this would happen. You've changed. And I'm not good enough to be related to you anymore."

"*I've* changed?" he exclaimed, aghast. "What about you? Who are those people?"

"They are my friends."

"Friends? They are confidence men and prostitutes."

"My friends have always been confidence men and prostitutes. Tom Fiddle was a confidence man. Don't you remember Tom Fiddle? He taught you how to read from the *Manchester Guardian*. And Polly and Midge, you used to play cards with them—what do you suppose they did for a living?"

"That was different."

By the time Stuart knew him, Tom Fiddle's career in chicanery had long ended and he owned the pub down the street. He didn't remember Midge so well, but Polly had been a quiet, tidy woman who prayed a great deal, nothing like the slatterns in the parlor.

His mother shook her head. "No, the only thing that's changed is you, Stu. You think you are so grand now. You look down on us, all of us."

Stuart's temper slipped away from his control. What happened to his industrious mother? Who was this indolent woman with no moral compass? "I wouldn't look down on you if you weren't drunk in the middle of the day!"

When Nelda Lamb died that winter of influenza, Stuart insisted that her remains be interred in Manchester, so he could pretend that the events of Torquay had never happened.

A pretense he'd upheld assiduously in the years since.

"I didn't like her when I found her," he said to Verity. "I never went back to see her again. When she died, when the people who cleared out the house sent her paintings to me, I had them put away. I didn't want to look at them. And then, after we talked about Bertie, I thought of her too. It was because of me that she'd had such a hard life, but she never once blamed me."

Verity came and put her arms about him. "I'm glad you forgave her."

"I can only hope she forgave me too."

"I know she did." She hugged him tight. "I'm a mother too. And we forgive everything."

Something in him unclenched. He kissed the top of her head. "I'll take you to see her grave sometime."

She laid her cheek against his. "Yes, we'll do that."

❦

Later that evening, as they lay in bed, warm and snug under the covers, they talked of their future.

"All this white is lovely. But we shall need to be much more practical in our own place," she said.

With a pang he realized that she wasn't talking about his house, since she could not live here openly with him. No one would take him to task for keeping a mistress, but when that mistress was Verity Durant, everything must be done with the utmost discretion.

He watched her carefully for signs of unhappiness, but her eyes were bright as she spoke of her plans. She would now finally have the time to write her magnum opus, a book of recipes and methods for professed cooks. Perhaps she'd poach a few of the kitchen staff from Fairleigh Park, train them some more, and open a tea shop that served authentic French and Viennese pastry. And later, when she had enough money, a school of cookery.

"You'll have a carte blanche from me, you know," he reminded her.

She smiled, a little ruefully. "I'm no longer used to spending anyone's money except my own. And besides, I like the security of an income."

"You are afraid of being at my mercy?"

"It's more pride than fear, I hope. I'm not ashamed—not anymore—of having such skills that would earn me a good living."

He brought her hands to the light and looked at them. She allowed him. The old scars and burn marks had faded with age, though there were new ones. Her calluses had become less pronounced and her skin much more supple than he remembered.

"I remembered your hands. I thought of them every time I held a soft hand untroubled by work."

"Now you tell me. I would have ceased my religious application of hand salve if I'd known," she said, her eyes twinkling.

He kissed her palm, tentatively, and was rewarded with a sharp intake of breath on her part. So the sensitivity of her hands hadn't changed. He glanced at her, mischief on his mind.

"Oh, dear," she said, pressing her palm to his lips again. "*Now* I'm afraid of being at your mercy."

Chapter Twenty-two

The man who'd seduced Lizzy two nights before rose from his breakfast table. "Lizzy?! What are you doing here?"

"I've come to see you, of course." She smiled through clenched teeth.

His expression was one of confusion and incipient worry. "You came all the way from Lyndhurst Hall by yourself? When? Does your father know where you are?"

The landlady left. Lizzy pushed the door firmly shut. She'd come the night before, fabricating some excuse about a bosom friend in need. Her father, alarmed—he'd had to announce the end of her engagement and she was not acting herself—had insisted on accompanying her. So this morning, while her father was in his bath, she'd ordered the footman who usually followed her on her morning walks to stay in the house, then left, climbing into the first passing hansom.

"You cur! You dirty, rotten scoundrel!" She gave free rein to her anger. "What games are you playing with me?"

"What are you talking about, Lizzy?"

He looked so gorgeous and so sincerely puzzled she didn't know whether to hit him or to cry.

"My former fiancé told me about your inheritance. He said I have nothing but 'ease and plenty' to look forward to in my future. Why do I hear about such a thing from him rather than you? What exactly are your intentions toward me?"

"To marry you, of course. I was just in the middle of writing to my youngest brother, to tell him the good news."

He went to the writing table and came back with a sheet of paper. She skimmed it. Various words jumped out at her. *Bliss. Soon. Marry. Bessler. Wonderful. Happy.*

"And the license is in my room, if you still don't believe me," he said. "And I would have left directly after breakfast for Lyndhurst Hall to speak with your father."

She exhaled. The worst fear in her calmed. But still she was upset. "That answers only one of my questions. Do you have any idea how wrenching this decision has been at times for me—to think of all the friends I'd have to give up because they would turn out to be fair-weather friends, and how my father would always have to worry because I'd married a poor man? You could have eased my mind at any point, and you didn't."

"It was never my intention to—"

She didn't let him finish. "You don't think very

highly of me, do you? You thought that if I knew about the money then my decision would be based solely on that."

"No! No!" He shook his head vigorously. "That is not true. I haven't told anyone other than Matthew and our baby brother, and Mr. Somerset knows only because he was my lawyer in the matter. My great-uncle—the one who put me in his will—is one of the most spectacular eccentrics of our time, fully capable of changing his mind at the last minute and leaving everything to his dogs—which he had done at one point, but the dogs died."

"Excuses, excuses. You didn't tell me because you didn't trust me."

"No, quite the contrary. I *was* tempted to tell you. But had I told you, I would have grossly misrepresented my situation. My great-uncle may be eighty-eight, but he is as healthy as a horse and could very well live another twenty years. Goodness knows, he's already outlived two sets of beneficiaries to his will—and that's not counting the dogs. How could I promise you 'ease and plenty' when neither might be forthcoming for years, perhaps decades? And how would you feel when nothing materializes? So I had to trust and hope that you would choose me, even given my current poverty."

She almost laughed when he mentioned the dogs again. Everything he said made sense—and was all easily verifiable via Stuart. She had to remind herself that she was upset with him.

"You could have at least given me a hint."

"I wanted it to be a surprise. If I told you, I'd become

anxious for it to come true—and I'm rather fond of the old bloke and don't really want him to give up the ghost yet."

She couldn't help smiling this time. He really was an adorable man. And now her cheeks warmed at having jumped to such far-fetched conclusions. "Well, now that's all cleared up between us, I'd better return to my house before the servants report my suspicious activities to my father and worry him."

"Your father is in London?"

"Yes."

"Then wait two minutes; I'll come with you. We'll fetch him and get married right away, since we already have the license."

Her jaw dropped. She grabbed him by the shoulders. "I think I have formed an attachment to you. You know, what the English call a desire to have symphonic concerts with someone at all hours of the day?"

He smiled. "And I love you too, darling."

❧

Verity and Stuart made tea and toast for breakfast. After breakfast, they returned to bed and made love again. Toward midmorning he got up, washed, and came back to the bedchamber to dress.

She lolled on the bed, still naked, and watched him. "My goodness, you look so handsome and so unbearably respectable. Why don't you shag me fully dressed right before you leave?"

"You've an amazingly rotten mind, my dear Madame Durant."

"I've had years to let it putrefy in fervent lust of you, my love," she said. "Now, where do you think you are going dressed like that?"

"To see my solicitor and put you in my will."

She set her chin on her palm. "What are you giving me?"

"Everything."

That made her sit up straighter. "Not Fairleigh Park too."

"Yes, Fairleigh Park too." He shrugged into his waistcoat.

Her mouth opened wide. "You will petition Parliament to break entail?"

He chuckled. "You are thinking of titular land, my love. Fairleigh Park is not that. The entail on it isn't even a primogeniture. My father gave Fairleigh Park to Bertie for the remainder of Bertie's life, and to Bertie's issue upon Bertie's death. But he also provided that should Bertie die childless, the estate will pass to me. I can renew the entail in my own will, but now I won't."

"Still, Fairleigh Park has always remained within the Somerset family."

"You are my family now," he said.

"You'll make me cry, you know," she murmured.

He came and kissed her. "For giving you things when I've no more use for them? You are too easy to please."

It had begun to snow during the night. Several inches of snow had already accumulated on the ground. She watched him leave from the bedchamber window and wondered how her heart could hold so much love without levitating her clean off the floor.

When he'd disappeared in the direction of Buckingham Palace Road, she quickly washed, dressed, and made ready to go out and buy provisions for their meals. The doorbell rang just as she reached the ground floor. She opened the front door. The cold air that gushed in was refreshingly clean for London; beyond the portico, snow fell luxuriantly.

"Is Madame Durant at home?" said a young, red-cheeked footman. Flecks of snow clung to him.

"I am she."

The footman bowed. "Mum, Her Grace the Dowager Duchess of Arlington requests your company."

She couldn't quite believe her ears. She looked at the footman again. But of course she should have recognized his livery the moment she opened the door. And she hadn't even noticed the crest on the brougham parked by the curb—her mind had been entirely on happier matters.

The dowager duchess worked fast—despite her uneasy thoughts the day before, Verity had not believed the dowager duchess would infer everything quite so soon. Her heart, warm and toasty a second ago, felt impaled by an icicle. She had to forcibly remind herself that the dowager duchess's power lay in the denial of privileges and recognitions—that she, Verity, had none left to be taken away.

"And what does Her Grace plan to do with my company?" she said, with a bite to her tone—she'd done nothing wrong, she didn't need to humbly suffer a lecture from the dowager duchess.

The footman looked nonplussed. Presumably those whose presence the duchess requested never asked why, but hopped into the nearest carriage and presented themselves before Her Grace at the earliest opportunity.

"I'm sure I don't know, mum," said the footman, sincerely indifferent.

She could say no. But what if the dowager duchess didn't want to lecture her? What if she only wanted to see Verity for some reason? Wasn't it often said that as people settled into old age, they looked more leniently upon those who had earlier given them great offense?

"If you will wait a minute," she said.

It was foolish to carry such hopes about the dowager duchess. But this wasn't a bad day for hope. It was a foolish hope too that had brought her and Stuart together again. She could afford to be hopeful today, no matter how unlikely the hope.

She put on her coat and climbed into the waiting carriage. There was an ermine carriage blanket inside, along with a brazier and a warmed brick for her feet. Gingerly she settled the carriage blanket over her knees—she hadn't touched anything quite so fine or expensive in years. Perhaps her hope wasn't so impossible, then: If the dowager duchess meant to give Verity a hard time, she need not have provided such comforts along the way.

The carriage left the curb, its motion smooth and easy, entirely unlike that of Verity's lurching heart. After she'd run away, she'd seen the dowager duchess only once, during the first months of her apprenticeship under Monsieur David. It had been at the wedding of a childhood friend of hers, and she'd been among the multitudes outside the church that morning, drawn by the pomp and pageantry of an aristocratic marriage. Seeing her old friend walking down the steps of the church arm in arm with her new husband had been devastating enough. Seeing the then-not-yet-dowager duchess nod with approval at the happy couple had crushed Verity's spirits for weeks.

It was less than half a mile from Cambury Lane to Belgrave Square. All too soon the carriage stopped. She took a deep breath and told herself not to be afraid. She was a grown-up woman who'd done decently for herself. And on this day when her heart overflowed with goodwill, she would be happy to see the dowager duchess—no matter what, they were still family.

As befitting their exalted station, the town house of the dukes of Arlington was an imposing structure, seven bays wide. Its portico spanned four bays and rose three stories high on columns that her arms could not entirely encircle. The carriage had stopped under a porte cochère. Verity was whisked out, past the marble entrance hall, then up the ormolu staircase into the grand drawing room.

Before she could quite take in all the changes that had been made to the drawing room—Where had the Gainsborough gone? Didn't the floor used to be parqueted in a starburst pattern, rather than a diamond one? And had the ceiling always been coffered?—a raspy but still imperious voice said, "You may leave us, Sullivan."

The voice came from a thin, black-clad figure at the center of the room. Verity did not recognize the white-haired woman whose eyes and mouth were deeply lined with age. Then she did. She blinked in shock at the ravages the years had wrought upon the Dowager Duchess of Arlington: She'd become an old woman.

The ebony walking stick right next to her was yet another sign of the encroachment of old age. Verity's heart tightened. Had it really been that long?

"Duchess," she said softly. "You sent for me?"

"You seem to have a special affinity for your employers," said the dowager duchess without preamble.

A familiar pain replaced the tenderness in Verity's heart. The dowager duchess might have aged, but she had not mellowed. A lecture it would be, then, whether or not Verity deserved it.

"Not true, Madame. Or I would have had the Marquess of Londonderry in my pocket," she answered, her tone almost as sharp as the dowager duchess's. She was surprised to realize she no longer quivered before the dowager duchess, the way she had when she was sixteen.

The dowager duchess chortled coolly. "A special affinity for your Somerset employers, then."

"Well, the elder brother was quite a man and the younger brother is too spectacular for words."

"Yes, the younger Mr. Somerset is a very fine, very

remarkable man. Your uncle, who was secretly a democrat at heart, had a great fondness for him. We would have been pleased had we a son like him."

This was generous praise indeed. "Then you cannot be too displeased that I have taken up with him."

"On the contrary. I am rarely so offended. Mr. Somerset's thoughtlessness in the matter astonishes me. He breaks up a perfectly sensible engagement in order to keep, as his mistress, a woman of your notoriety, on the eve of one of the most important votes in our lifetime, with the leader of the Irish already in a perilous position from his own ill-considered conduct.

"The fate of this government hinges on the Irish Home Rule vote. If it fails, the government will fall and we shall be relegated to the Opposition for an eternity—and I have worked too long and too hard to bring the Liberals back to power to allow anyone to endanger the government in this cavalier manner."

"Is it quite necessary to bring matters of the state into our discussion, Madame?" Verity dared to ask. "I fail to see what my rapport with Mr. Somerset has to do with the destiny of ruling coalitions."

"Do you so naïvely believe that your past will not reflect disastrously upon him? That it will not affect his effectiveness as the chief whip? He will lose Mr. Gladstone's confidence."

The dowager duchess studied Verity, her gaze level. "Power is perception, Vera. Mr. Somerset's power rests in large part on the perception that he is a man who does not make mistakes. In you he has made a disastrous mistake.

"Do you have any idea the prejudice this man has faced and overcome in his lifetime? Do you understand the sheer miracle that he has wrought to rise to his present position, with the portfolio of the Home Secretary to be entrusted to him upon the passage of Home Rule? There are few other men in the party with the reputation, influence, and moral authority to match him. Until he gave in to your temptation, he was on his way to 10 Downing Street."

"And you think I'm going to be the ruin of all that?" Verity said, a strong dose of scorn in her voice, although her heart was already sinking. The dowager duchess meant to take Stuart away from her.

"You *know* you will be the ruin of all that," said the dowager duchess. "But it's not too late yet. No one else knows. Stop this lunacy now. Leave. And you may yet preserve him for the highest office of the land. You know that is what he wants. That is what he has strived for all his life. Do not take it away from him with your selfishness."

"I am not selfish," Verity said, hating the note of defensiveness of her voice. "No more than you are."

"That is not a good comparison, for I am, and have always been, extremely selfish," said the dowager duchess, calm, serene. "But my selfishness does not imperil Mr. Somerset's good name, nor does it undermine his future. Yours will do all that, and more."

"I don't believe you," Verity said, trying to keep her voice level. The dowager duchess would exploit her emotions as weaknesses. "I have left him once already, for his sake. That was ten good years we could have had together. I will not leave him again."

"You will ruin him, then?"

Verity hated that question, hated the implication of her culpability. "There has always been much at stake. He knows it better than anyone. This is the decision he has made in spite of all the reasons to the contrary. It is not my place to second-guess his choice."

"It is folly on his part, and you know it better than anyone. You will hide behind his infatuation and be content to let him stumble. Have you no love for him?"

Verity's anger rose bitter hot. "Don't you dare question my love, you coldhearted witch!"

"But I do." The dowager duchess was glacial and implacable. "Your love is detrimental to him. It will bring nothing but dishonor and disgrace upon him."

"Say what you want. I will not leave him."

"Very well, then. I had hoped you would see reason, but I must say I did not expect it. I will speak to Mr. Somerset directly—he has always been a man of logic and rationality."

A black tide of fear rose in Verity. She remembered how respectfully he'd mentioned the dowager duchess's name. The good opinion of this woman mattered to him. And her influence—the influence of the Arlingtons—carried tremendous weight in Liberal circles.

"I need to know one thing, Vera," said the dowager duchess. "Will you let him go without further ado once he sees the light, or will you use tears and feminine wiles to make an already difficult situation even more difficult for him?"

Verity had never possessed *that* kind of feminine wiles. "I do not keep unwilling men about me," she said between clenched teeth.

"Good," said the duchess. "Then we understand each other."

"I will see myself out," said Verity.

"No, stay. Mr. Somerset will be here soon enough. You might as well listen to what he decides."

Stuart was already on his way here? Verity barely had a chance to be surprised before tea was brought in, along with sandwiches and cakes. She walked to a window that overlooked the snow-covered square. It was still snowing, but the new snow was no longer beautiful to her eyes, only desolate: a vulnerable canvas to be dirtied and defiled by passing carriages and careless pedestrians.

Three men in top hats and black cloaks trudged across the square in the direction of Arlington House. Her heart arrested, until she realized that none of the men was him. Perhaps the dowager duchess's minions wouldn't find him, since he'd gone to neither of his offices. If Verity could locate him first, she could persuade him to leave on an impromptu trip with her—somewhere, anywhere—to stave off the dowager duchess's grasp for just a few more days. But if the dowager duchess had had the house watched and him followed—

"Is it you who sends a bouquet of wildflowers to your uncle's gravestone every year?" the dowager duchess interrupted her thoughts.

Verity turned around, astonished that the dowager duchess would address her on something so inconsequential. She was even more astonished to see that the dowager duchess had moved to a different chair, which allowed her to better observe Verity.

"Yes, I send the wildflowers," she said, wary.

"I thought so. Only you would think to give him something like that."

"He liked wildflowers."

"Your uncle was very fond of you," said the dowager duchess. "Sometimes I think he loved you better than any of his own daughters."

Verity didn't know what response the dowager duchess intended to provoke, so she said nothing. As she turned back toward the window, her gaze landed on the framed picture of a pleasant-looking young man. It took her some staring to realize that it was her little cousin, whom she'd loved as a brother, all grown up.

"How old is Tin now?" she asked.

"Twenty-eight August last."

"Shouldn't he have married already?"

"Sometimes he is in a hurry to marry. But then he realizes the advantage of patience."

Verity glanced at the dowager duchess. "You mean you have rejected every girl he likes."

"I want him to marry someone who loves him for who he is, rather than what he is."

Verity chuckled bitterly. "That is an odd sentiment coming from you."

"That has been my standard for the spouses of all

my children. I've done very well by my daughters. I will do well by him too."

There was a long silence. Then, because she'd worried too much about it, Verity blurted, "Why do you have my son watched? I would like you to stop."

"He is my sister's grandson. Do you think the adopted son of a gamekeeper would have found a place at Rugby without my interference? Or that his life there would have been tolerable without the rumors I originated concerning his sire?"

"You used him to threaten me."

"I beg your pardon?"

"You used him to keep me in line, so that I wouldn't tell anyone who I was and embarrass you again, but I would never—"

A footman entered the room. Verity swallowed her rising tirade.

"Mr. Somerset has arrived, Madame," said the footman.

"Very good. Clear the tea service and show him in in two minutes."

When the footman was gone, the dowager duchess pointed to a Japanese screen set diagonally across a far corner of the drawing room. "There is a chair behind the screen. You will wait there."

❧

It seemed a long time before Stuart was shown in—Verity's eyes were cross from staring at a delicately painted crane. At last his name was announced. She clamped her hands between her legs to keep them from shaking and followed the sound of his footsteps across the floor.

"Your Grace," he said, his voice warm but puzzled. "You sent for me?"

"I did. Thank you for coming so promptly."

"I'm amazed you knew where I was to be found—it is not every day that I visit my own solicitors."

"I do have my means, Mr. Somerset. Please, take a seat."

"Is it something urgent?"

"It is certainly not something I wish to leave to the caprice of time."

"You have my full attention then, Madame."

"I sincerely hope so, for I need you to listen very carefully to what I have to say."

Someone came in and left. Verity heard the sound of water—the dowager duchess pouring tea.

"It has come to my attention that you have taken up with your cook," said the elder woman.

From across the length of the room Verity felt him stiffen in discomfiture.

"With all due respect, Madame, that is not something I will discuss."

She was gratified to hear that his voice had lost some of its warmth.

"I am not interested in the private particulars of your life, Mr. Somerset, but only the public ramifications."

"Miss Bessler and I have ended our engagement. I see no moral conflict to my 'taking up' with anyone."

"But it will not be interpreted that way. Once it is known that your cook is now your mistress, it will be naturally assumed that it was Miss Bessler's revulsion that led her to cry off the engagement. Lest we forget, her father is still well beloved among our rank and file. Your own prestige will suffer much in consequence."

The dowager duchess sounded so reasonable, so maternally concerned that Verity had to will herself not to despair.

"I see," Stuart answered, his voice guarded. "That would be most unfortunate."

"Ah, but it is not only unfortunate for yourself. It damages us all. Mr. Gladstone will be grieved to learn that you have so compromised your moral authority. He depends wholeheartedly upon you to lead the contest in the Lower House. We have no one else of equivalent skills and standing. Your diminished stature will severely wound any chance we might have of passing the Home Rule bill. Do you not agree?"

It was no use keeping her hands still, Verity thought vaguely, if the rest of her shook like the last leaf of autumn.

"We haven't much more time left," continued the dowager duchess in the absence of a response from him. Her voice was cogent, urgent, compelling. "You know the situation as well as I do. The Irish are restless. They will not abide English rule for much longer. This is our last chance to settle the question in peace and honor rather than in strife and bloodshed. Will you put one woman above the good of a nation?"

There was a long pause. Verity imagined her aunt

gazing intently at Stuart, her steely will seeking victory at all costs.

"Can the private happiness of one man truly be so deleterious to the well-being of many?" he asked.

Verity closed her eyes. Despite the evenness of his tone, she'd heard the bewilderment and dismay in his voice.

"Yes, it can," said the dowager duchess.

God Himself could not have spoken with much greater authority and conviction. Verity knew then that she had lost him. Bitter tears trickled down her face. The duchess knew that his greatest virtue was also his greatest weakness. The nobility of his character rested upon his absolute sense of duty.

"You are right," he said. "It can."

Her tears gushed now. After the Irish Question there would be other crises and other calamities—the ship of state sailed ever in dangerous waters. And there would never be a moment when he didn't need his moral authority and his stature.

"I'm pleased that you see my point so well," said the duchess.

Verity did not fail to notice the odd lack of triumph in the old woman's voice. Such a good actress she was— she would not gloat in front of him. She would savor it later, when she slapped Verity with her I-told-you-so.

"Thank you, Madame, for pointing out where I've been blind," said Stuart.

Verity covered her face, so as not to make any sounds. She would not give the dowager duchess the satisfaction of hearing her cry.

"You will send Madame Durant away, then?" said the dowager duchess, lightly yet commandingly.

"No indeed, Madame. I will marry her."

A dead silence greeted his words. Then Verity sprang to her feet. Something fell loudly. But it wasn't her chair. It came from the middle of the drawing room—and sounded like the dowager duchess's walking stick.

"What did you say, Mr. Somerset?" asked the dowager duchess, her voice uncharacteristically high-pitched.

"I said I will marry her, Madame," he said calmly. "Hiding her will allow speculations to proliferate. I will bring her into the open. I believe I might even be able to persuade Miss Bessler to be seen together with her. That should calm rumors about Miss Bessler's revulsion."

Yes! Yes! Yes! Verity stuffed her fist into her mouth to stop herself from screaming it out loud. She'd known she had entrusted her heart to the right person this time. She'd known it!

She climbed onto her chair just in time to see the dowager duchess rise from her seat. Stuart, who had been sitting with his back to the screen, rose also.

"Mr. Somerset, you have lost your mind."

"No, Madame. I assure you, I am in firm possession of all my faculties. You yourself said I cannot afford the loss of prestige brought on by an engagement that ends in ill feelings and an affair with someone of Madame Durant's particular . . . distinction. Every rumormonger loves an affair, but there is little to excite the imagination in a marriage. And while Miss Bessler cannot keep company with my mistress, I'm sure she will have no objection to a shopping expedition or two with Mrs. Somerset."

"A shopping expedition or two . . ." The duchess was never at a loss for words. She was now.

"With a special license we can be married within the week."

Verity had always liked Stuart's voice. Now she knew that he had the most beautiful voice in the entire world. *Within the week.*

"Mr. Gladstone will never stand for it." The dowager duchess almost sputtered.

"Do we speak of the same Mr. Gladstone, Madame, the one who in his spare time personally arranges for the rescue and rehabilitation of prostitutes? I should think he'd consider it splendidly done of me to make a vapid *hausfrau* of one of Britain's most infamous retainers."

"I will cede you that point," said the dowager duchess, more collected now. Verity's euphoria cooled a few degrees. The dowager duchess was regrouping. She was far from giving up. "Perhaps Mr. Gladstone, in his advanced age and eccentricity, would not mind your choice of a spouse. But you may be certain that he would be the only one. The rest of the Liberal establishment would be aghast. And it would be the end of your political career. You will not receive the Home Secretary's portfolio. You will not even retain your position as Chief Whip. And if you've ever entertained thoughts of 10 Downing Street, well, you need never entertain them again."

He said nothing. Did he waver inside? Did he realize that he would be giving up far too much for her? She dared not even breathe.

He retrieved the dowager duchess's fallen walking stick, and presented it to her.

"I understand everything," he said slowly. "And I accept it as a price I'm willing to pay."

"You do not understand." The dowager duchess stomped the floor with the walking stick. "She, and consequently yourself, will be shunned everywhere. Doors will close in your face. Opportunities will flee before you. Your life, as you know it, will be finished."

"No, Madame, my life will have finally begun. I do not need the blessing of the Liberal establishment to practice law. I do not need the approval of Society to keep Fairleigh Park. And I will gladly be shunned on her behalf."

Tears came again, hot and sweet. This was how a prince slew dragons for his princess.

"You are mad, Mr. Somerset." The dowager duchess's voice trembled.

"I have loved her from the moment I first saw her, Madame. She has left me and I have left her. And now that we are at last together, nothing, save death, will part us again. Not you. Not the Liberal establishment. Not the opinion of every last man, woman, and child in England." He bowed. "If you will excuse me, I've been away from her far too long this day already."

He turned and walked toward the door. At that moment, the dowager duchess did something unprecedented: She broke down and cried, and not silent, ladylike tears, but great, shuddering sobs that racked her thin, aged frame. Verity almost fell off her chair. Stuart turned around, aghast.

He rushed back to the dowager duchess's side. "Madame, are you all right?"

She turned her face away. Gradually, her sobs quieted to soft hiccups and then to complete silence. With great stiffness, she moved toward her seat. He caught up with her and silently offered his support. She leaned heavily on him and lowered herself with a hard grimace.

He bowed again.

"Mr. Somerset, please sit down."

"Madame, you must understand, there is nothing you can say to me that will make me change my mind."

"Yes, I quite understand that. I require only a few more minutes of your company. Will you humor an old woman?"

He hesitated. "Of course."

"You too, Vera, sit down. There is nothing more ridiculous than a grown woman standing on a chair," the dowager duchess said, without looking in Verity's direction.

"I beg your pardon, Madame?" said Stuart.

The dowager duchess, of course, did not answer.

Verity climbed down from her chair. But she couldn't sit. A dress, she needed a dress, simple and elegant and not too costly and—

"Do you remember, Mr. Somerset, what I told you about my brother-in-law and my sister the other day?" said the dowager duchess, her voice hoarse.

"Yes. They perished at sea together. You raised their daughter. And she died when she was sixteen."

"Her name is Vera. The Lady Vera Drake. And I never said she died; I said we lost her."

Utter silence.

"Do you understand now, Mr. Somerset?"

"My God, do you mean to tell me that—that—"

"Yes," said the dowager duchess.

Verity stumbled into her chair. She was sure the chair shook violently. She had to dig her fingers into the armrests so that she wouldn't be bucked off. Did she hear everything properly? Did her aunt just acknowledge her?

"The Lady Vera Drake was our joy and our despair. I worried about her constantly, more than I worried about my own four children altogether. Unfortunately, all my worrying was not enough. When she was sixteen, she conceived a child with a stablehand on our estate, who was himself only seventeen.

"The news shattered my well-run life. This was the beloved child of my sister, the beloved child of my husband's brother. I'd never been so grieved and so angry in my life—I had utterly failed in my duties to her, to my husband, and to her dead parents.

"Her pregnancy was a secret known to only myself, her governess, and the physician who had looked after the Arlingtons for thirty years. It became my overriding goal to keep it that way, for I had a plan to make things right again: The physician would diagnose her with a wasting disease that required a long trip abroad for recuperation, the baby would be fostered with a reliable family that would be lavishly compensated for treating the child well, and she would return to England, still only seventeen, make her debut, dazzle Society, and live her life as if nothing untoward had ever happened.

"In my anger and my great disappointment, I made a grave error. I moved her to a lesser Arlington property, but I did not tell her the rest of my plan. Instead, I told her that she was ruined. That I would transfer her to a remote location under lock and key and she would rusticate there in shame for the rest of her life. I meant to frighten her, for it was indeed a shameful thing that she had done. I wanted her to reflect long and hard on her conduct, and to be properly grateful for her second chance when she received it.

"But I frightened her too well. She ran away instead, with the child's father. We were able to trace their path to Southampton. And then they disappeared into the ether. My panic was complete. I swore the governess and the doctor into secrecy, and then I set out to craft the greatest lie of my life.

"We forged her death. In his grief, my husband's hair turned gray overnight. But I dared not tell him the truth, for fear of his disappointment in me. We held a funeral for her. Our lives went on, sadder and emptier. And I wondered every day what had happened to her, and what I could have done differently.

"And then, one fine summer day, almost seven years after she ran away, a young man came to call at Lyndhurst Hall. My husband was out on the estate. I received him alone. Awkwardly, almost stammeringly, the young man said that his cook had told him that she was the daughter of the ninth Duke of Arlington, and could that possibly be true?

"My panic returned in full force. My only thought at that moment was that my husband must not discover my deception. I showed the young man the grave that contained the body of a stranger that our physician had obtained from somewhere—I never asked where. I showed him a photograph of some other niece of mine. I offered to take him to see the same physician whom I'd sworn into secrecy. By the time my husband returned for luncheon, the young man had been thoroughly convinced that his cook was a liar. He told my husband that he had come to admire our gardens. We partook luncheon together and he left.

"The next day I went to London and hired someone to find out whether the young man's cook was indeed our lost niece. It was such a relief to know that she was alive and well, as was her baby. But the information my detective brought back also thrust me into a new dilemma.

"I learned that Mr. Bertram Somerset and my niece had been engaged in a liaison more than two years in duration, a liaison that ended abruptly after his visit—which led me to deduce that she had divulged her parentage in order to entice him to marry her, and that my denials had placed her in a most unflattering light and led to a rupture between them.

"I was desperate to bring her back into the family. But should we acknowledge that she was alive, she was still ruined beyond even what the power and prestige of the Arlingtons could repair. For that I needed a suitably situated man who could be prevailed upon to marry her. And yet that idea went against everything I held sacred about marriage: an institution not to be entered into except gladly, reverently, by two people longing to share all they have and all they are for all their days.

"Mr. Bertram Somerset would not marry her without the benefit of an alliance with the Arlingtons. Had she not been ruined, I would have resolutely forbidden such a match. But ruined she was, and he was the best candidate at hand. I agonized for weeks on end. At last I decided that I would swallow my principles, visit Fairleigh Park, and arrange for their marriage—the day after my annual ball.

"And then something unexpected happened on the day of the ball. She made a trip to London. My man, obeying my instruction to keep a close eye on her, followed her. I need not tell you what happened on that trip, Mr. Somerset."

Verity grew red hot. All these years, her aunt had known about her one night with Stuart—and would have thought of it every time she saw him.

"Why did you never tell me anything?" he said. "I was desperate to find her."

"With the difficult decision I'd made, I was severely disappointed in her. How could she yet again be so rash and reckless with her person? And with an absolute stranger, no less. For what? To avenge herself upon her former lover? I could think of nothing more stupid that she could have done."

"It wasn't like that," he said quietly.

"No, now I imagine not. But back then my opinion on the matter was harsh and unforgiving. I decided that she was quite unworthy of the ancient and illustrious name of Drake and that I would have no more to do with her in this life.

"But I could never bring myself to completely withdraw my detective from Fairleigh Park, and so I still received news of her and her child. Gradually I became impressed with tales of her extraordinary culinary skills and with her very promising child."

The dowager duchess sighed. "Three years ago, when my husband was on his deathbed, I confessed what I'd done. He was overjoyed—if he hadn't been so ill he would have gone to see her right then. I promised him that I would take care of her and the child for as long as a breath remained in me—and that Tin would take up that responsibility after my death.

"Which brings me back to the present. It is not true that I've never told you, Mr. Somerset. I did give you a hint when you came back to London after your brother's funeral. You still had no idea who she was, and I did my best so that you would seek a face-to-face meeting with her.

"But as always with Vera, I seem to misstep no matter what I do. From Fairleigh Park I received news that the two of you had been seen together at last. And immediately the next day you canceled your engagement to Miss Bessler. I was suddenly in grave doubt of the wisdom of what I'd done. For as I have related to you, there is much at stake, and I wanted to be certain that should you embark on this dangerous path, it is at least not for the sake of lust alone."

Verity was standing on her chair again. She saw her aunt raise a handkerchief to her still-red eyes. "But never did I imagine that you would be steadfast and determined enough to marry her. Now at long last, she can be restored to us, and we can be a family again."

The Dowager Duchess of Arlington rose. Stuart rose too. She embraced him tightly. "Thank you, Mr. Somerset. Thank you."

The dowager duchess pulled away and raised the handkerchief to her eyes yet again. "Now, Mr. Somerset, I am going to leave this room for a quarter of an hour. You will use it for your formal proposal of marriage. After this time you will not be allowed alone with my niece again until you are married. And, Vera, do not dawdle. We have much to do and little time. The family must meet. We must get you a proper wardrobe. You have yet to be presented at court. And there is the wedding to be held before the opening of Parliament. There is not a minute to lose."

❦

Stuart stood stupefied in the middle of the room.

And that was when Verity came out of nowhere and nearly mowed him down. She covered his face with kisses.

"I love you. I love you. I love you," said his beloved, between kisses. "I cannot believe what you just did for me. I cannot believe you would give up everything so we could be together. And you gave my family back to me. Now I can be there when Tin gets married. Now I can finally meet my cousins' children."

"I cannot believe you are who you are," he said, still flabbergasted. "I know she's admitted it and everything adds up. But I cannot believe it. I cannot believe I was right and your family really does go back to the Battle of Hastings."

"Wrong." She was laughing and crying at once. "And I'm shocked that you don't know better—we are older than that; we were already earls under Edward the Confessor."

Then she grabbed his hand and practically dragged him behind a screen at the corner of the room farthest from the entrances.

He took her face between his hands. "My God, how did you survive all these years?"

"Later, later, I'll tell you later." She wrapped her arms about him. "Now, shush and kiss me again."

"But I haven't proposed yet," he protested.

"Oh, forget the proposal. Hurry. Did you not hear what she said? Ridiculous old woman—chaperones at our age. And knowing her, she won't hold the wedding until the day before Parliament opens, just so the whole world can attend."

She reached for his trousers. He slapped a hand over hers, shocked.

"Here?!"

"You've a better idea?"

He stared at her a moment. "No, as a matter of fact, I don't. God, those will be some long nights ahead."

He pushed her against the wall and kissed her hard. And it was a swift, furious joining that sent her over the edge directly, and him only a few seconds later.

❧

They spent the remainder of the quarter hour trying to make themselves presentable again.

"You are giggling." She poked him in the arm. "I've never seen you giggle."

"I can't help it." He dissolved into another fit. "I shagged the Lady Vera Drake in broad daylight in the middle of the Dowager Duchess of Arlington's drawing room. My reputation will never survive it."

"Your reputation was headed for ruin the moment you met me," she reminded him.

He brushed a finger on her cheek. "No, that was my heart."

She cupped his face. "And what a mighty heart it is." There were tears in her eyes again. "I don't think I've ever told you this, but you are an extraordinary man."

"I but know what is important to me. And I should have known it much sooner." He linked their hands together. "Will you marry me, Verity, and make me the happiest man alive?"

"Yes. It will be my honor and my privilege and my heart's desire," she said.

He kissed her on each cheek, her forehead, the tip of her nose, and her lips. Then he looked into her eyes and smiled. "At long last, Cinderella."

Epilogue

In retrospect, people said it was a Cinderella story.

The wedding of Stuart Ralston Somerset and the Lady Vera Drake, daughter of the ninth Duke of Arlington, was certainly a fairy tale wedding. The radiant bride wore a gorgeous confection of satin and tulle the exact blue of her eyes. The bridegroom, for overcoming her dragon of an aunt in the name of True Love, had been elevated by popular imagination into a latter-day Prince Charming.

The happy couple chuckled over it on their wedding night—after they first spent half of it making delicious love, of course, as they'd hardly had a chance to see each other in the whirlwind weeks before. They were on a decidedly un-fairy-tale-like bed at a decidedly nondescript inn on Balham Hill, in Clapham, because of the groom's troubled conscience over a little lie he'd told more than a decade ago to the innkeepers: that he was the husband of the lovely lady staying with them, and that he'd done her wrong and must see her immediately, before it was too late, before she boarded the steamer that was leaving for Australia first thing in the morning.

"Are fairy tale princes allowed to grow bald and rotund?" asked the bridegroom. "Bertie was going bald. I could very well too, in a few years."

"What about me? The public would be aghast to see

Cinderella with a sagging bosom and a wrinkly face," said the bride, "which, I warn you, might not be that far off."

"This happily-ever-after concept is somewhat problematic," mused the bridegroom. "Will we have to be deliriously happy every day? Are we allowed to have lackluster days, or, God forbid, days when we look daggers at each other?"

Verity laughed and snuggled closer to him. "Yes, we are, we are. And this is not an end, but a beginning—the first day of the rest of our lives together."

"Amen," said Stuart. "You fancy another shag, your ladyship?"

About the Author

Sherry Thomas arrived on American soil at age thirteen. Within a year, with whatever English she'd scraped together and her trusty English-Chinese dictionary by her side, she was already plowing through the 600-page behemoth historical romances of the day. The vocabulary she gleaned from those stories of unquenchable ardor propelled her to great successes on the SAT and the GRE and came in very handy when she turned to writing romances herself.

Sherry has a B.S. in economics from Louisiana State University and a master's degree in accounting from the University of Texas at Austin. She lives in central Texas with her husband and two sons. When she's not writing, she enjoys reading, playing computer games with her boys, and reading some more.

Visit her on the web at www.sherrythomas.com.

Don't miss Sherry Thomas's
next captivating novel!

Look for

NOT
QUITE
A
HUSBAND

Coming from Bantam Books in 2009.

Read on for an exclusive sneak peek!

NOT QUITE A HUSBAND

on sale in 2009

Prologue

In the course of her long and illustrious career, Bryony Asquith was the subject of numerous newspaper and magazine articles, almost all of which described her appearance as *distinguished* and *unique*, and unfailingly commented upon the dramatic streak of white in her midnight-dark hair.

The more inquisitive reporters often demanded to know how the white streak came about. She always smiled and briefly recounted a period of criminal over-work in her twenties. "It was the result of not sleeping for days on end. My poor maid, she was quite shocked."

Bryony Asquith had indeed been in her twenties when it happened. She had indeed been working too much. And her maid had indeed been quite shocked. But as with any substantial lie, there was an important omission: in this case, a man.

His name was Quentin Leonidas Marsden. She'd known him all of her life, but never gave him a thought before he returned to London in the spring of 1893. She proposed to him within seven weeks of meeting him again. Another three months and they were married.

From the very beginning they were an unlikely pair. He was the handsomest, wildest, and most accomplished of the five handsome, wild, and accomplished Marsden brothers. By the time of his wedding, at age twenty-four, he'd had a paper read at the London Mathematical Society, a play staged at St. James's Theatre, and a Greenland expedition under his belt.

He was witty, he was popular, he was universally admired. Bryony, on the other hand, spoke very little, was not in demand, and was admired only in very limited circles. In fact, most of Society disapproved of her occupation—and the fact that she had an occupation at all. For a gentleman's daughter to pursue medical training and then to go to work every day—*every day*, as if she were some common clerk—was it really necessary?

There have been other unlikely marriages that defied Society's naysayers and prospered. Theirs, however, failed miserably. For Bryony, that was; she'd been the miserable one. Leo seemed scarcely affected. He had a second paper read at the mathematical society; he was more lauded than ever.

By their first anniversary things had quite deteriorated. She'd barred the door to her bedchamber and he, well, he did not wallow in celibacy. They no longer dined together. They no longer even spoke when they occasionally came upon each other.

They might have carried on in that state for decades but for something he said—and not to her.

It was a summer evening, some four months after she first denied him his marital rights. She'd returned home rather earlier than usual, before the stroke of midnight, because she'd been awake for forty hours—a small-scale outbreak of dysentery and a spate of strange rashes had kept her at her microscope in the laboratory when she wasn't seeing to patients.

She paid the cabbie and stood a moment outside her house, head up, the palm of her free hand held out to feel for raindrops. The night air smelled of the tang of electricity. Already thunder rumbled. The periphery of the sky lit every few seconds, truant angels playing with matches.

When she lowered her face Leo was there, regarding her coolly.

He took her breath away in the most literal sense: she was too asphyxiated for her lungs to expand and contract properly. He aroused every last ounce of covetousness in her—and there was so much of it in her, hidden in the tenebrous recesses of her heart, a beast barely held back despite steel bars an inch thick.

Had they been alone they'd have nodded and walked past each other without a word. But Leo had a friend with him, a loquacious chap named Wessex who liked to practice gallantry on Bryony, even though gallantry had about as much effect on her as vaccine injections on a corpse.

They'd been having excellent luck at the tables, Wessex informed her, while Leo smoothed every finger of his gloves with the fastidiousness of a deranged valet. She stared at his gloved hands, her insides leaden, her heart ruined.

"...awfully clever, the way you phrased it. How exactly did you say it, Marsden?" asked Wessex.

"I said a good gambler approaches the table with a plan," answered Leo, his voice impatient. "And an inferior gambler with a desperate prayer and much blind hope."

It was as if she'd been dropped from a great height. Suddenly she understood her own action all too well. She'd been gambling. And their marriage was the bet on which she'd staked everything. Because if he loved her, it would make her as beautiful, desirable, and adored as he. And it would prove everyone who never loved her complete and utterly wrong.

"Precisely," Wessex exclaimed. "Precisely."

"We should leave Mrs. Marsden to her repose now, Wessex," said Leo. "No doubt she is exhausted after a long day at her noble calling."

She glanced sharply at him. He looked up from his gloves. Even in such poor soggy light, he remained the epitome of magnetism and glamour. The spell he cast over her was complete and unbreakable.

When he'd returned to London, everyone and her maid had fallen in love with him. He should have had the decency to laugh at Bryony, and tell her that an old-maid physician, no matter the size of her inheritance, had no business proposing to Apollo himself.

He should not have given her that half smile and said, "Go on. I'm listening."

"Good night, Mr. Wessex," she said. "Good night, Mr. Marsden."

Two hours later, as the storm shook the shutters, she lay in her bed shivering—she'd sat in the bath too long, until the water had chilled to the temperature of the night.

Leo, she thought, as she did every night. *Leo. Leo. Leo.*

She bolted upright. She'd never realized it before, but this mantra of his name was her desperate prayer, her blind hopes condensed into a single word. When had mere covetousness descended into obsession? When had he become her opium, her morphia?

There were many things she could tolerate—the world was full of scorned wives who went about their days with their heads held high. But she could not tolerate such pitiable needs in herself. She would not be as those wretches she'd witnessed at work, wild for the love of their poison, tenderly fueling their addiction even as it robbed them of every last dignity.

He was her poison. He was that for whom she abandoned sense and judgment. For the lack of whom she suffered like a maltreated beast, shaking and whimpering in the dead of the night. Already her soul withered, diminishing into little more than this vampiric craving.

But how could she free herself from him? They were married—only a year ago, in a lavish affair for which she'd spared no expenses, because she wanted the whole world to know that *she* was the one he'd chosen, above all others.

Thunder boomed as if an artillery battle raged in the streets outside. Inside the house everything was silent and still. Not a single creak came from the stairs or the chamber that adjoined hers—she never heard any sounds from him anymore. The darkness smothered her.

Love me, Leo. Love me as no one has ever loved me. Love me until there are no more shadows in my heart.

He does not love you. He will not love you. There is nothing about you for him to love.

She shook her head. If she didn't think about it—if she worked until she was exhausted every day—she could pretend that her marriage wasn't a complete disaster.

But it was. A complete disaster.

One small lie—*This marriage has never been consummated*—would free them both.

Then she could walk away from him, from the wreckage of the greatest and only gamble of her life. Then she could forget that she'd been mired in an unrequited love as unwholesome as any malarial swamp on the Subcontinent. Then she could breathe again.

No, she couldn't. If she asked for and received an annulment, he would marry someone else, and *she* would be his wife and the mother of his children, not Bryony, forgotten and unlamented.

She did not want him to forget her. She would endure anything to hold on to him.

She could not stand this desperate, sniveling creature she'd become.

She loved him.

She hated both him and herself.

She hugged her shoulders tight, rocked back and forth, and stared into shadows that would not dispel.

❧

She was still sitting up in bed, her arms wrapped around her knees, rocking and staring, when her maid came in the morning. Molly went about the room, opening curtains and shutters, letting in the day.

She poured Bryony's tea, approached the bed, and dropped the tray. Something shattered loudly.

"Oh, missus. Your hair. Your hair!"

Bryony looked up dumbly. Molly rushed about the room and returned with a hand mirror. "Look, missus. Look."

Bryony thought she looked almost tolerable for someone who hadn't slept in two days. Then she saw the streak in her hair, two inches wide and white as washing soda.

The mirror fell from her hands.

"I'll get some nitrate of silver and make a dye," Molly said. "No one will even notice."

"No, no nitrate of silver," Bryony said mechanically. "It's harmful."

"Some sulphate of iron then. Or I could mix henna with some ammonia, but I don't know if that will be—"

"Yes, you may go prepare it," said Bryony.

When Molly was gone she picked up the mirror again. She looked strange and strangely vulnerable— the desolation she'd kept carefully hidden made manifest by the translucent fragility of her white hair. And she had no one to blame. She'd done this to herself, with her relentless need, her delusions, her willingness to gamble it all for a mythical fulfillment conjured by her fevered mind.

She set aside the mirror, wrapped her arms about her knees, and resumed her rocking—she had a few minutes before Molly rushed back with the hair dye, before she must arrange a meeting with him to calmly and rationally discuss the dissolution of their marriage.

Leo, she permitted herself this one last indulgence, a heartbroken widow at her husband's grave, sobbing his name in vain. *Leo. Leo. Leo.*

It wasn't supposed to end this way, Leo. It wasn't supposed to end this way.

Kalash Valleys
Near Chitral, Northwest Frontier, India
1897

The white streak was a slash of barrenness against the rich deep black of her hair. It started at the edge of her forehead, just to the right of center, swept straight down the back of her head, and twisted through her chignon in a striking—and eerie—arabesque.

It invoked an odd reaction in him. Not pity; he would no more pity her than he would pity the lone Himalayan wolf. And not affection; she'd put an end to that with her frigidity, in heart and body. An echo of some sort then, memories of old hopes from more innocent days.

She'd finished washing her hands minutes ago, but she hadn't moved from the edge of the stream. Instead she'd picked up a twig to trace random patterns in the swift-flowing, aquamarine water.

Beyond the stream fields of wheat glinted a thick, bright green in the narrow alluvial plain. Small, rectangular houses of wood and stacked stone piled one on top of another, like a collection of weathered playing blocks. Behind the village, the ground rose quickly, a brief stratum of walnut and fruit trees before the slope butted up against austere crags that supported only dots of shrubs and an intrepid deodar or two.

"Bryony," he said at last.

She went still.

So she hadn't known that he was there. With her it was sometimes hard to tell. She was capable of a surpassing obliviousness. But he did not put it past her to deliberately ignore him in public. It had happened before.

She picked up the rubber gloves she'd worn during the caesarean section and began to wash the blood from them. "Mr. Marsden, how unexpected. What brings you to this part of the world?"

"Your father is ill. Your sister sent several cables to Leh, and when she received no response from you, she asked me to find you."

She was still again. "What's the matter with my father?"

"I don't know the specifics. Lady Callista only said that doctors are not hopeful and that he wishes to see you."

She rose and turned around at last.

At first glance, her face gave the impression of great tranquillity and sweetness. Then one noticed the bleakness behind her eyes, as if she were a nun on the verge of losing her faith. When she spoke, however, all illusions of meek melancholy fled, for she had the most leave-me-alone voice he'd ever heard, not strident but stridently self-sufficient, and little concerned with anything that did not involve diseased flesh.

But she was silent this moment and reminded him of a churchyard stone angel that watched over the departed with a gentle, steady compassion.

"You believe Callista?" she asked, destroying the semblance.

"I shouldn't?"

She shook droplets of water from the gloves. "Unless you were dying in the autumn of '95."

"I beg your pardon?"

"She claimed you were. She said you were somewhere in the wastes of America, dying, and desperately wanted to see me one last time."

"I see," he said. "Does she make a habit of it?"

"Are you engaged to be married?"

"No," he said. Though he should be. He knew a number of beautiful, loving, unassuming young women, any one of whom would make him a warm, delightful spouse.

"According to her you are. And would gladly jilt the poor girl if I but give the command." She did not look at him as she said this last, her eyes on the gloves, which she patted dry with a cloth. "I'm sorry that she dragged you into her schemes. And I'm much obliged to you for coming out this far—"

"But you'd rather I turned around and went back right away?"

Silence. "No, of course not. You'll need to rest and re-provision."

"And if I didn't need to rest or re-provision?"

She did not answer, but bent down to stow the gloves and the drying cloth in her bag.

Weeks upon weeks of trekking across some of the most inhospitable terrains on Earth, sleeping on hard ground, eating what he could shoot and the occasional handful of wild berries, so he wouldn't be weighed down by a train of coolies carrying the usual necessities deemed indispensable for a sahib's travels—and this was her response.

One should never expect anything else from her.

"Even the boy who cried wolf was right about the wolf once," he said. "Your father is sixty years old. Is it so unlikely for a man of his age to ail?"

He'd acceded to Callista's pleas because in some archaic, chivalric way he still felt responsible for Bryony—for the failure of their marriage. Whether her father's condition was truth or fiction mattered very little: In returning her to her family he'd discharge whatever residual obligation his inconvenient sense of duty insisted that he owed her. Then he'd be free to forget her and move on.

She tightened the straps of her bag and buckled it shut. "It would be four months to go from here to England and back, on the off-chance that Callista might be telling the truth."

"And if she is, you will regret not having gone."

"I'm not so sure about that."

Her ambivalence toward most of Creation had once fascinated him. He'd thought her complicated and extraordinary. But no, she was merely cold and unfeeling.

"Chitral is one march away," he said. "We can reach it tomorrow. We'll need a day or two there for provision and coolies. Then we can start for Peshawar."

She looked back at him, her face an unyielding mask. "I did not say I'd come."

It was 370 miles from Gilgit, where he'd been peacefully minding his own business, to Leh, that much again back to Gilgit, then 220 miles from Gilgit to Chitral. For most of the way he'd done two marches a day, sometimes three. He'd lost a full stone in weight. And he hadn't been this tired since Greenland.

Fuck you.

"Suit yourself," he said. "I'm leaving in the morning."